THE RELUCTANT WIFE

L. STEELE

L. Steele

For the good girls,
who prefer a
morally grey, possessive bodyguard
who growls, "my wife."
I see you!

SPOTIFY PLAYLIST

Love Story (Taylor's Version) - Taylor Swift
    drivers license - Olivia Rodrigo
    You Should See Me in a Crown - Billie Eilish
    Arcade - Duncan Laurence
    Another Love - Tom Odell
    Stand By Me – Ben E. King
    Say You Love Me - Jessie Ware
    Like I'm Gonna Lose You - Meghan Trainor ft. John Legend
    Perfect - Ed Sheeran
    Yellow - Coldplay
    Somebody to You - The Vamps ft. Demi Lovato
    Clarity - Zedd ft. Foxes (Realizing love is messy but worth it)
    Good as Hell - Lizzo (The princess embracing her power)
    Butterflies - Kacey Musgraves
    Running Up That Hill - Kate Bush

PRIMROSE HILL

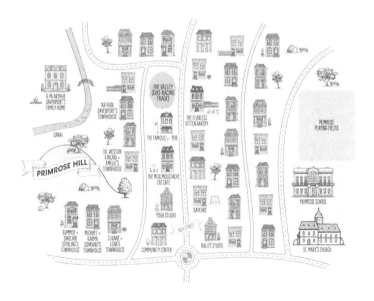

1

Aurelia

"Another espresso martini." I flutter my eyelashes at the bartender.

The man's gaze widens; his Adam's apple moves as he swallows. "Coming right up." His actions speed up. He pours the liquids into the mixer, then proceeds to shake it, adding enough oomph to his actions that I want to giggle. But I swallow down my mirth. Men are sooo predictable. He slides my martini across the counter.

My phone vibrates with an incoming call. I check the caller ID and make a face. *My worthless excuse for a fiancé is the last person I want to talk to right now.* I decline the call, slip the device into my purse. Then, to get the unwelcome reminder of what that call means out of my mind, I snatch up the martini and, raising it to my lips, down it in one gulp.

"Whoa." The bartender's eyes bug out. "That was quick."

"I was thirsty." I smile and notice with satisfaction when his color rises. "How much do I owe you?

"It's on the house."

I arch an eyebrow. "I insist." *I don't accept favors from anyone.*

When he hesitates, I dig into my purse, pull out a few notes and place them on the counter.

"Can I call you sometime?" His expression is pleading.

"My husband won't like that."

"You and I both know that's a lie, doll," a new voice interjects.

I glance sideways to find a man of medium height with thick shoulders and an even thicker waistline leaning against the bar. Catching my eye, he winks at me, a look of satisfaction on his wide features. *Ugh.*

Narrow eyes and a crooked nose, combined with his stout features and an ox-like neck, not to mention the gut hanging over his belt, give the impression that he might have spent all his time at the gym once upon a time but now has allowed himself to go to seed. He leers at me.

I stiffen. I draw myself to my full height, tuck my handbag under my arm and sniff. "Goodbye."

I sail past him. I'm sure I've made it and begin to relax, when a heavy hand descends on my shoulder. "Now, just a minute. I haven't finished talking to you, I—" the man begins to say, but I turn on him.

"Let go of me!" I tug at his hold and must take him by surprise, for I pull out of his grasp.

I see the intent in his eyes a second before his features twist. He reaches for me, but I evade him, then bring my knee up and bury it in his groin. The man cries out. I pull back, and when he begins to clutch at his center, I pivot and elbow my way through the crowd of people milling around the bar counter in the direction of the exit. Only, my progress is slow.

The hair on the nape of my neck rises. And when I turn, I spot my aggressor gaining on me. The man limps in my direction, an angry look on his face. *Oh, no!* Adrenaline spikes my blood. Fear squeezes my gut. I turn and plunge forward, trying to shove people out of the way. This is when I wish I were taller.

My five feet four inches puts me at a disadvantage. "Please, let me through." I shove at the woman standing in front of me. She moves aside, but then I'm faced with someone else. "Excuse me."

I shoulder my way through, only to crash into something so hard and so wide, I'm sure I've smashed into a wall. Only it's warm and covered with cloth that smells of fabric conditioner. And below that, I can smell the unmistakable muskiness of man, laced with something spicy that makes my mouth water.

Then the *thing* turns, and I'm at eye-level with corrugated slabs of muscle that stretch a black T-shirt so worn with age, there are tiny rips in the cloth through which I can make out flashes of skin. The heat from this expanse of chest reaches out and crashes into me, curling itself around me. I swallow.

My mouth goes dry. My throat feels like it's clogged with emotions I cannot identify. My head spins. *What's happening to me? Why am I reacting like this? I'm not going to faint. I'm not.* I draw in a sharp breath, and that spicy scent intensifies. I sway and grab at his arm to steady myself. His skin is warm, the muscles under the surface turning to stone. It feels like I'm holding onto a pillar of strength. A very live, very vital column of living flesh. The hair on the nape of my neck rises. I risk a glance behind me to find my pursuer is almost on me. *Argh!*

I hook my arm through that of the man I'm holding onto. Then, for good measure, I push my cheek into that expanse of steel that passes for his chest.

"Where were you, darling?" I cry. "I looked everywhere for you."

The planes under my cheek grow harder, if that's possible. I sense the surprise coursing through the man's body. He grows so still that, but for the warmth pouring off of him in waves, I'd swear he turned to granite. I'm sure he's going to push me away, but instead, he wraps his big arm around my shoulders and tucks me into his side. I fit so well against him.

The massive bulk of his body is comforting, and the scent of his very male presence is so arousing. I melt into him. For a few seconds, I allow myself to wallow in his nearness. I sneak a glance to the side to find my antagonist from the bar standing in front of me. He looks from me to the man next to me, then back at me. He seems confused. Taking advantage of his uncertainty, I pat the chest of the giant I'm leaning against.

Muscles jump under my palm. Ohmigod, he feels huge. So well built. I resist the urge to massage the skin under his T-shirt and tip up my chin. "This is my husband, and I warn you, he can get mean when he's angry. If you value your life, I suggest you leave."

Something that sounds like a chuckle reaches me. I could swear it comes from the giant, but the tension radiating off of his body indicates otherwise. I keep my gaze firmly on my adversary who scowls between us again.

He opens his mouth as if to say something, but the behemoth rumbles from above me, "You heard my wife. Best be off, or I'll have to rearrange your features."

My wife. He said *my wife.* My insides melt. And that voice? It's like dark chocolate poured over creamy caramel with a bite of whiskey added. My entire body seems to catch fire. I shiver. He must feel it because he pulls me closer. And I'm too shocked at my response and too bemused at how familiar it feels to be held against him; I dumbly stare at my antagonist who's gone pale. Sweat beads his forehead. With a last glance at the man next to me, he pivots and walks off. The crowds close in behind him.

Once again, we're surrounded by the hum of voices, and the sound of the music over the speakers. None of which penetrates this strange thrum of awareness that encompasses the two of us. We could be alone on our own deserted island among this sea of humanity.

Then, something crashes behind the bar. It cuts through the haze in my head. I push away and the giant lets me. I turn to face him, standing almost toe to toe in that throng.

"Thank you." I swallow. Then, because an imp of mischief pushes me on, I murmur, "Husband."

I raise my gaze to his, and further up, and up. I have to tilt my head all the way back and when I meet his eyes, I gasp. A deep green, so green it's almost black, but for those silver flares highlighting those emerald depths. So verdant, it feels like I'm peering into the depths of a lush forest. So intense, I'm sure I'm gazing into a swell of the Northern Lights that's going to soar down from the heavens and steal me away.

I gulp, take another step back, and stumble. He shoots out his arm and wraps his thick fingers around my bicep. Electricity ripples from the point of contact. His eyes turn almost black, the silver sparks crackling and turning almost gold, which is how I know he's experiencing the same level of awareness I am.

Then he releases me, and I miss his touch. "Thank *you*, *wife*."

His voice is pitched low and has an edge of harshness that grates over my nerve-endings. I shiver again. I try to tear my gaze away from his, but it feels like I've fallen down a rabbit-hole and there's no end in sight. My stomach bottoms out. My knees turn hollow. I sway toward him but stop myself before I crash into him again. I take in that high, intelligent forehead, that thick dark hair, which must be silky to the touch, the straight nose, those high cheekbones, which seem sharp enough to cut through glass, and then, that mouth. Oh god, that mouth, with the pouty lower lip that invites me to dig my teeth in and suck on it. Goosebumps pop on my arms. My stomach feels so heavy, and there's a hollowness in the place my heart should be.

I'm headed for an arranged marriage. In three months, I'll be walking down the aisle and getting hitched to my insufferable fiancé —a man I don't care for, and with whom I have no chemistry.

The least I owe myself is to find out how it feels to kiss someone I'm so deeply attracted to. And if it leads to something else? Well, I can only hope, right?

If I can find out how it feels to be with someone of my choosing, then you can bet, I'm going to do it. It's why I came to this bar in the first place, and I can't lose this opportunity. It's that thought which pushes me to lift up on tiptoe.

I grab at the front of his T-shirt and tug. I must take him by surprise, for he lowers his head enough that I can press my mouth to his. For a few seconds, it's like I'm kissing a stone. Then suddenly, he comes to life.

He fits his big hand to the back of my neck, the other to my hip. He draws me in close enough that my chest brushes his, then he tilts his head and deepens the kiss.

2

Ryot

Soft. And sweet. Like honey, powdered sugar, and candy. Her taste pours through my veins and lights up my blood. My heart begins to thud in my chest. My pulse rate heightens. I swipe my tongue over hers, and the taste of her intensifies. I haul her closer and her scent—like honeysuckle, vanilla and strawberries—invades my senses. My mouth waters. The blood drains to my lower belly. Fire zips down my spine.

This. Her. Here. I've been waiting for this moment for so long. I've been waiting for her forever, and I hadn't been aware. I need her. I want her. I have yearned for her. She is the antidote to my past. She is the reason I'm alive. She is why I was awarded a fresh lease on life when I knew I shouldn't have been spared at war. She's my second chance.

I feel like I've been drowning since the day Jane was killed on mission two years ago. I feel guilty I never loved her. Guilty that I was tired of the constant bickering in our marriage and wanted her gone. And when she died, the sense of relief I felt made me feel like some kind of monster. If we hadn't fought that day, she wouldn't have left on the mission that killed her. I hold myself responsible for that. Not even the fact that she betrayed me lessens the blame I've lived with since.

I punished myself by shutting down. I locked myself off. Never noticed another woman... Until now.

I firm my grip around the nape of her neck; she shivers.

I flatten my hand across her back, and her entire being shudders. So responsive. So pliant. She was made for me. Sensations course through my veins. I haul her closer, and when she whimpers, a fierceness grips me. She's mine. *Mine. Mine. Mine.* I growl deep in my throat and am rewarded when she melts further into me. She throws her arms around my neck and arches into my embrace. I allow myself to drink of her, to revel in her closeness. I know she must be aware of how I'm responding to her, but I'm unable to stop myself. I need her too much. I need her more than anyone I've ever met before and—I tear my mouth from hers. *What's wrong with me?*

Why am I thinking like this? I stare down into her shining eyes. It's like I'm looking into the heart of the very earth. A safe space. A place I can call home. I shake my head to clear it.

What bizarre thoughts are these? I've never felt this moved before. This touched in a way that makes me feel vulnerable, like I've exposed my deepest secrets to another. I cannot allow myself to feel this way. It's wrong. I release her so suddenly, she gasps. Her eyes round with surprise. The color rises on her cheeks.

The next moment, she pushes past me and, stepping between two groups of people, she heads for the door. For a few seconds, I watch her retreat. Then, as if we're tethered, I stalk after her. I muscle my way through the crowd, and those in front of me move aside as if sensing my impatience. Good thing, too.

I'm not sure why I'm so affected by her. I'm not sure why I feel like she means something to me already. *I just met her. I don't even know her name.*

I never felt this way about the woman I was married to... Being drawn so powerfully to someone else in a way I never was to her makes me feel like I'm doing something wrong. But I'm not; I know that. Yet each time my heart races at this new attraction, guilt follows closely behind, whispering about the past.

My steps slow down until I come to a halt. I watch as the woman who called me her husband heads out of the bar area and down the hallway.

She disappears from sight. My heart drops into my stomach. A strange nervousness grips me. An emptiness squeezes my chest. My breath sticks in my throat. It's as if I've lost a part of myself. I shouldn't follow her. But my feet don't seem capable of obeying the commands from my brain. I move forward, and when I step into the hallway, I spot her at the main exit that leads out onto the side.

As if she senses my presence, she looks at me over her shoulder. There's a challenge in her eyes. *Eh? What is she up to? What is she —?* She bypasses the exit and continues down the corridor.

I should let her leave and relish meeting her as a nice memory. After all, I don't know her. I've only just met her. I stand there, clenching and unclenching my fists. The next thing I know, I'm in motion. I take off hot on her heels.

I take in the sway of her hips under the dress she's wearing. It clings to her curves and reaches halfway down her thighs. The three-inch heels she's wearing draw attention to her shapely ankles. A thrill of anticipation pulses under my skin. Sweat pools under my armpits. I raise my gaze in time to catch her gathering her hair over a shoulder.

The creamy expanse of her back bared by the deeply cut 'V' of her dress has me entranced. She passes the line of women waiting for the ladies' room and continues until she reaches the door that must open out onto the back alley. When she steps through, I'm right behind her. The door slams shut. The sound echoes around the empty space. It sends a shudder of something through her—anticipation, fear? A mixture of both? She pauses. And when I place my hand on her shoulder, she shivers.

When I run my hand down the expanse of skin revealed by the plunging back neckline of the dress, she sighs. I slide my hand down the arch of her back. I want her so much. I want to push her up against the wall, lean into her and draw in her scent. And her skin — I swallow. That gossamer-fine, satiny-plush, buttery-smooth skin of hers. One touch and it'd stop the devil himself in his tracks. I'm only human. I pull her up against me, and she gasps.

I lower my head and drag my whiskered chin up the side of her neck. She shudders. And when I bite down on the lobe of her ear, she whines. The sound cuts through the haze in my mind. I raise my head and look around the empty alley. There are dumpsters opposite us, lined up like sentinels. A dog barks in the distance. The faint sound of voices, then a muffled crash as something breaks, reaches us through the door at our back. I wince. Then twist her around to face me.

She looks up into my face. And I know then, I must have her. Just one night; then I'll let her go. It's only to assuage this burning need inside of me. The kind I forgot I was capable of feeling.

"Come home with me," I growl.

Her gaze widens, then she shakes her head. "I can't."

"Why not? You want this. So do I." I knit my brows. "Unless I read your signals wrong?"

She blinks rapidly.

My heart sinks a little. I didn't realize, until now, how much I want this woman. I force myself to push aside my despair and focus on her features, "Did I read your signals wrong?" I prompt her.

She shakes her head. "I do want you."

The tension in my shoulders bleeds out.

She sets her jaw. "But I can't wait." Before the full impact of her words sinks in, she jumps up. I catch her. She wraps her legs around my waist. "Here"—she pants—"right here."

I hesitate.

She rises up, throws her arms about my neck and holds on. "I want you." Her lips tremble. "Please."

Her soft whisper slithers down my spine. My heart rate spikes. I turn and, shielding her back with the palm of my hand, I press her into the wall near the door we came through. She must sense the evidence of my need, for her lips part, then she raises her chin. I lower mine. Our mouths clash.

The kiss is everything the earlier one promised and more, so much more. Her taste permeates my senses; her scent fills my nostrils. The feel of her in my arms is heaven. I tilt my head and drink from her, feel the barrenness in my chest absorb the sensations and come to life.

Once again, I feel this...meeting is not trivial. It's meant to be so much more than this. More than a chance encounter. More than a fumbling fuck in an alleyway. I pull back and, chest heaving, stare into her flushed features. Her eyelids flutter open, and she looks back with dilated pupils. Her fiery red strands have fallen over her forehead, and something in the angle at which she's staring at me sends a ripple of awareness up my spine. "Have I met you before?" I frown.

She startles, then panic filters into her eyes. "Of course, not." She half laughs. The sound is feeble, and a flash of guilt laces her features. She pushes against my chest, and I let her down, taking a step back. I steady her until she finds her footing, then stay in place until she's put her clothes to right.

"You know what? Forget it." She tosses her head, "I don't think I want you, after all."

I allow a small smirk to curl my features and am rewarded by her glower.

"That's not what I read on your features earlier, Princess," I scoff.

An expression of alarm comes over her. *Huh?*

"What's wrong, you—" I grunt when she kicks me in the shin. It's not that it's painful as much as she takes me by surprise. Enough to distract me. So, when she darts past me, I don't stop her. By the time I recover and hurry after her, she's reached the mouth of the alley. It's the anxiety I saw on her face earlier that has me concerned. I don't think I said anything to warrant it. She was into me. She wanted it as much as I did. But something happened to make her anxious. And I need to understand what it was. At the very least, I need to make sure she gets home safely.

I run after her, turning the corner to find her racing up the sidewalk, past the entrance to the bar. I run toward her, then pause when she reaches a stately Jaguar with tinted windows and slips into the driver's seat. The car feels too formal for her, yet its elegance also befits her.

I rub at my temple. *Who is this mystery woman?* One who looks like an angel and smells like heaven—yet had the presence of mind to pretend I was her husband to get rid of unwanted attention—but kisses like a siren.

She's so full of contradictions, so full of life, so enticing that, surely, I won't be able to forget her. It's the first time a woman has made such an impression on me. The car drives past. The window on the driver's side lowers, and her gaze meets mine.

Despite the darkness, there's enough light from the streetlamp to light up her features. Her eyes sparkle like the color of bluebells after rain, like the richness of blue diamonds. Something so precious, so rare. My heart skips a beat. Our gazes hold. The chemistry sparks across the distance. Then she throws me a kiss.

The gesture is so saucy that I bark out a surprised laugh and pretend to catch it. The car pulls ahead, and she's out of sight. The taillights disappear around the corner. What a woman!

Slowly, the sounds of the city filter back into my consciousness, and with it, the breath I hadn't been aware I was holding whistles out. A flurry of wind catches some scraps of paper, lifting them into a whirlwind, causing them to dance in circles. Like my life. Like this emptiness left behind. I glance down and see my hand over my heart. Damn, I'm not given to maudlin gestures such as this. One kiss, and she's reduced me to a bumbling Romeo. I shove my hand into the pocket of my jeans.

It's not like me to give into such fanciful thinking. Whoever she was, she's gone. Good riddance. I'll never see her again. Never feel the press of those gorgeous lips against mine. Good thing, too. I don't have time for such distractions. I've sworn never to allow myself to be this susceptible again. I'll never allow myself to feel for another. Not after what I've been through. And yet—the way she felt in my arms. The way she molded herself to me. Those curves of hers that felt so right. So vital. So...everything. I shake my head. She's gone. Time for me to move on and put her out of my mind.

My phone buzzes. I pull it out of my pocket and bark, "What?"

"Be ready to report for your assignment at oh-six-hundred hours," my uncle's voice barks down the line.

It's as if I'm back in the Marines, and he's my commander. Only, I'm not, and neither is he.

"I haven't said I'm accepting the task," I remind him.

"Cut the crap," he scoffs. "It's not like you have other options."

"Not like joining a fledgling security agency yet to establish itself is an option."

He laughs. "*My* reputation precedes me."

Only a fool would take Quentin Davenport at face value. His tone masks an edge of steel. Q was the first in our family to join the Marines. It set an example for me and my brothers to follow. And all of us, except the youngest, Connor, joined the armed forces. And each of us retired after giving our best years to the service. None of us regret it. Though, dealing with the guilt of living while so many of others didn't is something I'm not sure I'll be over anytime soon.

"You're not going to join the Davenport group. At least, you're smart enough to not make *that* mistake," he admits. Q, like my older brothers Nathan and Knox, gave it a shot. But while both stayed on as CEOs of group companies, Q resigned his role. He agreed to stay on the board but channeled his efforts into setting up his security agency.

When I heard about it, it felt like a viable alternative to riding a desk—a possibility which has zero appeal. I squeeze my fingers around my phone.

Q is responsible for giving the order that resulted in Jane's death and that of her battalion on a tour of duty. When I learned this about my uncle, I vowed revenge. Then, I discovered he wasn't aware they were at the enemy site he'd given the orders to take out. I had it verified by other sources, too—he wasn't at fault. He's since apologized for his role in the matter. So, am I going to consider his offer?

"If I'm being honest, you'd do me a favor by accepting this," he murmurs.

I let out a derisive chuckle. "Laying it on thick, aren't you?"

Q huffs out a laugh. "Of course, if you're not ready to take on a role that you could perform with your eyes closed, then I understand. Perhaps, you need more downtime to take care of your mental health..."

The last thing I need is more time off. Frankly, I'm itching to be on a mission… Any mission. I miss the discipline of the Marines. I miss having a purpose. Former Commanding Officer that he is, Quentin Davenport is shrewd enough to know this. But I still have issues working with him. I hesitate.

On the other hand, he's right. I have no other option; nothing else lined up. And the need to wake up and know I'm going to be of service, albeit for a private client, is a lure I can't resist. I need something to get my mind off the past. Something to help me re-focus my attention. Something to test if I still have the edge. It's too attractive. It's why I snap out, "I haven't forgiven you."

"I don't expect you to." He blows out a breath. "But you need a goal, an objective to keep you going—" he says, unknowingly echoing my thoughts. "And I need good men I can count on. Besides, you don't want your training to go to waste. If there's one thing I know about you, Ryot Davenport, it's that you want to continue to protect those in need. But do you have the guts to accept this challenge? Do you have the courage to rise above your past and commit to moving on? Do you"—he hesitates—"do you have the fortitude to not just survive but to live once again?"

3

Aurelia

"Father." I curtsy to the King of Verenza.

We're on the top floor of a very well-known hotel owned by one of the Seven, a group of billionaires who are close friends with my father. It doesn't hurt that they gave him a huge discount. It's the only way we could afford to stay here. The truth is, the Royal Family of Verenza is a hair's breadth away from bankruptcy. It's one of the reasons my father is in London. To drum up funds from wealthy patrons.

"Darling, Aura." He looks up from where he's been deep in discussion with Fred Humphries, his First Minister, and another official looking man I don't recognize.

My father's familiar face breaks into a large smile. The warmth on his features is palpable. He's my only surviving parent. Seeing him reminds me of my mother, and my heart squeezes in my chest. Suddenly, I'm not twenty-three years old and a princess, but a daughter who goes for long periods without seeing her dad. He often travels on missions to further our country's diplomatic ties.

I want to race toward him and throw myself against his chest, but he's the king. Royal protocol decrees that I do not indulge in overt gestures of affection, not even when we're alone.

The meeting ends, and the official I don't recognize rises to his feet and bows. "I'll have the paperwork sent to you, Your Highness."

My father also rises. He holds out his hand. "Thank you, Mr. Singh. I am grateful the International Monetary Fund has accepted our bid for a loan."

Another loan? It's been less than a month since Verenza borrowed from the IMF. Things are worse than I realized.

Mr. Singh shakes my father's hand. "I'm glad I could be of help, Sir. But"—he hesitates—"speaking as a friend, I would advise you to pay off your loans before you borrow anymore; else it'll result in weakened investor confidence and a downgrading of your credit rating, which will only make it more expensive to borrow further." His features turn grim. "I'm sure you'll find a way to pay back your loans before you default." He bows once more at my father, then nods at Fred, before bowing to me on his way out. "Princess."

I turn on my father. "Is what he's saying true? Are we on the verge of defaulting on our payments?"

My father exchanges a look with Fred, then turns to me. "You don't have to worry about that, honey."

I blow out a breath. My father always dismisses any attempt I make to understand my country's financial situation. He's made it clear that my role is to be joined in an advantageous marriage. Given his traditional outlook, I know he'd never allow me to accept my publishing deal. But the size of the advance meant, no way, was I going to turn it down.

I can use the money to finance my living costs, as well as pay my team. It helps me do my bit to ease the financial strain on my father's resources, even if he's not aware of it. I lock my fingers together, hoping my nervousness doesn't show.

"Let me see you." He scrutinizes my features, and his own soften further. "You look so like your mother."

A thickness clogs my throat. I swallow around it. My mother died when I was ten. But memories of her are fresh in my mind. Her gentleness, her laughter, her thick auburn hair, which I inherited. I also get my curves from her. She was taller than me, statuesque. But other than that, I could be her doppelgänger. This is the first time my father's mentioned it though. Not surprising, considering I don't get to spend that much time with him.

"She'd have loved to see you all grown up and so beautiful." A tear slides down my father's cheek.

"Oh, papa." I close the distance to him but stop short of hugging him. Instead, I squeeze his arm.

For a few seconds, we stay that way. Then Fred clears his throat.

"Sir, you were going to talk to the princess about her security detail?" he urges.

So, my father didn't call me here to talk about my publishing deal. *Whew!* My secret is safe...for now.

"What about my security detail?" I incline my head.

"In light of the upcoming investiture of your brother, there is a lot of attention from the world press on Verenza and the Royal Family. So, we've made the decision to strengthen the safety detail for all of us," my father informs me.

"It's Viktor's investiture; not mine." I tip up my chin. "I don't need additional security."

"You're a key member of the Royal Family." My father flattens his lips. "You're as much at risk as we are." He and Fred exchange glances.

"Did something happen?" I look between them. "There's no need to protect me from reality just because I'm a woman," I point out.

Fred looks uncomfortable. My father's brow furrows. When he proposed an arranged marriage, I wasn't surprised. Sure, a part of me rebelled against it internally. But as a member of the Royal Family, I understood that my life partner would likely be someone decided upon by my father.

And when, I found out that my future bridegroom, who belongs to another European Royal Family, would invest enough money to ease my country's economic vows, I knew this was my chance to help my father. Besides, it's not like I could say no. My father made it clear this was his expectation of me.

If I'm lucky, Gavin will love me. Although, based on interactions I've had with him, that seems highly unlikely. To be fair, I can't imagine loving him either.

At least, my father decided to keep news of my engagement under wraps.

He and Gavin's father don't want to endanger the union in any way. Announcing it would mean too much media scrutiny. I, for one, am happy I don't have to contend with that. This also means I don't have to talk about my upcoming nuptials, which suits me fine. I'd rather not think about it at all.

Meanwhile, arrangements are underway for a wedding that will put the world's attention on Verenza. Only three more months of freedom, and then I'll be locked in a loveless match with that spineless tosser. Ugh.

I shove those thoughts out of my head and widen my eyes in what I hope is a beseeching expression. "Tell me what's happened, Papa. I deserve to know."

My father turns to Fred and nods. Fred sighs. He pulls a handkerchief from his pocket and mops his brow, despite the very comfortable temperature inside this hotel suite. "There has been a threat against you. This one shouldn't be taken lightly." There's a thread of anxiety running through his voice, which tells me he's rattled.

My stomach turns to stone. My heart begins to race. *Another threat? Oh no.* I can only imagine how this is going to turn my life upside down again. Every time one of these arises there's more security, more restrictions, more rules imposed on me, until it feels I can barely breathe. I feel the urge to scream and run out of there, but my mother's voice echoes in my head: *Spine straight. You're a princess. Never forget that.*

As always, it helps me find my composure. I tuck my elbows into my sides. "Any—" I clear my throat. "Any idea why I was targeted?"

Fred shakes his head.

"Is it because those who are behind the threat are anti-monarchists?" I rub at my temple. "Perhaps, it's because our people are upset at the growing cost of living? Especially, when they see me wearing my fancy clothes and taking part in high profile tours."

Like this current one to London, where I've been fulfilling up to three engagements a day. I've been seen at movie premieres, fund-raisers, and charity drives. It's to keep Verenza top of mind and drive tourism to my country. But from the outside, it can seem frivolous. Especially when so many are struggling to put food on the table.

When neither of them replies, I scowl. "So, that's it. I don't get anything else?"

"*Cara mia*, it will only upset you. If there were something you needed to know, I promise, I'd bring it to your attention," my father says in a soothing tone.

Verenza is an island adjacent to Italy. Hearing my father address me by that endearment, which is in Italian, the language my mother spoke with us, twists my heart. The fact that he uses it now also tells me that this threat is serious. Which scares the crap out of me. It also makes me want to find out more.

I shove aside the sadness that thoughts of my mother bring and protest, "But Papa—"

My father cuts me off with his raised hand. "I will not entertain further discussion about this."

"But—"

"My decision is final." He draws himself up to his full height. Once again, he's the King. The monarch. When my father gets this way, I know, it's near impossible to sway him. But I have to try.

I blow out a breath, then fold my arms across my chest.

He must see the stubbornness in my expression for his eyes soften. "Aura, I only have your best interests at heart. You know that, right?"

I allow my shoulders to relax, feeling unhappy that he felt I might ever think otherwise. "Of course, Papa."

He nods. "Good." Then he looks at Fred, who pulls out his phone and dials a number.

"Send him in."

The door opens behind me. Footsteps approach. The hair on the back of my neck prickles, but I bat aside the frisson of awareness that runs up my spine.

My father nods in the direction of the person who draws abreast. "This is your new bodyguard."

"Ryot Davenport." A deep, dark voice reaches me. A voice I recognize. A voice that turns my insides to butter and my thighs into a mass of quivering need.

No! No...no...no. Surely not. I draw in a breath, and his scent — dark, smoky and rich, like the smell of fine, worn leather, spiked with something sensual and slightly animalistic — confirms to me that I have not made a mistake. *This is him.* The man I met at the nightclub last night. The man I called my husband. The one who I kissed. And to whom I'd have happily given myself, except I came to my senses and fled the scene. And now, he's here. And he's my —

"Personal protection specialist." Ryot bows to the king. "That's what I prefer to be called, Your Highness."

My father seems taken aback, then nods. "Of course." He looks Ryot up and down. "You're Arthur Davenport's grandson and Quentin Davenport's nephew."

Ah, so he's part of the Davenport clan? They're one of the leading and most powerful business families in the country. So, what's he doing, working as a bodyguard? It's not for the money, that's for sure.

"I'd prefer to stand on my own merit," he retorts.

My father looks at Ryot as if seeing him for the first time and nods. "You have impressive credentials. You've been awarded the King's Commendation for Valuable Service, as well as the Conspicuous Gallantry Cross, and the Military Cross."

Ryot sets his jaw. "Those who died in battle deserve it more, Sir."

Whoa, not only is he the most charismatic man I've come across, but he's also humble when it comes to his achievements? He seems too good to be true. I narrow my gaze on him.

My father regards him with a considering expression. "Can you protect my daughter?"

Ryot tilts his head. "As long as I'm the princess' close protection officer, nothing and no one will get past me."

Is it my imagination, or was there a hard note to his tone when he said *princess*? Also, there is no doubt in my mind, he means it. So long as he's guarding me, I'm safe. Funny how, I don't know this man, but I already trust his ability to keep me unharmed. And it has nothing to do with the fact that I know how it feels to be held against his wide, firm, muscled chest. Also, why am I thinking of that encounter? I risk a glance in his direction then wish I hadn't because, *oh my god*, he's every bit as devastating as I remember him to be.

Green eyes, which seem almost hazel today, and remind me of the mesmerizing patterns on a snake's coils—*he's just as dangerous; I need to watch myself with him.*

There's a confidence that clings to him, a dominance that shimmers in the air about him, a self-assurance that's almost annoying because I recognize it well. It's the confidence that comes with breeding. With being born into a family that confers status on you. With not being used to taking no for an answer. With a trust, an unshakeable belief that you can have anything you want.

Only, he's not going to control me. And I don't want him as my bodyguard. The thought of this man who I'm so attracted to, in such close proximity to me? It both scares me and excites me. But I'm not a pushover.

I'm the Princess of Verenza and I, too, will get my way.

"I already have a security team," I try to reason with my father.

But he ignores me. He and Ryot are locked in some kind of staring match. They're taking each other's measure. At least, my father is. Ryot's spine is upright. His face could be carved out of marble, given how smooth his forehead is, how unmoving his expression is. And that absolute rigidity in his stance is a dead giveaway that he's ex-military. I didn't spot it the first time I saw him; I was too taken in by his good looks. Now, I can't not see it. And now that I know his background, I can see the experiences he's lived through in the shadows that cling to his eyes.

It speaks of nightmares he's faced and conquered. It signals that there's more to this man than being the scion of a well-known family and having the right blood line with all of the privileges that come from growing up as part of the upper class. None of which I knew when I met him last night.

I was drawn to him. There was this intense chemistry between us which surprised me. I wanted him enough that I would've let him bend me over and take me right there in that alley. I was sure I'd never see him again. Yet here he is. To say I'm shocked is putting it mildly. This is the epitome of a cruel joke the universe is playing on me.

Then my father nods, as if he's come to a decision. An understanding seems to pass between them.

Ryot's face is expressionless. It's my father who walks to me and takes my hand in his. "I will not compromise on your safety. You're my daughter, the light of my life. I could not bear it if anything were to happen to you. I need to ensure you're secure, and Ryot comes highly recommended. I believe he will keep you safe."

I search my father's features and see the worry in his eyes. The plea in his gaze, more than anything, renders all my protests moot. As a last resort, I throw up my hands. "You just met him, and you trust him for this job?"

My father looks past me and exchanges another look with Ryot. A small smile curves my father's features. "I couldn't have survived this long without sizing up someone in seconds. Besides, his track record in the military speaks for itself."

His words remind me of how Ryot protected me against the creep in the bar yesterday. My father's instincts are right. How can I argue with that? But I have to try. "I already have a security team guarding me," I remind him.

"They don't have the experience Ryot has." My father's gaze grows resolute. "With his level of training and background in the Royal Marines, he'll provide a level of safe keeping which will allow me to rest assured."

Damn. It's true, my existing security team is not the most competent. It's how I managed to evade them and get to the bar yesterday. The tension radiating from Ryot tells me he's thinking the same thing. Thankfully, he stays quiet. Which means, if he becomes my bodyguard, he already has something on me. Which puts me at a disadvantage, and which I don't appreciate at all. I firm my lips and decide to try to dissuade my father one last time.

"But Papa, you barely know him." I clasp my fingers together. "Are you sure this is a wise decision?"

Before my father can reply, Ryot draws himself up to his full height. "Your father is a good judge of character. He knows, I'll put my life on the line before I let anything happen to you, Princess."

4

Ryot

Her eyebrows shoot up. She seems taken aback by my declaration, and to be honest, so am I.

Images of our kiss from last night, of how her curves felt pressed against me, of how her lips clung to mine before she pulled away, overwhelm me. Her scent stayed with me and ensured that, despite jerking off a few times, I spent the night sporting a hard-on, unable to sleep.

I realized I would not be able to forget this woman. I needed to keep myself occupied so I wouldn't obsess about her. It's why I accepted Quentin's offer.

To think, the princess he referred to is the woman I met at the bar. I'd have done anything to take her home, and not let her go until I'd had her in every way possible. I am more powerfully attracted to her than to the woman I once married. My intuition tried to warn me not to wed her, but I ignored it. Now, it's telling me I should turn down the role of the princess' personal protective detail to prevent any conflict of interest.

But the thought of anyone else spending all that time in such close proximity with her is inconceivable. And the possibility that someone else couldn't protect her as well as I can is frightening. My stomach tightens.

After meeting with her security team this morning, it's clear to me, they are woefully unprepared for the threat posed to her, which I verified as credible. Given my background and experience, I can confidently say, no one is better qualified than me to protect her.

And while I cannot cross the line of the professional relationship between us if I accept the role of her security detail, at least, I can see her every day.

I regretted that I was unable to take her to bed, but now, I realize, it's the only reason I can keep my perspective about this job.

I was wondering why she ran; now, I'm thankful. It's why I'm able to accept this assignment with a clear conscience and a promise to myself to not overstep the line.

Her blue eyes narrow like she's aware of what I'm thinking. Then she sniffs. "I suppose that's part of your job description."

I incline my head. "Indeed, it is, *Princess*."

I infuse just enough sarcasm into the last word that she stiffens. She seems like she's about to retort when her father nods. "That's decided, then. You're my daughter's security detail and you report directly to me."

The silence stretches. Her expression reveals her unhappiness.

"Thank you for doing this for me, honey." The king's gaze gentles. "Knowing you are safe helps me do my job better."

The fight seems to go out of her. Her shoulders droop, "I love you too, Papa." She pivots and walks out of the room. I follow closely.

The door shuts behind us. She continues past the guards outside the suite and down the corridor to the elevator. She stabs at the button to summon the elevator.

"What are you doing?" I scowl.

"I'm heading out. What does it look like?" She stares at the indicator panel of the elevator.

"Not so fast. I must brief you on the changes made to your security arrangements." I growl, then curse myself.

She's my principal. I need to soften my tone instead of ordering her around. This is why I shouldn't have taken on this bodyguard gig.

"Why do I need to know that?" She tosses her head. "Surely, that's your job."

"I'm your protective detail." I strive for a neutral tone. "Your safety is my only concern. This meeting is to ensure there is nothing left to chance when it comes to your welfare."

"And I'm the princess." She looks down her nose at me which, given she's a head shorter than me, is no small feat. "I'm asking you to get out of my way."

This woman! She's magnificent when she's digging her heels in. A part of me admires her sass, and damn, if it doesn't turn me on further. I get my need for her under control and school my features into a firm expression.

"*I* am *your* security lead, and I ask that you follow me so we can meet with your security team and finalize the details of your arrangements." I can't stop myself from infusing enough authority into my voice that it comes out sounding less like a request and more like a mandate. She hears the command in my voice and glowers.

She opens her mouth, no doubt, to refuse, when a voice calls out, "Everything okay, Aura?"

I look past her to find the previous head of her security detail approaching us, his forehead furrowed.

The fact that he has been so lax with her security thus far—enough to allow her to go to a bar on her own and expose herself to danger—turns my insides to molten lava. I want to close the distance to him and swing at him, but that's not going to help the situation. So, I rein in my anger and draw myself to my full height.

What pisses me off more is that he called her by her nickname. I glower at him as he comes to a stop behind her.

The princess steps to the side, then affirms, "Everything's good."

"Smith." I fix him with a steely-eyed glare.

I took this assignment with the caveat that I'd bring my own team on board. Overnight, I reached out to my network of former Marines and pulled together a crew I trust.

I indicated to the king that I'd be in this role through the investiture of the crown prince, after which, we'd review it. The king agreed but insisted that Smith continue to lead on the security details for himself. Now, I content myself with scowling at him.

He thrusts out his chest.

The princess looks between us, a bored look on her features. She sighs. "Why don't I let the two of you compare dicks while I head on for my appointment?"

Her mentioning the D-word from those flawlessly made-up pink lips is both incongruent and a bloody turn on. Her jaw is set. There's a stubborn glint in her eyes. If it were up to me, I'd lock her inside and not let her out.

"I have a better idea. Why don't you and I discuss your security arrangements"—I nod toward the elevator car which has just arrived — "enroute to your appointment?"

5

Aurelia

I step into the elevator, followed by my new bodyguard. He punches the button for the ground floor, and the doors close. *Finally, some level of privacy!* I turn on him.

"What are you doing here?" I hiss.

"I'm your new personal protection officer, of course." He clasps his hands behind his back and regards me with an unwavering gaze.

My cheeks flush. I can't stop thinking of how he came to my rescue and saved me from that creep last night. Or how it felt to have his lips pressed against mine, to be plastered against his strong, broad chest. *Surely, he's not going to spill the beans on what happened, is he?* I gave my security team the slip and escaped. I shouldn't have been at the bar. I certainly shouldn't have kissed a stranger. No way, do I want my father finding out about what I got up to, either.

"What happened at the bar—"

"Will not be repeated." His tone is firm. His features assemble into a stony mask. There's a shutter over his eyes, which have turned into sheets of bullet-proof glass. He's saying all the right words. I'm a princess and he's…my bodyguard. Of course, I can't indulge in a relationship with him. Not when I must marry someone else. Not that it stops me from wanting this man.

Or wishing he'd acknowledge this thrum of chemistry spiking between us. Or hoping… He intends to repeat what happened yesterday between us. So even though it's a relief to realize he's not going to pursue the matter, I'm also disappointed to hear it.

"It was a mistake. I apologize for it, Princess." His tone is formal. His jaw is granite. He holds my gaze steadily, and there's nothing in his expression to tell me he recalls how our mouths clung to each other, how I hung onto his biceps while he kissed me with a dominance that I felt all the way to my feet. A lick of anger curls up my spine.

How dare he call what happened between us a mistake when I haven't been able to stop thinking about that kiss?

I dig my fingers into the handle of my handbag, then say in my best princess tone. "You chased after me. Why?"

He hesitates. "I wanted to make sure you got home safely. That's why I followed you out of the alley."

"That might be so, but it's not the only reason." I search his features. "I saw your face from the limousine, remember? And you looked gutted."

He arches an eyebrow. "I wouldn't put it like that."

"Then how would you put it?" I demand hotly.

"I admit, I wanted to take you home. Who wouldn't? After all, you were willing too." He shrugs. "I was surprised you cut and ran. I knew you wanted me, and—"

"And *you* wanted me," I remind him, trying to stay calm, when everything inside me wants to stab my finger into his chest and demand that he confess how much he was affected by that kiss.

"It was a moment of insanity." His features remain bland. "And when you left so abruptly, I felt compelled to make sure you were okay."

I search his face, frustrated that he's talking so calmly and logically when what I want is for him to throw me down and complete what we started yesterday... Which, going by the resolve on his face, it's clear is not happening anytime soon.

I blow out a breath. "So, that's it?"

"It has to be." He tilts his head, his face inscrutable. "I will not tell anyone what transpired between us, Princess. Your secrets are safe with me."

I should be grateful he's saying that, but frankly, I don't care. I wish... I could throw caution to the wind and have a hot, no-holds-barred fling with this man. Which is what I was hoping for when I saw him at the bar, wasn't I? At least that way, I'll have some memories to hold onto when I'm locked in my emotionless marriage. My stomach bottoms out.

I didn't realize how much I've been dreading my upcoming nuptials until I met this man. He's turned my world upside down, and he's not even aware of it.

It makes me want to chip away at his very irritating composure until he acknowledges that the kiss meant something to him too. Also, a part of me is secretly rooting for a replay of what happened between us last night.

He seems satisfied by my silence and jerks his chin. "It's best we meet every morning with your personal assistant to discuss your appointments, so I can plan the best course of action each day."

I suggested this to my previous security team, who disagreed with me. But then, they were rather incompetent and, even to my inexperienced eyes, seemed to make obvious slip-ups. With them, it felt like a game where I tried my best to evade them and, often, succeeded.

The thing is, I don't want a bodyguard on my tail at all times. *Although I might be more than willing to have this man on my tail.* I resist a smile that threatens to break free.

Still, I feel the need to not comply right away with his suggestion. Instinct tells me I need to carve out the boundaries on my terms, so he knows I'm not going to accept everything he recommends without questioning it. "What if I want to be spontaneous?"

His forehead furrows. A spark of anger in his eyes shoots a thrill of excitement down my spine. *Ha! He's not made of stone, after all.*

He holds my gaze with his startling green ones. "I can cope with spontaneity, but I also know your engagements are decided in advance, so there's no excuse not to share those with me. I can plan your safety escort around them."

Damn! This man knows his job. Which reassures me that I'm safe. It also makes me realize I'm not going to be able to get away with much with him around. More reason to hold my stance. I scowl at him.

His lips twitch. *Ugh!* No doubt, he's loving the fact that I thought I'd managed to put one over on him.

When he speaks next, his voice is mild. "It's important that you understand the security measures I will be putting in place to guard you."

I do understand, but I can't stop myself from baiting him.

Something about that inscrutable mask he's pulled over his features makes me want to see how far I can push him before he snaps. Something about that tightly leashed control, evident in the coiled muscles of his shoulders makes me want to disrupt it so he reveals that passion I felt last night.

"Hmph." I scoff, pretending a rudeness that I hope will upset him. "You do your job, and let me get on with my life, will ya?"

But does this man come any closer to losing his cool? Nope. He simply tips his head to the side, not looking very surprised with my defiance. Then, he reaches over and stabs the stop button, and the elevator screeches to a halt.

"What the—" I gape at him. "Did you just—"

"You leave me no choice." He turns slowly to face me. "We need to be in sync about your safety precautions."

I tap my foot. "There are people who will realize the elevator has stopped and call you—"

His phone buzzes as if to punctuate my words. I look at him triumphantly. *Yeah, yeah, I know. Not very princess-like of me to swear inwardly.* But I've spent my entire life trying to break out of the box people keep trying to put me into, and no bodyguard, however hot, and gorgeous, and drool-worthy he may be, is going to rein me in.

He pulls his phone from his pocket and growls, "Davenport."

A voice squawks on the other side.

"The princess and I decided it best to have our discussion in the most secure place possible, an elevator, which I searched beforehand to make sure there were no bugs."

He listens again to the voice.

"You can monitor us on the security cameras. We should be on our way in five minutes, at the most." He disconnects the call.

I stare at him open-mouthed. "You told them—"

"The truth. Which is always best, don't you think?" He pockets his phone, leaning a shoulder against one of the walls. "As I was saying, we'll meet every morning with your personal assistant to go over your schedule for the day."

I fold my arms across my chest and paste the most regal expression I can summon on my face. Not that it has any effect on him.

"You will always be accompanied by me, wherever you go. I will be present at all your meetings, internal and external," he says in a voice which brooks no argument.

I brush aside the resentment bubbling inside and say in a remote voice, "Whatever."

His forehead furrows but doesn't react to my less than enthusiastic response. "For safety reasons, my room will be in the same suite as yours in the hotel."

"Oh?" A shiver squeezes my spine. I hadn't expected that. It's exciting to think of this epitome of masculinity being so close.

"Also, once we have our morning meeting there will be no more changes to your appointments for that day," he declares.

My frown deepens. "That sounds very rigid."

"It's the only way to ensure all preparations are made to protect you throughout the day," he rumbles in that reasonable tone I'm coming to hate.

What he means is that there is no way I can make a last-minute change, then take advantage of the resulting confusion and slip away, like I used to do. Which was more a testament to their ineptitude than my innovativeness, if I'm being honest. It livened things up though. *And now*, that window of opportunity is gone too. A suffocating feeling squeezes my chest. I take a breath to calm myself.

"There have been enough threats in the past, none of which have played out." The words slip out before I can stop myself.

He face tightens. "Which doesn't mean this threat should be taken lightly."

"Yes, I get that. But what if you put these measures in place, and then, it turns out the threat was empty?" I lock my fingers together. "Meanwhile, there are even more restrictions on my life."

"What if the threat is real?" His voice is not unkind. "It's better to be safe than to regret the lack of security measures later."

It shouldn't be a big deal that my freedom is even more curtailed, but it makes me feel like I have even less control over my life. That sense of suffocation spreads to my throat, and I struggle not to panic.

I must let some expression slip, for his features soften. "This is for your safety, Princess. I am only as good as your cooperation. If you think these rules won't work for you, now is the time to speak your mind."

And disappoint my father? I can't do that.

"They're fine." I pull out my phone from my purse and pointedly glance at the screen. "Can you get the elevator moving? I don't want to be late for my appointment."

6

Aurelia

When I look up into his face, he's staring at me with those emerald-green eyes. I notice the flecks of silver in his irises, like light dancing on a forest floor. The dark depths to them hint at mysteries, at secrets he harbors, ordeals I can only imagine he's been through. He's seen war. Has killed men in the line of duty. In comparison, I've led a sheltered life.

The worst thing that ever happened to me was losing my mother. Yet, there are similarities between us too.

He served his country by joining the Royal Marines. I opt to serve mine by sticking it out in this role I was born into—a princess who might often come across as a figurehead but who can make a difference. It's something I remind myself every time I feel I'm in a gilded cage. Having tighter security is the price I have to pay for my privileged position.

His eyes narrow, and the ferocity of his gaze shoots delicious heat through my veins. I don't look away, though. Neither does he. Without breaking the connection, he leans in closer, closer.

Close enough for the heat of his body to wrap around me like an embrace, for the spicy muskiness of his scent to invade my senses, for those fine lines radiating from the corners of his eyes to stand out in relief. That familiar attraction between us roars forward and slams into my chest. I gasp and raise my chin. My lips tingle. My throat dries. His gaze lowers to my mouth and stays there. His eyes widen, and he hesitates, then he raises his hand, and my breath catches.

He's going to touch me. Touch me. Please. Instead, he slams a button on the elevator panel. The car begins to descend, which is the only reason my stomach bottoms out. It has nothing to do with his nearness, of course.

He pulls back, and tucks his arms into his sides, then turns to face forward. *Damn.* And I was so sure he wanted to kiss me.

The thought of our lips almost meeting has heat flushing my cheeks. The fact that he had me fooled makes me bristle.

I straighten my spine, square my shoulders and, as soon as the doors open, I brush past him and walk out. Only, with his long strides, he overtakes me.

He slows his pace, forcing me to slow down as well, then angles his body in the direction of the corridor that leads away from the main entrance. "It's safer to use the side-entrance. The car is waiting there."

He leads me out past the waiting security, toward a Rolls Royce, which is flanked by another two vehicles. None of which I recognize.

He dismisses the security personnel standing by the backseat and opens the door to the Rolls for me.

"The car you've been using will be driven by a member of the security team who will be following us." He explains. "*You* will be in this armored vehicle. It's safer for you."

I frown. "This feels like overkill."

"Better than *you* being killed," he says in a bland voice.

I blink. "Are you trying to frighten me?"

"Just stating the facts, Princess," he continues in that same overtly reasonable tone which sets my teeth on edge. "Your driver is trained in security measures and evasive techniques, so he can protect you, if the need arises."

"You're very thorough," I murmur.

This is not something the last team thought of. I have to appreciate this man's foresight. But it means I can't drive my own car. Having that small freedom taken away makes me feel trapped. My chest tightens. That feeling of suffocating returns. Stronger this time. It squeezes my guts and tightens around my rib cage. I struggle for a modicum of composure and take a few calming breaths. "Driving my car is one of the few times I felt free from constraints, but I understand why that's not possible anymore…"

Spine straight. You're a princess. I draw in a breath. *Thanks, Mom.* I square my shoulders.

"But don't expect me to fall in line and submit to your every whim." I tip up my chin.

Something flashes in his eyes, something carnal, and hot. Those green eyes turn a darker shade, a color that reminds me of the hidden depths of an underground spring. A fever spikes my blood. My throat dries. *Jesus, did he choose to misinterpret my words and give them an X-rated meaning? Or did I mean it that way without realizing it?*

A shutter lowers over his eyes and he's, once again, inscrutable. I want to demand that he not hide what he's feeling from me.

"Why don't we discuss this, enroute to your next meeting, which"—he looks at his watch—"I believe we need to be at in less than half-an-hour." He scrutinizes me steadily.

Once again, our gazes clash. I sense his will. The strength in his stance. The fact that I won't be able to cajole him into doing things my way, the way I do with my wider team. The car in front and behind has members of my new protective detail on either side.

"Your assistant Veronica will follow in a separate car." He shuts the door, walks around and gets in from the other side of the passenger seat. Then the chauffeur eases the car forward.

I press the button set into the door, and the privacy screen rises, cutting us off from the driver. With the heavy tint on the glass on either side, we have complete privacy.

"I expected you to be more upset that she's not riding with you. She certainly seemed put out about it," Ryot rumbles.

"Oh?" I glance out the window. Veronica and I use these car journeys to discuss details related to my schedule. It's easier to do that face-to-face, but if Ryot thinks it's better for her to be in a different car, I'm not going to fight it.

From her point of view, it would be simpler if she could be in the same vehicle as me, so I can understand her being upset about this.

For a few seconds, we drive in silence. He's sitting at ease with his big thighs spread out. taking up more than his share of the seat. He's...so huge, so male, so larger-than-life...so unreachable, and so attractive with his features composed into a mask.

"I understand these changes may seem like a lot. But it's why your father hired me." Those green eyes of his are impenetrable.

He's hiding in there, somewhere behind that professional mask he's donned. He's trying to pretend I'm just a job...which I have been for most of the people in my life—my child-minders after my mother passed, all of my father's council... Even my father, sometimes.

Most of them don't give me credit for knowing what I want. Many in my country see me only as a princess who'll one day marry well and bring money into the country.

This man, though? I'm not going to be a pushover for him. The fire, the passion, that explosive tension between us? All of it is real. Of course, I'm better off ignoring it, seeing as I'm going to be married soon. Besides, he's my bodyguard, and if I try to cross the professional line with him, he'll rebuff me. That said, I'm going to make sure he can't ignore the chemistry between us either.

I place my handbag on the seat beside me with exaggerated care. "Is that right?"

He nods, a wariness creeping into his expression. "I cannot take any chances with your safety. I understand how frustrating these new security measures must be for you, but I'd rather you be pissed off and alive, than not." His rough, dark voice grows deeper in timbre, and my pussy instantly responds.

Moisture pools in my panties, and my nipples bead. He's talking about safety parameters, and all I want to do is crawl into his lap.

It must strike him that my thoughts are elsewhere, for his jaw hardens. "Are you listening to me, Princess?" The frustration turns his voice even more rough, and my thighs clench. A shiver grips me.

When I raise my gaze to his, he freezes. I'm not sure what he sees there, but there's an answering spark in his eyes. And that's all the encouragement I need. I sidle closer to him, and before he can stop me, I lean up and press my lips to his.

7

Ryot

Softness, so soft. And sweet enough to make me feel I've dived headlong into cotton candy. And her scent. *Jesus.* Honeysuckle and vanilla. She smells like freshly baked shortbread. Like the first bite of a sun-ripened strawberry I long to indulge in. I allow her to brush her lips against mine once, twice. Fire ignites in my belly. My shoulder muscles coil, but I manage to not respond.

I curl my fingers into fists, tighten my muscles and will myself to stay still. A sound of frustration emerges from her throat. She bites down on my lower lip, and my cock instantly stiffens. A bolt of lust shoots through my veins. I've managed to hold onto my control, but fucking hell, when she presses her curves into my chest, and I feel the outline of her beaded nipples, something coiled inside of me snaps. I clasp my palm around the nape of her neck and take control. With my free hand I cup her cheek to hold her in place, then I tilt my head and lick into her mouth. With a moan, she parts her lips.

Instantly, I sweep my tongue over hers. I deepen the kiss, draw on her breath, and the taste of her fills my senses. She squirms in her seat, and I tighten my hold on the nape of her neck. I release her face, only to cup her hip. I squeeze, and she shudders. I pull her closer, swipe my tongue over her teeth, and a whine spills from her lips. Her little sounds of need go straight to my head. My thigh muscles harden, and I wrap my arm about her and pull her onto my lap. I continue to kiss her until it feels like our breaths are one, and our lips are melded together, and she's melting into me.

Then, the vehicle brakes, and it's like someone has thrown cold water on me.

Shock clears my mind of all thoughts. Immediately, I release my hold on her. Chest heaving, I stare down into her flushed features. Her auburn hair is tumbled about her shoulders, her lips are swollen, and the chain around her neck is askew. She looks like she's been thoroughly kissed. Satisfaction squeezes my chest, followed by anger. At myself. I stepped over the line. A few more seconds, and I might not have been able to stop myself from fucking her right here.

The only other time I've lost control with a woman was last night... With her. No one has made me forget my values, my principles, my standards like this before. No one has imprinted their presence in my life quite so deeply, so quickly. No one before has burrowed their way under my skin, causing me to lose my mind when I'm on a job. Not even Jane. Not one. Except this woman. I need to remember she's a job. This is a job, and she is my principal. I need to get a grip on myself.

"I'm sorry." I grip her hips, then place her back in her seat. I move away, closer to the window, ensuring there's enough space between us.

"*You're* sorry?" More color flushes her cheeks. Her eyes spark.

"I shouldn't have done that." I manage to infuse enough hardness into my tone that she flinches.

Then she gathers herself and tosses her hair over her shoulder. "Oh, lighten up, it was just a kiss."

"It shouldn't have happened." I tighten my jaw. It *wasn't* just a kiss. It was a slap-me-across-the-face and punch-me-in-the-guts, stomach-twisting-like-when-you-jump-off-a-helo kind of a kiss.

"Besides, it was I who kissed you, so—" She pops a shoulder.

"I responded to it," I say through gritted teeth.

"I'm aware." Her lips twitch. "We didn't do anything wrong, by the way."

Maybe not her, but I sure did. While becoming a personal protective detail does not require you swear an oath, I take it no less seriously. My ability to block everything else out and focus on the task at hand is what makes me good at what I do. By kissing her again, I confirmed that the touch of her, the taste, the smell, the little whimpers that escaped her as she tried to burrow into me are every bit as soul-shattering as I remember.

I shake my head to clear it. "Everything about this was wrong," I growl.

"What do you mean?" She furrows her forehead. "Surely, you've noticed that there's chemistry between us?" She waves a hand in the air. "It was a normal response. Besides, I was getting tired of your dos and don'ts. It was the only way to shut you up."

I glare at her, half angry, half turned on by her ability to stand up to me. She doesn't seem put off by my forbidding persona, one I perfected over the years to ensure I'd be obeyed without question. Of course, then I discovered the bossiness I used with my troops was also how I preferred to treat my partners in bed. I like to be in control. I like to dominate. I like my women to be subservient, to offer themselves up to me, to trust me to give them what they need. Power exchange is what gets me off. The kind this spoiled princess would never dream of.

"Don't do it again." I pull my phone from my pocket and peruse the messages which have come in from the rest of the team.

"What the—" She sputters. "You... You... Dare tell me what I can and can't do?"

"You're under my protection. Which means, you follow my directions."

She freezes. I sense the shock radiating off of her. Guess no one's ever spoken with such authority to her. She listened to her father's command earlier, but I got the sense that was only because he issued it in the role of King. On a personal level, it's clear she's run rings around him and, likely, everyone else who she's worked with over the years. But that stops now.

I need to keep the princess safe. The danger she's in is too real. I need my wits about me to protect her. I cannot allow myself to give in to my attraction for her, as that will only compromise my judgement and endanger her. Besides, I don't trust these feelings the princess elicits in me. I've never had them before, and damn, if that doesn't make me feel... Guilty? Confused? Frustrated? I don't even know. It's just so... Unfamiliar.

I'm not someone to be taken in by big blue eyes, creamy skin, and lush curves that make her resemble a Rubenesque painting. As long as I don't touch her again, don't kiss her, don't allow myself to be taken in by this electricity that sparks when we're near each other, things should be okay.

I'll be okay. I resist the urge to run my finger under the constricting collar of my button-down shirt; a uniform I was instructed to don to fit in with the rest of her detail, which I hate.

I'm not surprised when she scoffs, "Don't forget, you work for me."

"I work for your father, actually." I turn to her. "And if I were to tell him I need to curtail your comings and goings until this threat has been neutralized, what do you think he'd say?"

She glowers at me. That little fold between her eyebrows is back, and it's so fucking adorable. My fingers tingle to reach out and smooth it, so I shove my phone and my fingers into my pocket.

"Look, I don't mean to come off all heavy-handed. It's why I would have preferred to have a discussion with you, before jumping straight into being your detail, but your father insisted it was urgent."

"It doesn't matter." She turns away and glances out the window, giving me a view of the column of her throat. Creamy unmarked skin which, I can confirm, feels as smooth as butter. And were I to push my nose into the hollow of her neck, would her scent be more intense there? My already erect cock extends further in anticipation.

Fucking hell, I need to find my center, my composure. I need to push all thoughts of her out of my mind and get myself back in the game.

I roll my shoulders, draw in a few deep breaths, and when I feel more composed, I turn to her. "Please accept my apologies, Princess."

She turns slowly; there's surprise on her features. "In my experience, most alpha males who admit they're in the wrong—*if* they admit they're in the wrong—don't mean it. But apparently"—she looks into my eyes—"you do."

She thinks I'm an alpha male? Good. That means she knows what my expectations are when it comes to my woman. Not that *she's* my woman. Jane was my woman... Or so I thought, until she betrayed me. Aura though... She's my principal. *A job.* Someone I need to protect.

"The day I begin to believe I'm infallible is when it'll cost me my life."

She blinks slowly. "You mean—"

"My sole focus is to keep you safe. And I can do that better if I have your cooperation. It's going to be much trickier if we're constantly at loggerheads. And if that means—"

"—if you have to apologize, you'll do it to help you do your job well?" That glower in her eyes is back.

Damn, I'm botching this up again. I roll my shoulders. "I mean, I am sorry. I didn't take the time to explain my approach and discuss the parameters with you, only—"

"—I kissed you." She half laughs, then rubs at her temple. "I'm sorry, too. I didn't mean for things to get awkward between us."

"They're not."

She surveys my features. "You mean it," she finally remarks in surprise.

"I'm aware of what it's like to be constantly under pressure. Living in an environment where you're in the public eye, having to maintain an image while trying to be true to yourself, while also living up to your father's expectations is not easy."

She shakes her head. "You surprise me."

"Because I have enough emotional intelligence to understand

what it's like to spend most of your life under the microscope of public scrutiny."

She regards me with a quizzical expression. "I guess, I had you pegged as just muscle, but maybe, there's more to you."

"I'm *sure* there's more to you than meets the eye, Princess." Our gazes meet. The air between us spikes with heat. Her irises dilate. I have no doubt, if I were to touch her between her legs, she'd be damp and melting, and waiting for my cock. And if I licked her there, she'd be every bit as sweet, as evocative, as mysterious as the taste of her mouth promised.

Once more, my thigh muscles harden, my pants feel too fucking tight.

She leans in closer, but this time, I manage to pull my mind back to the task at hand. I hold out my palm. "Your phone."

"What?" She blinks.

"Give me your phone."

She must be more shaken than normal, for she digs it out of her purse, unlocks it, and hands it to me without hesitation. I slide the protective cover off, disable the built-in tracking app on it, then slip a bug between the cover and the phone.

"You have me under surveillance," she says in a resigned voice.

"You don't sound surprised."

She shrugs. "I often wondered why the previous team didn't insist on it, but hey, I figured I could enjoy my freedom for a little longer."

It's my turn to be taken aback. "So, you're not going to fight this?"

She looks at me with resignation. "Would it make any difference if I did?"

I shake my head.

"That's what I thought." She looks away. "Anyway, thanks for leveling with me." Her voice is remote.

But underneath, I hear the note of frustration and fear. For all her bravado, she's concerned about the threat, but she's trying not to show it.

It makes me want to reassure her. And take care of her. A fierce sense of protection overwhelms me, and I don't question it. She's my asset. It's my job to ensure she feels safe.

"Nothing will happen to you as long as I'm your bodyguard," I promise.

"Thought you preferred protective detail?"

I hear the chuckle in her voice and I'm glad it's helped lighten her mood, even if it's only temporary.

"I do. But in this case, bodyguard fits the role I've adopted for you, as long as I'm leading your security detail. The rest is semantics."

She nods. "I understand why my father trusts you… You're quite thorough."

"Experience. I've been in too many situations where going that extra mile with safety measures has made the difference between life and death."

She shivers. "You can be quite grim, you know that?"

"Best to be grim now if it means it'll help to ward off danger. If we keep things tight and have enough visible security around you, it will, hopefully, put off those behind this threat."

"You think whoever is behind it poses a real risk?"

I choose my words carefully. "Until my team and I track down and neutralize those behind it, we have to assume whoever is behind the threat wants to hurt you in some way."

"And you want it to seem difficult for them to get away with anything." She turns to me. Her features are composed. "You're hoping this will serve as a deterrent."

"I intend to ensure that it's almost impossible for them to get to you, but every protocol has a gap that, try as one might, cannot be plugged. Which is why additional precautions like this"—I hand the phone over to her—"work, even if the phone is switched off. Wherever you are, we can track you."

"Thanks." Our fingers brush, and she draws in a sharp breath.

Heat shoots up my arm, and I pull it back. This woman's dangerous. I need to ensure there is no other opportunity for us to be in such proximity.

"We're here." The driver's voice emerges from the intercom set in the partition. Like a fucking coward, I use the excuse to push my door open and slowly walk around to grip the handle on her side. I glance around, ensuring the team who have piled out of the cars in front and behind us have formed a cordon around us.

I wait a few minutes, scanning the area, until I think she's righted her appearance. Then I open her door.

8

Aurelia

I look up from reading *The Owl Who Was Afraid of the Dark* into the faces of the children in the room. We're at the inner-city school I handpicked for this engagement. I love children and, given a choice, I'd rather spend time with them than at yet another boring, official event shaking hands with dignitaries of state. I selected one of my favorite children's books and brought along my own copy to read to the kids. Not that all of them are interested in it.

One of the little boys is scribbling into his notebook with his pencil, another little girl has her fingers linked together and a frown on her face as she glances at the door. A third boy looks out the window. There are a few in the front who look back at me with blank faces.

At the back of the room, the teacher wrings her hands in distress, no doubt, worried that she's going to be called to the principal's office for not getting her class to listen to the princess who deigned to drop by.

"Woooo!" I cup my palms around my mouth and pretend to hoot. The little boy stops scribbling in his book and peeks up at me from under his eyelashes.

"Woooohooo?" I hoot again…this time, with a question mark at the end, in the hope of getting more of a response.

The little girl shoots me a sideways look. The boy who's been scribbling in his notebook lets the pencil drop from his hand.

Ryot, who's positioned by the doorway, flicks a glance in my direction. He's been still since he walked in, except for his head which constantly roves the room as if he'll find danger lurking in the corners. Our gazes meet and it's as if a truck slams into me, then he continues with his perusal of the space. The breath I didn't know I was holding shudders out.

"Wooohooo hoo hoo." I jerk my head toward the kids to find the same boy who was scribbling in his book earlier smirking in my direction.

He lowers his hands to his sides. "That's not what an owl sounds like."

"No?" I stifle my own smile. At last, I have their attention. "How does an owl sound?"

He obligingly cups his palms around his mouth and hoots. Some of the kids giggle.

Then, a girl and another boy join him, and suddenly, there are a bunch of them hooting back at me. I burst out laughing and hoot with them.

The hair at the back of my neck prickles. I sense his gaze and turn in his direction to find Ryot staring at me. There's a weird look in his eyes—one of surprise and confusion. Guess he didn't expect me to get childish with the kids? His gaze sweeps past me as he continues his perusal of the classroom. I feel bereft at once. Why is that? Why should meeting his eyes this way affect me so much? It's as if we're connected by an invisible thread that lets me know exactly where he is in the vicinity.

I push away thoughts of him and focus on the children. "One, two, three, eyes on me." I raise my hand in the air.

The reading continues without incident. I bid the kids good-bye and leave the classroom without meeting Ryot's gaze.

I wave at the photographers gathered outside the school but decline to comment.

The rest of my protective detail stand guard as I board the vehicle, with Ryot walking around to slide back inside with me. Within seconds, the entourage is on its way.

My phone vibrates with a message. I pull out the device and glance at the message from my assistant.

> Veronica: Your Highness, I am so very sorry I couldn't stay for the rest of the reading. I had to leave to take care of something. Rest assured; I will message soon with an update.

I frown. On the face of it, there's nothing wrong with her message. But her unfailing politeness often grates on my nerves. Still, she's good at her job, which is why I keep her on. On the other hand, even *she* gets to drive herself. I push that thought out of my head.

My phone vibrates again.

> Veronica: Some of the biggest clothing brands from Paris want to set up appointments for you to try on clothes from their upcoming collections. Would next month work for you?
>
> Me: Tell them I won't be needing clothes from them this season.
>
> Veronica: But Your Highness, you have always bought clothes from their new lines every year.
>
> Me: Tell them it's part of my drive to be environmentally conscious. I'll be recycling clothes from my wardrobe until further notice.

> Veronica: Are you sure, Your Highness? This is a great opportunity to have access to the latest fashion trends. It's bound to result in a boost to your social media profiles.

I frown. Sometimes I think Veronica is too taken in with the image of a Royal Princess. She's party to the sweat and tears that go into building my public persona, so she should know, that's all it is. A persona. But she seems too enamored by the glamorous front I try to present.

> Me: Thank you for your feedback. And you're right. It's a great opportunity. But at this stage it doesn't fit in with my plans so I'm going to have to sadly refuse.

Not to mention, I won't have the budget to buy from any of these brands in the near future. Not when my country is on the brink of economic collapse.

> Veronica: Of course, Your Highness. I will let them know.

My phone vibrates with an incoming call. I glance at the caller ID and wince. Then decline it. Within seconds, another incoming message pops up on my screen

> Gavin: Aura, why are you not answering my calls? Are you avoiding me?

Ugh! I can almost hear his whiny voice in my ears. I suppose, at some point, I need to take his calls. But not now. I flick a glance in Ryot's direction, then hurriedly slide my phone back into my shoulder bag.

"Everything okay?" Ryot asks.

"Of course." I accept a bottle of water from him and nod my thanks. I drink from it before capping it and placing it aside. "Is it normal for you to ride in the same car as the person you're protecting?"

He hesitates. "Only because of the recent threat. If something were to happen, I have more of a chance to protect you in such close quarters."

I nod slowly. "And inside there, did you actually expect a possible threat in a classroom filled with children?"

"It's when you least expect it that they strike. I wouldn't put anything past them."

There's a finality to his words, a hard edge which sends a jolt of fear up my spine. The bite in his tone warns me this is not like the other times when I've been threatened. *Oh, for crying out loud, how bad can the threat be?*

"This note I received; can I see it?" I'm sure he's going to turn down my request like my father and his team have done in the past.

Instead, he looks at me with surprise. "You haven't seen it?"

"My father and his courtiers prefer not to show me the threats I receive. They felt I should be protected. They insisted it would only make me worry more." I don't bother masking the frustration I feel about it.

His forehead furrows. "And what do *you* think?"

I blink. He's the first one to ask me that question. My father and his team prefer to talk down to me. My brothers stand up for me, but I'd rather not go to them with every single challenge I face. I prefer to fight my own battles, as much as possible. *Perhaps, he can help me with this one?* I'm not going to turn down help in this regard. "I think I should be allowed to judge for myself the level of danger I'm in."

"I agree. Understanding the severity of the threat you're under will help you understand why I need to implement certain security protocols." He pulls out his phone, swipes the screen, and hands it to me. I survey the picture open on the screen. It's a printout which simply states.

Princess Aurelia, you will die

. . .

A shiver runs down my spine. Seeing the threat in black and white ties my guts up in knots. Whoever wrote the note is serious. This is not someone who craves notoriety or who hopes to be tracked down and captured to gain a few seconds of fame. This...comes from someone who means business. Who won't stop until they complete their mission.

My throat dries. My heart begins to race. I draw in a breath, manage to find some composure, then hand the phone back to Ryot. "Where was it found?"

"On the pillow of your hotel room bed."

"What?" I gasp and snap my gaze to his. "You're joking."

The expression on his face tells me he isn't. "One of the house-keeping staff who came in to make up the room found it and raised the alarm."

"Shit." I sink back into my seat, then notice the strange expression on his features. "What? You thought because I'm a Princess I don't swear?"

His expression closes. "It is a surprise... Yes."

"Talk about stereotypes." I snatch my bottle of water and drain it before setting it aside. "No wonder my father seemed more upset than usual." I glance out the window. Unspoken is the fact that someone found their way past the existing security to leave that note on my bed. If I'd been in the room at that time—I shiver and lock my fingers in my lap.

"I'm sorry if I disturbed you by showing you the note." Ryot's voice is gentle.

"Bullshit. You're not sorry. In fact, you hoped showing me that note would make me fall in line with your protective measures."

I turn to look at him in time to catch the flash of something in his eyes. It confirms to me that I hit the bullseye.

"You're right." He holds my gaze. "In this, I don't agree with your father. It's best for you to see the threat so you can gauge for yourself the seriousness of it."

I turn away again. He's right. Seeing that note brings home the gravity of the situation. My father's priority has always been protecting me, and apparently, that means protecting me from worrying too. I understand his intentions, but if someone had shown me one of these threats, I would have taken them more seriously.

"You don't mind going against my father when he's the one paying your salary?"

I sense him stiffen. "I'm here to protect you and will do what I think is right to keep you safe, even if that means going against your father's directives."

Not too many people would have the courage to do that. He might be an arrogant, over-bearing and opinionated ass—but given how he saved me at the bar, I pegged him as chivalrous, maybe even fearless. Now that he's standing up for me against my father, I realize, he's macho not only in his looks, but also when it counts. He's truly brave and courageous. A real man.

"You're an astute woman. You deserve to know what you're up against. It will help you understand the measures I'm implementing for your safety."

That, more than anything, moves me. Of course, he's also doing it so I'm more cooperative, but regardless of his motives, I appreciate him treating me as someone who knows my mind and can decide what I want for myself.

Then another thought strikes me. "Does this mean I need to change my hotel room?"

Once more, his features turn expressionless. "This means, we'll be re-visiting the backgrounds of everyone on your team who had access to your hotel room. And yes, you'll be moving to a different hotel."

My jaw drops. "I am?"

He nods. "I'm relocating you to a boutique hotel. One which might not be as fancy as the one you were in, but where you will be safer and which I hope will match the style you are accustomed to."

I disregard the sarcasm in his voice. "And when were you going to tell me this?"

He has the grace to look shamefaced.

"You weren't going to tell me about this until we reached the hotel?"

"We are on our way there now," he admits.

I do understand the reasoning behind not going back to the hotel. Fact is, I wouldn't feel safe there either. So, I'm glad not to return. "You could have mentioned it to me earlier," I grouse.

"I didn't want to take your focus off the event you were headed to. And I am telling you the first opportunity I got."

I purse my lips. He's right, I admit grudgingly. I'm used to events in the public eye, but I still do need to focus my mind on it to give it my best. If he'd shown me the note or told me about the hotel change before the event, it would have broken my concentration, so he did the right thing. *Damn, I can't even get pissed off with him, can I?*

"Also, given someone made it past the security on your floor, it felt prudent to keep the details of where we were moving you on a need-to-know basis."

I incline my head. "You mean, you don't trust me not to share my whereabouts with, say, social media?" I raise my phone.

His lips quirk. "You wouldn't be stupid enough to do that."

"Thanks?" I scoff.

"I didn't think you were going tell anyone outside of your imme-diate circle, but I wanted to ensure not even your personal assistant, or anyone from your previous security team, would find out about it. Your father is, of course, aware of our plans."

"Not even Veronica?" I frown. "With all the planning we have to do, it would be helpful to have her staying in the same hotel."

"That's what she said too." He raises a shoulder. "It's only until we've completed a thorough check on everyone's background, and until we rule out their being involved with the last threat."

All at once, the meaning of his words sinks in. "You think someone within the team let the intruder have access to my room?" I ask in horror.

"I prefer not to engage in conjecture." His voice is calm, and I get the feeling, once again, he's trying to manage me...because I'm his client. *Grr.* That's the box he wants to stick me in, and he's not budging on it. I'm going to try my best to make him reconsider it, though.

Once again, I look out the window. The city passes by outside, and I spot the familiar sign of a well-known fast-food chain. The only time I've been to one was when I evaded security and sneaked out of boarding school with a friend. I was reprimanded by my father for it.

It was the fact that I might have endangered my friend's life that made me realize I needed to take more responsibility for my actions. I realized then, I liked to pretend to be like everyone else, but I wasn't.

But there are also benefits to my position. Like now, when I want something and not even my controlling bodyguard can stop me from having it.

I press the button for the intercom and speak into it, "Stop the car, I want to get out."

9

Ryot

When the car keeps moving forward, she lets out a sound of disgust. "Ask him to stop." She turns to me. "I want ice cream."

"You want ice cream?"

She sets her jaw and inclines her head toward the immediately recognizable fast-food chain. "Right now."

And that'll create a freakin' security nightmare. But based on the obstinate glint in her eyes, I realize, if I say no to this request, she's going to lose it. Of course, seeing her pissed off would be a turn on, but not being granted this ask might make her uncooperative overall. I weigh the odds. I don't want her refusing to move to the new hotel I picked out for her. No doubt, she's pushing the boundaries to find an excuse to not comply with my plan. And I can tell, suggesting we order at the drive-through is not going to cut it.

Agreeing to her wish means taking the risk of someone getting to her while we're in there... But I trust my instincts to keep her safe. Plus, the element of surprise means the person who threatened her won't know she's going to be there either. I pull out my phone and update Cole, my lead protective detail in the other car, about the change in plans. Thankfully, I had enough time to brief the team before taking over this morning.

Then I depress the intercom button. "Pull over, Alfie."

The chauffeur slows down, then eases the car to a stop.

"Wait for me." I jump out the car, but by the time I reach her, she's already out and striding up the sidewalk. This woman is so willful, I have a good mind to spank her... Only, I don't dare. And not only because she's my principal but also because she's likely not into any kind of kink.

Jane wasn't into the kind of kink I enjoy either; she made that clear. And the chances that the princess is into the kind of proclivities I like is...almost zero. Not that I wouldn't enjoy introducing her to it. I certainly didn't care enough for Jane to want to convince her. So why does it feel like I'd enjoy exploring it much more with the princess?

I have the sneaking suspicion *I* might like it too much with her. The thought wraps my chest in a vise and turns my cock to stone.

I shove aside all thoughts of how it would feel to have her across my lap, my palm squeezing her butt. I also keep my gaze off her tempting backside as she flounces forward.

Cole, who disembarked from the car ahead of us, has already gone ahead into the outlet to make sure it's safe. I lead the way and Brian, another member of my team, brings up the rear.

Cole holds open the door. I enter first and the princess follows me to the counter and orders. Then, she holds out her hand in my direction. I look at it, then back at her with a quizzical expression.

"Your credit card," she prompts.

"You want my credit card?"

Her cheeks redden. "I forgot to carry mine and I don't have cash."

I nod at her to step away, and when she does, I use mine to pay for the order. The counter staff hands the receipt to me. I glance at it and realize she bought ice cream cones for the entire team. Huh. That's a gesture I hadn't expected.

I urge her to the side. "I assume you know how the system works?"

She rolls her eyes. "You think, because I'm a princess, I've never been to a fast-food outlet?" Her gaze turns pensive. "I suppose, you think I'm spoiled because I insisted you stop the car. And despite realizing it would be a security minefield, I insisted you bring me here."

"It does create a security headache, given how we're in a roomful of strangers but..." I shrug. "You're allowed to blow off steam, given your situation. Besides, you bought cones for everyone. It tells me you're not self-absorbed, despite being born into luxury."

A streak of pink steals over her cheeks. Her eyes widen with pleasure. Then she tips up her chin. "Is that a backhanded compliment?"

"It's a compliment. Period." I chuckle.

Her number flashes on the screen. I step forward to claim her order then change my mind and hand the receipt to her. Likely, she doesn't get to do this often, so it'll be an experience for her to pick up her dessert at the counter. She shoots me a curious look, then approaches the counter and hands over the receipt.

The counter staff, hands her two carriers with seven ice cream cones stuck in them.

She thanks the attendant, who finally seems to notice the identity of the person she's serving. Her gaze widens. But before she can say anything, I touch the princess' elbow and steer her away from the counter. She doesn't protest, much to my relief. Once again, with Cole leading the way, we head out of the restaurant and onto the sidewalk.

"I'll pay you back for the ice cream," she murmurs.

"Don't worry about it." I open the door to the car, and she slides in.

I shut it and, with Cole keeping a look out, I round the car and get in next to her.

She lowers her window and calls out, "Would you like an ice cream cone?"

Cole turns, a look of surprise on his face. He glances at me, and when I nod, he steps closer.

"Please give one to your friend"—she nods in Brian's direction—"and two more for the others."

"Thank you, Princess," he murmurs.

She hands him one of the carriers, then raises her window, before pressing the intercom. "Please, can you lower the screen? I have ice cream for you."

I sense Alfie, the driver's surprise as the panel lowers. The princess leans forward and offers the tray. He, too, glances at me, and when I nod, he accepts a cone. "Thank you, Princess. These ice creams are the best."

"I know, right?" She beams at him.

He flushes and looks starstruck. A tendril of jealousy squeezes my guts. One I don't question too closely. I hit the button on my side and the panel rises, cutting off the view of his face. She turns to me, with shock on her features. "I was talking to him."

"Well, he was done talking."

"But—"

"Is that for me?" Without waiting for her response, I grab an ice cream cone and bite off a mouthful of ice cream.

"You could at least say 'thank you.'"

"Considering I'm the one who paid for it, maybe *you* should be saying 'thank you,'" I retort.

Her eyes widen. "That's not fair; I said I'd pay you back."

I soften my tone. "I know; you did. But I don't want you to pay me back, and I'm not looking for you to thank me. However, you should know that it's against protocol to offer food or drink to my men when they're on duty, but I'll allow it this time."

"That's not how it was with my previous security team," she tosses her head.

When I stay silent, she rolls her eyes. "Just because you're serious and boring, doesn't mean the rest of them need to be that way."

"If being serious and boring means it'll help to save your life, then

I'd prefer all of them be that way. Besides, I did stop when you asked for ice cream," I growl.

"Exactly. It's only ice cream. Lighten up, will ya." She licks up one side of the serving and, Jesus, the sight of her pink tongue slurping the frozen dessert sends the blood draining to my groin. I can't take my gaze off her mouth as she swipes her tongue over the confection. A bead of sweat slides down my temple. This...fascination with her has to stop. Why is it that, in the years I was married to Jane, I never felt this way about her?

"You're melting," the princess murmurs.

"What?"

She nods in the direction of my ice cream cone. I glance down, then curse when I find ice cream dripping down my knuckles. I lower my chin and lick it up, then look up to find her staring at my mouth. Without allowing myself to think, I slurp up some of the ice cream.

Her pupils dilate. The pulse at the base of her throat speeds up. Then, without breaking the connection, she proceeds to lick up the side of her own ice cream before circling the entire thing and ending with a swirl around the entire top of it. Heat shoots through my veins. I'm aware of leaning in closer to her and can't stop myself. She mirrors my move. We're so close, I feel her breath on my cheek. She closes her eyes, raising her mouth. My lips are so close to hers, I can taste her.

That's when Alfie's voice comes over the speaker, "Are we ready to leave?"

10

Aurelia

I startle. Both Ryot and I straighten. He looks away and, without losing a beat, he slaps the intercom button on his side. "Yes, let's head to the hotel."

He makes sure to glance out the window on his side and proceeds to demolish the ice cream in two big bites. I hope he gets an ice cream headache. Not that he'd ever let on. His expression is carefully blank. It's as if that heated moment between us never happened. *Damn. Is it that easy for him to pretend there's nothing between us?*

My stomach feels heavy. I glance down at the ice cream cone in my hand and find I've lost all appetite for it. I dump it back in the tray and resist the urge to fling it in his lap. He'd deserve it though... that...that...knobhead, grr. If only people knew the number of choice British insults I know, thanks to attending school in London. They'd realize, I'm not the sweet, innocent princess the media often makes me out to be. I plonk the holder with the now-melted ice cream on the seat between us.

"Is it that easy for you to switch off whatever you felt a few minutes ago and pretend nothing happened between us?" I fume.

"It is, because nothing happened." He speaks slowly, like I won't understand what he's saying.

"I call bullshit. You and I both know that we both felt...that pull. That attraction. That...same chemistry we both felt at the bar, and it's not something that's going to go away."

His forehead furrows. Then he turns to me. "I can't deny that you are a beautiful woman, and I find you attractive."

"But—?" I fold my arms across my chest and wait.

"*But* I will not cross the line between bodyguard and client. If I did, I'd be no good as your protector."

"What do you mean?" I purse my lips.

"Once I'm personally involved, I won't be able to keep my edge. I won't be able to make the right decisions when it comes to your safety."

"That sounds...far-fetched."

His eyes grow hard. "It's not. I need to keep my perspective so I can make the right decision under pressure. When it comes to you, I can't afford not to, do you understand?"

I scan his features, take in the vehemence in his expression. "Are you this committed to the safety of all your clients?" *Or is it just me? Say you're this protective because it's me, please?*

Instantly, a mask seems to drop over his face. His jaw turns to granite. "I always do my very best to safeguard my assets."

Disappointment squeezes my chest. "So that's all I am? An asset?"

"Isn't that obvious?" He pulls out his phone and begins to swipe across the screen, signaling the discussion is at an end.

I scowl. He's right, of course, but something tells me he's lying. He felt that insane chemistry which turned our kiss into a shooting star of flames. It rocked my world and made me realize what I'd be missing out on in an arranged marriage. This is the only time I will ever get to feel this way. Is it too much to hope for it to be reciprocated?

"I don't believe you," I say hotly.

I'm frustrated that we didn't get a chance to finish what we started, as the constant state of my arousal will testify to. And if I'm being honest, it wouldn't hurt to know that if there were a chance to have more with me, he'd take it.

He pockets his phone and raises his gaze back to mine. Those green irises of his blaze with something glacial that freezes me in my tracks.

"Don't mistake what happened at the bar for something more than what it was." His tone is hard enough to cut glass.

"Oh? And what's that?"

He clenches his jaw. "A potential one-time shag. In retrospect, it's best it didn't happen. You'd have wanted more, and that's something I cannot give you."

I flinch. It's as if he physically slapped me. "Did you just imply that I'm good for a one-night stand, and nothing more?"

He raises a shoulder. "Take it however you want."

"I... I..." I try to form a complete sentence, but my brain seems to have short-circuited. He's joking; he has to be. I felt him respond that night when I kissed him. Felt him kiss me back. Felt him deepen the kiss and drink from me like he couldn't get enough of my taste. And when I kissed him earlier in the car, I felt his heart thunder against mine. He's lying; I know it. But to hear him speak of it, you'd think it meant nothing.

"Yes, I had a physical response to you, but that's only to be expected. You're a beautiful woman, after all. But it didn't mean anything."

"Sure, it did. You can't say the response you had to me was something that has happened before."

"Are you searching for confirmation of your own attractiveness?" he drawls in that reasonable voice that makes me want to punch his beautiful face.

I fold my arms across my chest. "Don't pretend not to understand what I'm saying. It's not like everyone feels this way when they're attracted to someone else. This is different, isn't it? So why can't you at least say so aloud?"

"I'm doing it to protect you," he growls.

"Protect me? How?" I shake my head. "You're not making any sense."

"It's not only the fact that you're a princess—"

"And you're a Davenport. Your family is as wealthy as mine, if not wealthier."

He shoots me a curious glance.

"I might be insulated from a lot of the daily issues that people face, but even *I* have heard of the Davenport Group. My father holds your grandfather in great esteem. Enough to hire you as my bodyguard and trust you with my life, not something he'd do lightly. You may not be of royal blood, but in every other way, your family is as powerful as mine."

His brow furrows. "Your point being?"

"We belong to the same social class."

"You mean, we come from generational wealth?" There's a disparagement in his tone that raises my hackles.

"Are you one of those people who prefers to disown your moneyed background?" I take in his features, trying to understand him. He's so much more complex than other men I've encountered.

Thanks to attending boarding school in England, I've managed to have a more or less normal life. Well, as normal as can be when you go to one of the most sought-after private schools in the country, and when your fellow students come from the cream of British society. I didn't hit it off with them. Didn't form any lasting friendships with my titled peers who moved in the kind of rarified circles I was keen to avoid. And none of them had half as much depth as this man.

"Is that why you decided to serve your country?"

A muscle at his jaw tics. "I joined the Marines because I wanted to make something of myself. I needed to forge my own path."

"And now, you're a bodyguard."

"I'm a protector. It's what I do." He says it in a matter-of-fact voice, and I believe him. He's hardwired to be a guardian.

"You're different from anyone else I've encountered. You've seen the horrors of wars, and that can't be easy," I say slowly.

My previous bodyguards didn't have military experience, and I can see the difference in how Ryot holds himself. How he's always hyper alert. How he constantly scans his surroundings and takes in people in my vicinity, how the tension radiates off of him like every muscle of his is tuned into the environment to sense the tiniest threat. He reminds me of an apex predator in the forest who is always vigilant.

He doesn't respond—big surprise! —but his features close further. Guess he doesn't like to talk about it. Which is…understandable. It makes him an enigma, which makes him even more appealing, which also pisses me off. It's not fair that, even when he's being rude to me, I find him so irresistible. It's that which makes me shoot off my mouth. "Is it because I'm born into a family with royal bloodlines? Is that why you hate me?"

He blinks, and his features soften. "I don't…hate you."

"But you don't want to sleep with me, either?"

"It's not that I don't want to, but as I have explained to you, I can't. You're my principal, and I cannot cross that line. Besides—" He looks away, then back at me. "Your father trusts me to protect your life, and I can't let him down."

Something in his tone and his demeanor tells me he's hiding something. There's something else stopping him from acting on the attraction between us. Something more than professional etiquette. If I tell him more about myself, might he be open to sharing?

"Being a princess is not all it's cut out to be," I offer.

"Oh?" He looks at me with curiosity.

"Most of the men I meet are more interested in the fact that I come from a royal background. None of them are interested in me. It's not that I'm complaining about being born into the kind of status that most women would wish for, but"—I take in the attentiveness on his features—"but I'd give anything to be a normal girl and go on a date with a man I like, who's interested in me for myself, you know?"

He pauses. Then the set of his features relaxes. "I understand more than you realize," he admits.

"Given your family's background, I suppose you do." I nod. "And given your looks—"

"My looks?" he asks in an amused tone.

"You know what I'm talking about." I resist the urge to roll my eyes. "As I was saying, given your above average handsomeness and the fact that you come from a family of billionaires, I bet you have women falling over themselves to date you."

He straightens his spine. When he looks at me, his expression is remote. "I haven't been on a date in years," he finally says.

My jaw drops. "I don't believe it. Why, at the bar, we'd barely met when you asked me to go home with you."

Something flickers across his features. A look I can't quite interpret. Then he clears his throat. "That was...out of character."

It's clear, he's telling the truth. And my heart blooms in my chest. The fact that he asked me home when he wouldn't have normally done so makes me so very happy.

There's something in his eyes, a glimpse of desolation, a look of... Anguish? Of something that hints at secrets. It sets off a lightbulb in my brain.

"You're not... Married, are you?" The words are out before I can stop myself. I slap my hand over my mouth. "Oh my god, I'm sorry. I don't mean to pry, honestly."

I glance down at his fingers and don't find a ring. Or even a telltale band of lighter-colored flesh around his ring finger. *So... Probably not married, right?*

The muscle above his jaw twitches. A tightening around his eyes tells me I'm not far from the truth. But I also feel like I'm encroaching in his personal life when, clearly, he doesn't want to talk about it. I lower my hand and lock my fingers together.

"You know what? Never mind. I didn't mean to make you uncomfortable. Truly. Forget I said anything. And please accept my apologies for the intrusion."

He continues to stare at me, his features a mask of granite. The seconds stretch, then he seems to come to a decision. "I was married," he says in a remote voice.

I flinch. "You *were* married?"

He nods.

"And you're divorced?"

He slowly shakes his head.

"Then… Are you separated?"

His shoulders seem to swell. A nerve throbs at his temple. Then he looks out the window and mutters, "She's dead."

11

Ryot

I sense the surprise ripple through the space between us. Then there's silence. She doesn't offer me her sympathies, for which I'm grateful. There have been too many who've given me their meaningless condolences. They've always felt empty. For nothing could take away the anger and the regret I've carried around in my heart since I got the news about Jane's death. *I didn't mean to share that piece of information with Aura.* After Jane was killed on a mission, I literally stopped speaking for a while.

Not only because I was upset by her death, but also because I was relieved that I no longer had to pretend that I loved her. I didn't have to pretend that we were happy. I didn't have to pretend that our relationship wasn't falling apart. And the realization that I wasn't really sad she was gone—especially after how she betrayed me—made me feel even worse. But how could I explain such a selfish notion to anyone? It was easier to claim I felt responsible for what happened to her. Even easier to blame Q for his part.

The combination of emotions was a lot to process. It still is. My way of coping was by speaking as little as possible, and only when needed. That gave me a lot of time inside of my own head. I still haven't come to terms with all of it, but I'm beginning to accept it. I don't hate myself quite as much as I did two years ago, and I'm finding it harder to maintain a grudge against Quentin.

And I certainly don't talk about my past with people I've just met.

So why did I open up to Aura? Do I trust her enough? Is it the attraction between us addling my decision making? Or did my subconscious lull me into a false sense of being comfortable around her? Enough that I could confide in her?

Either way, I've crossed another line in our professional relationship, and I'm pissed with myself for that. Also, I don't want to talk about Jane with her. So, I pull out my phone and feign an interest in my email.

She doesn't intrude. Then after a few seconds, she does the same. The car inches through the city traffic. I directed the team to take a convoluted route to our destination. I'm not taking any chances with having anyone following us.

It's another forty-five minutes before we're drawing up to the hotel. This one's set in a quiet side-street on the edge of Regent's Park. It's also so exclusive that there are no signs indicating it's a hotel.

As soon as the car draws to a stop, I push the door open and jump out, then walk around to open hers. She slides her handbag over her shoulder, then straightens. She takes a few steps into the middle of the sidewalk in front of the two-story Victorian building, raises her arms in the air and stretches. Then bends over to touch her feet, giving me a view of her pear-shaped behind stretching the skirt of the dress she's wearing.

I remind myself I need to stop ogling her perfect butt, but I'm unable to look away.

Cole and Brian are already ahead of us, scoping out the area. Once more, Cole takes the lead, I walk next to her, and Brian brings up the rear. We guide her toward the side-entrance where another member of my team is holding the door open. Then, it's to the private elevator which whisks us to the top floor.

It's one of the reasons I chose this hotel. Her comings and goings can be private. There will be no hotel housekeeping staff allowed onto the floor either. Instead, I've organized a team of cleaners who I screened to carry out those duties.

As for room service? One of my men will deliver the orders and stay while the food is prepared, then deliver them to us. I'm not leaving anything to chance.

"What about my clothes? My luggage?" she asks without looking up from her phone.

"It's been taken care of."

"Of course, it has." Her voice is caustic.

Cole and Brian exchange glances, but I don't allow my expression to vary. I sense she's finding the changes unsettling, and that's understandable. If it helps her to take out her frustrations on me, that's fine.

When we reach the floor I booked out as a precaution, Cole leads the way to the double doors at the end of the corridor. On either side, we pass rooms where the rest of the team will be staying. When we reach the entrance to the room, I touch her shoulder and say softly, "Let Cole give the all-clear."

"You think there might be someone waiting in there for me?" She looks at me with a disbelieving expression on her face.

"Best not to take a chance."

She scoffs, then moves aside so my fingers slide off her arm. She's putting distance between us... Which is what I wanted. Let her think I'm still in love with my deceased wife. Plus, she's probably annoyed that I didn't give her advance notice about the changes I made to her security detail and the hotel. I wanted her to be pissed off enough with me that she wouldn't want to have anything to do with me. And it looks like I've succeeded. So why do I feel bereft?

Cole walks out of the suite and nods to me. "It's safe."

Before the words are out of his mouth, she's stomped inside the suite.

Once again, Cole and Brian exchange glances, but don't say anything. I appreciate their silence.

While I may have ensured she wants to keep her distance from me, it also means I'm not going to get her to cooperate willingly. The beginning of a headache drums behind my eyes, and I push it away. I follow her inside the suite which houses both our rooms and shut the door behind me.

She walks to the bedroom. I stand in the doorway. I should head on to my own room but I'm unable to move away. I can keep telling myself that I will not cross the line with her, but I can't stop myself from wanting to be in her presence. Anything to be close to her. To draw in her scent. To watch her graceful movements.

She throws her bag on the bed, kicks off her stilettos, then reaches behind her and begins to lower the zipper of her dress.

Get out of here. You shouldn't be here. I stay frozen to the spot. I can't take my gaze off the strip of skin she bares, and then there's the swatch of pink satin visible from between the zipper teeth. *Is that the strap of her bra? Holy hell that* is *her bra.* The blood rushes to my groin. My cock extends.

I should make a noise and protest. I should tell her that she's my principal, and this is all wrong. But my throat is too dry. The words I'm trying to form get stuck in my gullet. The connection between my brain and my tongue seems to have been severed. I can't stop staring as she begins to slide her dress down one arm. And when the curve of her shoulder is bared, a jolt of lust pulses through my veins.

I'm so hard that the length of my cock stabs into the zipper of my pants. A bead of sweat slides down my temple. I want to move, but my feet are stuck to the carpet. I curl my fingers into fists at my side, willing myself to look away. This is wrong. She's teasing me. Taunting me. Showing me what I'm missing.

I want to strip the clothes from her and take in every inch of that soft skin. I yearn to have her naked and writhing under me as I drag my knuckles across the curve of her hips, over her fleshy backside, and down the seam of the melting triangle between her legs. My shoulder muscles turn to boulders. My thigh muscles feel like they've turned into concrete. I'm so fucking turned on, every cell in my body seems to have turned into sparks of electricity.

Then she turns and glances at me over her shoulder. Her eyes are big, blue seas of want, her lips are parted, her breath comes in small pants, and I realize she's as turned on as I am. Her gaze clashes with mine, and whatever she sees there draws a moan from her lips. She pauses in the act of pushing the dress off her other shoulder. The first is already bared, with the dress caught in the crook of her elbow. She's unable to proceed further.

I glare at her, and the color fades from her cheeks. Her shoulders rise and fall. She's waiting...waiting...for me to tell her what to do next. She may have started this act of her undressing to get a response out of me, and she succeeded, but she's unable to move further without my command. I stay silent, not responding to her seduction, and her expression turns uncertain. Her features pale further. She forces down a swallow, her throat visibly constricting. Then she lowers her arm to her side, and finally her gaze.

There you are.

She might come across as defiant, obstinate, and willful, and no doubt, she'd have to be all of that to survive being in the public eye. She'd have to have a mind of her own to make it through the trials of being born into the Royal Family, where the path of her life was decided for her even before she was conceived. We're similar, in that regard.

We both come from privileged backgrounds. We've carried the weight of expectation on our shoulders. We've had to struggle hard to find ourselves, to carve out our own identities, in the face of being told very clearly what we can and cannot do. Only difference is that I like to be in control. I need to be in charge, whether it was leading my platoon or driving a mission, and now, when it comes to sex.

This became more important after the nightmare of being on the front lines. I got together with Jane under pressure cooker conditions while on a tour of duty. By the time I realized it didn't feel the same when we were between missions, we were married.

And though I tried to give our relationship my best shot, whatever little chemistry had been between us fizzled out. We fought all the time. I knew we needed to get a divorce, but I kept putting it off.

The guilt of wanting her out of my life, then having that wish come true, in the most final way possible, made me feel terrible. I took turns blaming myself for what happened to her, then blaming Q for sending her to her death. Only, he was doing his duty. I get that now.

He didn't realize his choices would end in so many deaths. Logically, I know I'm not to blame for Jane's actions, either. But I wanted her out of my life, so it's easier for me to forgive Q than myself.

Either way, it's enough to put me off future relationships. I don't deserve love with someone else, and I don't want to be betrayed again. I refuse to trust anyone else again and risk being hurt.

I can't deny that the carnal side of me desires Aura. But she's my principal, and that changes everything. I promised her father I'd protect her, and until I find the person behind that threatening note and complete my mission, I will not touch her.

A trembling grips her. I slide my jacket off, walk over to her and drape it over her shoulders. "I don't fuck innocent little girls; and definitely not those who like to top from the bottom."

12

Aurelia

That was a week ago. I'm still not over the fact that he called me a little girl. Or that he felt I was topping from the bottom. I do know what he means by it. I've read enough spicy romance books and seen enough porn to realize he was alluding to the fact that he's dominant. Which is not a surprise. If he thought that was going to dissuade me —he can think again.

The fact that he could initiate me to the pleasures of sex and do it in such an interesting fashion has sent my libido into overdrive. Also, I'm pissed that my seduction attempt didn't work. Again! I refuse to be embarrassed by my behavior though. I gave it my best shot. So what, if it didn't work? I can try again, and differently. I'm nothing if not persistent.

Not that I've done so yet. Instead, I've gone about my daily routine without raising any further objections. And though I do feel a little resentful that he must approve my public engagements, I know it's the best way of staying safe.

He continues to ride with me in the car to and from my appointments. Smelling his dark scent and being close to him in that enclosed space has me drenching my panties in a way that's seriously embarrassing. Not that he's speaking to me much. We've exchanged maybe five full sentences since that day, and all of it is related to my security arrangements. After we return from my daily appearances, I don't see him.

I don't even hear his movements, though he's in the next room, with only an interconnecting door separating us. I was so bored, I forced myself to use the gym in the basement of the hotel. Under the watchful eye of a security guard who was not Ryot, which meant, I promptly lost interest. I ate a few meals in the restaurant downstairs and even had a late-night drink at the bar a couple of evenings, but it became such a hassle when security had to go down and assess threats before I could go. And when it became clear Ryot wouldn't be the one accompanying me there either, I didn't venture back.

I miss that man more than I care to admit. I've taken to watching TV and yes, I admit, also watching porn and masturbating while thinking of my big, dark, handsome bodyguard. None of which is helping.

I've worked myself into a state of such arousal, and my thoughts are so jumbled, that I know I need to speak to someone about it.

I throw off the cover, then sit up in bed and shove the pillows behind my back to support me. I stare at the interconnecting door between our rooms, which he made sure to lock after himself. As if I were going to head into his room? I snort to myself. Nope, I need a different way to approach him. Nothing as amateurish as my last seduction attempt.

Reaching for my phone, my gaze falls on my laptop, and I rub at my forehead. I should have started writing my next novel. Given I'm not going out in the evenings, I should make the most of my time and, at least, start brainstorming ideas for the book, but I haven't been able to get myself into the mood to do it.

I'm too busy worrying about the bill we're running up for this trip. This hotel is just as luxurious as the previous hotel, but it has a smaller number of rooms. And Ryot booked out all of them on this floor for our stay. I could remind my father we can't afford it, but he'd insist—rightly—that this is the best way to ensure my safety. I can't argue with that. But it means he's probably spending money we can ill afford to cover the costs. Which makes my forthcoming arranged marriage and the money that will come with it even more unavoidable. My spirits plummet.

I need to get my mind off my upcoming nuptials, so I grab my phone and videocall my friend, Zoey.

I met her at university. She's one of my best friends, and my editor. No one knows my inner thoughts more than she does.

She and her two friends, Harper and Grace, welcomed me into their circle, and being with them helps me feel more 'normal' and less like a princess. I dial her number, and it keeps ringing. *Shoot, is it too late to call?* I am about to hang up, when she answers.

"If it isn't Her Royal Highness, herself." Her image appears on screen.

I wince. "You promised you'd never call me that."

"Considering you're calling me close to midnight, I think it warrants the title, eh?"

"I'm so sorry." I slap my forehead. "I couldn't sleep, and it was only after your phone started ringing, I realized how late it is, and—"

"Relax, Aura, I was kidding you." She stretches and yawns.

"Woman, are you still at work?" I glance around what I can see of her surroundings and can make out the bookshelves in the background, as well as the coffee maker she keeps on the shelf at the far end. "You *are* still at work," I exclaim.

"Someone has to make sense of your meanderings and turn it into a coherent narrative." Her eyes gleam with a wicked glint.

I grab my phone, then push my legs out of the bed and, standing up, I begin to pace. "How bad is my writing? Are you going to send me pages and pages of revisions that I'm going to have to spend weeks fixing?"

She laughs. "Firstly, no, it isn't bad at all for a first book. And I wouldn't have approached you to write a novel if I didn't know you're talented and have been writing since the first day I met you—"

"But—" I begin, but she cuts me off.

"I know how much you love to read spicy novels, and you have so many drafts completed and gathering dust on your hard drive. And remember, you're publishing under a pen name, so no one is going to know."

I gnaw on my fingernail. "I'm still worried. What if someone finds out it's me writing?"

I only accepted the publishing contract when she named an advance that took me by surprise. It's good money, which I'll use to help foodbanks in Verenza, who've reported a ten-fold increase in their services in the last six months. "If anyone were to find out—"

"I promise, your penname's identity will be kept secret."

"Thanks, Z." I stop by the window and glance out at the park opposite. It's dark and, but for the lights on in the courtyard below, everything is quiet.

"What's on your mind, hmm?" She walks to the tiny counter at the back of her office and, placing the phone such that I can see her, she sets about filling her kettle.

"You mean, other than the threats made on my life—"

"You've had threats on your life?" She places the kettle down with a thump and snatches up her phone. "Are you okay? What happened?"

"Relax." I half laugh. "I'm fine. I have a new team, led by a new security guy who's bossy and overly cautious when it comes to my safety, so I'm sure I have nothing to worry about."

She doesn't seem very convinced. "How long have you been getting these threats? And why didn't you tell me sooner."

I turn away from the window and, walking over to my bed, I throw myself down on it. "This is not the first time I've received them. Remember that stalker years ago in Verenza who the local police managed to track down?"

She nods.

"I would have dismissed this as something similar, only this time, the note was left on my pillow in my hotel room."

"Oh, my god!" Her eyes round. "In your hotel room?'

"Which is why Ryot insisted I move hotels to be safe."

"Ryot?" Her forehead furrows.

"Ryot Davenport. His family owns the Davenport group. He's loaded, and god knows, he doesn't need to work for a living, but he's a former Marine and now, he's into this body-guarding business. Just my luck that my father trusts him."

"Ryot Davenport?" She seems taken aback. "My friend, June married his brother Knox. And another friend, Skylar married his other brother Nathan."

"Whoa, you know him?"

"Only what I heard from my friends." Her gaze is troubled. She seems like she wants to say something more but is stopping herself from doing so.

"What's on your mind?" I search her features. "Out with it, Z."

She places the phone back on the counter and switches on the kettle. While it starts to boil, she moves away so the noise doesn't intrude on the conversation. "These Davenport men can be quite pushy."

"Tell me about it. The man has been making unilateral decisions on my behalf and informing me after the fact. It's so annoying and yet"—I shake my head—"I can't stop myself from admiring him for it. No one has ever ordered me around the way he has. And I find it hot, and for the life of me, I can't understand why."

She gives me a funny look. "So, you hate him, but you also like him?"

I nod slowly. "I have conflicting feelings for him. It pisses me off when he decides something related to my security arrangement, and I have to fall in line. By the same token, I admire him for the fact that he does what he thinks is right and is not worried about being fired by me or my father. It helps that he doesn't need the money. I can't help but wonder if he's doing it because he needs to feel a sense of responsibility?"

"Responsibility?" She turns back to her kettle and pours the hot water into her cup.

"He went to war out of duty for his country. Now, it seems, he's transferred that duty to his 'principal.'" I make air quotes with my fingers. "I'm convinced he needs to be on some kind of a mission to feel alive."

"You seem to have spent a lot of time analyzing him..." Her lips curve in a smile.

"Only because the man's swept into my life and played havoc with his security measures." I make a face. "Then there's the fact that I met him at a bar the night before he arrived."

"A bar?" She pauses with the cup halfway to her mouth. "You met him at a bar? Did something happen between the two of you?" She peers into my face.

When my cheeks heat, her jaw drops. "Something *did* happen."

"It was only a kiss," I murmur.

Her eyes gleam. "You guys kissed?"

"So what?"

"So, you're blushing." She smirks.

I toss my hair over my shoulder. "Fine. So, it was an amazing kiss. But it was before he became my bodyguard. He has since told me, *clearly*, we can't be involved, since I'm his principal and it goes against his code of ethics to have any personal relationship with his clients. So"—I pop a shoulder—"can we talk about something else?"

"Sure." She nods. "Why don't we talk about how you got to a bar? I thought you're not allowed to go to public places because it's a security risk?"

I burrow further into my pillow. "My previous security team weren't the smartest. It was easy for me to slip past them."

She frowns. "Was it worth the risk?"

"If it means having an evening of freedom and experiencing what it means to be 'normal'"—I make air quotes with my fingers— "then yes, it was worth it." *I also hoped I'd find someone I was truly attracted to —enough to lose my virginity.*

I might have to settle for an arranged marriage, but this way, I was making sure I had some control over my life. Plus, it was also the ultimate FU to the rules imposed on me.

I make a face. "I won't be able to do so again. Ryot insists I have a chauffeur drive my car. He's part of Ryot's team. No doubt, he'd go running back to Ryot if I asked him to drive me somewhere. Which is why I'm stuck here in this hotel room."

"Aww, I'm sorry, Aura. But it is safer for you not to go traipsing around at night."

"You're right." I worry my lower lip with my teeth. "Whoever sent the note, they mean business." The stakes are high, and I'd be stupid to ignore the security measures Ryot has set down. "But if I don't get out and do something soon, I'm going to go crazy," I half mutter to myself.

"Perhaps, the girls and I could go out to dinner with you. Why don't you speak to Ryot about it?"

13

Ryot

"No, you can't go out with your friends," I say through gritted teeth.

We're standing in the living room of the suite. It's my self-designated neutral area and the only part of the suite I allow myself to enter.

Seeing her belongings strewn around the bedroom, not to mention the sight of her unmade bed, makes me want to throw her down on it and cover her body with mine. Her scent is overpowering in the space, and I have this primitive need to jerk off on her to mark her as mine. The result? I don't trust myself to be alone with her. I've made sure not to be alone with her since the day she undressed in front of me.

On the positive side, there have been no notes left in her room. Given I booked out the entire floor and have my team staying in all the rooms, as well as having two of them guard the entrance to our suite around the clock, no one should be able to get to her. I've also employed some of the best investigators in the business to track down the person who left the note in her previous room. I will not rest until I neutralize this threat to her. I'm doing my best to keep her safe.

I managed to avoid her all day until she finally cornered me.

"I'm tired of having my meals by myself in the restaurant downstairs. And if I'm forced to have another late-night drink *alone* in the empty hotel bar, I'll scream." She pouts.

Damn! That 'O' shape of her pink lips makes me wonder how it'd feel to have it wrapped around my cock. I shove the thought out of my head and focus on the princess.

"You were by yourself because we cleared out the space for your safety," I say in my most professional tone.

"Whatever." She tosses her head, then fixes me with a regal look on her face that makes me want to kiss it right off.

My cock hardens further. *Down boy. Get your head back in the game.* The one at the top of my neck, I mean.

"My point is, I need some time away from this hotel." Her tone turns pleading. "Besides—" She widens her gaze. "You have an entire battalion guarding me. Surely, I'm safe on an evening out at a restaurant? Nothing can happen to me when you're around, can it?"

And now, she's trying to appeal to my pride in a bid to have me loosen the reins on her. I'm not falling for *that* gimmick.

"I will not compromise on your safety," I growl.

"Exactly. If you're there, I'm sure you'll stop anyone from coming near me. So, I have nothing to fear, right?" She flutters her long, thick eyelashes at me, and my chest squeezes.

Goddam, this woman's a witch. There's no other explanation for why I lose my composure around her.

"There's a limit to my effectiveness. If I take you somewhere public, it raises the chances of the person who wrote that note tracking you down. I'm trying to ensure your security."

"And I can't spend all evening cooped up in here—"

"You have the gym and the pool, and the salon within the hotel—"

"I need to go somewhere *not* within this hotel. If it weren't for the work events, I'd've gone crazy by now." She throws up her hands. "I can't believe I said that. Do you know how much I hate most of those commitments? But being cooped up here, I actually look forward to being out there and on display."

I knit my eyebrows. "I thought you liked being out and about, meeting people?"

"Oh, I do. Especially when it means I can read to kids in school or meet children in the hospital and raise funds for them; it's very fulfilling. But it can also grow tedious, you know? After a while, it gets tiring to put on another dress and go to another society event."

"So, why do you do it?"

She rubs at her temple. "It's my responsibility to represent Verenza overseas and create awareness of it as a tourist destination." She shrugs. "It probably seems like I'm complaining too much. After all, anyone would want to be in my shoes, wearing designer clothes and cavorting around with important people. I'm sure I seem spoiled to you." She looks uncertain.

Her insecurity tugs at my heart. I want to reassure her that she has a point. Even those who're rich and titled have their issues. But I don't move. If I touch her, I won't be able to stop myself from holding her close and kissing her. And there's only one way that can end.

Suddenly, she perks up. "Wait, what if my friends come here instead?"

I hate to crush her enthusiasm, but I respond, "Sorry, Princess. No one is supposed to know where you are, remember?"

Her shoulders drop, and she sighs. She trudges to the window and peeks out. She cuts a forlorn figure, standing in her yoga pants which cup her shapely arse and outline her gorgeous fleshy thighs. She's wearing a T-shirt which proclaims: *Bow down, peasants!*

It had me chuckling when I saw it, but I managed to contain my mirth. Especially because I was distracted by how it stretches across her impressive rack and showcases her nipples. Damn.

She's not wearing a bra, that much is clear. I almost told her off, then managed to stay silent at the last moment. She's my principal, after all. And she's doing it purposely to distract me, too. I'm not going to give her the benefit of realizing that she succeeded, either. If

I did, it would only encourage her to find new ways of torturing my composure.

She looks magnificent and way too sexy to be shut in here on her own for the night. Especially since her event for the evening was cancelled at the last moment.

My chest tightens. I feel her frustration like it's my own. Which...is wrong. I can't let myself be this tuned into her. But she is my principal, and although my primary responsibility is to keep her safe, I'd also like to see her happy. And when she flattens her palm against the window and presses her forehead against the pane, my mind is made up.

"You want to get out of here?"

She looks up at me, a dejected look on her face. Then, my words seem to sink in, and she spins around. "Do you mean that?"

I arch an eyebrow. "Not going to repeat myself, princess. If you want to leave this room and do something different—"

"I do." A big smile breaks out on her face. Her blue eyes sparkle. It's like the sun's rays bouncing off droplets of a waterfall and casting a rainbow in the sky. My heart stutters. My stomach ties itself in knots. I can only watch with a mixture of bemusement and arousal, and something resembling resignation when she bounces over to me and throws her arms about my neck. "Thank you. Thank you. Thank you."

I tuck my elbows into my sides and will myself to stay unmoving. I pretend I don't feel her breasts pushing up against my chest, or her scent playing havoc with my senses, or my cock pushing up against the zipper of my pants, wanting to nestle into the sweet triangle between her thighs.

She must sense my state of arousal though, for she freezes. Her neck muscles tighten. For a second, she stays there, plastered against me from thigh to hip to chest, then she begins to back away.

I should let her go. It's wrong that I'm so attracted to her when I still haven't come to terms with the death of my wife. I feel like I've compromised myself by kissing her, even *after* I found out she's my principal. If I do so again, there'll be no turning back. And yet, when I take in her trembling lips and her big, blue eyes, every fiber in my being throbs with the need to have my arms around her...just one more time. *Surely, it won't mean anything?*

I plant my hands on her hips and hold her there. A shudder grips her. And when I raise her so her feet no longer touch the floor, and position her over the bulge at my crotch, she whimpers. *Jesus.*

The sound goes straight to my head, and yes, also to my groin. I feel myself harden further. She holds onto my shoulders, then brings her legs around my waist, and locks her ankles behind my back. And when she raises her head to mine, her blue eyes turn turquoise. There's no mistaking she's turned on. Not when the pulse at the base of her throat flits like a butterfly caught in a spider's web. And I'm the spider? I certainly want to ensnare her. I want to tie her up and eat her up. I lower my head to hers, and when my lips almost brush hers, I stop. I draw in her sweet breath, and my pulse rate spikes. *Honeysuckle, vanilla and strawberries.* "Is that your shampoo?"

"What?" She blinks.

"Honeysuckle, vanilla and strawberries; your scent drives me crazy."

"It's the lotion I use on my skin. It's made specially for me."

Her words remind me that she's a princess. And I'm her body-guard. And we each have our duties to fulfill. If I ignore my instincts, I'm going to pay for it. Like I did with Jane. I shouldn't have married her. But the overwhelming emotions of being with her while on a mission blinded me. Every day, I regret not thinking through that decision. I can't get carried away again.

I manage to keep my conflicted emotions off my face. Then, instead of kissing her, I straighten and walk toward her bedroom. I stop at the entrance, lower her to her feet, then step back. "Boots, jeans and a jacket."

"Now you're telling me how to dress, hmm?" She doesn't seem put off by it. If anything, her pupils dilate.

"You like it when I do," I point out.

She seems about to deny it then nods slowly. "I've never liked it when anyone else told me what to wear," she muses. The expression on her face is surprised. And so adorable. My heart kicks in my chest. My thigh muscles coil. I am in serious trouble. This is not just a physical attraction. It's something more.

It involves real feelings. The kind I didn't face with Jane. I didn't plan for this kind of complication. If I touch her again, not only will I be breaking my professional code of ethics, but I also won't be able to walk away from her. And I'm not ready for that kind of long-term relationship. Not again. Not after everything that went down with Jane. Not after how she betrayed me. Thankfully, I came to my senses before I kissed Aura again. One touch of her lips again, and I'll lose my judgement completely. I need to let her down, gently.

"Good." I dip my chin. And before I can stop myself, I've kissed her forehead.

Goddamn, I shouldn't have done that. But the tenderness I feel for her is overwhelming. Combined with the protective instincts she arouses in me, it makes me want to get her out of here to a place where she'll be safe. Where we'll be free to explore this potent attraction between us. But we both have responsibilities to fulfill.

So, I step back and nod at her. "I'll see you at the elevator in ten minutes."

14

Aurelia

He's agreed to take me out, which is awesome. But what caused him to change his mind? He's been insisting I stay inside every evening. And initially, he refused to let me go out to dinner tonight. Then, he offers to do so himself?

My head spins. He's so confusing. I could have sworn I felt that iron control of his thaw. I thought he was going to kiss me, but he settled for a peck on my forehead. Not that it matters; the touch of his lips sparked goosebumps on my skin.

Maybe none of it matters. I'm getting to go out with him. It's not a date. He said it's not a date. But it sure feels like one. I can't stop myself from doing a little skip as I jump into the shower. I'm going out with my hottie, tall, dark, and brooding bodyguard and that makes me so happy.

And yes, he was right when he pointed out I find his bossy attitude a huge turn on. When he told me what I should wear, liquid heat pooled between my legs. My stomach flip-flopped. My nipples turned into points of need. My body reacted to his words with an excitement that caught me by surprise. In case it wasn't already obvious, I'm not the kind of woman who hands over control willingly. But with Ryot...

The chemistry clouds my brain and sharpens my instincts at the same time. With Ryot... The thought of having him command me and take charge turns me on. It also pisses me off. *Why does it have to be the most closed-off, unapproachable, unreachable man I've ever met who has this effect on me? And why do I have to be so attracted to him? And why do I find myself fantasizing he's the royal I'll be marrying? It's ridiculous. And why is it that every part of me wants to please him by arriving at the elevator at the time he specified?*

All the more reason *not* to obey him.

I take half-an-hour to get dressed. Really, who can get dressed in ten minutes, *amiright? Didn't stop me from following his directions in terms of what to wear though, huh?* I survey my reflection.

I'm wearing my favorite blouse, jeans, a leather jacket, and a pair of Doc Martins. I slip my phone into the pocket of my jeans. On impulse, I push the jacket off my shoulders and throw it aside. I grab my cross-body purse, then flounce out of the suite.

I nod at the two men posted there. Then walk down the corridor to where he's waiting for me next to the elevator. He's wearing worn combat boots, faded jeans and a chambray shirt, over which he has his own leather jacket that's seen better days. He's also carrying a smaller one in his hand. When he spots me, he holds it out.

My jaw drops. "How did you know—"

"That you wouldn't wear a jacket?" His lips twist. "You're so predictable, Princess."

"I'm not predictable." *It was just a lame attempt at rebellion.* For some reason I feel compelled to test boundaries with this man. I should have known he'd never let me get away with it. I stuff one arm into the jacket sleeve, then the other.

He smooths the jacket over my shoulders, then punches the button of the elevator. The cage arrives at once.

When the doors open, he gestures for me to enter and follows.

I cross my arms over my chest. "I'm. Not. Predictable." I feel the need to protest. Predictable is boring. And if there's one thing I've tried to make sure I'm not, it's boring.

His lips twitch. "How did I know I'd have to carry a jacket for you?"

"Lucky guess?" I grumble.

When a chuckle rolls up his throat, I stare. The sound is so warm, so masculine, it sends a cascade of sensations coursing through my bloodstream. Also, he's smiling, and it lights up his face and reveals a tiny dimple in his left cheek. Ugh, he cannot be that perfect to look at, can he?

"By the way, I completed screening your team, and everyone checks out," he rumbles.

"That's a relief." Some of the tension falls off my shoulders. Guess I was more stressed than I realized about the possibility that someone from within my team could have been responsible for that note.

"I alerted your closest team-members that you are not to be disturbed this evening. I've told them where to reach us in case anything urgent comes up."

That's thoughtful of him. "Thank you," I murmur, "although it would be nice if *I* knew where we'd be." He just smirks.

When the elevator doors open, he steps out. I follow him to the side-entrance. Brian, who's been waiting by the door, pushes it open. He, too, is dressed in boots, jeans and a jacket. When I walk out, I find Cole dressed similarly, standing by a bike.

He hands a helmet to Ryot and one to me, then goes over to the bike in front and, retrieving his own helmet, pulls it on. Brian follows suit and straddles the bike behind us. Ryot straps on his helmet, raises the visor, then throws his leg over the Ducati.

"Hop on." He pats the seat behind him.

What the —? I stare with my mouth open. Riding behind Ryot on that mean-looking machine is the last way I imagined this evening would unfold. I've always wanted to ride a motorbike, but so far, have never had the opportunity. I couldn't buy one because: one, I couldn't bring myself to spend that much money, and two, I'd never be *allowed* to buy one. And even if I somehow managed to do so, I'd never be allowed to ride it.

I approach him, eying the machine and the gorgeous man astride it with suspicion. "How did you guess —"

"That you've never been on a bike before but have always wanted to?" He grins, looking all too pleased with himself. "Another lucky guess?"

Whoa. The flash of his white teeth against his lips sends a spurt of need spiraling in my belly. "No, seriously, tell me. How did you know I'd love to get on a bike?"

He scans my features. "You wanted to get ice cream from a fast-food chain when you could have asked for one from any gourmet restaurant or brand, but you didn't."

"So?" I frown.

"Then, there's the fact that you love driving your own car because it gives you a feeling of being free." He shrugs. "It wasn't a stretch to conclude that you'd love being on a bike." Something in his eyes makes my heart skip a beat.

He was paying attention to me. He noticed my quirks and my reactions. He spent time thinking about what I'd like to do. He might have offered to get me out of the hotel because of pity and, perhaps, a sense of responsibility to keep me, as his principal, entertained — enough so I'd be more amenable to toeing the line with his security measures.

But offering to take me on his bike? That...is something he planned for.

A boatload of emotions squishes inside my chest. I stand there, staring at him dumbly, unable to move. *What does this mean? Does it mean anything? Am I reading too much into his gesture?*

"Get on, Princess. I know you want to." *Was that supposed to sound so suggestive?* He hits the ignition, and the bike roars to life. The sound throbs through my veins and settles in my bones; it shoots a burst of excitement up my spine. *Damn. He's actually going to take me for a ride?* My heart feels like it's going to burst out of my ribcage. I'm pathetically happy, and that gives me pause. Also, I want to put up a token protest, so he doesn't think I'm going to obey everything he says—even though that's probably the truth.

"Why can't I drive the bike?" I tip up my chin. "Why do I have to sit behind you?"

"Because it's my bike?" He revs the bike again. "Coming or not?" I move toward the bike, and he guns it forward.

I stumble back. "What the hell?"

He smirks. "Sorry about that."

He doesn't sound sorry, at all. *Asshole.* I gauge the distance toward the bike, then take a step toward it. Once again, he allows the bike to jump forward.

"Ryot, what are you doing?" I slap my hands on my hips and glower at him.

He laughs. It's a full-throated, very manly laugh that has me looking at him in amazement. This playful side of him is one I have not seen before. Is this how he was before he became a Marine. Before he lost his wife? Was he this carefree? This spirited... This roguish? *Oh god. He's so damn sexy like this.* Also, my pussy is now completely wet. I wish I could feel the vibrations from that laugh between my legs. I bet I'd come just from that sensation. Also, why can't I stop thinking of his head between my thighs? And this when he's treated me so...so... normally? He doesn't give a shit that I'm a princess. He's not polite around me. He doesn't hold himself in check. He speaks his mind. He tells me what to do. He tells me off. He reprimands me. Chastises me. Cajoles me into doing exactly what he wants. And...I love it.

Butterflies take flight in my chest. I close the distance to his bike and straddle the seat behind him.

"Hold on. And make sure you lean into the turns when I do." He reaches behind to grab the back of my thigh and pulls me snug against him. I'm now hugging his thighs with mine. And my core is flush against his very tight, very hard backside. I lock my arms about his waist. His lean, sculpted waist; I can feel his chiseled abs through the leather of his jacket. Then he guns his bike, and it leaps forward.

With a squeak, I tighten my hold about him. I sense him chuckle again. And when he slides onto the road and races forward, exhilaration bubbles in my blood. Cole zooms off ahead of us on another bike, and Brian keeps pace behind us on his.

We might be on bikes, but he's keeping his security formation. I can't help but be impressed. He's not going to compromise my safety, even now. We weave through traffic. When we get on the highway, he guns the bike forward. I whoop. The freedom. The thrill. The edge. The brush with danger that being on the bike brings spikes my blood with adrenaline. *I'm out of that hotel room. I'm free.* Ryot zips past a few cars, then a truck, and exhilaration bubbles up my throat. I'm on a bike, and no one passing by knows I'm the Princess of Verenza. I'm just another girl holding my man tightly as we head out to who-knows-where.

I cling to him, allowing myself to relax so my body flows with his. We ride for about half an hour, then he takes the next turn off, and my body leans into the turn with his. We continue down another road, then emerge onto one that skirts the Thames. In the distance, I can see Tower Bridge, or London Bridge, as it is wrongly called by tourists.

He slows down as we near it, but instead of stopping in front of it, he turns into a side road. A few more minutes, and he pulls up in front of a doorway. He switches off the engine and kicks down the stand. I jump off without waiting for him and notice that Cole has already parked his bike to the side. He walks over to stand by the doorway. Brian comes to a stop a few feet behind us. He dismounts and walks past Cole, then through the doorway.

I'm about to follow him, but Ryot stops me with a touch on my elbow. "Let him make sure it's safe."

Pinpricks of awareness course out from the point of contact. I pull away, studying the quiet street. It seems to be residential with overhanging trees. There are a few cars parked up the road, but other than that, there's no one around.

Why did he bring me here? It doesn't look like the entrance to a restaurant. Some of my excitement fizzles away. I thought he was bringing me somewhere special, but this looks like an ordinary London house. My shoulders droop. Disappointment coils in my belly, but I shake it off. At least, I'm not eating dinner from room service while watching TV. That has to count for something, right? I'm outside. I just rode on a motorcycle with my body wrapped around Ryot's!

I take a deep breath, relishing the fresh air, so different from the recycled hotel air I've been breathing over the last week.

Before I can ask Ryot where he's taking me, Brian walks out of the doorway and nods. He holds the door open, and Ryot indicates I should move forward.

I step into the hallway and realize the space is bigger than it seemed from the outside. There's a winding staircase that leads up to a landing, and above that is a roof with skylights set into it. He brushes past me and walks up the staircase. "Careful, the steps are a little steep," he warns.

I follow him, trying to keep my eyes off his butt and failing. Bet he stares at mine when I walk in front of him, too. I've felt his eyes on me. I push that thought away. I follow Ryot onto the landing on the second floor and through the short hallway through what seems to be the door to an apartment.

When I step in, my breath catches. It *is* an apartment... But there's no furniture. Except for a table set for two with a candle in the center and two chairs, both angled toward a stunning view. And what a view it is! Massive floor-to-ceiling windows frame a view of the Thames and the beautifully lit Tower Bridge in all its glory.

"Wow." I hook my jacket on the coat rack and deposit my purse on the entryway table. Then walk past Ryot toward the window. I come to a stop next to the table and take in the sight of the iconic landmark. My breath catches.

Ryot—who's also taken off his jacket—walks up to stand next to me. For a few seconds, we gaze at the monument.

"I've never seen it from this viewpoint before," I whisper.

"It's a secret," he says in a soft voice.

"Thanks for sharing it with me." For some reason, tears drum at the backs of my eyes, and I blink them away. I don't know why I'm feeling this emotional. Maybe, it's the fact that the spectacle of the London bridge is so breathtaking? Or it's that he was thoughtful enough to arrange for me to see it? "It's beautiful." I whisper.

"It is."

Something in his voice makes me shoot a sharp glance in his direction, and our gazes hold. And connect.

Instantly, the air between us heats. My heart seems to descend to the space between my legs, the pulse loud and insistent. I sway toward him, and Ryot... He leans in. He lowers his head, I raise mine, when footsteps sound.

"Good to see you, Ryot."

I spring back, but not before I catch the annoyance and the disappointment on Ryot's face. It's my only consolation for not being able to see that kiss through to fruition. I turn to find a tall man with dark hair and intense features looking between us.

"Princess Aurelia." He bows. "James Hamilton, at your service."

He turns to Ryot, then closes the distance to him and slaps him on the shoulder. "Davenport, about time you crawled out of the hole you've been hiding in."

Ryot jerks his chin, then the two of them shake hands. "Thanks for doing this on such short notice."

"Anything for you, man."

A glance passes between the two, then it's James' turn to nod. He turns to me. "Ready for dinner?"

15

Ryot

"You got a Michelin-starred chef to cook for us?" She glances toward the kitchen where James has disappeared.

"He's a good friend of my brother, Knox. They served together in the Marines."

I'll also admit that it was a spur-of-the-moment decision. When I realized how at the end of her tether she was, I knew I had to get her out. I spoke with James during the time it took her to get dressed. And it didn't hurt that she took longer than I specified. It gave James enough time to get himself and his staff over to the apartment to set up the table and get the food organized.

I pull out a chair. She walks over, and slides into the chair, her movements graceful. I scoot her forward, make sure she's comfortable, then walk around to take my own chair.

Cole, who followed us in, nods in my direction. He steps out then shuts the door behind himself as he leaves. I know he and Brian are standing guard outside. Given there have been no other incidents since that last threat and since I'm in the room with the princess, we agreed she should be safe, at least for the next few hours. I have to admit I'm happy to have some privacy with her.

She glances around the space with an appreciative sigh. "This is a beautiful spot and the view—" She shakes her head. "It's incredible. Who does this place belong to?"

When I don't answer, she turns to me, understanding filtering into her eyes. "It's yours."

I nod. "I bought it with the money I saved up when I was in the Marines. I haven't gotten around to furnishing it though."

She looks at me with curiosity. "You didn't want to use your family's money?"

"Does that surprise you?"

She shakes her head. "It makes me jealous of you."

"Why's that?" I frown.

"I'd give anything to be able to have a normal job, earn my living, and be independent. But unlike you, being part of the Royal Family comes with a set of responsibilities which I cannot run away from."

"You could leave if you wanted." I reach for the jug of water between us and fill up her glass, then mine.

"Thanks." She reaches for her glass of water and takes a sip before setting it down. "You mean, turn my back on my father and brothers, and my country?" She blows out a breath. "The thought has occurred to me more times than I can count, but"—she taps her fingertip against the glass—"my mother made me promise I wouldn't let down the House of Verenza. So"—she looks at the still empty wine glass—"anything else I can drink?"

James approaches the table wheeling a small cart with two Champagne flutes and a bucket of ice containing a bottle of my favorite drink. "I believe these bubbles that Ryot ordered will be to your liking, Your Majesty." He pops the cork and pours the fizzing liquid into both flutes before setting them on the table. He sets the bottle in the bucket and steps back. "Your starters will be out shortly."

"Thank you." She smiles at him.

James smiles back before nodding in my direction and heading back inside.

"A bit imperious of you to think you know my tastes?" She sniffs.

I merely reach for my flute and raise it.

She huffs, then raises her own. She takes a sip, and her gaze widens. She swirls the liquid over her tongue and swallows. "That's…. Very good."

"I chose it especially for you."

She takes another sip and closes her eyes, savoring it before swallowing. "It's fresh and crisp and there's a hint of"—her eyebrows draw down—"of…"

"Honeysuckle, vanilla and strawberries," I offer.

It's why I messaged James to choose this vintage.

"That's right." She sips some more, then—in a very unladylike gesture which brings a smile to my face, and which I take as proof of her loving the Champagne I chose for her—she drains the rest of the glass.

"Can I have more?"

"After you eat your first course."

She narrows her eyes. "Are you now directing when I drink alcohol?"

"Only because you ate very little lunch, and I don't want the alcohol to go to your head."

Her lips part. She looks both taken aback and turned on. With her flushed cheeks and flashing eyes, she's a mixture of sass and hesitant need to accept that she likes being told what to do. And it's such a fucking turn on. My cock thickens. My thigh muscles ripple.

On impulse, I reach over and place my hand on her free one. "You relish being told what to do."

Apparently, I can't hold back this evening. When I decided to bring her out to dinner, my intention was to keep on the right side of the bodyguard/principal boundaries I set for myself. But hearing her whoop for joy and then feeling her arms clasped around my waist as she clung to me on the bike weakened my resolve.

I told myself this wasn't a date, but who am I kidding? It's definitely a date, given the lengths I went to, to find a place that's special yet secluded enough to be safe for her. Not to mention, calling in my years-old favor with James and asking him to cook us this meal. And when I saw the pleasure on her face as she took in the sight outside the window, my reservations melted away. *I can't be this close to her and not show her how well I can read her. There's no harm if I tell her what I want to do to her, right? I could indulge myself, for just this evening, can't I?*

Her lips firm. She opens her mouth to speak, and I lean in and raise my finger to her lips. "Don't deny it. Your heightened breathing and the way your pulse speeds up at your throat tells me you enjoy when you're not given a choice."

The pulse at the base of her throat speeds up.

"Deep inside, you long to hand over the reins to someone more dominant. Someone who'll help you relax into your own pleasure. Someone who'll take care of you, and protect you, and punish you when you're out of line. Someone who'll tell you off when you test boundaries and put you in your place. Someone who'll make you beg for what you most desire." *Someone who I hope is me.*

Her pupils dilate. She's riveted by my words. Hanging onto every syllable. And fuck, if that doesn't turn my cock into a raging column of steel.

She pinches her fingers around the stem of her Champagne glass and the skin stretches over her knuckles. "And I suppose that person is you?"

I incline my head, holding her gaze. The air between us crackles with unspoken need. Sparks seem to zing between us. The blood pounds at my temples, at my wrists, even in my fucking balls. A few more seconds, and I'm going to haul her to me, and kiss those soft lips of hers until she can't think straight. But not yet.

Not ever.

Dammit. What the hell is the matter with me? Once more, I've forgotten myself in her presence. I need to...control myself better. I slide my palm from hers and lean back in my seat.

This was a bad idea. I shouldn't have said anything to her. She's tying me up in knots and confusing my train of thought. I've never been this...indecisive before. Never. Regret coils in my belly. I can taste the bitterness of remorse at the back of my tongue.

"It could have been"—I look away, then back at her—"if I hadn't taken this position of being your bodyguard."

Her gaze narrows. Confusion laces her features. I shouldn't have overstepped the boundary I set for myself. I thought I could give her a feeling of being free; instead, I'm going to hurt her. And all because I can't fucking hold onto my control when I'm with her.

I toss back my Champagne, hardly tasting it, then fix her with an unblinking glare. "There cannot be anything between us, Princess."

"So, you keep saying." She juts out her chin. "Yet you're the one who implied that I need someone dominant to bring my desires to life."

"I'm sorry. I shouldn't have said that...even if it is true. But, the fact remains, I can't do it. I can't allow myself to be that person, however much I might want it."

She seems stricken, then firms her lips. "You keep using the fact that you're my bodyguard to throw up walls between us. But I think it's because you're still not over your wife. That's the real reason you're too scared of acting on your instincts."

Anger squeezes my guts. My stomach churns. I grab the bottle of Champagne and top off my glass, then push the bottle aside. It's a testament to how preoccupied she is that she doesn't insist I also top her up. I take another fortifying sip of the bubbles and place my glass down carefully. "You have no idea what you're talking about. You don't know how things were between us."

"So, tell me." She leans toward me. "I want to understand, Ryot. I know I have no right to ask you this, and I wish I didn't care so much about your answer, but I do. I want to understand *you* better. That kiss meant something to me. And despite my best efforts, I've begun to care for you. And you must feel something for me. You must, at least, consider me a friend. Otherwise, you wouldn't have brought me here today. So—" She looks at me earnestly. "Talk to me. Tell me what's on your mind."

I glance away. I wish I could tell her how I felt about Jane. How if I hadn't come home between tours at the same time as her, we never would've had that argument. I wouldn't have pissed her off enough that she'd call up her commanding officer and insist that she leave right away. I wouldn't have picked up the phone when it rang a few days later to find that she and her platoon had been taken out. I wouldn't be left with the memory that she'd been unfaithful to me for a while by the time she died—which was why we were fighting before she left.

I knew I'd made a mistake within weeks of marrying her. I realized then, I had never been in love with her. I didn't want to be with her, but I was so stubborn, I thought I could make things work. Meanwhile, it was clear she didn't care. I wonder if she ever cared at all. I wonder whether I did? Maybe that's why I felt ...nothing— *nothing*—when I got the call. Nothing other than the lingering anger at her infidelity. And then the shame at being so relieved that she wasn't coming back. The worst part was the crippling guilt that followed because, really, wasn't I responsible for her going on that tour, in the first place?

How I wish I could tell Aura all of this. How I wish I could confess to her all that I feel foolish for marrying Jane, angry she cheated on me, guilty our fight caused her to go back early which led to her death, a failure for not making my marriage work, and ashamed for not even caring that she's dead. Nope. Not happening. I'm not even ready to admit most of that to myself.

I toss back the rest of my second glass of Champagne and wish it were something stronger. I never talk about Jane. The fact I even shared this much with the princess when I haven't discussed it with my brothers is something I don't want to question too closely.

"So, you did love her?" She asks softly.

"It's complicated." I look away then back at her. "I realize, that's not a real answer, but it's the only one I can give you right now."

James returns, negating the need for more conversation. He slides a plate in front of her. "Seared Scallops with Cauliflower Purée and Truffle Oil, for your Highness and"—he places another in front of me—"Lobster Bisque with Cognac and Tarragon for you, Ryot." He steps back and looks between us. "Enjoy." He turns and leaves.

She looks at her plate. "You ordered for me?"

"I'm aware that you don't have any food allergies and that you happen to love any fish-based dish."

She looks at me strangely. "How did you find that out?"

"I checked your file."

She looks crestfallen. What her file didn't mention is how much she loves Champagne. I found that out from her family chef. I used my position as her personal protective detail to find out everything I could about her.

"For the record, I also love seafood."

"Hence..." She nods at my dish.

I pick up my spoon. Unable to stop myself, I lower my chin and inhale the aroma of the bisque. When I make a sound of appreciation deep in my throat, she shivers. The blood drains to my groin.

Damn! Her responsiveness will be my downfall. And it's wrong of me to be this horny when I've been thinking about just how much I fucked things up with Jane, and how happy I am that she's not in my life anymore. Of course, I wouldn't have wished her dead, but...
Annnd, now I feel guilty again. Good times.

I shove aside my attraction for the princess, then take a spoonful of the soup. The rich, creamy, and savory flavor coats my palate. The aromatic notes of onion, garlic, leek, and carrot add a subtle layer of complexity, which both satisfies me and makes me want more. James is a genius.

I scoop up the last of the mixture in the bowl, then tear off a piece of bread that's on the accompanying plate and soak up any remaining drops with it. I bring it to my mouth, savoring the last drops, then look up to find she's looking at my lips. Her own are parted, her cheeks flushed. And when I drag my thumb across my bottom lip, she gulps.

"Don't you like your food?" I nod toward her almost untouched plate.

She ducks her head, and spearing a scallop, brings it to her mouth. When her pink tongue flicks out to lick it off her lips, my scalp tingles. My skin feels too tight for my body. Nope, not going there. I glance away, trying my best not to be affected when she hums under her breath. "This is really good."

"It is." My voice comes out strangled and I clear my throat.

She peeks up at me from under her eyelashes and when she sees the expression on my features, she flushes further. Our gazes lock, and she freezes. A look of yearning glitters in her eyes.

Unable to stop myself, I reach over and slide the fork from her fingers, then pierce another scallop and bring it to her mouth. She parts her lips, and I place it on her tongue. She licks off the tines of the fork, then chews. When she swallows, I can almost feel the suction around my cock. This time, I'm helpless in the wake of the need gripping me.

I spear the last scallop and bring it to her lips. When she's licked the fork clean, I place it on her plate, then lower my hand and wrap my fingers around her throat.

16

Aurelia

He squeezes his fingers gently, and I can feel the imprint of each finger against my throat. A shiver pinches my shoulders. My ribcage compresses. My lungs burn, and I'm sure I'm going to burst into flames any moment.

I can't believe my seduction technique is working. When I saw his reaction to my appreciation for the food, I realized I had to lean into the chemistry between us. The fact that our surroundings are so romantic gave me the courage to follow my instinct. Given he's made it clear that he won't cross the line of professionalism, that he's made it clear he's not going to be the one to dominate me, I was sure he'd shut me down again but... Looks like he's reached a tipping point.

"You're so fucking sexy." His voice is low and hard and sends another burst of sensations pulsing under my skin. He flattens his thumb over the pulse at the hollow of my throat. It's an act that puts him in control. Which makes it seem like he could get me to do anything with his touch. If he asks me to drop down on my knees, I'll do it right now. If he asks me to spread my legs for him, I will. My heartbeat spikes in my ribcage. My nipples are so hard, I'm surprised they aren't tearing through the fabric of my blouse.

"Slip your fingers into your panties and touch yourself," he says in a low hard voice. Goosebumps scatter over my skin. "There are no cameras in the room."

I flick a glance in the direction of the doorway. "James might enter any moment."

I turn to find him watching me with an inquisitive expression. "He might," he acknowledges.

I hold his gaze steadily for a few more seconds. *Is that going to stop me from touching myself?* A quiver courses through my body.

"How do you feel about that?" His question seems innocent, but that watchful edge to his gaze tells me it's anything but. "Does the thought of someone finding you in a compromising position turn your pussy into a melting mass of need?"

My core clenches. My thighs turn to jelly. I'm panting. I can hear my heaving breaths, but I'm so turned on, I'm past being embarrassed. When I nod, those green eyes spark. It's like lightning caged in those beautiful irises.

"Who'd have thought the poised Princess of Verenza was an exhibitionist, hmm? Now"—he eyes me with a hungry look in his eyes— "touch yourself."

Instantly, I brush my fingertips over my throbbing center. I cry out.

"Good girl."

I whimper. His words feel so very good.

"Such an obedient little slut," he nods with satisfaction. "You're so wet, I can smell your arousal from across the table."

What the—? He called me a slut but that only spikes my arousal further. The impact of his words resonates through my mind and ricochets around my chest.

"I want to lick up the seam of your melting pussy. I want to stuff my tongue inside your slit and taste you. I want to bite down on your swollen cunt so you can feel me all the way to your nipples. I want"—his nostrils flare—"I want you so badly, my balls hurt."

"So why don't you fuck me?" I tip up my chin, daring him—hoping, wanting, *needing* to push him past the point of no return. *If I dare him, will he oblige me?*

He releases his hold on my neck and snaps, "Pull your fingers out and hold them up."

I want to refuse him. I want to demand that he collar my throat with his fingers, but the glare on his face insists I obey him. I withdraw my fingers and lift them up.

He locks his fingers around my wrist, brings my hand close to his face, then bends and sniffs my fingers. His eyelids sweep down. He inhales one more time. "Such a fucking aphrodisiac."

He closes his mouth around my fingers and licks them off. My toes curl. My pussy feels so bereft. I squeeze my thighs together to stem the emptiness between them. He senses my movement, and his eyes glitter.

Spots of color smear his cheeks. "You know why I can't." He lets go of my arm and sprawls back in his seat.

"Can't or won't?" I grip the edge of the table. "I'm tired of your teasing me, tired of your saying one thing and doing another."

His gaze flicks down to my chest. His eyes widen. *What the hell is he playing at?* I glance down to find a bead of light flickering over the left side of my chest. *What the hell is that?* Before I can continue, he throws himself over the table and takes me down.

I cry out. The next moment, the window explodes. The sound echoes through my mind, along with the reverberations when my head collides with something hard and immovable. Then, he locks his arms around my waist and squeezes me to his chest so tightly, I gasp. My ribcage hurts. My pulse rate shoots up. My stomach bottoms out. *What's happening?*

More glass shatters. Shards pour over us, and I whimper. Then, I'm being rolled out of the way and to the side.

I hit the wall, and then something heavy and warm pushes me back. My nose is buried in the strip of skin revealed by the lapels of Ryot's shirt. I breathe in his dark musky scent and focus on the beating of his heart which thuds against my chest. It mirrors the racing of my own. His weight pins me down, and his hard thigh is pushed up between mine. And while I should be in shock, the fact is, I'm too aware of how every inch of his ungiving male body covers mine.

How his hips are fitted over mine. How the hard ridge at his crotch stabs into the sensitive area between my thighs. My pussy turns into a sloppy mess. And despite my sudden realization I've just been shot at, despite my intensifying fear that the shooter is probably still lurking out there, I can't stop myself from straining against him as I try to get closer to his heat. For a few more seconds, I stay pinned down by him. Then footsteps approach.

"Ryot, Princess, are you okay?" A gruff voice — Brian's, I think — asks from somewhere over us.

"Go after him, don't let him get away," Ryot barks without taking his gaze off my features.

"Cole is already in pursuit. I just wanted to check on you first." Brian pivots and darts off.

Ryot pushes up on his arms and scans my face. His jaw is hard, and his green eyes have turned almost grey as he stares into my face. He looks pissed off and afraid. Very afraid. "Are you okay?" he growls.

I want to nod but, perhaps, I'm still in shock. Or perhaps, I'm too aware of the evidence of his arousal throbbing between my legs. Either way, I'm unable to say or do anything. His forehead draws down.

His gaze grows fierce. "Aura, are you okay?" He cups my cheek. "Talk to me. Are you hurt?"

He called me by my nickname, and oh god, it feels so good. So right. A tear squeezes out from the corner of my eye. His eyes turn stormy. Sparks flare deep inside. Gold and silver, and I can almost see lightning flash in them. Almost on cue, thunder rumbles somewhere in the distance, then the pattering of raindrops against the balcony outside reaches me.

"Nod if you're fine," he orders. His voice is harsh and bossy, and so insistent. It cuts through the noise in my head. I manage to jerk my chin.

His shoulders relax. "Jesus, you had me worried." He lowers his head and presses a quick kiss to my forehead. "Follow my lead."

He begins to crawl toward the open doorway, sweeping aside the glass shards in his way. I follow him. Once we're through the door and to the hallway, where we're no longer in plain view of the window, he rises to his feet. He holds out his arm. I take it, and he hauls me up to my feet.

When I stumble, he simply scoops me up in his arms. I should protest and tell him I'm okay. I'm the princess who swore to never become a helpless, sweet, defenseless woman who needs a knight in shining armor to save her but— The truth is, my legs feel too weak to support me, and my head is still spinning from what I know was an attempt on my life. *Oh god, the note. They weren't bluffing. Did they follow us? What do they want?*

If Ryot hadn't been here, I'd be dead right now. He saved my life. Another shudder grips me. I can't seem to stop myself from shaking.

"Ryot, I… I'm scared." My voice trembles. I'm ashamed that I feel so vulnerable. But right now, it feels like he's the only unshakeable, strong, secure thing in this world.

"I am not going to let anything happen to you." He looks into my face with his intense gaze. "You hear me, Aura? I'll take a bullet for you."

"You almost did." My mouth feels like it's filled with sawdust. My stomach heaves. My features crumple, and I push my face into his chest as the tears flow down my cheeks. *Don't break down. I have no business going to pieces like this.* But oh god, as the shock settles into my bones, I feel like I'm going to fall apart. He holds me close and wraps his arms about me, tucking my head under his chin. He lets me hold onto him and weep in big sobbing gulps.

"There, there, darlin'. You're safe. I'm not going anywhere." He kisses my forehead, then my eyelids. His touch is comforting. It also inflames my senses and turns my nerve-endings into little balls of fire. *Damn. I almost died. He almost died defending me.* And I can't stop myself from wanting him in the most carnal of ways.

"You're in shock." He pulls me closer, then turns to face the man standing in front of us.

"We need a—"

"My car's waiting at the back entrance." James' voice.

I glimpse his shuttered features, then he slips a key fob into Ryot's pants pocket and hands over our jackets and my purse. Ryot nods his appreciation, his features grim. "Thank you."

Before the words are out of my mouth Ryot starts leading me down the hallway through the kitchen to what I assume is the fire escape.

I feel discombobulated, like I'm somewhere far above, watching this scene unfold. I cling to Ryot as he descends a set of stairs. Then we're at ground level. He walks swiftly down the alley. A car beeps, and he stops in front of a Mercedes AMG. He sets me down on my feet, but I cling to him.

"We need to get you into the car and away from this, baby."

His voice is gravelly, and the endearment is...unexpected. And the way he threw himself between me and whoever was firing to protect me—while making sure to cradle my head so I wouldn't hit the floor—was such a tender gesture. *He wouldn't do that unless he cares for me, right?* A fresh trembling crashes over me. He pulls me in even tighter, until my nose is, once again, buried in his chest. And the hardness of his sculpted torso is imprinted into my skin. His heat surrounds me and pins me in place.

"We can't delay further. I have to make sure you're away from here. The shooter, might be lurking around."

I shudder, then draw in a deep breath, filling myself with great gulps of Ryot-scented air. Then I nod. "Okay," I say, the sound muffled against his chest.

"Okay." He kisses the top of my head, then steps back and pinches my chin. He surveys my features, which must be tear-stained, and my swollen eyes, and his features soften. "It's going to be fine."

I nod.

He lowers his chin, and as if unable to stop himself, he presses a hard kiss to my mouth. Before I can respond, he pulls open the door to the car and ushers me inside. Then, he leans over and straps my seat belt, before shutting the door and walking around. He slides into the driver's seat, turns the ignition, and eases the car forward. He turns onto the main road and guns the engine. Several more turns, as if he's trying to confuse anyone following us, and then he joins the traffic on the highway.

"Where are we going?" I relax into the seat, the tension oozing out of my shoulders and leaving me exhausted. I yawn, nestling my cheek into the soft leather seat.

"A safe house." He steps on the accelerator. "Sleep. I'll wake you when we get there."

17

Ryot

It's my fault this happened. I never should have let my guard down. How could I have taken her out of the hotel when I know the level of danger she faces? How could I have indulged my attraction for her and arranged for that date when I know the threat comes from a credible source? How could I have given in to her needing a change, knowing it was breaking protocol?

After the shooter fired at her, James and I exchanged one glance and agreed, without speaking, that the situation had turned even more serious. It was best to get her out of there and to a place no one knows about. Not even my team.

No one, but me and my brother, Tyler, who I messaged and informed of my plans.

Cole updated me earlier. Neither he nor Brian found any evidence of the shooter. Which confirms to me that whoever we're dealing with is better than I originally gave them credit for.

Since the princess' team was vetted by me, I saw no harm in

sharing our whereabouts, so they could reach her, if needed. I curse myself. I shouldn't have done that.

On the other hand, the list of suspects has been narrowed to the inner circle. One of them must have leaked details of the princess' movements.

Until I figure out what's happening, I'm not going to trust anyone other than, Tyler.

I drive through the night and arrive at my safe house in the early hours of the morning. She's sleeping so peacefully, and the shadows beneath her eyes are so pronounced, I decide to carry her into the house. This place is off the books.

I paid for it through a company that cannot be traced back to me. This is the one time I dipped into my inheritance. Instinct had warned me that, at some time in the future, I might need to get out here.

I place her on the bed, unlace and remove her Doc Martens, and cover her up. For a few seconds, I watch her chest rise and fall. Her eyelashes curl over her cheekbone; her cheeks are flushed. At least, she's no longer pale. She'll likely be exhausted when she wakes up, though. I place a glass of water, along with a bottle of Tylenol next to her on the nightstand. Then I tuck the duvet around her and walk out.

I head down into the kitchen, fill a glass of water from the tap and drink from it, then place the glass down on the counter. I step out onto the patio, pull out my phone, and video call my brother.

Tyler picks up in two rings. "Are you okay?"

There's worry in his voice.

"I'm good."

"Assume this is a secure line?"

"Don't insult me," I scoff.

"No harm covering all bases. When you're in the middle of a tricky operation, it's surprising how much detail can slip."

I stiffen. "If this is about what happened to Jane —"

"It's not." His voice softens. "Don't get all worked up about it. I'm simply watching out for you and your principal."

It's strange how I'm no longer as disturbed about hearing her name emerge from my lips as I was even a few weeks ago. Is it because of... Aura? Because the princess is occupying my thoughts, and has clawed her way under my skin and into my heart? If I had any doubts about what she means to me—that assassin's bullet put them to rest.

The moment I spotted the telltale crimson pinpoint of the laser sight quivering over her heart, my entire being went into overdrive. My pulse sped up, my heartbeat spiked, adrenaline flushed my blood stream, and I moved without conscious thought.

Thank God, I managed to take her down and shield her body from the worst of the impact. I heard the bullet break the glass of the window and shatter the water jug before it punched through the overturned chair where she'd been seated and embedded itself in the floor.

I felt the vibrations from the hit deep in my bones. Every cell in my body snapped to attention, every instinct ringing out in alarm. I managed to roll her away, against the wall, until we were out of sight of whoever might be out there. And I covered her body with mine. She was silent under me, but for the hammering of her heart, which confirmed to me she was alive. And despite the danger of the situation, my body was drawn to hers. I was painfully hard, and my cock insisted on nestling happily between her thighs.

I cursed myself and wanted to pull away, but then she squirmed under me. She pushed herself up and into me, flattening her gorgeous curves against my much harder body, and I almost came in my pants. I was so conscious about her and hated that I couldn't turn off my response to her. I enjoyed it too, and berated myself for it, and—

"Ryot, you there?" My brother's voice interrupts my thoughts.

I bring myself back to the present. "Sorry, you were saying?"

He scrutinizes my face with a worried expression. "You holding up okay?"

"It's been a long day." I rub the back of my neck. "I need you to help me find who's behind the shooting. My team has come up short, and the king's security has nothing on it either."

"On it already. I've reached out to the best investigators who're part of Karina Beauchamp's team."

"Karina…?" *Where have I heard that name before?* The realization kicks in. "She's connected to Sinclair Sterling…" Who's our friend, and someone who Arthur trusts—something which is a rarity.

"That's right." He nods. "She has a highly specialized team who're working with Cole and Brian. I should have something for you in the next forty-eight hours."

"Make that twenty-four. I've bought us a little time by bringing her here, and keeping it secret to minimize any chance of leaks. This place has the best security possible." I know, because I put it in. "But whoever is posing a threat to her life is not to be underestimated." I gave in to her pleas. I broke my own rule of not taking her anywhere where her security could be compromised. And I lost my focus, so enamored with her, I forgot to be vigilant for any attacks. And look what happened?

It almost cost me her life. It's because I'm attracted to her. I've lost perspective, and that's what I feared most. I'm unable to keep my infatuation with her separate, and it's beginning to affect my decisions.

Only… It's too late to walk away from her. I won't be happy handing over this assignment to anyone else. I can't trust anyone else to protect her. Which means, I'm going to have to shadow her even more closely, until the threat to her life is neutralized. I won't be able to get out in the field and track down whoever shot at her. I'll have to rely on my team and Tyler. If there's anyone I'd trust with my life, it's him.

I love all of my brothers, but Tyler is the one who feels emotions as deeply as I do. Perhaps, because he's the only one of us who has a child?

"You did the right thing by taking her away, but it's a temporary measure," he cautions.

"It is." I blow out a breath. It would make my job much easier to tell her to cancel her appointments so I can keep her in one room and, preferably, lock the door behind me so I can make sure no one else enters. But that's counterintuitive to what having a protection detail is about. I wouldn't be doing my job if I made her compromise on her lifestyle.

I need to fold into her comings and goings and be as nonintrusive as possible, while protecting her. Of course, with the awareness flaring between us, it's not like I could simply blend into the background. No matter how inconspicuous I try to make myself, I'm too aware of the attraction between us. And she seems to know exactly where I am at any point. The more I try to avoid looking at her directly, the more she insists on trying to get my attention. I notice it all. Every twitch of her lips, every exaggerated sway of her behind, every time I have to pass by her and a whiff of her scent leaves me with an enormous hard-on that's unseemly. It's why I've given her a wide berth. But I couldn't pass up the opportunity to take her out to dinner, could I? "I'm going to keep her here for as long as I can, but until the threat against her is neutralized..." I shake my head. "Damn, I'm so pissed off. I bent enough rules that I gave the gunman the perfect opportunity to shoot at her."

"But you got her out of harm's away."

"And I can't afford to put her in his crosshairs, again," I say grimly.

"Don't be too hard on yourself." Tyler half smiles. "Though I should say, it's a relief to find you back in the land of the living."

"What do you mean?"

"After Jane, you appeared to bury your feelings and hide away."

"I didn't hide. I was living my life," I snap. And yes, I spent time withdrawing into myself, not speaking much to anyone while I tried to come to grips with what happened. Not that I'm going to admit to that aloud.

"Were you, though? You were pissed off with Quentin for his role in the attacks on her. You got into fights with him, in your compulsion to make him pay."

All of which is true. "I needed to blame someone. Quentin fit the bill. I held him responsible for what happened to Jane's battalion when, really, he was only doing his duty."

"It's understandable that you were so grief stricken you weren't thinking straight. In fact"—his brow furrows—"it's why I was surprised to find you were joining the security agency."

"It seemed the lesser of the two evils." The other being joining the Davenport Group. Which would have meant more contact with my grandfather, which I'm keen to avoid at all costs. "I was beginning to realize that I couldn't hold Quentin responsible for something that was out of his control." *Or perhaps, I got tired of being angry and alone and decided I needed to move on with my life.*

"It's good you took up the mission. The best way to heal is to feel needed, to know you're valued. To contribute to something larger than yourself."

I head back inside the kitchen, reach for the bottle of whiskey on the shelf over the counter and pour myself a drink. "Is that why you decided to join the Davenport Group?"

It's his turn to wince. "I joined because I need stability for Serene. I'd be lying if I said having her in my life didn't force me to grow up and face my responsibilities. Plus, being the CEO has perks. I can set my hours, and I can work from home when needed.

"Still having nanny problems?" I snicker.

He arches an eyebrow. "Glad you find that amusing. I'll have the last laugh, though, considering I'm witnessing you falling in love."

I give him a strange look. "You do realize I was married once?"

Tyler inclines his head. "Are you telling me you were in love with Jane?"

When I don't reply, he merely nods. "I rest my case."

"How did you guess?" I give him a strange look.

"The ring you inherited from our grandmother; you didn't give that to her."

Arthur's wife left each of us brothers a ring from her jewelry collection. She also gave us instructions that we were to give it to the woman with whom we fell in love. It never occurred to me to give it to Jane. That's how uncommitted I was to that relationship.

When I stay quiet, Tyler sighs. "It's okay to admit you didn't love her. You don't have to feel guilty for what happened to her. You couldn't have stopped her from going on that mission, and you know it."

"If I hadn't fought with her, she might not have felt compelled to sign up." I glance away.

"As a former Marine, I don't need to tell you that we're all aware of the risks when we embark on that life. You know better than to blame yourself for what happened."

I rub the back of my neck. I want to believe him. A part of me knows he's right. Another part of me can't get over the lingering guilt that coats my insides. Perhaps, I never will. I take another sip of the Macallan. "Either way, who said anything about falling in love?"

Tyler's features gentle. "You deserve to be happy, Ryot. If you're given a second chance, I hope you won't be so afraid of what happened in the past that you'll shut yourself off from possibilities."

His words send a tremor of hope through my guts. I make sure to bat it away and scowl at him. "I don't need you telling me what to do. You focus on finding who was behind the hit on the princess. Leave the rest to me."

"But—" he begins to protest.

I hit the screen and disconnect the call. Fuck. My brothers are nosy so-and-so's. You'd think, being the alpha males they are, they'd keep our discussions on safer topics. But fuck, do they love to gossip. And they're up in each other's business. To be fair, despite pulling away from my family after Jane's death, even I kept tabs on Nathan's, and Knox's, not to mention, Quentin's love lives. I also agreed to attend Arthur's family Sunday lunches, as a way of keeping up with everyone. Much as I might protest, I'm cut from the same mold. I toss back the rest of the whiskey, then place it on the counter and turn back. My breath catches.

She's standing inside the doorway by the table pushed up against the wall. The moonlight streaming in from the windows kisses her figure, and casts shadows on the valley between her breasts, on the dip of her waist and the hollow between the tops of her thighs. *Fuck my life.* She's naked.

18

Aurelia

His gaze rakes me from head to toe, his perusal slow. There are no lights on but the glow from the stars outside bathes him. It picks out the silver in his irises, which seem to glitter as he devours me with his eyes. The air between us sparks with unsaid emotions. My pussy clenches. He takes a step forward, and another. The force of his presence seems to fill the space and circles around me, lassoing me in place. He drags his gaze up my legs to the space between my thighs and stays there. A throbbing sensation tightens my veins. He glides closer, still closer. Stalking me, holding me in place with intent writ in every angle of his chiseled body.

I'm aware, I'm naked. I'm aware that he's a predator who's looking at me like I'm his next meal. And I have a sneaking feeling he's going to love to play with me first. I must have been crazy to think I could walk in here without any clothes on and expect to leave without facing the consequences of taunting him.

I might be royalty, but he's the king of all he surveys.

He's an alpha male used to getting his way. An apex beast, at the top of the food chain.

His arrogance, his dominance is imprinted in his every lethal step. In how his chest planes bunch, stretching the shirt he's wearing, straining at the buttons. He's abandoned his jacket and undone the top three buttons, and I can make out the trail of hair that disappears into the lapels. His shoulders seem to swell. His powerful thighs strain his pants. And the bulge between them is massive. I stare openly at the virility he wears like a badge. The man's packing. No wonder he has such a swollen ego. It's not the only part of him which is swollen either.

A snicker escapes me, and he inclines his head, the movement sharp. His gaze is even sharper as he raises it to my face.

Our eyes clash, his green with gold and silver sparks in their depths. In this light, they seem hazel, almost surreal. An alien from another world who's come to carry me off to his lair and have his way with me. A gust of wind blows in from the open doorway to the deck. Goosebumps pop on my skin. He stiffens, then spins around and walks back to slide the door shut. He pivots and prowls toward me again.

My belly twists. My toes curl. The blood thrums at my temples, in my veins. My nipples tighten. My breasts ache. He pauses in front of me, so close the heat from his body singes my skin. A buzzing sensation gathers in my lower belly. My breath comes in short, choppy bursts. He reaches down and unfastens his belt buckle. The scrape of the leather against fabric as he pulls it off lights up my nerve-endings. The hair on the back of my neck stands on end. Then, without taking his gaze off my face, he folds the belt in two and thwacks it against his palm. I gasp.

He nods in the direction of the table next to us. "Bend over."

"What?" I squeak.

"You knew you had me when I couldn't take my eyes off how you licked the food off your fork with your pretty pink tongue at dinner. You knew if I saw you without your clothes, I wouldn't be able to resist you."

"Y-you can't resist me?"

His features take on a tortured expression, then he shakes his head as if to clear it. "I told you I cannot overstep the line between protective personnel and principal and jeopardize your safety. Yet, you persist in finding ways to tempt me. You insist on shaking my concentration. On shredding my control so I can't do my job of keeping you safe. Ergo you put yourself in danger. And I cannot have that." He wraps his free hand around the belt fold and stretches it.

The hiss of the leather against his palm causes a strange yearning to jolt up my spine. My pussy clenches painfully. My knees tremble. I should be afraid of what he can do to me. Of what he's asking me to do for him, but I want so badly to please him. Want to feel that leather against my skin. Want to feel his hands on me. Want him to control me. *Gah! What's wrong with me? I don't bend for anyone. But him? What about him? Will I bend for him?*

"You've been disobedient. I told you, whatever is between us cannot come to fruition. Not until I've completed my assignment as your bodyguard. But you did not listen to me. You decided to force the issue by seducing me. You decided to take matters into your own hands. And now, I'm going to take *you* in hand. I'm going to punish you for disobeying me."

"You're punishing me because I prevented you from doing your job? Because I tried to seduce you, and you fell for it? You realize how illogical that is?" *And how perfect.* This is what I wanted all along. I was never spanked as a child, and that he's going to be the first to deliver it with a belt turns my insides to mush. I want him to be so focused on me. For him to lose his mind until he could no longer resist me. Only now, I feel like I've been caught with my head inside the lion's mouth.

I try to laugh but it comes out as little more than a little thread of noise. One that causes him to flare his nostrils. Oh my god, he can smell my fear and my arousal; I'm sure of that.

He tilts his head as if considering my response, then jerks his chin. "Do it." His gaze is hard, his jaw set. His green eyes are now more gold than silver. Oh, he's turned on. I can see it in the way the tendons of his throat stand out in relief. The way a nerve ticks at his jawline. The way a bead of sweat trickles down his temple.

Whoa, he's reached the end of his tether. He looks like a man undone. I wore him down. I'm finally going to get my way. He's going to make me submit to him. To someone who's earned the right to be my master. To someone who's shown me that he's more dominant than me. And it feels so right. I feel like I'm going to go up in flames with the sheer anticipation of the moment.

I risk a glance at that package between his legs, which seems to have grown bigger, thicker, wider, straining at the zipper of his crotch, and saliva pools in my mouth. My fingers tingle. Unable to stop myself, I reach out to touch it, and he flicks the belt across my knuckles.

I cry out, pull my hand back, and cradle it against my chest. He didn't hurt me. The leather barely licked my skin. It's the shock that he did it that surprised me. I stare at him with wide eyes. The expression on his face doesn't reflect what he did.

"I won't ask again," he growls in a low, dark voice.

I shiver. *Oh god. Oh god. Oh god. Am I going to do this?* I swallow, then turn and place my palms flat on the table and fold. My cheek meets the flat wooden surface.

"Good girl."

I shudder. That yearning in my stomach flips into a full-blown flame of need. A trickle down my inner thigh signals how turned on I am. Then he kicks my feet apart. I draw in a sharp breath. Before I can find my bearings, a crack across my backside makes me cry out.

"The hell!" I glare up at him from the corner of my eye. "What are you doing?"

I know *exactly* what he's doing, but I want to challenge him to get more out of this. I want to rile him up, so he won't hold back. This might be the only chance I have to be with him like this, and I'm going to make the most of it. I want to experience everything with him... For just this one night.

"Are you going to take your punishment and show me how much you want this? Or"—he looks me up and down—"are you going to straighten and walk away, and I'll never again attempt to share how it can be between us?"

I swallow. The line of fire across my butt cheeks sizzles and sparks. The contrast between it and the cool air that envelops my backside ramps up my desire.

My thighs tremble. My pussy continues to leak like an open faucet. My body wants more, but my mind cautions that if I agree, I'm turning a corner in this relationship. It's a line once crossed... I can't retreat.

He seems to understand my thought, for he nods. "This changes everything." His voice is remote, almost clinical. If I thought he was the strong, silent type, now there's also a dark edge to him I only sensed earlier, which attracted me, but which he's only revealing to me now. Is it because he used the belt on me? Is that pulling back the layers he likes to throw up between us? Is this the only way I'm going to see the real Ryot? The one I'm so attracted to. My instinct says yes. My body says... *Fuck* yes. I nod slowly.

"Say it," he snaps.

"Yes—" I swallow. "Yes," I say in a hoarse voice, "I want you to whip m—" I cry out again, for even before the words are out of my mouth, he's brought the belt down on my backside, again and again. And he's not holding back. Each slap of the belt against my butt sparks a fresh wave of discomfort, followed by a burst of pleasure which arrows straight to my core. It turns my pussy into a sea of desire, with waves of need that lap against my clit. My thighs shudder. My nipples pinch into points of longing. A craving builds up deep inside me. It swells and grows tighter, curling in on itself. Tautening, knotting itself into something so much more intense. I begin to pant.

My chest heaves. Sweat trickles down my spine. And yet, he doesn't stop. He continues to slap the belt down, alternating between ass cheeks, and with each welt, the yearning inside me grows fiercer. More enormous and more potent. I sense a power greater than me gather inside of me, and when he brings the belt down on my pussy, the shock is so sudden, I orgasm.

I cry out, squeeze my eyes shut and slap my palms into the

surface of the table. Waves of intense pleasure pour over me like nothing I've faced before. All those orgasms I've had thanks to my trusty vibrator have nothing on the gratification he's brought to me. I shudder, aware of the mewling noises which escape my lips. My toes curl; my knees quiver.

I begin to slump, when he squeezes his big palm around my hip and holds me in place. Then, he slides a finger between my swollen pussy lips. Shockwaves cut through the buzz of fulfillment in my mind. And when he brings his finger to my face and smears my cum on my lips, it feels...so decadent. So...erotic. I lick the taste of myself off my mouth, and it's surprisingly sweet. When I furrow my brows in surprise, he simply leans down and brushes his mouth over mine.

It's soft, just a whisper, gone so quickly, I chase after it, but he shakes his head. "You have to earn the kiss, Empress." He stabs his finger in my direction. "Stay there."

Empress. I love that nickname.

What I'm not sure about is the imperious tone of his voice. So bossy. I want to protest that he can't order me around, but... I allowed him to spank me. And enjoyed it. And climaxed. Ripples of aftershock convulse through my body. Apparently, I *think* I don't like to be bossed around, but any command from him, anytime he asks me to do something in that bossy voice of his, anytime he's controlling... It turns me on so much. It's so confusing. I mull over the possibility that I like it because he's the one who's so demanding? It's only when it comes from him that I feel like I must obey... My head spins.

I hear him moving around. He opens and closes a drawer, then there's the sound of the tap running in the sink. He walks around to stand behind me. Something cold and wet is placed over my smarting bottom. A moan of relief escapes me.

"Feels good, hmm?" He keeps the wet towel pressed into my butt cheeks, and the lingering pain fades. Then he takes off the towel and smears something over my ass, and the discomfort recedes completely. "Aloe Vera," he answers my unspoken question. "It'll soothe the skin, so you're ready for your next spanking."

"What?" I jerk my chin to stare at him over my shoulder to find he's smirking.

"Very funny." I want to be pissed off, but really, the gleam in his eyes and the slight curve of his lips elicits a smile from me. "Can I straighten now?"

"No." He shakes his head.

"No?" I frown.

In response, he pulls me upright then turns and scoops me up in his arms.

The way he maneuvers my body like I weigh nothing. Holy shit. It makes me feel small and delicate. Which is refreshing, given my curves. I love it.

"Oh," I squeak and hold onto him. He strides out of the kitchen like I weigh nothing. And how I love that. I am not defensive about my curves, but I also know I don't fit the conventional picture of a rail thin, Disney princess either. I dress to show off my curves. And have made it my mission to support charities that help women with self-esteem issues. We don't owe the world how we look, but sometimes, it's difficult to hold onto our self-confidence when the media dictates that we look a certain way.

"I can walk," I murmur.

"Let me take care of you."

19

Ryot

I carry her to her bed, and tuck her in. When I turn to leave, she catches my wrist. "Stay with me?"

She stares at me from under eyelids which are heavy with desire and laced with a satiation I'm responsible for. A tightness tugs at my lower belly. A melting sensation squeezes my chest. The sensations feel deep. And so very real. So very uncomfortable. I don't dare put a name to it. Instead, I choose my words carefully.

"I'm not strong enough to stop myself when it comes to you. And if I go any further, if I allow myself to take what you offer, I will be no good at protecting you." I give in to the plea in her eyes and sit down next to her.

I'm fighting a losing battle when it comes to resisting her. It's frustrating, but also a relief to admit this to myself and to her. Doesn't resolve this conflict I have of my personal feelings versus my professional role.

"I can't understand why you think if you fuck me it's going to impair your efficiency." She scowls. "Personally, I think you're using it as an excuse because you already know that you're falling for me." She releases her hold on my wrist, and it's my turn to grab hers.

I twine my fingers through hers, knowing even this little show of affection is a weakness, but I'm unable to hold back. The anger on her face, the frustration in her features, and that hint of sadness in her eyes tug at my heart. I know she's right. I *am* already involved with her—I have been since I saw her at the bar, where she claimed to be my wife. For a few moments there, I allowed myself to be transported to a reality where she was mine, and it had felt so right. I wanted it to be true, which is why I kissed her back. But then she left, and I didn't think I'd see her again. Until I realized she was to be the principal.

"I could have backed off the moment I realized you were the person I was assigned to protect, but I didn't."

Her forehead furrows. "I don't understand."

I'm irritated with myself for being so attracted to her, wanting to resist her, but being unable to do so, and paying the price for it by putting her in danger. I allowed her to distract me and look how that turned out. She was almost shot. If something had happened to her, I'd have never forgiven myself.

A bit too late for morals, given I also spanked her. And God help me, I enjoyed it more than I should. I'm on a slippery slope when it comes to her. Question is, can I make a last-ditch attempt to stick to my principles? For her sake? For her safety?

"You might think I could both fuck you and protect you, but the two cannot go hand in hand. My ability to keep you safe depends on my being able to make quick, impersonal decisions, and once it gets personal—once it gets more personal than what it is now—I'm of no good to you."

"So, you're saying—"

"I'm saying that I knew I was attracted to you, and it would have been best if I'd turned down the role of your bodyguard. But the thought of anyone else spending all that time with you was not something I could stomach."

Her forehead clears. A small smile plays around her lips. "You were jealous?"

I incline my head. "I knew no one else could take care of you better than me. And I wanted the opportunity to, at least, be able to see you every day." I rub my thumb across the tender skin over her wrist and feel the beating of her pulse. "But the moment we fuck, I lose the ability to be objective. Do you understand?"

She scoffs.

"It would be normal for you to feel emotions for me under the charged situations that we've been thrown into. You've been under a lot of pressure, and it was telling on you. You needed... A way to blow off steam."

"Blow off steam." She tugs on her hand and this time, I release it. "You thought I needed to blow off steam?" Her voice is soft. Her blue eyes turn icy.

Fuck, I'm definitely not handling this right.

"Look"—I hold up my hands—"the threats on your life are causing you to reach out to someone who you think can protect you—"

"Which is you?"

I nod. "And it's normal to feel things more deeply. All the more reason for us to keep our distance."

"Even after you spanked me?" she asks in a low tone.

"Especially after I spanked you. I saw you naked; it took me by surprise." I can't stop my gaze from straying down her body, covered by the duvet which is unable to hide her curves completely. "I realized the images from what happened earlier were not letting you sleep." I rub the back of my neck. "You were so tense, so unhappy. You were hurting, I knew I could help you." I lean back. "I did it the only way I knew."

"By whipping me with your belt?" She tips up her chin, a defiant look on her face.

"Yes."

She seems taken aback by my response.

"Fact is, you're submissive—"

She begins to protest, but I cut her off.

"Your body recognizes my authority over it. And after the way you followed my lead and orgasmed, I'd fathom a guess that your logical mind also understands it. The dominant in me acted on instinct. I needed to help you unwind. I had to help you let go. And you did, beautifully."

"And you're going to walk away from me like it never happened?" She grimaces. "Did that mean nothing to you?

"It means a lot. It means too much. And that's the problem." I cup her cheek. "Trust me on this, please. I need to step back now."

It's too late to step back, you're already involved. I shove that thought out of my head and focus on her.

"I know it's going to hurt you. But I can... *We* can salvage the situation. We can find a way to keep our relationship professional... Or as professional as it can be. This way, I can continue to be your bodyguard. This way I can protect you." I take both her hands in mine. "Please, help me take care of you. Help me keep you safe. Can you do that?"

20

Aurelia

The expression on his face signaled there was no changing his mind about the matter. Besides, there was a tone of anguish running through his words. And he said please. Which surprised me, enough that I found myself holding back further arguments on the issue.

He peered into my eyes, and even though I didn't nod my agreement, he took my silence as acquiescence. He released my hand, rose to his feet and stalked off toward the doorway of the bedroom. I held my breath and urged him in my mind to turn and look at me. But he didn't. He walked off, leaving me alone. I was sure I'd toss and turn, but to my surprise, I fell asleep.

When I wake up, the sunlight slants through the crack in the curtains. I reach over and grab the phone from my bedside table. Ryot must have plugged it in; it's charged. Notifications fill the screen. There are missed calls from Gavin, *ugh!*; from my brother, Viktor; from my assistant Veronica; from Zoey; as well as a ton of voice messages and text messages. I swipe and read the first.

Fred: Your father sends his apologies for not
being able to message you directly, but he's
held up in meetings. He's glad you're safe
and is being briefed by Ryot on the situation.

I know my father loves me, but the fact that he didn't think it was
important enough to call me or message me directly after the incident
yesterday is not surprising. Disappointing, but not surprising. I read
the next message.

Viktor: Are you okay Aura? I spoke to father,
and he gave me the news. He assured me
you were fine. But an attempt to assassinate
you? Jesus. I'm taking the first flight to
London.

I sigh in frustration even as a fond smile tries to curve my lips. Of
course, my older brother wants to swoop in and save the day. But the
last thing I want is him landing here and making a big fuss.

When my mother passed, I coped with her loss by becoming
independent and trying not to rely on anyone else, while also trying
to take care of my father and brothers. I've tried to become the
woman in the family and fill in her role.

My father dealt with her absence by throwing himself into
building the future of Verenza. Viktor compensated by becoming
protective of me. Once he grew to adulthood, though, he started
spending time away from home. He also decided to work his way
through a revolving door of women.

As for my middle brother Brandon? He doesn't get along with
my father and has distanced himself from the family.

It's been years since I've seen him, even though he's kept in touch
with me on occasion. No doubt, the news hasn't yet reached him in
whatever corner of the world he's in.

I know better than to think he'd reach out, but a part of me still
hurts that he hasn't. I shake off the sadness and message Viktor.

Me: I am fine. My security intervened and saved my life. It could have been much worse, right? 😌 Seriously though, you don't need to come. Your diplomatic mission is more important.

I open the next message.

Zoey: Hey bish, I thought we were supposed to go out to dinner, but you disappeared on me. Are you okay?

Good question. Between the shooting yesterday and the note left on my pillow at the other hotel, I feel unbalanced.

Why are these people after me? Are they anti-monarchists? Or is it something more personal that prompted the attack? Why do they want me dead? What harm have I done to them?

A queasy sensation clenches my stomach.

I grip the phone tightly and take a few deep breaths. *I'm fine. I'm here. Nothing happened to me, thanks to Ryot.*

As long as he's with me, I'll be okay. That sense of confidence his presence brings me is no longer a surprise. I may not have known him long, but I'd trust him with my life. He almost took a bullet for me. And it has nothing to do with how he spanked me and brought me to orgasm yesterday. My bottom throbs in recollection. It's a pleasant soreness, not painful at all. As I wriggle into the bed, the chafe of the sheets against my butt sends a flurry of heat to my clit.

That orgasm relaxed me enough that I could sleep and wake up refreshed. I'm not sure how I feel about the fact that he seems to know me better than I know myself. Especially when he came so close to giving in and taking me. I saw the conflict on his face and almost felt sorry for him. But we're here alone, and I can't lose this opportunity to get him to fuck me and take my virginity.

And what about your upcoming arranged marriage? Shouldn't you mention it to him?

If I do, he's going to be angry with me. No way is he going to fuck me. Nope. He's too honorable for that. *And I'm a heel for thinking of seducing him while engaged to someone else. Then again, does it count if it's a marriage of convenience to someone I don't even like?* I press my fingers to my forehead. *The bottom line is, I want him.*

I want...something to hold onto for when I'm trapped in a love-less marriage. This is the only way I can control my future. And he's said he wants me too. He'll probably be upset if I don't tell him I'm engaged, but if I do, he might not want anything else to do with me. Which means, I'd miss out on being with him, even if it is temporary, and I can't bear the thought of that.

I'm a terrible person. My conscience would never let me rest. I have to tell him. Maybe later, though?

I message Zoey to let her know I'm fine and pick up the next one from my assistant.

> Veronica: Thank God you're safe. I was so upset when I found out what happened. I am so sorry.
>
> Me: I am fine.

Instantly, the dots on screen jump around. Then a message pings back.

> Veronica: Were you hurt? I feel responsible. I should have accompanied you to where you were going, Your Highness.
>
> Me: You shouldn't feel responsible. It's no one's fault what happened. And no, I wasn't hurt.

Just shaken, but I'm not going to tell her that.
The dots jump around again.

> Veronica: Still, I feel like if I were there I might have helped somehow.
>
> Me: That's sweet of you. You're already a big help in managing my schedule.

Veronica's been a lifesaver. When my former assistant suddenly quit a year ago, I needed someone to replace her asap. The recruitment agency the palace worked with sent through a bunch of resumes, but they weren't satisfactory. That's when I coaxed the palace to advertise on the official Royal Family website for the first time.

The two assistants I shortlisted from the entries and offered the job to dropped out. I then met with Veronica and, while I wasn't a hundred percent happy with our chemistry, I put that down to the fact that her personality is so different from mine.

On paper, she was a perfect candidate. She ticked all the boxes. And because I urgently needed someone, I decided to proceed with her. My former security team screened her. And so did Ryot and his team. So, if there were anything suspicious, it would have shown. Besides, she's never given me any reason to be dissatisfied with her performance.

> Me: Please put out a statement assuring everyone that I am fine and that the people of Verenza will not be defeated so easily. We are strong and we will survive this. Please post it to all my social media channels.

Ideally, I should record a video message, but given I don't have any cosmetics with me to appear halfway decent on screen, this will have to do.

> Veronica: Of course, Your Highness. BTW, Ryot messaged to say you're in a safe place and on his advice I cancelled your appearances for the next five days. I hope that's okay...

I frown. *He cancelled my events? Without checking with me? That's taking things too far. How dare he take this liberty?* It feels like someone dumped a pail of cold water on me.

I sit up, and the last vestiges of sleep fade away. I push off my cover and rise to my feet. Taking in my naked form, a blush sears my cheeks. Also, I'm pissed with myself. I'm grateful for the orgasm, but making decisions related to my schedule without consulting me is not something I'll tolerate.

I spot a bathrobe, along with a pair of jeans and a sweatshirt folded on the chair next to the bed. He must have left them for me. I shake them out and when I hold them against my body, I realize they're my size. And they're brand new, with the labels attached. So, that rules out this belonging to any girlfriend. *How did he manage to swing this? And did he do this because he was being thoughtful?*

I should find his actions controlling but it turns me on. For someone who hates restrictions imposed on my life, I find Ryot ordering me around very hot.

Besides, I don't fancy wearing the same clothes I was wearing yesterday. Not when they remind me of the assassination attempt. My stomach clenches, and my knees feel rubbery.

Assassination attempt? Is it right to call it that? Aren't assassinations only supposed to happen to public figures who are important? I've never thought of myself that way. But what happened yesterday makes it clear that *someone* thinks I'm important enough to shoot at me. Another tremor of fear squeezes my chest. I brush it aside. I am safe, for now. And I feel rested.

I pull on the bathrobe and walk into the bathroom, shutting the door behind me. The space is smaller than the size of the bathrooms I'm used to, and the furnishings are basic. But everything is clean. There's a sink with a hot and cold tap. A mirrored cabinet above it. An old-fashioned clawed tub stands to my left. There's a shower cubicle tucked away into the wall behind me. And thick towels are hung over the rack next to the sink. I walk over to survey myself in the mirror.

A stream of condensation along the top tells me he already showered. There's one used toothbrush, along with toothpaste, next to the sink. I pull open the mirror, and finding a new toothbrush, snap it open. I brush my teeth, shrug off the bathrobe and step into the shower. I use the soap, which doubles up as a shampoo, and wince when I massage it into my hair. Without any conditioner, my hair's going to be a mess, but at least I'll be clean, right? Besides, it smells like him.

I sniff at the liquid in my palm. It's dark and musky with a trace of cloves and cinnamon. It reminds me of how he smelled when he held me close and protected me from the assassin's bullet with his body. It turns me on and makes me feel so very close to him. Like he's right here in the shower with me. I lather up and run my fingers over my swollen nipples down my waist to my tender ass. The touch sets off ripples of pain-pleasure which arrow to my core.

My pussy turns into a triangle of need. I slide my fingers inside my cunt and, supporting myself against the wall of the shower, I begin to masturbate. *He said I can't come onto him, but I can get off to thoughts of him, right?* I imagine the water from the shower running down the ridge between his pecs, down to the trail of hair arrowing down to that magnificent specimen of manhood... Which I'd do anything to wrap my fingers around. Assuming my fingers could circle his cock, that is. Instantly, my inner walls clench.

Just thinking of his glorious cock sends tendrils of heat up my spine. I begin to pant and imagine him, with his thick fingers around the distended head of his cock, as he begins to stroke himself from root to head again and again. I see his thigh muscles bunching and the tendons of his forearms flexing as his shaft grows bigger and thicker, and I imagine him growling as he comes. It's enough to send me over the edge. I push the knuckles of my free hand into my mouth as I follow him over the edge.

Jesus, this climax was nowhere as intense as the one I experienced when he spanked me, and nowhere as satisfying, but it's still better than the ones my formerly trusty vibrators bestowed on me. *Gah.* The man has spoiled me for self-induced climaxes. Another reason he's the right person to be my first.

An arranged marriage to European royalty means there's an unspoken expectation I'll be a virgin. I'm determined that my first time will be with someone of my choosing.

And him? What about how angry and upset Ryot is going to be when he finds out about your upcoming nuptials? I'll have to make him understand. I *hope* he'll understand that it was my choice to give my virginity to him. What I feel for him is so powerful, I cannot even fathom giving it to anyone else.

As for Gavin finding out? Given the lack of chemistry between us, I doubt he'd even notice. And if he did, I'd explain it away with a vibrator.

A part of me is aware that this is not very princess-like behavior. My mother would not be happy about my decision. But I'm confident she'd understand my need to create a few memories that are only for me.

I finish my shower, then dry off. Wearing the same bathrobe, I head back into the room. I want to defy him and not wear the clothes he left out for me, which would mean going down in the bathrobe, which feels too close to being naked. So, I swallow my pride, pull on the fresh underwear along with the jeans and the sweatshirt, which is incredibly soft.

I slide my phone into my pocket, then walk out and head down the stairs. The scent of coffee draws me to the kitchen.

I step in to find he's standing at the stove. Good Lord, he's wearing a pair of grey sweatpants pulled low. The material stretches across that tight backside and to his powerful thighs and makes me woozy. *Maybe that's because I'm hungry?* Sadly, his chest is not bare. But he's wearing a black T-shirt that's been washed so often, it's threadbare. Lucky me.

It stretches across the breadth of his shoulders and clings to the hard planes of his back before dipping in at his trim waist. My mouth begins to water. My fingers tingle. My mind is busy taking mental snapshots that I can add to my spank bank. And after the stunt he pulled by cancelling my appointments, that's all I'm going to allow myself.

I take a couple of steps in his direction when he turns. His green eyes lock with mine. The impact is almost physical. I gasp and come to a standstill. My heart leaps into my throat. I'm unable to move. Unable to say anything. I simply take in his clean-shaven face and his wet hair, which he's finger-combed back. An errant lock of hair has fallen over his forehead, and I so want to go over and smooth it back. I swallow, trying to get a grip on myself.

His expression softens. "Good morning," he rumbles.

"'Morning," I mumble.

He takes in my pink cheeks, but probably assumes it's due to the shower I just took, for he merely nods toward the table. "Have a seat."

I begin to shuffle over, then stop myself. *How annoying that I'm tempted to obey him. How annoying that I want to please him.* I push aside the instincts and glower back. "You cancelled my events?"

He tilts his head. I expect him to look guilty. Instead, he picks up the carafe of coffee and a cup. He walks over to the table and, placing the cup in front of me, he pours me some.

The bitter, aromatic scent of the liquid makes me almost cry with joy. He places a small jug of milk next to the cup, along with a bowl of sugar, then looks at me with polite curiosity. My gaze is drawn to the coffee, and I find myself edging toward it. When I reach the table, I can't resist. I sink into the chair, pour in the milk, and add three spoonfuls of sugar to the coffee. I stir it, set the spoon down, then raise the cup to my mouth and take a sip. Rich. Sweet. Complex. Dark. I moan. "This is good." I take another sip, then look up to find him watching my mouth with hungry eyes.

"It's my favorite coffee," he states.

"It's very good." My voice breaks, and I have to clear my throat. He looks away, and I collapse back as if released from a tractor beam. Whoa, everything about this man is intense. And distracting. I frown. "You didn't answer me."

"Was there a question?"

He turns back to the cooking range, and making a batter of the powdered eggs pours it into the skillet.

"You can cook?" I blurt out, then mentally smack myself. *Nice, such a clever observation.*

"I learned to cook so I could eat palatable food."

The enticing smells of eggs and bacon frying wafts over, and my stomach rumbles. By the time I've finished my coffee, he's placed a heaping plate in front of me and a twin in front of himself. I eye the scrambled eggs, accompanied by bacon, baked beans, a sausage, and hash browns.

The toaster oven dings. He heads over to it and returns with a plate of toasted whole wheat bread slices, which he places between us, next to the butter and jam which are already there. He ensures we have cutlery, then tops up our coffee cups before taking his seat.

"Eat up." He nods at my plate.

My stomach rumbles, but I tear my gaze away from the food and fix him with a glare. "I have a question." I fold my arms across my chest. "Did you cancel my appointments for the day?"

"And for the next five days." He nods.

I blink. "That was *my* schedule. *My* meetings. My team and I spent weeks, in some cases, months, arranging them."

"None of them are more important than your life," he says in a reasonable tone.

Anger squeezes my spine. I'm pissed that he seems so unruffled and unrepentant about making this decision without informing me. And I'm even more angry that he's right. I shove that last thought aside. "I wish you'd consulted me first."

He nods. "I'm sorry, I did it without asking you."

Eh? I pause mid-tirade. *He's already apologized to me, so why am I surprised that he is willing to do so again?*

"After you were asleep, I realized that it would be much safer if we holed up here for a few days, until things cool off. But I didn't want to wake you. I did text you though, so you'd see the message when you woke up."

"You did?" I frown.

"I also plugged in your phone and left it to charge on your bedside table."

"I noticed. Thanks." I smile weakly before pulling out my phone and scrolling through the rest of my messages. Sure enough, there's one from him, updating me on what he's done. *I must have missed it.*

"This"—I hold up my phone—"is not a consultation. This is a...a directive from you."

"It's a recommendation, as your head of security."

I rub at my temple. "I understand why the events needed to be called off. I'm also aware that I don't have the necessary wardrobe on hand to go to the appointments." Not to mention, I do not want to put myself on display, not when the person who took a shot at me is at large. "What I'm not happy about is that you took that unilateral decision without discussing it with me."

Ryot takes in the play of expressions on my face. A look of consternation comes over his features. "You're right."

My eyebrows shoot up. "You agree?"

He nods. "I'm not going to argue my point when I'm wrong. I was… Influenced by my concern for you."

He squares his shoulders.

"I shouldn't have made that categorical decision. I'm sorry. I was —" He seems at a loss for words. "I was upset and angry. I thought I'd failed you. I allowed myself to be distracted and slipped up on my duty to protect you. I felt responsible for what happened. I could not have lived with myself if you'd been hurt in anyway."

His jaw hardens.

"I probably wasn't thinking straight when I messaged your assistant and told her to cancel your appointments. I didn't think through how it might come across to your team or how it might upset you."

He looks away and draws in a few deep breaths. When he looks back at me, his features are contrite.

"It was wrong of me to make that call on your behalf. My…my personal feelings for you interfered with my professional judgement." His forehead furrows. "It won't happen again."

I'm so taken aback by the fact that he explained himself, I stare, bemused.

"Do you forgive me?" he asks softly.

My anger dissolves in the face of his contrition. And the fact he admitted that his feelings for me influenced him… Wow! Coming from this man who's held his emotions so tightly in control since he assumed the role of my bodyguard, is unexpected. And thrilling.

"You do forgive me, don't you?"

The worry in his voice lights a trail of warmth under my skin. My heart blooms in my chest. *Oh, my god.* After all these days of yearning to see some sign that he recalls the passion of our first kiss, I am overwhelmed. I try to speak but my tongue refuses to cooperate. My brain is digesting everything I've heard from him. Struck dumb, I can only nod.

His shoulders relax. "Thank you."

I shake my head. "Thank you for thinking on your feet. I wasn't in any shape to make any decisions yesterday. And I certainly can't face turning up for those meetings today. You did the right thing."

He peers into my face and, when he realizes I mean it, his forehead smooths out. "I did want to suggest one more thing."

I look at him, waiting.

"It would be best if all communication with your team went through me." His tone is firm but soft.

I rub at my temple. What he's suggesting is for my own safety. But it means losing another freedom.

"It's only until we track down whoever is behind the shooting."

Hearing him say that sends another shudder down my spine. "You're convinced someone from within my inner circle is involved somehow?"

He nods. "Given I'd mentioned it to them, it seems probable someone shared details of where we were headed with the perpetrators. I don't want to take any more chances with your safety."

I'm more than a little gutted at what he's implying. If I can't trust those in my inner circle, then who can I rely on? *You can trust Ryot. And Zoey, and your friends. And your father. And your brothers.* I have people I can lean on. The thought reassures me.

I nod. "Okay."

The tension leaches from his shoulder. His lips quirk. "Thank you for believing in me, Princess. I won't let you down."

"I know you won't," a flood of feelings grips my chest. My heart feels like it's going to burst. My cheeks grow warm. I have never felt this close to anyone before. It goes beyond physical attraction. This is something more. I trust him with my life. I want more. But I can't have it because I must marry someone else.

Tell him, Aura. Tell him you're engaged.

Given Ryot has information about my background and must have made his own enquiries too... *There's no way he doesn't know I am, right? And if it doesn't bother him, then who am I to bring it up?* I convince myself.

Besides, if I mentioned it to him, our dynamic would change. This closeness I feel with him, would be gone. This understanding and affection that's developed between us would be shattered. Right now, I can't bear that. No, I'll tell him later, when the time is right.

"I have another question." I nod toward my clothes. "These are my size; how did you manage that?"

"I reached out to a clothes-shopper my sister-in-law, Skylar, uses and gave her your size. She packed enough clothes to last a few days, including some formal wear. I had my brother, Tyler, deliver them to me early this morning."

"Your brother knows where we are?"

He hesitates. "I'd have preferred no one knew, but if I did have to take someone's help, it would be Tyler. He's a former Marine, and I'd trust him with my life... And yours."

Something about how he says it is so sincere, so absolute, I believe him. I am grateful to have clothes in my size. And I appreciate that he was thoughtful enough to think this through. "Thank you."

"We're safe here. There's an electric fence around the property, plus a complete array of cameras and drones, all of which are linked to the security app on my phone. And to Tyler's phone, as well. Nothing can get in or out without our knowing. Given the security, we don't need to be confined to the house either. We can move about the grounds freely."

He's so thoughtful, that lightness in my chest expands until it fills my entire body. It confirms to me I made the right decision in not telling him about my upcoming nuptials. I don't want to spoil this moment between us.

"Thank you," I say softly.

He inclines his head. "You should eat." He nods in the direction of the heaped plate he set in front of me.

I pick up my knife and fork and cut up a piece of the sausage, along with a bit of the hash browns and baked beans. I fork it into my mouth, and the flavors explode on my palate. The sausage is juicy and well-seasoned, with a blend of herbs and spices, the baked beans are sweet and tangy, and the hash browns are crunchy. I couldn't tell this came from a can and frozen ingredients. "Whoa. This is surprisingly good."

His lip twitch. I can tell by the crinkling of the lines around his eyes that he's pleased by my compliments.

I concentrate on eating for the next few minutes, and so does he. When I've finished more than half of what's on my plate, I lean back with a sigh. "I'm full."

"You're sure?"

21

Aurelia

> Veronica: Your Highness, I was wondering if you had any thoughts of your schedule for the next few days. People are asking for confirmations.

> Me: All my movements need to go through Ryot.

> Veronica: I'll message him. But if you had any preferences on which events you'd definitely be attending, then please do share.

I frown. Veronica can sometimes be very persistent. Which is the hallmark of a good assistant, right?

> Me: I've already indicated that to Ryot. It's best to check with him.

A few seconds go by. The dots on screen jump around and stop. Then jump around again.

Veronica: Of course, Your Highness.

There's another missed call from Gavin. But thankfully, no text message. Maybe he's given up trying to reach me? Hah, probably not. And it's so cowardly of me to avoid him... But I don't want to talk to him. It's only going to remind me of how much I don't want to marry him. And why I have to. And I don't want to be reminded of my duties and responsibilities. Not when my engagements for today and the next few days have been cancelled. Not when, for the first time in a long time, I have hours stretching out in front of me with nothing planned out.

So, when Ryot suggested he'd show me the sights, I readily agreed.

I pulled on a jacket, socks and hiking boots, all of which fit perfectly.

The fact that Ryot got my size right is something I don't want to examine too closely.

I pocket my phone and, as we draw away from the house, I begin to relax. He, on the other hand, remains as watchful as ever.

Being out among the trees and seeing the droplets of rain from last night glinting off the leaves feels therapeutic. By the time we reach the waterfall on the property, a half hour walk through the forest surrounding the house, the images from yesterday's incident have subsided in my mind.

It's a beautiful space with a pool of clear water and trees surrounding it. Most of the path here was uphill, and by the time we arrive, I'm sweating. Enough to pull off my jacket and shoes and wade in. I turn in time to see him strip off his own jacket. Only, he doesn't stop there.

I watch as he pulls off his combat boots and socks. He reaches behind himself and pulls off the black T-shirt he wore this morning. He pulls out his cell phone and places it on the ground, along with his gun, then shucks his jeans.

He places the gun he's been carrying on top of his clothes, then straightens. I didn't realize he had a gun on him. Of course, he does. He's my bodyguard. And undressed and wearing only his boxers, the sheer power radiating off of him is overwhelming.

For a second, I allow myself to take in the breadth of his shoulders, his heavily muscled chest planes with the dog tags nestled in the V made by his impressive pecs; the corrugated abs of his six — Or is that a nine-pack? The mouthwatering 'V' of his Adonis' belt, the flex of his biceps, and the powerful coiling of his thighs as he walks into the water and past me.

He continues on until the water laps at his waist, before turning to smirk at me over his shoulder.

"Come on in, the water's amazing," he calls out.

It looks way too cold for me. "You go ahead; I'll stay here." I walk up the strip of stony beach at the edge of the pool and, stepping onto the grass, seat myself.

He looks like he's about to protest, then shrugs. "Suit yourself."

Turning, he dives in. I strain my eyes, waiting for him to surface, and when he doesn't, I begin to worry. I count to ten. Then thirty. By the time I get to sixty, my heart is in my throat. Could he have hit his head? Gotten his leg tangled in a tree limb? He saved my life yesterday, and here I am, standing uselessly while he could be drowning right in front of me.

I jump up and call his name, but there's no reply. My heart bangs into my ribcage. My blood pressure shoots up. When I've counted to a hundred and twenty and he still hasn't surfaced, I'm beside myself with panic. I strip off my clothes. When I'm down to my bra and panties I wade in, then dive into the water.

The cold hits me like a slap across my face and my body. My breath catches. My skin feels like all the pores are closing down, my skin drawing tight over my flesh like armor. I open my eyes underwater and look around but don't see anything that resembles him. And my lungs are nowhere as strong as his. In seconds, I rise to the surface and find myself face-to-face with him. My heart rams into my ribcage. My pulse booms in my ears. I'm so relieved that my knees go weak.

"Where the hell were you?" I begin to yell at him but end up taking in water and going under. He grabs me under my armpits and drags me back to the surface. I shove my hair out of my eyes and glare at him. "Why did you disappear like that?"

He seems taken aback. "I was underwater and lost count of the seconds, I guess."

"Quit showing off, will ya?" I slap at his chest. "You scared me."

"I'm sorry," he says softly. "Truly. It felt so good to be back in the water, I lost track of time. I'm a Marine, remember?"

His voice is genuine, and his expression contrite. Seeing yet another human side of him sends a flurry of sensations to my extremities. I'm still angry with him. And upset and… The remnants of that panicky feeling squeeze my belly.

"I thought you drowned—" I swallow. "I thought—" I shake my head. I don't know what I thought. But for a few seconds there, I thought I'd lost him. And that turned my stomach to stone, and shattered my heart, and a sinking feeling came over me. Like a black void had swallowed me, and I couldn't imagine ever escaping. It felt like the end of the world. Like things were over before they'd even started. Like…my life as I knew it had changed irrevocably. A feeling which still clings to the deepest recesses of my mind. I felt so powerless, and it shook me.

My confusion, anger, and vulnerability must show on my features, for his own grows serious. "Hey, come here." He pulls me close, and I sink into his chest. I wind my arms about his neck and let him take my weight. And when he boosts me up, I wrap my legs around his waist.

The tears fall from my eyes, first slowly then gathering speed. I turn my face into his chest and allow them to come.

"I thought I was never going to see you again," I sob.

I was congratulating myself for pulling myself together after what happened yesterday, but this… Thinking he'd drowned sent me over the edge. All the shock from yesterday, the trauma I absorbed, bubbles up and spills over. The distress I tried to lock away boils to the fore. It feels cathartic, and very indulgent, to let myself break down and have him hold me.

I sense him rubbing circles over my back and tuck my head under his chin. "I'm so sorry I scared you; I didn't mean to," he whispers into my hair.

His voice is so soft, so tender, it only makes me cry harder.

"Let it out, baby. Let it all out." He carries me out of the water, and when he reaches the grass, he sits down with me straddling him. I cling to him, and he runs his fingers down my hair, murmuring words I can't make out.

The comfort in his actions and his tone, in how he wraps his big arms about me and holds me so close... It allows me to feel cherished and safe. Enough to let all the frustrations inside me flow out. When the tears finally stop, he continues to hold me.

The heat of his body cocoons me, surrounds me, and he's the only thing anchoring me to this world. He's the antidote to the black void that threatened to swallow me.

I feel safe. There's that word. *Protected. Cherished. His.* I hiccup, and he continues to swipe his hand down my back, soothing me. That musky, spicy scent of his surrounds me. I draw it deeply into my lungs, allowing it to calm me further. He smells like every erotic dream I've ever had. And like security. Yeah, I've never felt as shielded as I am now in his arms.

Pressed into his chest, with my thighs plastered against his sides, and the throb of something hard and insistent stabbing into the space between my thighs... *The throb of something hard and insistent stabbing into the space between my thighs?*

I draw in a sharp breath, and just like that, the safe, content feeling transforms into something hungry. Something erotic. Something insistent which makes my nipples tighten, turns my stomach to a seething mass of desire, and my pussy into an insistent throb of need. I look up to find he's staring down at me with green eyes that are almost black with lust. They mirror the depths of the water I thought had swallowed him up.

And maybe I'm overreacting, but I don't question this need to hold him, and touch him, and lick him, and feel him, and make sure he's here. I tip up my chin. "Kiss me."

His forehead furrows. A tortured expression flits across his features. "I'm trying to do my job here, Princess." He cups my cheek. "I'm trying to do the right thing. I'm trying to make sure I don't get so involved that the next time I need to protect you or make decisions, which could mean the difference between life and death, I don't hesitate."

I frown, trying to make sense of what he's saying. *Didn't he admit that his feelings for me have already affected his actions? And shouldn't a stronger connection between us mean he'll protect me even better? How can I convince him of that?* I don't even know what words to use but... Something desperate inside of me insists that this is my chance.

We're far from everything that defines me. Here, I'm not a princess, and he's not my bodyguard, and I'm not engaged. I've never felt something this powerful for anyone else before. And maybe, we can't have a future together, but I can seize this moment, can't I?

"Please," I whisper. "I want you. Please, Ryot."

His jaw hardens. A nerve throbs at his temple. I see the struggle in his eyes a second before that wall I've sensed before slams down, and I know I've lost him. And a part of me can't accept it. I refuse to let him turn away. If I let him walk away now, I'll never have this opportunity again, when I'll feel so close to him. Closer than I've been with anyone before. Closer than I'll ever be to another human. And I want him. I need this. I *must* have this. So, I tip up my chin and fit my lips to his.

22

Ryot

One touch of her lips, and I know I'm in trouble. Since I met her, I haven't stopped thinking about our first meeting and how the first time I saw her face it felt like a gut punch.

How her scent had awoken something primal inside of me. How it'd felt to pull her into my side and feel her melt into me like she belonged there. How right it felt to call her my wife. More than it ever felt with the woman I once married. How it turned me on to spank her. How satisfying it was to have her climax under my ministrations. How we fit physically and emotionally. How, the connection between us is more than just sexual.

Then, I kiss her deeply and I realize I was wrong. Her mouth is softer than I remember. Her breath sweeter. Her taste more complex. She feels perfect pressed up against me, with her arms and legs wound around me like she has no intention of letting go.

How can I ache this badly to be inside of her? How can I feel this deeply connected to a woman I've known for only a few weeks?

I look into her eyes and sense the mirrored emotions in hers. She feels this connection too. These unseen bonds that tether us, growing stronger with every passing second. And once I make love to her, I won't be able to pull back.

Once I'm inside of her, my judgement will be compromised. Then, how am I going to protect her? I keep my elbows tucked into my sides and my mouth in a straight line.

She nibbles on my lower lip, and my cock twitches. I want to grab her and fit her over the aching tent in my crotch, but when I don't move, she stills.

I hear her swallow; know the precise moment the fight seems to go out of her. She pulls back. Her lips turn down; her chin wobbles. When the light in her eyes dims, my chest compresses. *Damn.*

She has this power to gut me, to cut me off at the knees, for when she's upset, it's like the entire world is wrong. I'll do anything to keep her happy. I'd burn the world to keep her safe.

I'm going to hunt down those who tried to shoot her and wipe them out from the face of this earth. I'm going to ensure they never come after her again.

She's here in my arms, and it feels so right. It hasn't felt this good with anyone else. Not even Jane. I've borne the guilt of her death for so long. Don't I deserve a rest from it?

Don't I deserve to stop thinking of all the possible ways I could have changed things? Don't I deserve a few minutes of happiness? Of being with the woman who's come to mean so much to me from the moment I laid eyes on her?

Also… I can't refuse her.

Not when she's in my arms, and needy and wanting. I can't turn her down. Not now.

No matter that once I make love to her, it won't be easy to walk away from her. And despite my judgement being compromised, I won't be able to give up this assignment. I'll have to cross that bridge later. Even if it means I'm going to hate myself after this, I can't hold back.

Fuck my sense of propriety. Fuck the principles I've lived my life by. None of that matters in comparison to making her happy. As long as I can give her what she wants and wipe that fear from her eyes, even if it is for just a little while, it'll be worth it.

She begins to pull away, and I place my palms on her hips.

A shiver runs down her back. Her breathing quickens. She raises her gaze to mine, and those baby blues of hers are like the depths of a clear lake. I'm sure I can see my entire universe in them. "Princess, this is so wrong—"

Her shoulders droop.

"But—"

"But—" A flare of hope lights up her eyes.

"But I can't say no to you anymore."

Her lips part, a look of surprise, then delight, then anticipation, and finally, exhilaration flit across her features. Then I frame her jawline, lower my chin, and fit my mouth to hers. She gasps, and I swallow the sound, then thrust my tongue between her lips. Slowly. Slowly. I take my time exploring every single corner of her mouth, sucking on her and drawing in her essence. I tilt my head, deepening the angle of the kiss, and she melts into me. She opens herself up, and I possess her and pour all my longing into the kiss. She whimpers and writhes in my lap. I hold her in place over my aching cock. And it's better than I hoped, for the warmth of her cunt steams up the wet layers between us. She digs her fingers into the short hair at the nape of my neck, then drags her fingertips across my neck, and I growl, "I want you, Princess."

"Fuck me," she mewls against my mouth. "Please, Ryot." Then she presses her breasts into me, and feeling her nipples stab into my chest turns my entire body into a tsunami of fire. I release my hold on her long enough to grab the clothes I discarded earlier and smooth them out next to us. Then I flip her onto them, cushioning her head with my palm. She looks up at me, surprise in her eyes, her lips parted. And when I reach behind her to undo the hooks of her bra, she throws it off. I glance down at the goosebumps on her chest. "You're cold. I should take you back and—"

"No." She surges up and grips my shoulders, then pulls me down on her. "You'll warm me up."

The heat between us is certainly steaming up the water on our bodies. I trace a drop which drips down her cheek to the edge of her lips, then whisper kisses down her throat to the valley between her breasts. I lave a circle around one nipple. She mewls and thrusts her chest up, and when I finally close my mouth over her nipple, she cries out. I suck on it, and she locks her ankles around my waist and begins to hump the bulge in my boxers. I pull back and she groans. "Don't stop."

"I'll fuck you when I'm ready, and not before."

She scowls, and looks so disgruntled, I chuckle.

"It's not funny, I'm… I'm in so much pain; it hurts."

"Good." I cup her other breast and squeeze.

She shudders. "You're a tease."

"Just getting started." I pinch her nipple, and she moans. And when I roll both nipples between my fingers and twist, she cries out.

She arches her back, pushing her breasts up and further into my hands while squirming and continuing to hump my now very hard and extended cock that's threatening to stab its way out of my boxers. I cup her breasts in my hands, and press them together, then bend and take both nipples into my mouth. I pull and tug and suck. She moans loudly and pants, turning me on even further. I kiss my way down her almost dry stomach to her belly button, and when I lick into the dent, she shudders, digs her fingers in my hair and tugs. The little flashpoints of pain stab down my spine. My balls tighten. I lean back, so she's forced to part her legs. I grip the waistband of her panties.

"Up," I order.

She raises her hips. I roll the scrap of lace down her thighs, sliding back enough that she can knock her knees together so I can pull off her underwear.

She begins to close her legs, but I lock my fingers around the outside of her thighs and hold them apart. "Let me look at you," I order.

A blush makes it way down her neck, but she obliges. And when I stare at the succulent triangle of flesh between her legs, she whimpers.

The little noise she makes turns my cock into a hard column of need. I could come in my boxers just from listening to the obvious sounds of her being turned on, but not yet. First, I need to worship her. I need to make her climax. I need to ensure she's so aroused and relaxed that when I enter her, my size doesn't cause her discomfort. So, I bend and bury my nose in her pussy.

23

Aurelia

"Oh my god."

He sniffs deeply, and the gesture is so carnal, so erotic, so everything, my pussy contracts. Moisture trickles down between my inner thighs. He instantly licks it up, and when he looks up, there's satisfaction on his features. The sight of his head between my thighs is so titillating, my entire body seems to turn into one long drawn-out moan of desire. Without breaking the connection of our eyes, he releases his hold on my thighs, only to pull apart my pussy lips. Then he licks around my swollen clit.

I cry out. A jolt of heat spirals up my body. And then he swipes his tongue up my slit and begins to eat me out in earnest. Sensations crowd my mind. My scalp tingles. My stomach ties itself in knots. It's so good. So agonizing. I grip his head to hold him in place because I want more. Also, it feels too much. The pleasure pinches my nerve-endings, fills my belly, and squeezes in on itself. The knot deepens, tightens, and when he stuffs his tongue inside my channel and rubs the heel of his hand over my clit, electricity explodes out from the contact. The climax sweeps through me, and I sob. My entire body feels like it's on fire. The orgasm has me in a vice, which suddenly loosens, and I float down to earth. When I open my eyes, it's to find he's staring down into mine.

"You okay?" he murmurs. His lips and chin glistening with what must be my cum.

He catches me staring at his mouth and his lips quirk. "You're a squirter, baby."

"What?" I blink.

"Didn't know that, did you?"

I shake my head dumbly. Then he kisses me, and I taste myself on his lips, and those vibrations in my lower belly start up again. He kisses me deeply and with such enjoyment, it's like he's eating his favorite dessert. But there's also tenderness in it, and an assuredness which tells me he knows exactly how to play my body. It's so arousing and unexpected. And then, still kissing me, he reaches between us and slides his thick digits inside me. He weaves them in and out, and I shiver. Goosebumps pop on my skin, and it's not because I'm cold. Quite the opposite. A bead of sweat slides down the valley between my breasts. The heat from his body snaps around me and binds me to him, and it feels like I'm next to a furnace. His kiss deepens and it feels like he's swallowing me whole.

He slides the fingers of his free hand down between my ass-cheeks to play with my forbidden entrance, I shudder. It's...filthy, I should hate it, but... The very illicit nature of the act excites me further. I'm so turned on, the sensations chasing themselves inside me and stabbing at my insides with a forcefulness that holds me in thrall. I strain against him as that pressure in my womb grows bigger and wider until it seems to fill every part of me.

When he slips another finger inside my channel and curls his fingers, I orgasm at once. He swallows the groan of pleasure that wells up my throat. He continues to use his thumb to massage my clit as I shudder and shiver and allow my climax to heat my blood. I slump into the ground, my muscles so relaxed, I feel like I've turned into jelly. He finally tears his mouth from mine. His green eyes glitter a rich emerald, the sparks in their depth like lightning in a storm.

"You're so beautiful." His voice is gravelly. The pulse beating at his temple tells me he, too, is close to being undone.

"Fuck me, please," I beg.

His jaw tics. Then he releases me and, rising to his feet, steps out of his briefs. His long, thick, hard cock juts up against his lower belly. The head is purple and swollen, and beads of pre-cum glisten at the tip. The vein that runs up the side throbs, indicating just how turned on he is. And the length and the thickness of his cock... It's beautiful. A work of art.

I'm glad I'm so aroused because, surely, he's going to struggle fitting it in. Yet the rigidness of his thighs is a testament to his self-control. He's made me come twice, while denying himself the same. It only makes me want him even more.

Standing over me with sweat clinging to his shoulders and droplets of water from his swim trickling down his sculpted belly, his arms held at his sides, he resembles a warrior. He is the ultimate pinnacle of manhood. He's so alpha, it makes my teeth hurt, and my stomach flip-flop, and my pussy turn to mush. The yawning emptiness in my belly increases in severity until it threatens to engulf me. I make a sound deep in my throat, and instantly, he responds.

He goes down on his knees between my thighs, then hesitates. "Are you on the pill?"

When I shake my head, he reaches for the pocket of his jacket on which I'm lying.

He retrieves a condom, and a part of me wonders if he came prepared, knowing this would happen. The other part, the one too far gone with desire, rejoices in the knowledge that there's nothing stopping him from taking me. The crinkle of a wrapper, and he sheaths himself.

Then he reaches down and positions himself at my entrance. For a second, he stays there, looking deeply into my eyes. And it's so intimate. Almost more intimate than the actual act of penetration. It turns me on even more. I reach up and trace his beautiful mouth with my thumb. He nips at my digit. I feel the tug all the way deep in my belly. He kisses my thumb, then he grips my hip. He propels his hips and breaches me in one smooth move.

I gasp. He's big; he feels bigger than I anticipated. And despite the fact that I'm dripping, the pressure on my inner walls feels tremendous.

"Take a deep breath for me," he orders.

I do.

"Another."

I oblige. There's no question of my disobeying. The muscles at his jaw pop. A vein stands out at his forehead. I realize, then, how much he's holding back, giving me the chance to adjust to his size. Even now, he's focused on my pleasure.

And my heart... It stupidly stutters. *This is more than fucking. This is so much more than just a one-off encounter. I wish it could be more. I wish... I told him earlier that I'm engaged.* I wince. *But I wanted this with him. I wanted to know what it would be like to consummate this overwhelming attraction between us. The kind that is a once-in-a-lifetime connection. I didn't think this through.*

Didn't think there could be anything more between us. But then, I didn't think he might want something more lasting with me either. How is he going to react when I tell him?

Likely, he'll be annoyed that I wasn't upfront with him. *But it's not like we promised anything to each other. And given I'm not yet married and the transactional nature of the engagement, do the rules of monogamy even apply here?*

The thoughts whirl around in my head.

Either way, my conscience tells me I owe it to him to be upfront. *And I will. Just not yet. I can't. Not when I want to make the most of these moments with him.*

I'm going to hold these images of him looking at me like I'm the most beautiful thing in the world. Of the tenderness in his eyes as he braces himself over me. Of the lust on his features as he thrusts inside me, the tension in his jaw as he struggles to find control, as the emotions on his face mirror the confusion I feel inside. I wonder if he realizes his mask has slipped?

"You okay?" His tone is rough and strained and yet, there's a tenderness to it that ramps up my confusion even more. *What have I done? Why did I lead him on so?*

His eyebrows know. Concern flickers in his eyes. "Answer me, Aura. Does it hurt?"

I shake my head, knowing I need to reassure him, or else he'll pull out, and I don't want that. "I'm good," I whisper. "Really good."

Some of the tension drains from his shoulders. "You're so wet, baby. So tight. You feel so fucking good. You make me feel like I'm your—" His brow furrows. "Am I your first?"

I stiffen. When I stay silent, his gaze widens. "I *am* your first?"

He begins to pull out, but I lock my ankles around his waist. "Please, don't. I need you, Ryot."

"You should have told me." His gaze grows wary. "Why didn't you? I'd have taken more care with you."

"You made me come. Twice." I half smile. "You're taking care of me plenty."

He studies my features, but to my relief, he doesn't resist the inevitable. He cups my cheek then kisses me again. Long and slow and deep. The feel of his lips, of the sweetness, the tenderness, the sheer devotion in his kiss sinks into my blood. It's drugging in its passion and arousing in its attentiveness. In how he holds my face like I'm fragile, while his cock throbs inside me as evidence of his desire.

Then he pulls away, and when he peers into my eyes, the connection between us feels even more raw. More genuine. More real. It feels like he's peering into my soul. And I know, whatever is happening between us is changing me in a way I couldn't have fathomed. He begins to move slowly inside me. Pulling out until he's balanced at the rim of my entrance, then pushing in with such intent, I can feel every pulsing centimeter of his shaft sinking into me. He presses in, until he hits a part hidden deep inside of me. Shivers of delight sweep up my spine. My thighs tremble. I groan; so does he.

"That feels—" I begin.

"—so bloody good," he says through gritted teeth.

We look at each other, and something passes between us. Something that arrows to my heart and warns me—*this, whatever it is between us... Is different. This is not what I expected when I set out to find a way to sleep with him. This is so much more serious.* But I'm not going to regret it. Not when this sensation of being joined with this man in a way that feels almost cosmic is something I'll never find with anyone else. His green eyes turn emerald. Silver sparks flare in them. Then, he drags his hand up my arm and urges me to clasp his shoulder. "I'm going to fuck you now."

24

Aurelia

He pulls out and stays poised at the rim of my slit again. This time though, he kicks his hips forward and buries himself inside me in one sweet move. Tendrils of sensation flare out from the point of contact. Liquid heat shoots through my veins. I dig my heels into his back, feeling the muscles bunch and flex as he begins to fuck me in earnest. Each time he sinks inside me, he hits that secret spot deep inside of me. A place where only he has been. The friction is devastatingly stimulating and so very intimate. Sweat beads his forehead, and not once does he look away.

This connection between us is so personal, it heightens my awareness of him. Of how he's watching me closely every time he sinks into me, how he varies the angle of his hips to hit my clit, how he balances himself on one arm to keep most of his weight off while still pinning me with his cock and his hips, and those long, deep, smooth thrusts like a dance we've choreographed before. Vibrations shudder out from where we're joined and curl in on themselves. That familiar tightening in my lower belly signals I'm going to climax. Again. Yet he continues to drive into me. And the next time he impales me, that pressure inside me shoots up and out to my extremities.

He holds my gaze, pushes in again, then growls, "Come with me."

He plunges into me, and the climax crashes over me. The orgasm builds up my spine and bursts in a shower of sparks. I hear myself cry out as if from a distance. And yet he hasn't closed his eyes; neither have I. He holds my gaze and, with a hoarse cry, follows me over the edge.

I feel him grow even more hard inside me. His shoulders shudder and he lowers his forehead to mine. A bead of sweat slides down his temple onto my cheek. For a few more seconds, we stare at each other.

"Wow." I swallow. "That was—"

"Incredible." One side of his mouth quirks. He presses his lips to mine. A butterfly wings brush of a kiss. Then he kisses the tip of my nose, and my eyes before he pulls out.

He falls onto the grass next to me. His chest rises and falls, his breath coming in pants. For a few seconds, we stay silent. As my heart rate returns to normal, the sounds of the waterfall creep into my consciousness. Then, he sits up. I open my eyes to find him pulling off the condom. He ties it off and slips it into the pocket of his jacket. Then, he rises to his feet and holds out his hand. I take it. He pulls me up. For a few seconds we survey each other. Then he pulls some stray leaves from my hair and smooths it down. His touch is soft. And so gentle.

It makes me feel even worse. I swallow down the ball of emotion in my throat and glance away. "I look—"

"Thoroughly fucked," he says with satisfaction.

I flush further. The pride in his voice is so damn arousing. I'm so aware of his naked body and his strong presence. It makes me want to sink into him and forget about my responsibilities. *If I burrow into him further, perhaps, I can hide from the fact I've been promised to another?* It's not as if I have any fondness for my betrothed, so I don't think I'm cheating.

Besides, it's more of a financial commitment than emotional. Ryot probably won't care either way. *Will he?* Taking in the possessiveness in his eyes, a shiver of apprehension climbs up my spine.

To mask my thoughts, I bend, pick up my jeans and slip them on, then my sweatshirt, before pulling on my socks and shoes. I stuff my wet underwear in the pocket of my jeans and my phone in the other. When I look up, it's to find he has also finished dressing.

He holds out his hand. "Come 'ere."

The command in his voice insists I obey him. My legs seem to carry me to him independent of my instruction. I place my palm in his, and he pulls me close. He searches my features, then cups my cheek, and before I can protest, brings me in for a kiss. Instantly, I melt against him. I can't hold out against the feel of his lips against mine and the scrape of the calluses of his fingers against my cheek.

"You all right?" he whispers against my mouth.

I nod. Once more, his tenderness is my undoing. To my shock, I sense tears well up and swallow them away. *Self-pity? Really? I've never given in to feeling sorry for myself. So why am I feeling so confused? This discombobulated. It was just sex...wasn't it?*

He senses my bewilderment, and his forehead furrows. "Losing your virginity is a big change. It's okay to feel emotional about it." When I don't reply, he sighs. "You can talk to me. I'm not going to pass judgement, I promise."

Droplets of rain hit my face, but I ignore them. That he's so understanding only makes it worse. Also, I am so embarrassed because I feel like I misled him. "Can we talk about something else please?" I beg.

He searches my features, then nods slowly. "I'll let it go. For now."

"Thanks?" I begin to pull away, but he doesn't let me.

"You're going to be okay, Princess. I'm going to keep you safe."

"So, you'll stay, despite the fact that we slept together?"

He nods.

"You're not going to leave me because you feel your judgement is compromised?"

His gaze grows serious. "My decision-making capacity is bound to be influenced by the fact that I have...feelings for you, but I'm going to have to deal with them."

My heart somersaults into my throat. It's the second time he's referred to his feelings for me. *Oh. God.*

This is terrible. I mean, it's amazing that he has feelings for me. I do too, for him. But...this is getting so complicated. "There... There's something I need to tell you, I—"

The raindrops increase in intensity. He looks up, then takes my hand in his and pulls me along. "Let's get out of here first."

"But I... I... I'm enga—" I have to run to keep up with him. My breath comes in pants. I'm unable to speak and have to focus on not tripping.

By the time we reach the back door to the house, we're both soaked. He pulls me under the awning. We look at each other and burst out laughing. For a few seconds, our gazes meet. That familiar bubbling sensation squeezes my belly. My pussy begins to throb. The heat in the air turns the raindrops on my skin into steam. A current of need invades my blood stream.

I sway toward him, and he slides his hands down my waist to my butt. His hands squeeze my ass cheeks. I shiver. And when he draws me up on tiptoe, I go willingly. He lowers his chin and presses his mouth to mine. I part my lips, and he deepens the kiss.

I close my eyes and give over to that drugging feeling only he can elicit in me, when suddenly, I'm free. The next moment he's turned around, so I'm hidden by his broad back. There's no mistaking the tension that emanates from his big body. He pulls out the phone from his jeans pocket, glances at it, and swears.

"What is it?"

He doesn't reply. Instead, he pulls open the backdoor and urges me in. "Stay there."

"Wait, what?"

He shuts the door after me, but not before I notice the gun in his hand. My heart sinks into my stomach. Did he spot something on the security cameras connected to the app on his phone? Through one of the windows, I spot him heading around the house and toward the front door. I head through the house, and when I reach the front door, I crack it open enough to see what's happening. A car drives up the driveaway and parks in front of the house. Then the driver's door opens, and a very tall, broad-shouldered man steps out. By his resemblance to Ryot I guess it's his brother? *What's he doing here?*

My question is answered when the door to the front passenger's seat is flung open. A familiar figure exits the vehicle.

Oh no! My heart sinks from my stomach all the way to my toes. My pulse rate shoots up. *I knew I should have told him about my upcoming nuptials sooner. Now, it's too late. Now, there's nowhere to hide.*

Spine straight. You're a princess. And I've gotta face the music. I can do this.

I fling the door open and walk out, just as Ryot steps on the patio.

The next second, Ryot pushes me behind him. I peek around his broad back to find the man whose calls I've been avoiding, holding up his hands. Ryot points his gun at him.

"D-Dont shoot," he stammers, his chin trembling.

Oh, no! This can't be happening. "Ryot!" I grab his bicep. "Please, lower your gun."

Ryot glares at the man standing in the driveway. A nerve pops at his temple. "Who're you?" His body is rigid. There's tension radiating from him. I can feel the coiled muscles under his skin. So hard. So strong. So… *Mine.* And soon, he's going to hate me.

I step around him. "Hello Gavin," I say with resignation.

That seems to get through to Ryot, for he stiffens. He still doesn't take his gaze off the other man. "You know him?" Then, he puts his arm out to prevent me from approaching the other guy.

"I do." I nod.

"No matter," Ryot growls. "Don't come closer. Not until I've checked out your background."

"Don't be ridiculous; I'm her fiancé."

25

Ryot

"Fiancé?" I look the man up and down. He's shorter than me, and skinny. Pale skin. Blonde hair which is beginning to stick to his forehead because of the rain.

He's wearing a suit which, while an expensive cut, hangs on him. He has the gangly look of a boy who has left his teenage years behind in chronology, but his body has yet to catch up with that reality.

Also, the look on his face is one of anger and confusion. And while I recognize the aggravated expression of self-importance in his eyes, there's no hint that he's lying. I sense her agitation by my side, and when I glance at her face, she's looking up at me. In her blue eyes, there's helplessness and guilt. *Jesus.* "You're engaged?" I growl.

Before she can reply, the other man bursts out, "Yes, we are." He looks between us. "Who're you?"

I ignore him and stare into her eyes. She doesn't refute what he said, and she doesn't answer my question. But she doesn't need to.

The remorse in her eyes is all the answer I need. *She didn't tell me she was engaged. Of course, she didn't need to. We fucked. Once.*

She doesn't owe me anything. So, why does it feel like she deceived me? And why wasn't this information in her file? More to the point, was I beginning to see a future with her?

Nope, not possible. I know I was developing feelings for her, and yes, she gave me her virginity. And perhaps, the fact I was her first made me certain that what we have meant something to her too, but I guess I was wrong.

"I can explain." She reaches for me, but I take a step away from her like I've been scalded.

I glare at Tyler. "Why did you bring *him* here?"

His forehead furrows. "He called Veronica, who reached out to the First Minister. He called me."

He half bows his head toward the princess, "Your Royal Highness. I'm Tyler Davenport, Ryot's brother."

She manages a small smile and acknowledges him.

Of course, the two haven't met. I was too pre-occupied with this latest development to introduce them. *Finding out that the first woman you're attracted to since your wife died is engaged to someone else, can do that.*

I thrust out my chin in Tyler's direction. "I warned you; the location of the safe house was not to be disclosed. Also why didn't the First Minister call *me*? More importantly," I shoot him a sharp look, "why didn't you message me before starting out?"

His gaze is troubled. "We agreed to route all communication from the King through me, and I was to avoid messaging you to prevent any chance of a leak, remember?"

How could I have forgotten?

"The king insisted that I bring her fiancé to her, so he could accompany her back to Verenza, where he believes she will be safe." Tyler's frown deepens.

I was worried about being distracted by her because it might compromise my ability to my job. I was right. Apparently, I'm so taken in by my feelings, I wasn't able to do my job properly.

I take another step away from her. "My job here is done."

"Ryot, *please*. I can explain." She follows in my footsteps.

I ignore her. I pivot and stalk into the house. I'm done with this charade. I opened myself up for the first time since Jane, only to find I've been taken for a ride.

Tyler follows me in and grips my shoulder. "Wait, that's not all."

"Whatever it is, I'm not interested," I growl.

"You will be in this. The king has insisted you accompany the princess and her, uh—fiancé."

"Not happening."

Tyler looks uncomfortable. "Arthur insisted that you go."

"Like I give a fuck what the old man thinks?" I sneer.

"Also, he's, ah, holding a dinner tonight at his house in honor of the princess, and he insists the three of you attend."

"What bullshit," I snap.

Tyler shifts his weight from foot to foot. "You know Gramps. He's...adamant that you attend."

"It's not safe for her to leave here."

"He's asked Quentin, Nathan, and all of our brothers to be in attendance, and to provide protection."

I scoff.

"In addition to your own team, of course."

Resentment floods my senses. Also, anger and a sense of disbelief. "If the old man thinks he's going to call me, and I'll come running—" My phone buzzes. I ignore it. "I'm responsible for the princess' protection, and I say it's dangerous for her to leave this safe house."

"Now, look here—" her asshole fiancé sputters.

I give him a look so poisonous, he cowers.

"Ryot, please, give me a chance to explain—" Aura begins to speak at the same time.

I sneer, "Not interested," and she subsides. But not before she aims an angry look in my direction. *Good. That makes two of us who're pissed off.*

My phone stops, then starts again, adding to the confusion.

"You should take that," Tyler murmurs.

"Oh, for fuck's sake." I pull out the device to shut it off, then realize it's my grandfather calling. *Of course, it is.* "I'm tempted to ignore the call. I *should* ignore the call."

"Don't," Tyler warns. "Better to face the old man now than later, when it's only going to make things worse."

I hesitate. He has a point. Arthur is not the kind of man who can be ignored. In fact, he'll only take it a sign of encouragement and double his efforts in trying to reach me. Likely, he'll find a way to make my life miserable in the meantime, too. If that's possible. I walk away from the rest and answer the call, "What?"

There's silence, then Arthur's chuckle floats down the phone. "Is that anyway to talk to your ailing grandfather?"

"Last I heard, you were given a clean bill of health."

He was diagnosed with lung cancer six months ago, but they caught it in time. He's now on targeted therapy, and the disease is in check. He'll need to take pills for the rest of his life, but it hasn't affected his lifestyle in any way. If anything, Arthur's tried to pack even more into his life. He's found himself a girlfriend—not that the Harley driving, shit-kickers-wearing Imelda would appreciate being described as that. He also took on the project of getting his as-yet unwedded youngest son and grandsons married off. I'm proud I've held out so far.

"At my age though, it's like the lottery. You never know when the disease might rear its head again." He coughs.

"One can only hope," I mutter. "Wait, did the doctors say something?"

"Nope, but that doesn't mean I don't have much time left." His voice sounds morose. I have a sneaking suspicion he's playing me, but I find my mood softening anyway.

"You'll likely outlive us all, old man." I drag my fingers through my hair.

When I glance up, it's to find all three of them watching me—the princess with a mixture of anger and hope in her eyes, the fiancé with confusion and apprehension, and Tyler with an expression that says, *I told you so.*

I glance away and scowl into the phone. "If you're calling me about this so-called dinner—"

"I'm expecting you there with the princess and her fiancé," he says in an imperious voice that sets my teeth on edge. Clearly, the dominant part of us is something we inherited from Gramps, given how weak my father was in front of him. Also, I have no intention of obeying him.

"No," I snap.

"Thought you'd say that." The old man's voice is filled with satisfaction. He anticipated my response, and he doesn't seem upset. In fact, he almost seems to relish my defiance. The hair on the back of my neck rises.

"What are you up to?" I growl.

"Me?" he says in an innocent voice. My instincts warn me he's going in for the kill. Sure enough, his next words are, "If you don't bring them to my place for dinner tonight, the king will withdraw the contract for security from Quentin's company."

"What?" I blink.

"Which means, you won't be going to Verenza to keep an eye on the princess."

I draw in a sharp breath.

"Her fiancé will be accompanying her, of course."

Frustration knots my belly.

"And if you don't continue as her bodyguard, there'll have to be someone else who'll be in close quarters with her, keeping an eye on her."

Fucking hell, Gramps has my number. *Am I that obvious?* Most likely, he's trying to rile me, but that doesn't stop me from tensing up. My insides churn. *Someone else taking over for me? Someone else living in close proximity with her, accompanying her to her public engagements? Someone else breathing in the same air as her?*

A sharp burst of anger shoots through my bloodstream.

"It might even be her old head of security, who could be reassigned by the king to her protection detail."

"That bastard doesn't know his arse from his elbow," I growl.

"Of course, there's no one as effective as you'd be in this scenario, but I believe the king's words were 'needs must,'" he adds in a casual tone.

The old man is playing me. And I'm taking his bait. I'm aware of it and am unable to stop it. I squeeze my fingers around my phone with such force, the cover cracks. "The fuck do you want?" I growl.

"Language," my grandfather admonishes, then in the same breath says, "it's not me who wants anything; this is the king's diktat."

"You expect me to believe that?" I sneer.

"Believe what you want. Bottom line, you need to bring the princess and her fiancé to dinner tonight, or else you forfeit the role of her bodyguard."

I clench the fingers of my free hand into a fist. *Goddammit.* I hate ultimatums. And yet, he's putting me on the spot, and he knows it. "It's not safe for her to be back in the city."

If he realizes it's a capitulation on my part and that he's won this round, he doesn't show it. "You'll be with her, as will the rest of your team, not to mention your brothers, many of whom are trained military personnel. And you'll, no doubt, take all of the necessary precautions to ensure her safety. She'll be fine."

"I wish I shared your confidence." I roll my shoulders, trying to displace the stabbing pain that's crawled between my shoulder blades. It's a sign that I'm on alert, and I welcome it.

"Not like you to doubt yourself." Gramps' voice softens.

"They almost got her the last time." I squeeze my eyes shut, recalling the pain, the anger, the helplessness, the sheer impotence I felt when I saw the crimson pinpoint of the laser sight on her. "If it hadn't been for—"

"You," he interrupts. "You were there, and you saved her. You'll make sure nothing happens to her."

"I was lucky the last time." I crack my neck.

"Not like you to be so diffident. I understand, when it's someone you have feelings for—"

"Feelings? I don't have feelings," I lie. But he's right. Where she's concerned, my emotions are firmly in the mix, but I'll be damned if I'm going to let him know that. Besides, that was before she told me she was engaged. I'm not going to let myself continue down this path, now that I know she's going to marry someone else. And then, there's the fact she didn't mention it to me. The combination of which tells me, I need to keep my association with her strictly professional from now on.

"Of course not; a slip of the tongue." Arthur's voice is bland. "When it's someone you feel responsible for, of course, it's normal to be a little shaken. But it means you're going to be even more on guard from now on. You're best suited to be her protection."

He's right. In the silence that follows, I sense Arthur nod. Then a new thought strikes me. *Why did the princess' engagement not make it into her file? I had my team screen her and everyone in her circle before I signed on to this assignment, and no mention of a fiancé was flagged.* I straighten. Unless— I walk out of earshot of Tyler and Aura, then turn my back on them.

"You made sure news of her upcoming nuptials didn't show up on her background check," I growl into the phone.

The silence lengthens. And it confirms what was a glimmer of suspicion in my mind. For really, who'd have the power and the motivation to do such a thing but Arthur?

"Don't insult my intelligence by denying it," I snap.

"I won't," Arthur admits.

What the hell? I pull the phone from my ear and stare at it. I knew my grandfather was a meddling bastard but this... This is going too far.

"Why?" I bark into the phone. "Why did you do it?"

"Why does it matter so much to you that she's engaged?" Arthur retorts.

I blink. "It doesn't."

There's more silence. Then, Arthur's voice comes down the line again. "The king requested that her engagement not be mentioned anywhere, including in any review of her past."

I rub at my temple. "Why would he do that?"

"He was worried, if news got out, those who mean to hurt the Royal Family might try to break up the engagement."

My guts churn. My stomach ties itself in knots... The thought of her belonging to anyone else turns my insides to ice. *But she was never yours to begin with. She doesn't owe you anything. You never should have over-*

stepped your professional boundaries by sleeping with her. Now, you must pay for your transgressions.

It's my turn to stay quiet.

Arthur heaves a sigh. "If I'd known you'd get personally involved with her, I'd have—"

"I already told you, I'm not personally involved with her," I say through gritted teeth.

"Whatever you say." To my surprise, he doesn't push it. "Right, then. I'll expect you here; six p.m."

He disconnects. I pocket the phone, square my shoulders, and snap my gaze to Tyler. "We're going to London."

I brush past them and head inside.

"Wait. Ryot." She follows me in. "We need to speak."

26

Aurelia

"I can explain," I increase my pace so I can keep pace with his longer stride. He takes the stairs two at a time, with me right behind him.

"Aura," Gavin calls from behind me.

"I'll be back," I call out over my shoulder.

Ahead of me, Ryot stiffens, then doubles his speed. By the time I reach the landing, he's disappeared into the room where I slept last night. *He's really pissed with me. And I deserve it. But surely he can listen to what I have to say?*

"Ryot!" I burst into the room. "Can you give me a second?"

He ignores me and, walking to the closet in the corner, pulls out a duffel bag. It's half full, so perhaps, this is the bag that Tyler dropped off?

He picks up the clothes I wore yesterday from the chair where I placed them and shoves them inside, along with the Doc Martens I wore.

"What are you doing?"

He continues to move around the room, stuffing the charger of my phone into the bag, and zips it up. Then, he snatches a second duffel from the closet. He heads into the bathroom and emerges with some toiletries which he stuffs inside, along with the clothes he was wearing yesterday. I walk over and grip his arm.

He shakes it off.

My heart sinks into my stomach. I feel like someone took a battering ram to my chest. I shove away the hurt and plant my feet. He's going to listen to me, even if I have to force him to do so. "Can you at least do me the courtesy of giving me a few seconds of your time?" I cry.

He drops first one bag, then the other, on the floor between us, and slaps his hands on his hips. His stance is belligerent. He fixes me with his gorgeous green eyes, and in them, I see disdain. And an accusation I know he's right to level against me.

That sinking feeling in my stomach spreads until I feel it's swallowing me up completely. I'm sure my frustration must show on my face, but he doesn't acknowledge it. His green eyes turn into glacial sheets that resembled frozen absinthe. He could cut me with his glance. Tear my heart to pieces.

Oh wait, I did that to myself already. I am the Princess of Verenza, but I am also human. I make mistakes. And this...might be the most expensive one of them all. But I'm going to try to fix it. I must fix it.

I hold up my hands. "Ryot, I'm sorry. I really am, for not telling you about the betrothal."

His jaw grows harder. That tell-tale nerve throbs at his temple. Anger radiates off of him, mixed with icy contempt. He seems to grow taller and looks more forbidding than I've seen him before. I deserve his derision.

"I thought you knew about my impending marriage. I assumed my engagement would have been mentioned in my file." Somehow, my reasoning, which I used to convince myself, seems lame. Even to my ears.

His eyes blaze, but his voice is barely audible. "You thought I'd fuck you, knowing you were engaged to be married? You think I'm a cheater?"

I draw in a sharp breath.

His lips twist. "Couldn't find anyone else to help sow your oats, so you decided to use me, did you, Princess? I was attracted enough to you that you could seduce me. I was a willing dick on which you could lose your virginity, is that it?"

"That's not fair, I—" I wring my hands. "The attraction between us did take me by surprise. It's also what confused me, and I was swept away by my feelings for you, and—"

"Feelings? Don't talk to me about feelings." A nerve pops at his temple. "You led me to believe you were available. I had no reason to doubt that. I was taken in by your innocence. There was no mention of your engagement in your file either, because your father had it removed."

My father didn't want to publicize this engagement. So, it's not a surprise he had it removed from my file.

I glance away, then back at him. "This marriage is a business transaction."

His gaze narrows.

I feel my courage slip. Feel my stomach tremble and taste the bile on my tongue. *Nope. Not going to be sick.* I square my shoulders. I am going to see this through. I am going to face his wrath, even if I feel like running away and hiding. Even if a part of me wants to throw myself at his feet and beg him for forgiveness. And ask him to do anything he wants with me, except— Seeing the scorn in his gaze, I'm not sure if that's the right move.

No, I won't lose his respect for me any more than I already have. I'm going to face up to him. I'm going to own this. I have to. I need to…find a way to make him understand.

"My father drilled into me and my brothers that, as part of the Royal Family, my happiness is secondary to my responsibility to my country."

A flicker of something crosses his gaze. Just enough, I know I've gotten through to him.

"You were a Marine. You know what it is to believe in a cause that's larger than yourself."

He doesn't nod. But he's still listening, and he hasn't walked away, which I count as a win.

"So, when my father told me that Verenza's economy has been shrinking over the past decade and that we urgently need an infusion of money, and asked me for help, I couldn't refuse."

"What does that have to do with—" His brow smooths out. A glimmer of understanding dawns in his expression "He wants you to marry that fuckface in return for—"

I nod. "Gavin belongs to a Royal Family in Europe who are no longer recognized by their country. They live in exile. They have access to familial wealth. Enough that if our two families were joined by marriage, they'd be willing to provide an infusion of money into Verenza. In return, they'll once again be recognized as royalty and be accepted by their peers; and Gavin gets a title."

"So, you took the hit for the family?" he drawls. There's not an ounce of sympathy on his features.

What did I expect? That he'd understand my point of view and forgive me right away?

"My father told me what was needed of me, and I chose to do it out of duty. I have no feelings for the man I'm supposed to marry. And when I met you... the way I felt—" I swallow. "I knew then, I couldn't just settle for an arranged marriage without being with someone with whom the chemistry was off the charts. So yes, I wanted to give you my virginity."

His features turn to stone.

"I admit, I lied by omission. But I thought you knew. Then, I reasoned, if I reminded you that I was engaged, you'd never sleep with me."

"You're bloody right, I wouldn't have." His voice is so harsh it feels like a whiplash. I flinch.

"I'm sorry, I hurt you. I truly am."

He narrows his gaze. "Are you?"

"I am." I take a step in his direction, wanting to go to him, but the tension radiating off of him forms an invisible wall I don't dare attempt to scale. I settle for holding his gaze and infusing everything I'm feeling into my voice.

"I wasn't thinking straight. I was being selfish. I panicked at the thought that I might never get a chance to be with you." I swallow. "I knew, if I gave you my virginity it would be incredible. I thought I'd have, at least, some memories to hold onto when things got tough in the future. I wanted something just for me."

He listens to me without a hint of emotion on his features.

I wring my fingers. "Only, I didn't realize how thoughts of you have become so much a part of me that I'll never be able to forget you." I lower my chin. "I knew it would be intense with you, and it was. It was *everything*."

A nerve throbs above his jawline. He doesn't say anything, and I wring my hands. I feel terrible for what happened. *How could I have been this selfish? How could I have not realized how much it was going to affect him when he found out about my upcoming marriage? How could I have been this blind to how much anguish this was going to cause him?*

"I am so sorry, Ryot. Please, can you forgive me?"

His left eyelid twitches. "You used me. You didn't care what that would do to me?"

"I... I..." I'm not sure what to say. Nothing I say is going to help redeem this situation. I'm the one at fault. I made a huge mistake. I was only thinking of myself. "I... Somehow, I thought it wouldn't mean much to you."

I flinch as I say the words, realizing just how self-absorbed and insensitive I sound. And I am all of that.

"I'm to blame. It's all my fault. I was only thinking of myself. Guess for all my hate of my background and privilege, I've acted exactly like how an entitled, pampered person born into money would." I hang my head.

I feel horrible inside. My stomach twists in on itself. I taste bile on my tongue and am sure I'm going to be sick. And then, as if I can't stop myself, like a gush of vomit, the words pour out.

"Somehow, I thought you'd welcome the chance to sleep with me, then walk away." I laugh bitterly.

OMG, that sounds terrible. I can't believe that my self-esteem is so in the toilet I would think that. Worse, how could I say that aloud to him?

He glares at me.

"I know that sounds terrible. And I'm not saying you're callous enough to have done that, but it's also not like we made any promises to each other either."

His jaw clenches.

"And don't most men welcome the chance to walk away after sleeping with a woman without any strings attached?" My voice tapers off.

With each word I speak, his gaze grows fiercer.

When he speaks, his voice is hard enough to cut glass. "You thought I'd sleep with you and that it wouldn't affect me, so you decided not to tell me that you were going to marry someone else? You didn't give me a choice in the matter."

I flush. I'm an awful person. I judged him so harshly. I should have known better. He's been nothing but kind and considerate toward me, and I assumed the worst.

I *did* hurt him. And I hurt myself even more. I feel a gaping hole in my chest, like someone just ripped out my heart. And that someone was me. I deflate. Still, I have to explain myself.

"I'm sorry I made assumptions about what you would or wouldn't do. I'm sorry I didn't give you all the facts and allow you to decide for yourself. I really am."

Anger, then something like sympathy, flashes in his eyes. How confusing. He looks at me like he's seeing me for the first time.

"It's one thing that you thought my being with you wouldn't mean anything." His voice has a tone of resignation. "What bothers me more is that's what you thought *you* deserve."

27

Ryot

"What do you mean?" Her forehead creases.

Not only is she putting herself down, but she's not even realizing that's what she's doing. Doesn't she know she's beautiful? Addicting? She's the most perfect woman in the world, and she's not aware of it.

"Do you think so little of yourself that you can't believe I might want more than a one-time sexual encounter?" I say slowly. "Well twice, if you count the earlier spanking."

Her cheeks flush. Her pupils dilate. She's remembering how it felt to be bent over that kitchen counter as I spanked her with my belt and made her orgasm. And again, as I made her come twice before I took her virginity.

I'm almost not sorry I gave in to my baser instincts and fucked her. It was the most incredible experience of my life. It was sublime. It's something I, too, am going to remember for a long time. Likely, the rest of my life. Especially since I won't be repeating the experience; not now that I know she's taken.

But if she weren't promised to another? I'd never let her go. I'd tie her to the bed and not let her loose until I made love to her over and over again. Until I used the dominance she's so attracted to, to make her do everything I ask of her. Until I make her orgasm over and over again, filling her with so many endorphins, she'll barely be able to walk.

She must sense some of my thoughts, for her blush deepens, and she looks away. She squeezes her thighs together, and I have no doubt she's wet and hurting, wanting and ready for my cock again. The blood thrums in my veins. My cock lengthens. Of course, my dick is ready to disregard the fact that her fiancé is waiting downstairs and take her right here. I close the distance to her, and she doesn't flinch. She tips up her chin, defiance in her features, a glitter in her eyes.

She's not afraid of facing up to her mistakes. She's courageous enough to stand up to my authority over her body. It takes a princess and the imperiousness that comes from her upbringing to confront my controlling manner. Still, her breath hitches, and the pulse that speeds up at the base of her throat tells me she's feeling the tug of my power.

She's tasted how it feels to submit to me. To hand over control to what I can do to her in the bedroom, and revel in the freedom that comes with it. Too bad, I'm not going to explore that further. I shove my thoughts aside. "What concerns me most is that you don't think enough of yourself to anticipate that I might want more."

"Oh." She seems taken aback. "Do you... Do you want more?"

"You mean, more than bending your tight little body to my ministrations to make you orgasm?" I peer into her features. "Like showing you how I can take you to the edge and not allow you to come, to have you panting and writhing and moaning under me, and still not let you get your satisfaction?"

She swallows.

"Like looking behind the sass and seeing the submissive who wants to be told what to do in bed?" A fierce ache cleaves my chest.

"Like looking into your eyes and seeing the woman who I'd do anything for?"

Her gaze widens. There's longing in her eyes. A yearning I recognize. A need. A pining. A craving.

"Question is, do you?" I ask, knowing I'm putting her on the spot and hating myself. But also, not seeing any way out. I certainly didn't expect to bare so much more of my emotions to her. But I meant everything I said.

This complex, gorgeous, stubborn, spitfire makes me feel off balance in a way I've never felt before.

Her gaze bounces around the room, then she lowers her head.

"Don't bother answering," I say, half angry, half resigned.

The one woman who stirred something in me since Jane died, and of course, she's unavailable. It's poetic justice. I deserve it for being responsible for what happened to Jane.

She hunches her shoulders. "I... I wish things were different."

So do I. I recognize the sadness in her tone. The regret. The remorse. And I feel it too. "You deserve every happiness, Princess. Congratulations on your upcoming nuptials," I say in a formal tone.

She jerks her glance up. Her eyes glisten. I hate myself for hurting her. I want to tell her I want everything I said earlier, and more. I want to demand that she break off the engagement, but I will not. It's not for me to ask that of her. I know what it is to sacrifice everything in the name of duty for your country. This is her calling, and I will not stand in the way of it.

"I won't say I forgive you for what you hid from me, but I understand how difficult it is when you're bound to fulfill your obligations to your country. It's not an easy role you have, Princess. You carry an enormous burden on your shoulders. It's not an excuse for your keeping news of your engagement from me. But I also won't hold it against you."

Tears fill her eyes. "Ryot."

My heart seizes up. My fingers tingle to reach up and wipe away the drop of moisture that clings to the corner of her eye, but I stop myself. "It's not worth your crying, Princess." I soften my tone. "You have your duty to your people, and I have mine—to protect you."

"You'll continue as my bodyguard?" There's hope in her eyes.

And I want to say no. I want to say I can't bear to be with her and watch her with someone else. That my grandfather can go to hell. I don't care if I'm defying his orders, but I will not accompany her and her fiancé to Verenza. That if I see her fiancé touch her, I'm going to break his arm... But I don't. *Am I really going to put myself through this?*

Am I going to inflict the worst kind of pain on myself—for once, take on the role of masochist instead of sadist, which is my natural inclination? Fuck. I curl my fingers into fists at my sides and nod slowly. If something were to happen to her, I'd never forgive myself. I wouldn't be able to live with myself. I've lost one woman who was important to me. I will not let that happen again. So, I nod. "Until I track down those who want to harm you, I'll stay on as your bodyguard." *There isn't anyone else I'd trust with your safety.*

"Thank you." She swipes at the corners of her eyes. My ribcage tightens. Once again, I have to stop myself from taking her in my arms and kissing her pain away. *She's the principal. I'm the bodyguard. This is the only relationship we have.*

I head for the door and hold it open. "It's best we leave. We're expected at my grandfather's place for dinner."

"Your grandfather's place?" A crease forms on her forehead.

I rub the back of my neck. "I'll fill you in on the way."

28

Aurelia

"I don't understand why we have to go to this dinner," Gavin whines from the seat next to me.

Tyler is in James' car ahead of us. We're in the armored car, Tyler drove over.

Ryot, who's driving, stiffens. He filled us in on where we're headed and explained that Arthur and my father decided we need to appear at the dinner at Arthur's place before we head to Verenza.

Gavin seems to have conveniently forgotten the conversation, for less than an hour into the journey, he's begun to voice his protests.

I scowl at him, hoping he'll shut up. Not that he takes the hint. Instead, he begins to fidget in his seat. "Why can't we head back to Verenza? The jet is waiting for us. We could be airborne within a few hours and be back in time for dinner." He turns to me with a pleading look in his eyes. "You know how much I already consider Verenza home. I already miss it."

"You've been away for less than twenty-four hours. You'll survive," I say rudely.

"But, Aurelia, I promised my friends we'd be hosting them at the palace this evening."

I ignore him.

The silence in the car stretches. Then, Gavin begins to squirm around in his seat. It's an attention-garnering tactic on his part, and I try to pretend I don't notice. But he continues to shuffle around. I blow out a breath and turn back to him. "What is it?"

"I have to piss."

"What?" I blink.

"I need to pee, Aurelia," he says in that prissy voice I hate. *Jesus, he's really getting on my nerves.*

Before I can answer, Ryot's deep voice interrupts. "We'll pull off at the next exit for the amenities."

"You want me to use the public lavatories?" He gapes.

Ryot and I exchange a glance in the rearview mirror.

"It's either that or hold it in until we reach Arthur's place in the next hour," he drawls.

Gavin glowers at him, then pulls out his phone and, muttering under his breath, pretends to get busy with it.

Ryot calls Tyler to update him, then takes the next turn off.

Gavin's phone pings. I glance at it, not because I mean to pry, but it's the instinctive response to look at a device when it calls your attention. I notice Veronica's name on the message he's received. *Huh? She's in touch with him?* He notices me looking and angles his shoulder so I can't read the words on the screen. *Hmm.*

They've met a few times that I'm aware of, but I didn't think they'd know each other well enough to text each other. Then again, Tyler mentioned that Gavin called her, trying to find out about my whereabouts. Which is strange. He could have called Fred or my father directly. Perhaps, he couldn't reach them?

The car turns off the highway, and I put it out of my mind.

A few minutes later, we pull into the rest area behind Tyler's car.

"Hold on," Ryot cautions. "Tyler is sweeping the place to make sure it's safe."

Tyler stalks out of the entrance and nods at Ryot, who steps out and opens my door.

Ryot and I walk up the steps and follow Tyler into the service area. There's no one else around.

"Tyler cleared the area temporarily," Ryot clarifies.

"Very efficient." I search his features, but if I thought that shared commiseration over Gavin's whining eased things between us, I was mistaken. Ryot's features are hard. His gaze is impersonal.

"Your safety is paramount to us, Princess," he says in a formal tone, then leads us in the direction of the restrooms.

Tyler opens the door to the men's room. Gavin disappears inside.

"Uh, guess I might as well—" I head toward the ladies' room, but Ryot reaches it first. He holds the door open. I walk through and cross the floor to one of the cubicles.

When I emerge, he's waiting inside the doorway; his gaze is, however, fixed on the distance.

I walk to the sink, wash my hands, and dry them. When I turn, it's to find he's not looking at me. My heart sinks.

Of course, it's my fault. I withheld the fact that I'm engaged. He has every right to be upset with me, for ignoring me. But my stupid heart is not able to bear it. Not after how, just this morning, he made love to me. *He said he has feelings for me. Twice. Which must mean he's been thinking of me as much as I have of him, right?*

And what about his wife? Did he have feelings for her? He must have, right? That's why he married her. I can't ask him about it, can I?

It doesn't sound right, no matter how much I'm dying to know. I can't be that intrusive. Especially not after how I hurt him. *But I can't bear him not even looking at me. I can't.*

I wash my hands, dry them, then glance at his reflection in the mirror. I turn, lean my hip against the counter. "Ryot... I know I messed up. I was so wrapped up in my own stuff that I completely ignored how my thoughtlessness would cause you pain."

He stiffens. His expression grows even more severe.

"What I did wasn't okay, and I'm truly sorry for that. But please, don't avoid me. I can't bear it."

The planes of his chest grow rigid. His jaw seems like it's carved out of ice.

Oh no, by reminding him of what I did, I'm only making it worse.

I hang my head. My chest is so heavy, it feels like my center of gravity has moved there. The backs of my eyelids burn. I will not cry. I will not.

Spine straight. You're a princess.

Not even my mother's voice pulls me out of the black hole I seem to have fallen into. The silence in the space grows and pushes down on my chest until it feels like I'm carrying the weight of the entire world. I can't bear that remote expression on his face. I can't imagine how much he's hurting inside. And selfishly, I can't bear the thought of him not forgiving me for what I did. I can't.

"Please. Please say something," I croak.

Something in my tone must get through to him, for he blows out a breath. A beat. Another. Then slowly, he turns his gaze on my face. There's a bleakness on his features. A hopelessness that makes me want to hate myself all over again for not having come out and told him about my upcoming nuptials from the beginning.

I have been so selfish. Nothing is worth this wounded feeling I see in his gaze. Not the memories I'd hoped to hold onto. Not the fact that I gave my virginity to a man I wanted. If I could do it all over again, I'd suck it up and not keep him in the dark.

"Jane, was pregnant when she was killed in action," he says flatly.

His words are a sucker punch. I feel like I've been kicked in the stomach. "Oh, my god." I slap my hand over my mouth.

"I didn't find out about it until later."

I lower my hand to my side, then turn to face him. "I'm so sorry, Ryot. More than you can imagine."

His gaze turns stark. The pain and anger in his eyes freezes the air in my lungs. Then he pivots and walks out of there.

That dejection in his features was real. *He must have loved her. And she was pregnant. No wonder he's so devastated.*

No doubt, keeping my engaged status from him has only added to his trauma.

I have no doubt now that this thing between us is over.

29

Ryot

"You're not ready for this meeting with Arthur." Tyler pours water into a glass and hands it to me. I toss it back, wishing it were something stronger. Not that I'm going to let myself drink on the job, especially when it's her life on the line.

"Thanks for pointing out the obvious," I growl.

Tyler merely tops up my glass with more water, then places the jug back on the counter.

We're in the reception room. A space Arthur only uses when he has formal company, like that of the King of Verenza. Speaking of, "I haven't seen Gramps since we arrived."

"He's closeted with the king. No doubt, the two of them are involved in some kind of business negotiation." He takes a sip of water from his own glass.

A frisson of unease spirals up my spine. I push it aside, then glance about at the people milling around. As soon as we arrived, the princess disappeared into the guest room Arthur assigned her so she could freshen up.

The fiancé, too, was allocated a room, on the other end of the corridor from her. Members of my team are keeping guard at each of their doors. They have instructions to bring them both down when they're ready.

I wanted to follow her to her room, but if I had, I wouldn't have been able to stop myself from holding her in my arms and kissing her, after turning her over my lap and spanking her for that lie by omission. And that stopped me. I need to get over her, but the more I try not to think of her, the more she pervades my thoughts.

Connor, my youngest brother has chosen to make an appearance, now that he's back from one of his many work-related trips. He insists it's related to the research he must undertake on behalf of the Davenport group's biotech company he heads up, but we, his siblings, suspect he's a spook for the British government. Not that he's ever confirmed it to us. He's talking to Brody, my second youngest brother, who wears a dissatisfied expression on his features. Not that any of us are happy to be here. But when Arthur commands us to turn up, we can't disobey him. It's not that we're afraid of him, but all of us respect the old bugger—enough to fall in line when he asks us to do something.

Not far from them, my oldest half-brother Edward and his wife Mira are talking with my Uncle Quentin and his very pregnant wife Vivian. Nathan and Skylar complete the group. It's as if there's an unspoken rule that all married couples are on that side of the room and the rest of us bachelors have been shunted to the far end. Or maybe, we decided to give them a wide berth. None of us are in a hurry to give up our single status.

In my case, it's because I'm not the same person I was when I met Jane. In Tyler's case, it's because he's focused on bringing up his daughter Serene. "Found a nanny yet?" I can't resist asking.

He groans and rubs a hand over his face. "Found one, and she's left already."

"Whoa, that's a record. This one lasted what, a month?"

"A week. It's not that Serene is a difficult child, but she doesn't take very quickly to her nannies, and most of them seem to give up trying within a few days." He runs a hand down his face. "Good thing Sinclair's wife Summer was happy to watch her while I'm away. Especially since she misses Michael and Karma's kids."

"And Michael, any idea how he is?" Michael's wife Karma passed away six months ago. After that, he took his kids and moved back to his hometown in Sicily. No one has heard from him since. Summer was close to her niece and nephew. Given Karma & Michael used to live next door to them, it's no surprise she misses them so much.

"I spoke to him a month ago, and he didn't sound good." Sinclair joins us. "I told him we'd come visit, but he wouldn't hear of it. We haven't seen him since…that day at the hospital."

I wasn't there myself, but by all accounts, it was heart-breaking. Michael refused to let anyone see Karma's body. "I wish he'd, at least, agreed to have a funeral for her." Sinclair sighs. "It would have given Summer some closure. But not only did he not allow Summer to say her good-byes, he cut off all ties with us." Sinclair walks behind the bar counter and pulls out a bottle of Macallan sixty-year-old whiskey.

"That's Gramps' stash, which he happens to be very possessive about," I warn.

"He told me I could help myself to any of it." Sinclair pours the whiskey into tumblers. As if it's a signal, Connor and Brody stalk over and snatch up the glasses.

"You know why Gramps decided to host the King of Verenza?" Brody drawls.

Sinclair surveys his glass of whiskey, "They move in the same circles, and the King of Verenza trusts Arthur. At least, that's the official line. Then again, it's well known that everything Arthur does is with the goal of getting you lot married off." He looks at me meaningfully.

I roll my shoulders. The expression on Sinclair's face says it all. He's implying Gramps has set up this meeting in the hopes of hastening my getting hitched a second time.

I glower at Sinclair. "He's aware I'm not ready to marry again."

"Have you known Gramps to let that stop him?" Connor scoffs.

I rub the back of my neck. "There's something strange about this entire evening. The fact that Arthur called me up and ordered me to bring the princess and her fiancé here, a day after I took her to the safe house—" I shake my head. "I know he has something up his sleeve."

"There's an electric fence around Arthur's property. Our entire team has taken up position around it. There are cameras monitoring the perimeter around the clock," Tyler offers.

"I'm tracking them via an app on my phone, remember?" I snap.

"My point is, the place is guarded with more security than the White House." He pops a shoulder. "Not that it means you can relax, but just saying, she's safer here than anywhere else."

He has a point. At the same time, I'm fairly sure Arthur's going to spring a typical Arthuresque surprise on me. All the more reason to keep my wits about me. I step back from the counter. "I'd feel better if I checked in on the princess."

Connor stares at me. Brody chuckles. The men look at me with expressions varying from surprise to disgust to a knowing grin.

"What?" I glare at them. "It's my responsibility to ensure she's safe."

"From her own fiancé?" Connor smirks.

"If need be, yes."

Tyler chuckles, then turns it into a cough.

"If you have something to say—"

"Just that it's best you go and check in on her. Perhaps, you'll be able to relax after that?" Brody mutters with only a hint of sarcasm.

Fact is, my wanting to ensure she's safe is an excuse. I've been with her nonstop since I took her to the safe house. I've gotten used to having her by my side, smelling her scent, hearing her voice, being in her presence. Not having her with me feels like I'm missing a part of myself. I need to lay eyes on her like I need to breathe.

"I think I'll do just that." I reach for my glass of water, empty it again, then place it on the counter with a snap.

I turn and, ignoring the jokes from the rest of my brothers, head out of the room.

I walk up the steps, to the second floor, then down the corridor to the room allocated to her. Cole is on guard outside her room.

"Her fiancé is in there with her," Cole offers.

Fucking hell. That nitwit is in her room?

He's her fiancé, he's entitled to be there with her. Anger, and that hated jealousy I've felt so often since I found out about her status as an engaged woman, stabs it's claws inside my chest.

"Uh, would you like to be on guard instead?" Cole asks without any change of expression on his face.

"What?" I stare, unable to make sense of his words.

"You're here to relieve me, aren't you? It's time for my break."

As his words sink in, I nod. He pulls his cigarettes from his pocket and brushes past me.

Oh, right. He's giving me a chance to be alone to mourn the future I cannot have with my princess. He's allowing me to save face, giving me a reason to skulk outside her door, wondering how my life has been turned inside-out all over again? Good man. There's no better than a brother-in-arm who says so much without words. I feel lucky to call him my friend.

I pivot and stand to attention with my back to the door, scanning the area for any possible threats.

Voices emerge through the closed door. I recognize her feminine tone along with the fiancé's whinier one. And because I don't have an iota of decency in me, not when it comes to finding out more about their relationship, and because, of course, if I have more knowledge I can protect her —*sure, keep telling yourself that* — I press my ear to the door and listen in.

30

Aurelia

"Yes, I was alone with him in the safehouse. So what?" I slap my hands on my hips and stare at Gavin.

"So what?" His expression darkens. "I've seen the way you look at him."

I blink slowly. My fiancé is not the most intelligent person on this planet. So, if even he picked up on the vibes between Ryot and me and felt the need to confront me about it within hours of meeting us, it means I'm going to struggle to keep a lid on whatever happened between us. Not that I want to. Given a choice, I'd dump Gavin and pursue this...whatever it is with Ryot. It feels too premature to call it a relationship, considering we only fucked.

Yes, I've begun to call it fucking, rather than making love, in the hope that it will make it feel more impersonal. Not that it's helped. I haven't been able to forget how it felt to be below him, surrounded by him, his body heat holding me in thrall and his dick pinning me to the ground, his gaze searing me, looking deeply into my soul, such that I know I've changed forever.

I avert my eyes because I can't trust that my emotions won't show on my features. I thought I learned to hide my true feelings, thanks to the time I've spent evading the media and putting on a face in front of them so they never see what I'm truly going through, but being with Ryot has stripped me of the barriers I normally throw up between myself and the world. Being with him has made me feel more vulnerable. Enough that I'm no longer confident I have it in me to hide my true sentiments. I walk over to the mirror and survey myself.

Thanks to the clothes and, even more importantly, the make-up Veronica delivered, I feel suitably dressed for the evening.

She told me Ryot arranged it. Once more, he was thoughtful about my needs. More reason for me to feel awful for not having told him about my engagement.

Not that I'm sorry for the memories I now have. *Will it be enough to last a lifetime, though?* I take in the forlorn look on my face. *Perhaps not. But I'll have to deal with it. I'm strong enough to do that. Aren't I?*

"Aurelia…" Gavin comes up to stand behind me. "Do you have feelings for him?"

I spin around and frown at him. There's a strange expression on his face as he scrutinizes my features. "Do you?"

I pretend to laugh. "What are you talking about?"

He searches my eyes, and a look of understanding comes into his eyes. "You do… have feelings for him."

"Gavin, I—" I want to lie to him, but can't bring myself to do it. Instead, I look away, then back at him. "You're right. I do."

He flinches. "I suppose, it was bound to happen." His mouth turns down. "I hoped we had a real chance. One where we'd get married and, perhaps, even fall in love." His gaze turns contemplative. "It didn't take long for me to realize that I'd never have a chance with someone as beautiful and as bright as you."

"Oh, Gavin," I gasp.

I didn't think he had this level of self-awareness.

He straightens his spine. The expression on his features is more resolute. He looks older. More mature. Not as sniveling. Not as much of a gutless twat that I'd defined him as.

"I kept trying to reach out to you, to find a way to hold your attention. To perhaps, even try to woo you, but I was hopelessly out of my depth," he rubs at the back of his neck.

I shift my weight from foot to foot, "You shouldn't blame yourself. We were both pawns in the plan our fathers had to benefit their agendas. I did it for my country. I thought I could put my own feelings aside for the sake of the future of my people, but then, I met Ryot and—" I wring my fingers, not sure how much to reveal. I don't want to rub in the fact that I have such powerful feelings for Ryot.

Once again, Gavin surprises me, for a shrewd look—one I did not think him to be capable of—comes into his eyes. "He swept you off your feet."

I blink. "Umm... Uh... It's just that—" I hesitate; my training as a princess means I can't let myself be this heartless.

Yet, I didn't tell Ryot about my upcoming nuptials. I can tell myself it's because I thought he already knew, but that's just an excuse. I never made sure he knew because it was easier to justify what I wanted to do already. That was so out of character for me. *Was I so affected by him that I forgot all of my principles and decided I had to have him, even if I hurt him in the process? How could I have done that?*

As I struggle with my thoughts, he holds up his hand. "You don't have to explain yourself."

His muddy brown eyes glint with a kind of resolve I haven't seen on his face before.

I blink at his more confident demeanor. This version of Gavin is a far cry from the complaining, spoiled persona he's adopted thus far. A frisson of unease crawls up my spine.

"And you..." I observe him carefully. "You're not—"

"The lily-livered, blithering, wimp I led you to believe?" His lips twist. "I figured the only way I had of forming a relationship with you was to act weak. I hoped to play on your emotional need to be the one who takes care of me—"

"—until you were controlling me?" Understanding dawns on me.

"You think you're so smart. You thought you could go behind my back and sleep with someone else, and I wouldn't notice? You didn't realize I was the one who was manipulating you all along. If you think I'm giving up my chance at marrying into royalty and getting a title, you're wrong."

Oh, my god. Just my luck that my wimp of a fiancé turns out to be a narcissistic, greedy, ass.

"I believe I might have underestimated you," I say carefully.

"Enough to sleep with your bodyguard while avoiding my calls," he says in a hard voice, which is very un-Gavin-like. Strike that. This is the real Gavin. The man who whined and moaned, and acted like he didn't have a backbone never existed.

The silence stretches. My skin prickles with unease. "I do not owe any explanations to you for any relationships I had before the wedding."

"Oh?" He looks at me with curiosity, and something else in his eyes that amps up my discomfiture.

"Let's call off this... sham of a wedding, and I'll pretend you weren't disrespectful to me."

He inclines his head as if contemplating my words. "I have a better idea." Something in his tone alerts me. My senses snap to attention.

"You do?" I strive for a casual tone.

He nods slowly, then cups my cheek. "Kiss me."

My skin crawls where he's touching me. "What?" I cough, then take a step back so his hand drops away. "What do you mean?"

"It was a simple request. I'm still your fiancé, and we haven't even kissed."

It didn't sound like a request. I search his features and find he's serious. A twinge of discomfort squeezes my belly. I thought Gavin was harmless. Now... I'm not so sure.

"I thought we agreed, we didn't care about that side of our relationship." I take another careful step back.

He follows me, crowding me. I swallow.

"*You* didn't care about it." His gaze turns flinty. "I remember telling you that once we get married, I expect us to sleep together. And now you've fucked another man."

I wince at the crudeness of his tone but decide it's prudent not to respond. I badly want to flick my gaze at the door, but that would only alert him to my thoughts of escape, so I don't.

"Given we are still engaged, surely, you should give me a chance as well?" he says in a decisive voice, which again, I don't recognize.

"A chance?" I frown. "What do you mean?"

"To fuck you."

I reel back from the vehemence in his words. From the tension that colors the air.

I hurt his ego. And like any person who's insecure, he hates losing face.

My only way out is to lean into the persona of the haughty princess I've perfected over the years. *Don't show how scared you are. You can handle this.*

"Don't speak to me like that," I say in an icy tone.

His features turn ugly. "Ah, that virginal outrage. When you and I both know you're not one anymore."

"You're crossing a line," I say in a low voice.

"Did I say something wrong?" A hurt look joins the anger in his eyes. "Did you think I was stupid enough not to notice when I'm being cuckolded?"

I stay silent, not wanting to compound the situation further with my denial. Running from the truth is what landed me here in the first place. So, I'm done with that.

He curls his fingers into fists at his sides. "I demand to sample the goods I was promised."

Just my luck that my ass of a fiancé turned out to be a narcistic idiot who wants retribution. "How dare you say something so crude?"

He looks me up and down in a way that makes my skin crawl. "The least I can get out of this is sex with my fiancée."

Jesus, what have I gotten myself into? I don't regret giving my virginity to Ryot, not one bit. And I will not let this asshole make me feel guilty for it. I realize now, I was wrong to sacrifice myself on the altar of my father's wishes. *If I'm not happy, how can I serve my country?*

Surely, my father wouldn't want me to be sorrowful. Surely, he'll understand why I can't marry this... this wanker?

I tip up my chin and summon my haughtiest princess look possible.

"I will not demean myself by entertaining this conversation further. My father is waiting for me downstairs. It's best if I tell him that our marriage is off. If you'll excuse me." I brush past him and toward the bed, where I pick up my purse.

I take a step toward the door when he grabs my arm. He swings me around with enough force that I lose my balance and plonk down on the bed.

"What's wrong with you?" I tug on my arm, but he only squeezes it harder. "You're hurting me," My heart slams into my ribcage. "Let me go, you asshole." I kick out my leg, but he evades it with a litheness I would not have attributed to him.

How could I have misjudged him this badly?

I continue to thrash around, and when he leans his weight on me, I begin to panic in earnest.

My heart leaps into my throat. Adrenaline spikes my blood. I open my mouth to scream, when he's pulled off of me.

31

Ryot

I grab Gavin and throw him aside. He lands on his back on the carpet and groans. He begins to rise, but I'm on him. I plant my foot on his neck and hold him in place. The bewildered look on his face is replaced by anger. He grabs at my leg and tries to pry me off. I merely press down more of my weight, holding him in place. Fear creeps into his eyes. "I... I...wasn't doing anything... She—"

"Shut the fuck up. You were trying to force yourself on her." My chest hardens. A pressure begins to build behind my eyes, and I lock my fists at my sides. "I shouldn't let you live." I begin to bear down my weight on him. He begins to choke. His features turn red, but I don't let up.

"Ryot, don't. He's not worth it," she cries. I hear her, but my anger has me in a chokehold. I continue to glare at him and note he's beginning to turn purple.

"Ryot, stop. Please." I hear her footsteps, then she tugs at my arm. "Please Ryot. Let him go."

"He was rude to you. He disrespected you. He refused to take no for an answer. He deserves to be put out of his sorry life."

"I agree. And believe me, I'm pissed off at him too. But choking him is only going to draw attention to the Royal Family, and scandal could overturn everything my family and I have been working for all these years. Not to mention, what could happen to you." Her voice cracks on the last word. "Please, Ryot, let him go."

The urgency in her voice cuts through the noise in my head. I look up into her pale but resolute features. "There are other ways to punish him."

"I'd rather kill him right now, so he pays for what he did." My voice is remote. I'm aware of a cold sensation weighing down my chest and my stomach. It's as if I've slipped into a full body armor made of ice. One which has infused my veins and sunk into my very cells. My mind is fixated on one thing. He made her uncomfortable. He pushed himself on her. He hurt her. The woman who is not only a real-life princess but the queen of my life. *He. Hurt. Her.*

"Ryot," she says softly. "Let him go. Please. I promise. We'll make him pay."

Our gazes meet and hold. The strength in hers, the resilience, the grit I see in her eyes is not a surprise, because of course, she'd be such a peacemaker. This is such an Aura thing to do. It makes me appreciate her sense even more. She may have been brought up in luxury, but the experiences she's been through have developed a strength of character in her I can relate to. I might have come to her help, and I'm glad I did, but even if I hadn't, she'd have found a way to help herself. She's no shrinking violet, my woman. She's her own knight in shining armor.

A small smile curves her lips, and I have a feeling she's read my mind. I jerk my chin, then take my foot off Gavin's neck. He draws in a sharp breath.

As he lays there gasping, the princess and I continue to be locked in this strange meeting of our gazes which communicates without words. The air between us heats. My pulse rate jumps. And when her fiancé jumps to his feet, she closes the distance to me.

I place a proprietorial hand on her hip and pull her close. She melts into me. She wraps her arms around my waist and lifts her chin.

"Stop you can't—" Gavin clutches at his throat, which now carries my shoeprint, and fuck, if that isn't satisfying.

I shut out his voice and lower my head. I press my lips to hers, and when she parts hers, I sweep my tongue in. The kiss goes on and on, and when I slide my palms down to her butt and bring her even closer, she squeaks. But she doesn't pull away. We kiss until our breath's mingle and I'm lightheaded. When we finally break for air, she stares at me with flushed features and swollen lips.

I tuck her into my side and turn to her fiancé. "In case there's any doubt, I took her virginity." I add that, just to see his face fall.

Next to me, I sense a shiver gripping her body. *Is she remembering how it was when we came together? Does she realize it was as big a deal for me that I was her first?* I've never understood why virginity was important for some people... But the fact that there's no one else who's known her this intimately makes me want to hold onto her and never let her go. And then, seeing how her fiancé tried to take advantage of her roused my protective instincts in a way I know I can't shove aside. It's a dangerous line of thinking; one I'm helpless to do anything about.

"You— She—" Gavin shakes his head again, a look of despair on this face. He levels his gaze on her. "Look here, I understand the two of you have been intimate. But I'm willing to overlook it if—"

She fixes him with her best princess stare and tosses her head. "I'm not."

32

Aurelia

"I'm sorry, Papa, I know this means his family will not invest in Verenza. It's going to affect the future of our country." I wring my fingers together. "But I can't marry him. Not when he did what he did—" I swallow and gather my thoughts. "And not when I have feelings for someone else."

I'm conscious of Ryot's gaze boring into me, but I don't dare look at him. If I do I'm going to lose my courage. And I need every bit of it to get through what I have to say. I'm done not being true to myself. From now on, I'm going to say and do the right thing, no matter how difficult.

Spine straight. You're a princess.

I appreciate my mother's advice even more now. *Perhaps that's what her words really mean? To be a true princess, I need to start by staying true to myself.*

"I can't start my married life on a lie. That would be disrespectful for everyone concerned, including you."

Gavin shuffles his feet. He opens his mouth to speak, but Ryot glares at him, and he subsides. Ryot hauled him to Arthur's study where my father was waiting for us. I followed them and narrated what had happened.

So far, my father hasn't said anything. Once I started speaking, his gaze slid away from me. Now, his forehead is furrowed. A look of disappointment crosses his features. *Oh, no.* My heart sinks.

"I truly am sorry, Papa. I know how disappointed you must be." I swallow.

My father leans back in his chair. He and Arthur were seated in front of the fire in Arthur's study, deep in discussion when we arrived.

Arthur walks over to his bar, pours out a finger of whiskey in a tumbler, then returns, handing it over to my father. "Your Highness, perhaps this will help?

My father nods his thanks and takes a sip, then stares into the contents of his glass with a contemplative expression.

Arthur resumes his seat in the armchair twin to my father's.

A log crackles in the fire. The silence stretches. I sense Ryot's perusal from across the room where he's standing next to Gavin. His stance makes it clear that he's watching Gavin. I have a feeling he wishes Gavin would try to escape so he'd have a chance to bury his fist in Gavin's face. To be honest, I'd like that a little too much myself.

Ryot's made sure to put himself between Gavin and me, and while I'm sure Gavin won't try anything, I'm thankful for that.

The longer my father doesn't speak or meet my gaze, the more my stomach ties itself up in knots. My nerves are so stretched, I'm sure they're going to snap. It's clear my father is not happy. *I've disappointed him. I've compromised the future of my country.* My shoulders droop.

"I know this is not what you want to hear." I look away, then back at him. "I know how much you were relying on the money coming in from Gavin and his family. But how can I go through with this marriage when I know he's not the one for me?" I plead.

My father finally looks at me. His jaw is tense. There's also resolution in his gaze, like he's made a decision. My pulse rate goes into overdrive. *If he asks me to marry Gavin anyway and sacrifice my future for the betterment of Verenza, will I do it? Especially knowing I'll never feel the way I did with Ryot with anyone else?* I can't help myself; I glance at Ryot.

He, too, must read my father's expression, for his jaw hardens. He takes a step in my direction, but Arthur shakes his head. Ryot glares at his grandfather. Then, in direct contradiction of his grandfather's order, Ryot walks over to stand next to me.

Arthur's eyes gleam in a pleased expression. How strange.

As for me? I'm glad to have Ryot near me. But also, I don't want to make this entire situation worse. Before I can say anything, my father places his glass on the accent table. There's a look of such anger on his face that I flinch.

Then he glares at Gavin. "Get out."

Relief fills me. The tension gripping me drains away, and I sway. Ryot instantly grips my shoulder and steadies me. He doesn't remove his hand, and I don't pull away either.

Gavin's features turn hard. He looks older than his years. Or perhaps, he looks more like himself. I realize now that the innocent boy persona he likes to wear is an act and this is the real him.

"If I walk out the door so do the millions my father was going to invest in Verenza."

"Out." My father points to the door. "Is that clear enough for you?"

Gavin seems taken aback for a few seconds, then he turns to me with an ugly look on his face. "You are going to pay for this, you whore."

My father draws in a sharp breath. But it's Ryot who closes the distance between them and grabs Gavin by his collar, hauling him up until he's barely touching the floor with the tips of his Italian loafers.

"Apologize. Right now," Ryot growls.

Gavin's features grow purple; he makes a choking sound.

"What was that?" Ryot glares at him.

"S-sorry," Gavin stutters.

Ryot throws him out of the room. Tyler, who's on guard near the door, shuts the door after him.

Ryot walks over to me. "Sorry about that."

I shake my head. "He's at fault, not you." I am so glad my father supported my decision. But below the relief is this gnawing worry. I'm conscious of what this means for Verenza's future too. I walk over to my father, and when he opens his arms, I walk into them.

It's a testament to how upset he is that for the first time in a very long time, he hugs me. I hug him back tightly. When he finally releases me, I step back.

"Thanks, Papa," I murmur.

"I'm glad you're okay." He kisses my forehead. Then, straightens and nods in Ryot's direction. "Thank you for taking care of her."

Ryot, who's been watching the entire scene unfold with a stony face, bends his head in a half-bow. His eyes are hard, and his jaw is set. He seems angry.

Silence descends, broken only by the crackling of the fire. The firelight bounces off the rows of books which line one of the walls of the study.

The wall on the opposite side features a partially shredded painting by a famous British graffiti artist. It used to feature a girl with a balloon, until famously, when it was auctioned, the artist caused the bottom half of the painting to disintegrate. It only increased the value of the artwork exponentially. I had no idea Arthur was the owner.

He strokes his chin from his position in the armchair. He also notices my interest in the painting. His lips quirk. "Imelda, my girl-friend, loves the original street version painted by the artist, all of which have either deteriorated or been removed."

I incline my head. "This is considered the definitive version. I didn't realize the owner agreed to sell it."

His smile widens. "It took some coercion, but —" He raises his shoulder, leaving the rest to my imagination.

Ryot scowls at his grandfather. "We're not here to talk about your art investments."

"Indeed, we're here to talk about the future of Verenza"—Arthur sends a significant look in Ryot's direction—"aren't we, grandson?"

Something passes between him and Ryot. Something which sends a frisson of apprehension down my spine.

There's some kind of silent communication taking place between the two of them, and for some reason, I suspect it might have to do with me.

Ryot's shoulders flex. His biceps stretch the sleeves of his jacket further. He has changed into a freshly-pressed suit, tailored to his dimensions, and black in color. In contrast, the white of his shirt almost glows. His tie is a muted grey. It should look dull, but the flecks of green hidden in the material bring out the green in his eyes.

His eyebrows knit, and his look turns fierce. "You don't get to play with my and the princess' future," he growls.

"Me?" Arthur assumes an innocent expression. One which is so patently false, a giggle bubbles up. Or maybe, that's because I'm nervous, because there's something taking place here, something I can't quite put my finger on.

My father's eyebrows rise, but Arthur doesn't seem surprised. The silence stretches. A log breaks in the fire. It seems to be a signal, for my father rises to his feet.

He walks over to me and takes my hand in his. "I am sorry I put you in the position of needing to marry Gavin. I should not have put the responsibility of saving the future of our country on your shoulders."

"But I wanted to help. I'm the princess of Verenza. It's my duty to do what is needed to help my country. But now"—I wring my fingers—"now, I feel like I'm risking our future with my decision."

My father shakes his head. "The responsibility for our nation's future does not rest solely on your shoulders, Aurelia."

I shake my head. I'm relieved to not have to go through with the arranged marriage to Gavin, but the thought of having undermined the financial security of my country sits like a stone in my stomach. "I could have made a difference, and quickly," I say softly.

My father's expression turns contrite. "It's true, it would have been a silver bullet of sorts to have Gavin's family bring their familial wealth into our country to help with our reserves. That does not mean I will allow my daughter to sacrifice herself."

"Thank you, Papa." It feels good hearing that from him. Yet, that part of me which has always put country before myself wishes things were different. "If only there was more, I could do—" I fold my arms about my waist.

Arthur leans back in his seat, a thoughtful expression on his features. I don't know him well but having grown up exposed to the politics amongst my father's closest advisers, I can spot someone who enjoys manipulating people a mile away. And Arthur counts among them. And based on how Ryot is watching him carefully, I'll bet he feels the same way.

"I should not have put you in a situation where you felt compelled to agree to an arranged marriage." My father looks pained, then seems to get a hold of himself. "Either way, marrying Gavin is out of the question." He turns to Ryot. "Thank you. I owe you for keeping my daughter safe."

Arthur drums his fingers on the armrest. "It would seem Ryot is personally involved when it comes to the princess."

"The fuck do you mean?" Ryot asks in a cold, hard voice.

"Language," Arthur comments, his tone mild. He fixes his gaze on Ryot. "How did you know when to come to the princess' aid?"

Ryot sets his jaw. "I was outside her room."

"You were?" I ask, surprised.

A flicker of movement crosses his eyebrows. "I was on guard."

"You were?" I am repeating myself. But I thought he was pissed off with me. I thought, after the stunt I pulled, he'd never want to see me again. But he walked to my room to check in on me? I rub at my temple. "I…uh, I didn't expect that."

"No matter our differences, you're my principal. I wanted to make sure you were okay." His expression turns even more remote. "Your safety is my primary concern."

I flick a glance in the direction of the two older men to find them watching both of us with curiosity.

"Of course." I swallow. He was doing his duty. Ryot is too much of a professional. There's too much of the Marine in him to leave anything half done. He felt responsible for my safety because he took on the function of my bodyguard. That's the only reason he came to my room. "I'm glad you were there. You didn't come a moment too soon."

"You never should have gotten engaged to that tosser. He's beneath you."

I agree. I don't think I was wrong in agreeing to marry him. It was the only way I knew to help my country. But meeting Ryot changed everything. Well, I got my unvoiced wish. The marriage is off. And my country is no better off. I've just put the future of my people at risk.

Panic wells up. I force myself to draw a few deep breaths, try to force myself to calm down.

"You, okay?" Ryot asks in a low voice.

I manage a nod.

"You sure?"

I take another few deep breaths. Then, when I feel more in control, I meet his gaze. "Yes."

He studies my face and the expression on his gentles. "Whatever it is, we'll get through this. I promise."

I stare. *When did the two of us become we?* Not going to lie, it feels amazing to have Ryot in my corner. If only, I could keep him in my life forever. *Wishful thinking, but hey, a girl can hope, right?*

I'm conscious of the two older men watching us, but it doesn't stop me from holding Ryot's gaze. There's lingering anger, but it's mixed with something indecipherable. Something I can only classify as longing? And something more...calculating. Like he's weighing options and has come to a decision. It makes me wonder what he's thinking. Before I can ask, there's a knock on the door.

Tyler opens it, exchanges words with someone, then accepts something from the newcomer. It looks like a piece of paper in a transparent bag.

I know then, it's another anonymous note. My pulse begins to race. Sweat beads my palms.

"It's from the same source who sent the last note, I assume?" I'm proud when my voice doesn't quiver.

Tyler reads it, his jaw firms. He walks over to Ryot and passes it to him. The look on Ryot's face has the hair on my arms rising. His features turn to granite. His left eyelid twitches. Anger pours off of him. Whatever he's read in the note isn't good. And the fact that he's pissed off on my behalf is reassuring and hot. And turns me on. My stomach flutters. That familiar warmth encroaches in the space between my legs. I'm careful not to squeeze my thighs together; not when we have an audience. He nods at Tyler, who turns to me.

"One of the guards chased away a man trying to break in."

My heart rate kicks up. "Oh." I swallow. "Was he... Do you think he's my—"

"We don't know if it's the same person who wrote the note and left it in your hotel room, or if it's tied to the shooting, or if it's someone else who tried to break through the security here." Tyler's tone is gentle. "They did, however, find this note, which we assume the intruder dropped before he escaped."

I hold out my hand. "May I see it?"

33

Ryot

"I'm going to hold you hostage and torture you...BITCH. I'm going to make sure you regret the day you were born."

Those are the words in the letter. And I didn't want her to be exposed to them. But I will not deny her agency in her own safety. I will not patronize her. I know from experience, it's best to be open with the principal in matters such as this. Doesn't mean I don't want to protect her from the venom in the words of that note.

I hand the note to her. She reads it and pales. I take the note back from her, then lead her to the couch and guide her to sit.

I accept the glass of water Tyler poured for her, exchanging it for the note, and hand it to her before sitting beside her. Tyler brings the note to the king.

Once she's drained the glass, I take it from her and place it on the coffee table. "Better?" Not caring that my grandfather and her father are watching us with avid curiosity, I take her hand between both of mine and rub her much colder palm.

212 L. STEELE

She turns to me. I'm pleased to see that, while she's still pale, her gaze is clear. *She's a fighter, my woman.* I can't stop myself from thinking of her in those terms. Not when every part of me is coiled with anger and ready to go to battle for her. Not when I want to track down the person who sent her the note and tear them limb from limb.

"The tone of the note; it feels personal." Her expression clouds. "Or is that my imagination?"

I exchange a look with Tyler, then lower my gaze to her. "It does feel vindictive. But I'd rather not jump to any conclusions until my team has analyzed it further. We've also been running additional checks on everyone in your inner circle. That now includes Gavin."

She pales further, then nods. "You're right to do that, of course." Her voice slips on the last word, so I know the note has shaken her more than she's letting on.

I glance at Tyler, and without having to say anything, I'm pleased when he nods. "I'm heading out to confer with the team and find out what we can about this intruder." He slips out the door.

"We'll track down whoever is behind this. I promise you that."

She twines her fingers between mine.

I sense the king stiffen in surprise. When I look at Arthur, he has that familiar crafty look on his face, the one I've spied right before he comes up with one of his schemes. I glower at him.

He chuckles. To my relief, he doesn't say anything. But he seems extremely chuffed with himself. A prickle of distrust cascades through my veins. I shove it aside and focus my attention on the princess.

"We'll make sure they never get to you. My team and I are going to track them down and throw them behind bars, where they'll never harm a single hair on your head. This, I promise."

She nods, then takes a deep breath, and when she looks up at me, her gaze is resolute. "I know you will."

Our eyes connect, and once again, I feel that pull toward her. That feeling of something inevitable that binds us together. That sensation that we fit.

Aura's hand trembles. I squeeze her fingers, trying to communicate without words that she should not worry about anything. She shakes her head. "Everything is going wrong. My marriage would have brought much needed money into the country. But that's not going to happen now."

Anger squeezes my guts. I take in the disappointment in the downward slope of her shoulders, in how her lips turn down, and I'm so pissed off. She should not be bartering her future in this way. She should not be holding herself hostage for the sake of her people. And yet... Isn't that what I did again and again? I put my life on the line for the safety of my fellow citizens. I can't blame her for doing the same. She's the princess of her country, after all.

But she's also mine. *Mine. Mine. Mine.* I reel back as the realization sinks in. My insides are in turmoil. My guts churn. She's mine, and I almost lost her. *Only you never really had her, did you?*

If her bastard of a fiancé hadn't turned out to be such a heel, it's likely she'd have gone through with the wedding and I... I would have realized too late that I hadn't tried my best to stop it. I never would've forgiven myself for not stepping in and making her mine. And why? Because I was blinded by pride. I was attracted to her, and she gave me her virginity, and it meant something to me. But the fact that she didn't mention she was engaged bruised my ego. I was so overwhelmed by the blow to my self-esteem, I was ready to let her walk away from me. I'd have lost her, and by the time I realized I should have found a way to make her break her engagement and, instead, marry me— *Whoa, hold on. Am I really thinking this?*

Why am I not running away screaming from that thought? Why don't I find the prospect of being hitched again, and to her, alarming? Why is the idea of using the opportunity to make her my wife so appealing?

More to the point, am I going to do something about this opportunity I've been offered? Am I going to seize the moment and use every resource I have to tie her to me? Am I going to use this moment to acknowledge that, since I first saw her, I haven't gotten her out of my mind? That I need her in my life? That her engagement broke up for a reason? That I'm the man she must marry? That I'm the only one who has the resources to help her?

And if I don't do so? If I don't step up now and make a claim for her? Could I live with myself? Would I forgive myself for having the chance and squandering it? No. That cannot happen. There's a reason I've been afforded this window, and I cannot let it go.

She winces, and I realize I'm squeezing her hand.

"Sorry." I loosen my hold enough to relieve the pressure but don't let go of her. "I might have a solution to your problems," I murmur.

My phone vibrates. I pull it from my pocket, and there's a message from my brother.

> Tyler: One of the team spotted the car the suspect got away in. The person is masked but we managed to get a few images from our security cameras. Quentin's on the case. He's reached out to his contacts in the police to issue an APB. We'll track him down.

I slip the phone into my pocket, then nod in the direction of Arthur and her father. "If you don't mind, could the two of you give me a moment to speak to the princess in private, please?"

I stare at Arthur until my grandfather deciphers my silent message. He jumps up. He wears such a pleased expression, I wonder if he didn't set up events to unfold so I'd be led to make this exact decision.

Not even Arthur could have predicted how her fiancé would act, so I highly doubt it.

When the door shuts behind them, Aura turns to me. "What is it you wanted to talk to me about?"

I choose my words carefully. "We Davenports are only five times removed from the Royal Family of England. In fact, our family fortune outshines that of the King of England."

"Okay?" Her forehead creases.

"It's also no secret that we have business interests in every continent, other than Antarctica."

She looks at me carefully. "You're saying that—"

"My brothers, my uncles, and I are equal heirs to the Davenport fortune. In fact, I have a seat on the board of the Davenport Group. And we're always looking for new countries to invest in," I say slowly.

She stays silent, then a flash of understanding lights up her eyes. She pulls her hand from mine, and I let it go.

I need her to understand what I'm going to propose. I need her to realize I'm not manipulating her. Well, not completely.

Apparently, my grandfather has taught me well. He's going to be proud of what I'm going to propose. But I'm not doing this for him.

I'm doing this for her. And yes, also for myself. If I didn't use this chance to get what I want — which is her — I'd be a fool.

This is good; this is right, I can fix this for her; I know what to do. I can have her and make her mine.

She lowers her chin. "Are you saying you'll invest in Verenza?"

"I'm saying, I'm on the board of directors, and my recommendation to invest a billion dollars a year over the next five years in your country will be taken seriously." And when Arthur, no doubt, adds his voice to mine, the rest of the board will agree.

She rubs at her temple. "That's…much more than what Gavin's family would have done. And their investment timeline was in months, not years."

"Don't speak that asshole's name in front of me," I growl.

She nods, then locks her fingers together. "What you're offering will mean a great deal to my country."

I stay silent, allowing her to process my suggestion.

Then the crease in her forehead deepens. "I assume you want something in return?"

I rise to my feet and begin to pace. "That latest note you received indicates that whoever is behind the threats is escalating. I'm concerned about it. To ensure your safety I need to be by your side. And there's only one way I can do so without any questions being raised about my presence." When I face her again, she's looking at me with a strange look in her eyes.

"I... I'm trying to follow what you're saying, but"—she laughs nervously—"I'm afraid my brain's not able to keep pace with the conclusions my mind is drawing."

I walk over to her, and when I drop down to one knee in front of her, her eyes widen. I take her hand in mind again and look into her eyes. "Marry me."

34

Aura

"What?" My jaw drops. "You want me to marry you?" I whisper.

He nods.

There's no denying the intensity in his eyes. He's not joking. He's serious about this proposition.

My heart begins to race. My pulse flutters like the wings of a hummingbird.

First, he offers to invest the kind of money which will help my father pay off the country's debts and invest it in the future of the citizens. But to marry him in return? *Holy shit.*

I was sure I was headed for a marriage of convenience where I'd hate my spouse. But for Ryot to be my husband? My head spins.

I've been attracted to him from the moment I met him. He's the only man I've ever wanted. To be his wife, to share my life with him, to share his bed... It feels too good to be true.

I pull away from him, and instantly miss his touch. I ignore that and search his eyes. "Why would you do this? What's in this for you?"

Say it's because you love me. Say you proposed to me because you want me to be your wife in every sense of the word, because you want me. You need me. You can't live without me. Please.

Something flickers in his eyes. Surprise? Confusion? It's banked at once. He rises to his feet and sits next to me. "Would there need to be something in it for me? Could I not do this because I want to?"

But why *do you want to? Couldn't you just say it's because you love me? No...because he doesn't love me.* My heart sinks. My stomach heaves. I fold my arms about my waist, as if that's going to help me contain my disappointment. "Given how you've blown hot and cold with me. Given how you've insisted on maintaining a professional line between us, I'm not sure what to make of this change of heart."

Also, it's clear you're not over your wife's death. Not that I'm going to say that out aloud.

"Isn't it enough that I care for you? And I can help you?" he asks slowly.

Yes, he cares for me, but he doesn't *love* me. Likely, what he feels for his dead wife is holding him back from committing completely. And I'm *not* going to be second in his affections. I'm *not* going to compete with a ghost for his attention.

When I stay silent, he stares at me intently, as if trying to read my thoughts. "What if I told you that this is a good business opportunity for the Davenports? With Verenza's economy the way it is, there are bargains to be had. I have no doubt, The Davenport Group will more than recoup what we invest in your country. Besides, it'll get Arthur off my back." He half smiles. "When he finds out that you and I are getting married, he'll throw his weight behind my proposal to get The Davenport Group to invest in Verenza."

If I needed further proof that he's not doing this because he's fallen for me, here it is. He doesn't care for me the way I do for him.

My head hurts trying to make sense of everything. "You've made it clear thus far that there's no future for us. And now, you spring the prospect of my marrying you. It feels...too sudden."

Exasperation flits across his features, then his expression shuts down. The hard planes of his face don't allow me to read whatever he's thinking. "I'm offering you a chance to save your country from the brink of financial disaster."

"In return for marrying you?"

He nods slowly.

This *is* Ryot I'd be marrying. The man of my dreams. Only it'll be another marriage of convenience. This time, I'm not repulsed by the man I'm going to marry, but in some ways, it feels worse because I'm in love with him, and he doesn't reciprocate the sentiment.

How can I have everything and yet, nothing? My spirits droop. "And during the time we're married, would we have separate bedrooms, or—"

He shakes his head. "Afraid not, Princess. If we maintained separate lives my grandfather would never buy into our marriage." He leans back. "More importantly, I can't protect you if I'm in a different room. The intruder got to your bedroom in the hotel, remember?"

I look away. "So, no separate bedrooms?" I curl my shoulders inwards, trying to understand what he's suggesting. "Does that mean—"

"That we share a bed? Yes," he says in a firm voice.

A frisson of heat curls in my lower belly. My thighs clench. Nope, I'm not averse to that part of the bargain at all. "And does that include—"

"Yes."

I whip my head in his direction to find he's serious. "You're saying yes to—"

"Sex." He nods. "The chemistry between us is off the charts. I'd be a fool to think we could keep this platonic. Especially after I've already had you."

"We had each other," I point out.

"Indeed." His lips twitch. "And since you're not averse to my particular brand of domination, it should make things very interesting."

Anticipation pinches my veins. *Jesus, how can we be having this conversation in such a polite fashion when my skin feels like it's on fire?*

"So, what do you think?" He drums his fingers on his massive thigh.

What do I think about marrying the man of my dreams, when his proposal is not based on love? I want to laugh and cry at the same time. I want to demand that he not hide from his true feelings from me. I know how it felt to have him look into my eyes as he made love to me. And it *was* making love. *It was.* If only he'd acknowledge it, I'd be the happiest woman in the world. But things are never that easy, are they?

Spine straight. You're a princess.

Now, more than ever, I need to follow my mother's advice. So, I fold my hands in my lap and survey him with a measured gaze. "You're asking me to marry you, but you're still a stranger in many ways."

His jaw tics. I'm sure he's going to point out that I thought I knew Gavin and look how that turned out. But he doesn't push his advantage. Instead, he leans back. "What do you want to know about me?"

This isn't the way I envisaged finding out more about Ryot, but I'll take it. "Your wife; tell me about her."

He seems taken aback, then resigned. He rises to his feet, heads to the bar, and pours himself a shot of whiskey. Guess he's no longer on duty? Or perhaps, he needs the hard liquor to be able to talk about her. That sinking sensation in the pit of my stomach intensifies.

"Would you like something to drink?" he asks over his shoulder.

"The same." I nod.

He pours a finger of the amber liquid into another tumbler, then walks over to hand it to me.

He throws back the liquid in his own, then squares his shoulders. "What do you want to know?"

"Everything. How you met. How she...died. Whatever you're comfortable sharing with me, that is."

35

Ryot

Touché, Princess. I don't blame her for using this opportunity to find out the parts I would not have willingly shared with her otherwise.

I turn away, needing to retreat into that part of myself deep inside where I can shield myself from the hurt in recounting what happened.

"You already know that Jane was pregnant when her platoon was taken out."

She nods, then sets her glass aside without touching the drink.

I draw in a breath, then steel myself. Best to rip off the Band-Aid and lay it all out there; there's no easy way to say it.

"The child wasn't mine. It couldn't have been because we hadn't slept together in over a year. We'd been having trouble with our marriage."

"What?" She presses her knuckles into her mouth. "The child was—"

"Likely, the father was her platoon captain. It emerged later that they'd been having an affair."

She pales. "I'm so sorry. You must have felt so betrayed by her. Add to that, I didn't tell you about my engagement. That must have made you feel duped all over again."

I roll my shoulders. She's right. And yet, hearing the anguish in her voice, that tightness in my chest which I've been carrying around since that tosser of her now ex-fiancé turned up, eases.

"It's true, I was pissed off, but now that I'm thinking about it calmly, I realize you were under no obligation to tell me about your engagement. Not when I'd made it clear I couldn't have a relationship of any kind with you. It's not like we'd made any promises to each other before we slept together."

Unfortunately, it's not as easy to forget what Jane did to me. Time, they say, heals, but my guilt around Jane's death continues to eat away at me.

As if she's read my mind, she rises to her feet and walks over to stand next to me. "What happened with Jane wasn't your fault. You can't hold yourself responsible for her death, Ryot."

"If only that were true." I move away because being that close to her, smelling her scent, and feeling the heat of her body is doing crazy things to my libido, clouding my mind, and turning my brain to mush. And I need my wits about me to complete this sorry story of my past. "You don't know what you're saying." I begin to pace.

"Then, explain it to me," she says in a soft voice.

I sense the empathy in her tone, and that makes me angry. I don't deserve her understanding. Not when I know I'm to blame for what happened. "When we first met, I thought the chemistry between Jane and me was explosive."

She winces, visibly enough that I notice.

"I know, now, it's nothing compared to this attraction between you and me," I murmur.

She shakes her head. "This is not about me. Please continue."

I blow out a breath. *It is about her. It's very much about her.* But I don't say that aloud. "In retrospect, I put it down to the fact that we met on tour. Fighting for a cause, confronting your enemies, and going to sleep not knowing if you'll live to see another day, can have an unusual effect on people."

She stays quiet, letting me speak.

"When we returned from the first mission we served on together, both of us thought we'd found someone we might want to spend our life with. We thought we had so much in common. Especially our responsibility to the Marines and to our country. We were married within three months of meeting."

"That *is* quick."

Not as quickly as us discussing getting hitched within weeks of meeting, but I hold that comment back too. "We got married at City Hall between deployments, and it was all fine. Until we returned and set up house and found we couldn't get along." I laugh. "Both of us signed up on the next tour. We ended up meeting again while in service, this time on a peace-keeping tour in Cyprus. The sparks flew again. We thought we were over the worst. But when we returned and tried to function as a couple without the stress of war, it turned out, we weren't compatible."

Understanding flits across her features. "It only worked when your relationship was under the kind of pressure that life and death situations imposed on it?"

"Seemed like it." I hesitate.

She regards me closely. "There's more, isn't there?"

Yep, my woman's smart. She read between my words and sensed I'm not telling her everything. I walk over to the bar, pour myself another finger of whiskey, and take a healthy swig.

"Did it have to do with…your, uh… Need to be in control?" She approaches me and comes to a stop next to me.

I laugh, the sound bitter. "If by that you mean, my need to be dominant, then yes."

She flushes a little. I glance at her face to find her pupils dilated. And when she squeezes her thighs together, I realize she welcomes the prospect. The fact that she enjoyed being spanked and orgasmed so quickly is also a giveaway. But that we're able to talk about it openly is an unexpected bonus.

I toss back the whiskey in my tumbler and place it on the

counter. "Jane wasn't into the power exchange part of our relationship. She said she took enough orders at work and didn't want to do that at home, too." I'd known it and disregarded it.

I tried to fit myself into a box for her and look how that had turned out. It's one more reason I need to be upfront with Aura about it. Best to not go into this relationship—even if I am presenting it as one of convenience—without being open about my expectations.

"Right," she says in a low voice.

I return to stand in front of her. "I take it you don't feel that way?" Now seems the right time to ask about it, given we opened the doors to this conversation.

She shakes her head.

A tendril of hair is stuck to her cheek, and I reach down and tuck it behind her ear. An electric current runs up my arm at the contact. A corresponding shiver grips her.

"It's been more than two years since her platoon was taken out. And when I received her personal effects, there was a picture of a sonogram, and correspondence with her gynecologist that showed that she was pregnant."

"I'm so sorry." This time, when she reaches for my hand, I don't shake it off. She twines her fingers with mine.

"The worst thing is, I didn't feel anything when I got the news. No grief. No regret. Just relief that we wouldn't have to pretend to be married when I returned from my mission." I crack my neck, knowing I've never made myself this vulnerable before to anyone else.

"Before she left on that last mission, we had a big fight. One which ended with her signing up for that tour, despite the fact that she'd just gotten home. It was one of the few times we happened to be home at the same time. And what a disaster that was."

I squeeze the bridge of my nose.

"You can argue, she might have signed up for that operation anyway, but the fact is, our argument tipped her over. It also caused me to pull out of my next mission 'cause I didn't want to risk running into her while on duty."

I half laugh.

"So, I lived, and she didn't. And logically, it doesn't mean I'm responsible for what happened, but tell that to my sense of fair play."

"It's understandable." She leans toward me. Her scent intensifies —richer, sweeter, deeper—and it goes to my head.

"You can see why I wasn't rushing to get married again." I roll my shoulders. "That is, until I met you and wanted to make you mine."

She bites the inside of her cheek, as if my being open with her about my feelings makes her uncomfortable. Her next words confirm it to me, "But this would be a marriage of convenience. It means you don't need to have feelings involved." She peers at me from under her eyelashes.

"Maybe I don't *need* to, but I *do* have feelings for you," I point out.

She releases my hand. Her brow furrows, a crease forming at the bridge of her nose.

Apparently, she doesn't believe me. I firm my lips.

Seems my insistence on not crossing the professional line between us has left her unable to understand how much I want her.

There have been too many instances these past few weeks when I thought I'd lost her. I can't let that happen again. Once we're married, I'll win her over. I'll use my charisma—and sexual prowess —to ensure she's addicted to me. I'll ensure she'll never want to leave.

All I have to do is get her to say yes.

"It's a good deal, Princess." I infuse confidence into my voice. "You get to bail your country out of the problems it's mired in. I satisfy my grandfather's wish to see me married off and have the satisfaction of bringing the despots who're after you to heel. Not to mention"—I allow myself a small smile—"the sex would be a bonus for both of us. It's a win-win situation, all around. So, what do you say?"

36

Aurelia

The breath whooshes out of me. I can hear the blood banging against my temples. Nervousness grips me. *Am I really going to do this? Agree to marry him?*

This way, I get to be with him. That's better than nothing, isn't it? And perhaps, he might even come to realize that he *does* love me? He may have not said it aloud, but the way he looked into my eyes when we made love—*and it was making love*—tells me he does.

He confided in me about his past, which is huge. He's also been open enough about his expectations when it comes to sex. That he's dominant is not a surprise. If anything, it increases my anticipation about that part of our relationship. This is the most optimal outcome possible. *Now, all I have to do is make him realize that he does love me.* My throat burns as I fight back my feelings.

"Hey, you okay?" He sits down next to me on the couch.

"It's okay if you need to cry." He folds his arm about my shoulders. "Not that I can stand to see your tears. But if it helps relieve some of the pressure you've been under, then by all means, let 'em flow. Lean on me."

The gentleness in his tone brings a lump to my throat. A pressure knocks at the backs of my eyes.

I slip my arm about his waist and turn my face into his shoulder. And it feels so good. So right. The strength in his body bleeds into mine. My blood heats. The solidness of his chest invites me to sink into him. I draw a breath into my lungs, aware I'm sniffing him and unable to stop myself. He feels so reassuring. So unshakeable. It feeds my own confidence. There's a whisper of a touch on my head, and I realize he's pressed his lips to my hair. My heart melts in my chest. My bones feel like they're turning to mush.

I burrow further into him, enjoying the closeness, feeling his heartbeat echo mine. He wraps his other arm around me, his grasp tightens, and I become aware of how I'm plastered to him. How my breasts are flattened against his chest. How his muscles are rigid, and his biceps feel like they're made of granite. He seems to have turned to stone. And when I lower my hand to his crotch, I gasp. The thick column tenting the fabric is hot and vital, and bigger than I remember. I'm so turned on, I'm panting. My body feels like it's about to self-combust.

"What are you doing?" he rumbles.

"We should seal the deal, don't you think?"

His body stills. Except for the rise and fall of his chest, he's completely still. "Does this mean you'll marry me?" His voice is a deep, dark vibration in his chest that curls around my nipples and pinches my nerve-endings, making my clit throb.

"Yes," I whisper.

Instantly, he releases me, only to wrap my hair around his hand and tug. I gasp. My head falls back. Pinpricks of pain radiate out from my scalp and arrow to my pussy. My clit throbs; my pussy lips seem to engorge. I'm held immobile by his grip, my throat bared to him in a gesture of submission.

"Say it aloud so I can hear you properly," he orders. The command in his voice sends a delicious spiral of want to my core.

"Yes." I tip up my chin. "Yes, I'll marry you."

"Good girl," he rumbles.

A whimper escapes me. And when he bends and drags his nose up the column of my neck, I shudder.

"Let's get one thing clear; you don't give the orders. Understand?"

I nod.

"Out there, you might be the Princess of Verenza, but when it's just the two of us, I'm your Master."

The confidence in his voice is an aphrodisiac that turns my pussy into a melting mess.

"You're mine to do with as I want. Mine to punish if you disobey. Mine to reward when I decide you've earned it. Understand?"

The dominance in his words lights a million fires in my body. I'm burning up. My breath coming in short quick pants.

"Say it." He yanks on my hair.

I yelp, more in surprise than in pain. "Yesss," I hiss. "Yes."

In response, he bites down on the side of my throat. It's a gesture of ownership. And possession. And control. And so hot.

"Anyone could walk in on us, but I know the thought of that is only going to add to your arousal," he growls.

A shiver ripples up my body. The flames in my belly seem to leap up to my chest. He must sense how turned on I am for he leans back and stares into my features. "You're my lusty little plaything aren't you, Empress?'

I nod. Him calling me his plaything should definitely not ramp up the need in my body, either.

He kisses the very place on my skin where he bit me, and a low moan bleeds from my lips.

He places his other hand over where mine is wrapped around his length through the crotch of his pants. And when he squeezes down, his shaft seems to thicken and fill my palm. He swipes my palm over the steel pillar, and my nipples tighten. My thighs quiver. He drags his nose up the exposed column of my throat, and I shudder. My chest rises and falls. I squirm around, trying to get closer, and he laughs.

The sound vibrates through his chest and sinks into my blood. It ripples across my skin and turns my knees into jelly.

He continues to drag my hand over his swollen shaft and pins me in place with the hold on my hair. The fact that he's able to control my movements with such little effort ratchets up my need. I try to turn my head to look at him, but he clicks his tongue. "Patience."

I huff.

It draws another chuckle from him. The gravelly, very masculine sound slides down my spine and settles between my legs. Everything he does seems designed to increase my arousal to fever pitch. I wriggle in place, trying to inch closer, but his hold on my hair tightens. Pinpricks of fire skitter across my scalp, and that turns me on even more. My toes curl, and my clit throbs. I swear, I'm going to come just from the anticipation.

"Oh no, you don't," he whispers into my ear, as if he can read my mind. Then, he curls his tongue around the shell of my ear.

I groan. "Oh god."

"He has nothing to do with it." Ryot licks his tongue into my ear, and the pleasure is so intense, my eyes roll back in my head. Who knew these places of my body would be so erogenous? Under my hand, his length grows even bigger. My mouth begins to water. He feels so thick. So full.

The need within digs its claws into me and twists. "I want you inside of me," I whimper.

"Not yet." He grabs a cushion from the couch and drops it on the floor between his feet. Then, with his hold on my hair, he urges me onto it on my knees. He holds my hair back from my face with one hand and nods at his groin. "Show me how much you want it."

I scowl up at him. *Seriously?*

"Or are you too inexperienced to give a blowjob?"

I scoff.

He laughs.

That sounds like a challenge. I'll bet he knows I'll never shy away from one. I reach over and lower the zipper of his pants.

He lifts his hips enough for me pull down his trousers and his boxers. His cock springs free. Fully erect, he's thicker and longer than I recall. As I stare at him, he seems to grow even bigger.

A vein runs up the underside, and the head is almost purple, with a drop of precum clinging to it. I bend my head and lick it up. A shudder grips him. *Hmm. That's interesting.* I drag my tongue down the throbbing length and up again. This time, a groan is torn from him. I look up to find he's watching me with green eyes that have turned almost golden with lust. His lips are parted, his eyelids hooded. Holding his gaze, I close my mouth around him.

"Fuck," he swears. The way his hips surge forward, I know I have him. He's so big, I have to open my mouth really wide to take him inside. His hold on my hair tightens another fraction, enough for my scalp to tingle and for goosebumps to pop on my forearms. He spreads his legs wider, and I lean in. I take him further inside my mouth, and his gaze narrows. Silver sparks dot those greenish-gold eyes of his. He's so turned on, the lust radiating from him in waves lassoes around me, and I still. For a few seconds, we watch each other, then he guides me forward. His touch is firm, no hesitation whatsoever, and when his dick slips down my tongue and hits the back of my throat, I choke. Spit drips down my chin, and tears squeeze out from the corners of my eye.

"Breathe through your nose," he orders.

I draw in a breath, and the burning sensation in my throat begins to fade. He pulls on my hair, easing my head back until his cock slips out to balance on my lips.

"You okay?" He scans my features.

I nod, grateful for his concern. He wants to be in charge, but not at the cost of my comfort. Which is why he also made sure to cushion my knees. The combination of caring and dominance is exhilarating. It's reassuring he's in charge. It's arousing that he's monitoring my response and adjusting his demands accordingly. To be at the cynosure of his attention is exhilarating.

He continues to watch me. He must see something which reassures him, for he nods. He eases me forward, and this time, when his dick slips down my throat, I swallow.

"You're so tight, baby." His shoulders swell. He manipulates me with his hold on my hair and begins to fuck my mouth. Each time he moves me forward, his shaft dips down my throat, and he eases me back until he's balanced on the tip of my tongue. He watches my mouth as if fascinated by how his cock disappears inside of it. "You're gorgeous," he says through gritted teeth.

Considering the strings of spit dripping from the corners of my mouth, I'm not so sure, but I'm also not in a position to comment, considering my mouth is full of his cock. His movements increase, and I hold onto his thighs for support. He's using me for his pleasure. He's reduced me to a hole that he's decided to use at his will, and it should make me feel cheap. It should make me feel like I'm nothing more than a fuck toy—and the fact that I *do* feel that way is also strangely arousing.

My pussy is dripping, my panties soaked, and my nipples are so hard they hurt. Every part of me is focused on where we're connected. The dark taste of him, the spicy scent of him mixed with the musky scent of his arousal, the very male thickness of him filling my mouth and pressing against the walls of my throat. My stomach trembles; my thighs have turned into cords of yearning. The hollow between my legs gapes.

I'm so empty, and the contrast with the fullness of him in my mouth drives me a little crazy. Frustration grips me. I dig my fingernails into his thighs. But his muscles are like rock, and they hardly make a dent. Still, he must notice, for he raises his gaze to mine. His movements speed up. He stuffs his dick into my mouth over and over. And oh god, I can feel the tug of my climax as it squeezes out from my center and up my spine. That's when he pulls out completely.

37

Ryot

I pull out a handkerchief from my pocket and begin to clean her chin and around her swollen lips. The fact that it's a result of how she took me down her throat makes my cock weep. I'm so hard, it's painful. My balls feel like they weigh a ton. I'm going to have to jerk off soon if I want to get my head back in the game.

"You didn't come…" Her forehead furrows. "Did I do something wrong?"

I pinch her chin, so she has no choice but to meet my eyes. "You were perfect."

A flush stains her cheekbones. "I was?"

I allow a small smile to curve my lips. "You're a good girl who sucked me off so well."

The pulse dances at her collarbone. "But I'm so —"

"Horny?"

She nods.

"Good."

Her mouth falls open. "Good?" Her voice is strangled. Her blue eyes are round and filled with such shock, I chuckle.

Then, because it's too tempting, I lower my head and press my mouth to hers. Instantly, she melts into me. I can taste myself on her lips, and fuck, if that doesn't make me almost come. I pull back hastily and reach down, tugging up my boxers and pants, and zipping myself up.

She must finally realize that I meant what I said, for her lips tighten. "You're doing this on purpose."

I nod.

"You don't care that I'm so aroused that I can hardly think straight."

"I do care. A lot. In fact, that was the entire point of this exercise."

"What?" Her cheeks turn crimson. "Y-y-you... How could you?"

"It's called edging, baby. I want to build up your need over and over again, and when I finally let you come, it's going to feel so good." I rise to my feet and help her up, and when she stumbles, I hold her shoulders until she regains her balance. "I promise, this will heighten the enjoyment."

"It doesn't feel very good," she gripes.

"No pleasure without pain, baby." I kiss her hard, then set her back from me.

"You're doing this to show me who's in charge?"

"Maybe."

"You want to teach me to obey you, is that it? You want to show you have power in this situation? That you...you...call the shots."

I pretend to think for a moment, then nod. "Yes, and yes. All of the above."

She snaps her mouth shut. "You're an asshole."

I laugh. "Yep."

"And...and...a brute."

I half bow.

"I can't believe you're leaving me like this," she snaps.

"Trust me, I feel the same." I take her hand and press it to my groin, where the evidence of my arousal tents my pants.

"Oh." The red on her cheeks changes to a shade of pink that's so damn delectable, it makes me want to throw her down and have her right here, but that's not going to help with building the anticipation for her. "This is hard on me, too, as you can see."

She rolls her eyes. "If you expect me to commend you on your pun, prepare to be disappointed."

I grin, then release my hold on her hand and tuck strands of hair behind her ear. "How about this? I promise you, this is to heighten your gratification."

"Whatever." She tosses her head. "Maybe I'll get myself off."

"Oh no, you won't. You won't come without my permission." I bend my knees and peer into her eyes. "Your orgasms are mine, Empress. Only mine."

Her breathing roughens. Her pupils dilate, and I can feel just how aroused she is by my command.

"You're bossy." She tips up her chin. "And that shouldn't turn me on, but it does."

"And I fucking love how spirited you are, you know that?"

Her features soften. "You make me feel like I don't have to apologize for who I am."

The wistfulness I see in her expression gives me pause, "Why would you do that?"

Her smile is tinged with sadness. "I grew up with a stream of nannies trying to tell me how I should dress and behave like a proper lady. After all, I'm the Princess. I'm the example for all little girls to look up to. I'm the epitome of their dreams. I'm Disney royalty, come to life."

"Only, that made you feel restricted?" I hazard a guess.

"I was upset that, while I had to take lessons in etiquette, my brothers didn't have to do the same." She smooths down the fabric of her dress. "Viktor was off studying for his MBA at Harvard while Bran took a gap year."

She locks her fingers in her lap.

"To be fair, Viktor tried to reason with my father and his advisers. He tried to point out that the image of the docile princess dressed in pink and glitter was outdated. He wanted me to have the option of working in my father's administration. My father was open to it, but his team of advisers felt it would project the wrong signal to the 'Royal marriage market.'" She makes air-quotes.

When she sees the question on my face she clarifies, "The Royal families in Europe tend to look to each other to find a match. We belong to different countries, but our goals and values are often the same." She shuffles her feet. "It's not that I'm complaining... Well, not too much, that is. And it's not that I was interested in studying further, but it would have been nice to have the option."

"And if you'd had a choice, what would you have done?"

"An MFA in writing. Or perhaps, a course in entrepreneurship." She half laughs. "I'm not saying it would have come in useful. I realized, no matter how much I fought the inevitable, I couldn't escape the fact I was born into the Royal Family of Verenza. I also learned about the financial troubles my country was facing. I wanted to help, and it seemed inevitable that a good match would bring money into the country, and I would be fulfilling my duty."

"I admire your sense of responsibility." I cup her cheek.

She seems taken aback by my praise. "It was never a choice to shirk it. Not when I could single-handedly make such a difference to my people. It was the next best thing to being the head of the state."

"And now, you're getting married to help your father and your people." I scan her features. "How do you feel about that?"

She purses her lips. "It could have been worse. I could have had no choice but to marry Gavin."

"Don't make the mistake of stroking my ego," I say wryly.

"It's already big enough." She looks at me from under her eyelashes.

I can't stop myself from smirking. "And with good reason,"

She lets out an exaggerated sigh, but her eyes spark with humor.

"Feeling better?"

She tilts her head. "Was that to distract me from how turned on I am?"

"Is it succeeding?"

She hesitates. "Not...really."

"Good." I chuckle.

She slaps at my chest. "Stop it."

I place my hand over hers. "Never."

Our gazes hold. The chemistry between us, which always simmers under the surface, sparks. The air in the room heats. She sways toward me. I pinch her chin and lean in for a kiss when there's a knock on the door.

"Ryot?" Tyler's voice reaches me. "Arthur and the king are here."

I'm tempted to tell him, and them, to fuck off. But given this is Arthur's study, that might be tricky.

I have no doubt, he will agree to my proposition, but it doesn't hurt to play nice until the investment agreement is signed. And I want that for my Empress.

I bend and kiss Aura hard. "You ready to face the collective?"

38

Aurelia

"I am *so* not ready for this," I groan into the phone.

I'm perched on the counter of the bathroom adjoining the guest bedroom at Arthur's place, which I'm using to tidy my appearance.

I'm delaying leaving by calling Zoey and updating her on the latest developments.

She was, naturally, taken aback by my proposed marriage to Ryot.

"I know better than to talk you out of this, since you're doing it for your country." She looks into my features. "It's not going to stop me from worrying about you."

I look at her gratefully. "You're an awesome friend, Zoey."

I slide off the counter and walk out of the bathroom. Then, because I'm not ready to head down, I begin to pace. "At least, it's not Gavin I'm marrying."

If I repeat it enough, I'll convince myself that it's the only reason the thought of being married to Ryot fills my heart with excitement.

"Hmm"—she looks at me with a speculative expression—"did something happen between you and Ryot?"

I flush and must look guilty, for her eyes round. "Oh, my god, you slept with him, didn't you?"

"It's more accurate to say we slept with each other," I say primly.

"And you enjoyed it, so that's why the thought of marrying him is appealing to you?"

"You sure you don't want a second career as a shrink." I laugh.

"I'm an editor; that makes me part psychologist. The number of times I have to calm down authors and help them figure out the reasons for their writer's block alone qualifies me for that particular role." She chuckles. "But... I have to ask you again, are you sure you want to do this?"

"You mean do I want to let Ryot use the Davenport fortune to rescue Verenza?" I ask only half-sarcastically.

A line appears between her eyebrows. "I mean, do you want to marry Ryot?"

I think about it, then nod. "If I'm being honest, the idea is far from repugnant. Would I prefer that he's marrying me because he loves me? Yes. But given he's going to help afford an entire generation of Verenza a future where they don't have to ration food and are able to access healthcare provided by the state, not to mention the chance to study in state-run schools and take their place on the world stage..." I tilt my head. "It wasn't a difficult decision, at all."

She sighs. "I worry that you're, once again, sacrificing your happiness for the sake of your country."

"That *is* the meaning of being a princess. It was drilled into us that we need to put our country before our personal happiness, every single time. It is the only way to ensure the continued survival of my family." My voice rises as I warm to my topic. *And yes, being married to Ryot is going to be totally awesome, but I'm playing it cool. I don't want Zoey to guess just how much I'm looking forward to it. I'm not sure why.*

Her gaze grows fond. "I admire you."

I scoff, "Now, you sound like Ryot."

Her gaze widens. "He said he admires you?"

"More precisely, my sense of responsibility."

She seems nonplussed. "That's...unexpected."

I nod. "Right? It takes a secure man to say that. Given his macho persona, I didn't expect him to have the maturity to recognize the softer emotions men often seem to run from, let alone say them aloud. It's because I compared it to his duty while in the Marines." But then, Ryot has surprised me every step of the way.

"True masculinity is being able to call out your feelings, something most men forget," she agrees.

"For all his strong, silent, almost forbidding exterior, Ryot can be gentle and intuitive in a way that blows my mind." I confess. *And other parts of me too.*

The man is an annoyingly enticing mix of alpha-maleness and tenderness. He's grumpy and growly to the world, but when it comes to me, there's a softer side to him that takes me by surprise every time. I smooth down the fabric of my dress, trying to order my thoughts.

"Anyway, it is what it is." I shrug. "I didn't ask to be born into this family, but since I was, I have a responsibility." *And so does he.*

He promised to look out for me, and if marrying me is what it takes to keep his word, then he's going to do it. As long as the people after me are out there, he'll stay with me. And after that—? I'll have to cross that bridge when I come to it. Meanwhile, there's a tiny part of me hoping he doesn't track down whoever it is; that they just disappear, and he sticks around because he hasn't found them yet.

There's another knock on the door. Shoot, I lost track of time talking to Zoey. "I have to—"

"—go." She nods.

"I'll be in touch." I blow her a kiss, then disconnect the call. Walking to the settee, I slide my phone into my handbag, then take it in hand, walk to the door and open it.

"Your Royal Highness." Veronica curtsies.

I resist the urge to roll my eyes. "I've told you many times, you don't need to call me by that title. You also don't need to curtsy."

Her expression turns crestfallen. "B-but, Ma'am, protocol and the dignity of your office require that I do."

Sometimes, I forget that Veronica is from Verenza. She's used to having royalty in her life. I'll bet, like many of the citizens of my country, she looks upon the Royal Family as having almost mythical proportions. The media makes sure of that.

Little does she know the sacrifices it takes. Little does she know how unnatural it is to be born into this family and have everyone bow and scrape around you or treat you like you've achieved something extraordinary by being born into this life. A life that's mine purely by accident of birth.

"Besides, you're a real-life princess," she bursts out.

Yep. She's totally brainwashed by the hype surrounding the Royal Family. "Being a princess is not all it's cut out to be." I sigh. "While it might seem dazzling and very Disney-like, the reality is, I'm hemmed in by restrictions and feel like I'm living in a gilded cage."

She pinches her lips together. "I'd give anything to live a single day in your shoes," she huffs. Then her cheeks redden when she realizes she spoke out loud.

"Would you?" I ask, more curious than upset with her words. Perhaps, a little creeped out at the fervent look in her eyes. She's always been over-committed to her role. But I don't recall her being this fascinated by the royalty aspect of my life before.

Her gaze lights up. "It's the only thing I've wanted to be since I was five." She nods vigorously.

Something in her tone sends a prickle of unease down my back. "You want to be a princess?

"Only in my dreams. I know, it's not possible in real life." She flashes me a smile that's so over-eager, it makes me take a step back. Then, she laughs and adds, "Unless you know of a prince looking to marry..."

What?! Did she sabotage things because she wants to be with Gavin? Was it her idea to send him to the safe house? Maybe she was hoping he'd catch me doing something with Ryot, call off the wedding, and then, she could swoop in? My thoughts whirl about in my head.

When I don't respond, she continues.

"It's why, when I saw the job advertised on the Royal Family website, I applied right away. And I'm so glad I did." She locks her fingers together, adulation evident on her features. "I didn't think someone as ordinary as me would ever be able to work in proximity to such beauty and status, but here I am. Too bad about Gavin, of course."

Something in her tone pings another flurry of disquiet across my nerve-endings. *Why does she care about Gavin?* For that matter, why would he call her to get to me? Surely, he knew how to contact Fred directly. I mentally shake my head.

This is ridiculous. I've already been through this. He probably couldn't reach Fred and was anxious to locate me. I'm letting my fears cloud my thinking.

Veronica has been nothing but helpful since she joined my team. So what, if she's overzealous at times. She's my assistant; she's supposed to go the extra mile to ensure I don't mess up my schedule, right?

"Not that you could have married him; not after what he did to you. And this, on top of the threat and the assassination attempt?" She shakes her head. Her features take on a look of concern, and she bites her lip.

Her running through the list of events that have shaken me in the last few weeks pumps up my blood pressure. My stomach churns. My fingers tremble, and I have to lock them together. She's right. It *is* a lot. To be threatened, shot at, and then to have your hitherto harmless fiancé turn on you, while having to maintain the princess façade with the media, is enough to cause *anyone* a nervous break-down. *No wonder, I'm getting suspicious of her.*

"You poor thing. You must be so shaken." Her gaze is earnest. "I'm so sorry you're going through this."

She seems really concerned about me. The expression on her features feels genuine. Enough for me to push aside my unease. *While we have a strictly professional relationship, it stands to reason that something as big as Gavin no longer being in the picture would warrant, at least, a comment from her, right?* I push aside the concern—what's done is done —and hold my bag out to her.

She accepts it. "They're waiting for you, Your Royal Highness."

She bobs her head again. On the other hand, her bowing and scraping sets my teeth on edge. It feels so... Insincere.

"I am the princess. I'm allowed to be late, aren't I?" I say in a haughty tone to mask the annoyance I feel.

Once I go down there, and we announce to the world that I'm marrying Ryot, the word will be out, and there'll be no turning back. *Remember Verenza and how it's citizens are going to benefit.* It's all going to be worth it. And meanwhile, I get to be with Ryot. I get to benefit from the orgasms, when he decides to bestow them on me, that is. And if I'm lucky—and persistent—I'll be able to convince him this is not just a marriage of convenience but a forever relationship. A shiver of anticipation pinches my nerve-endings, but I don't dwell on it.

I need to focus, not on the sexy things Ryot has promised to do to me, but on my upcoming nuptials.

Meanwhile, Veronica looks at me with that strange light in her eyes. It's fangirling; I need to let it go. She's so taken in by the 'Royal Princess' image I try to portray, she can't see behind the façade I present to the world. Unlike Ryot, who figured me out right away.

He understands my insecurities and what it takes to live this role I've been born into. Too bad, he has his own ghosts preventing him from embracing this connection between us. Ghosts which, by the way, I intend to banish. Meanwhile, I'll take what I get, and as long as it benefits Verenza, it'll all be worth it.

"Come on." I walk past her. "It's time to face the music."

39

Ryot

"I assume this makes you happy?" I turn on Arthur.

We're in Arthur's study with the family in tow.

Arthur's seated in another armchair, this time, in the one closest to the living room fire. In addition, the heating has been turned on. The room is like a furnace. I wipe the bead of sweat from my brow, then loosen the tie around my neck. You'd think, after years in the Marines, I'd be comfortable with a formal suit, but ties are the bane of my existence. They make me feel claustrophobic. Which I take as a weakness, but which I'm told is normal for many who've seen action.

Arthur's Great Dane, Tiny, lolls on the floor next to the fire. His tongue hangs out, and he watches us with curiosity.

"If you mean, you marrying the princess, I'm proud of you for coming up with the idea." Arthur raises a glass of water to his mouth.

His hand trembles. For the first time, I notice the dark circles under his eyes. He's also hunched a little, tiredness writ in the angles of his face. Despite his diagnosis, the treatment Arthur has been undergoing has kept the disease in check. It also hasn't impacted his lifestyle, which makes it easy to forget he's not completely well. In comparison, his girlfriend Imelda, who's standing behind him, looks a picture of health. The firelight plays off her slightly plump features and highlights the pink streaks in her short hair. She's wearing her usual outfit of cargo pants and shit-kickers.

No dressing up for Imelda; not even for royalty. Her only concession is the pink blouse she's teamed with the cargo pants. The entire outfit should look incongruous, but she manages to pull it off. When Arthur raises his other hand, she grips it.

He seems to draw strength from her, and his face brightens. "I couldn't have done better myself," he murmurs.

"Not sure if I take that as a compliment," I retort.

Tyler snorts from his on-guard position near the door.

Brody and Connor, who're standing on either side of me, look between us with interest. We're crowded around Arthur and Imelda.

Nathan and Knox are standing behind a Chesterfield which holds both of their wives. The king and Fred are deep in discussion on the other side of the room. Their voices are muted.

Quentin's out, ensuring the security team has the place sewn up tight, to prevent any repetition of what happened earlier. It's one of the reasons I feel a little more at ease.

Sinclair is sprawled in a recliner near the Chesterfield. All of them are following our discussion with avid curiosity.

"You're losing your touch, Gramps," Connor declares. "I'd have thought it would be you instead of Ryot coming up with the idea of marrying the princess in return for investing in Verenza."

"The last thing I want is to become predictable, especially since the lot of you seem to be able to see through machinations," Arthur says in a mild voice. "I'd rather you boys emulate the kinds of tactics which have kept The Davenports going for more than three quarters of a century. My father—rest his soul—was Machiavellian when it came to the survival of the company. And while I hated his efforts, when I grew older, I realized he'd done the right thing. I don't apologize for what I do to keep my bloodline intact. And I'm even more proud that you boys are following my example."

Brody and Connor watch me carefully.

"I'm nothing like you," I growl.

"Oh?" Arthur inclines his head.

"I'm marrying her because it's the only way to stay close to her without arousing suspicions. It's the only way to keep her safe."

And to get you off my back about getting hitched.

Outwardly, I say, "Besides, The Davenport Group is always looking for places to invest. Given the economic condition of Verenza, there are bargains to be had. It's a strategically sound decision."

"That it is," Arthur says slowly.

"But it's not the only reason you suggested the match." Tyler smirks.

And I thought he was on my side. I flick a dirty glance in his direction. "What's that supposed to mean?"

"Figure it out yourself," Brody murmurs.

"If you want a clue, he's talking about the fact that you're giving another shot at that ol' four-letter word, beginning with 'L,'" Connor quips.

"Jesus. Fuck."

"Language," chastises Arthur.

I spare him a look before digging my fingers in my hair and tugging. "Have you guys turned into avid Hallmark movie watchers? Is that where this is coming from?"

Connor chuckles. "If it doesn't apply to you, why are you so upset? Unless—" He pretends to study me closely. "Unless...there's a measure of truth in what I said?"

"What? Of course, not," I snap, then notice the sly look in my youngest brother's eyes. Trust Connor to pull your leg when you least expect it.

"Asshole," I growl.

He chuckles, then slaps at my shoulder. "It had to happen at some point, given the sparks between you and the princess."

"What do you know about that? You haven't seen us together."

"Didn't need to." He nods in Tyler's direction.

I whip my head toward him to find a sheepish expression on his features. "You told him?"

"And me," Brody pipes up.

"Et moi." Imelda smirks.

"Didn't have anything else more exciting to gossip about? And seriously, Imelda, I wouldn't have expected you to indulge in such trash."

"But I'm a gossipy old woman at heart." She flutters her eyelashes at me.

And I'm going to marry a princess.

"I think he needs another drink," Connor says as he peers into my features. "Do you think he needs a drink?" he asks no one in particular.

"He looks pale, he might need a drink," Brody agrees.

Tyler walks over to the bar, pours a finger into a tumbler and brings it over. "A wee dram for some liquid courage?" He holds it out.

I glare at him. Then think better of turning it down. I need all the help I can get. I snatch the glass from him and throw back the liquid before tossing it back to him.

He snatches it from the air. "Feeling better?"

I hold my finger up at him. The sound of the door opening reaches me. The hair on the back of my neck rises, and I know it's her. I draw in a breath, then another. Then turn and meet her gaze. She stands inside the doorway, head held high, her spine erect.

She combed her hair back, and not a strand is out of place. She refreshed her makeup, and her lipstick is immaculate. Nothing remains of the flushed woman whose swollen lips indicated she'd allowed me to use her mouth in a way that does not befit a princess. She's, once again, the regal royal, who supports charities and graces events with her presence to drive up their newsworthiness. *Damn. It makes me want to go over and muss her up again.*

The rest of my family rise to their feet. Everyone bows, including Tyler. When Arthur begins to rise as well, she shakes her head. "Please, stay seated." Then she turns her gaze on me. I haven't followed my family's example. She scowls at me. *Does she expect me to bow to her?*

And when I slowly rise to my feet, a look of wariness comes into her eyes. I stalk toward her, aware that every gaze in the room is following us, and not giving a damn.

When I come to a stop in front of her, she tips up her chin and fixes me with a haughty gaze.

I lean close and say softly, "No can do, Empress. Don't expect to treat me like one of your subjects and get away with it."

I cup her cheek and, before she can pull away, I kiss her soundly. Her lips are stiff, and for a few seconds, she stays unyielding. Then her mouth opens. And when I sweep my tongue inside, she melts into me. I hold the back of her head to keep her in place and kiss her thoroughly. When I straighten, her cheeks are flushed, her breathing erratic. Her eyes are glazed with need, and she stares at me with a confused look. There; much better.

I stay there for a few seconds, until her eyes clear. "What was that for?" she says breathlessly.

"Can't I kiss my wife-to-be?"

She flushes. The pulse at the base of her throat speeds up. But her gaze is confused. She's still coming to terms with our upcoming nuptials.

Then she tightens her lips. "They're waiting," she says in a voice which trembles a little. *Good. I'd have been disappointed if she found her composure so soon after that kiss.*

I hook her arm through mine, then lead her into the room.

The king approaches us. He kisses her on each cheek, then eases back on his heels. "Do you definitely want to go ahead with *this* wedding? You are under no obligation to do so. I will find another way of paying off the country's debts, *cara mia*."

The princess takes in his features. His eyes are haunted. There are hollows under his cheekbones. He seems to have aged in the last few hours. If the Davenports' investment isn't forthcoming, it'll put him in a very difficult situation.

I know Aura cares for him too much to put him through that.

And I care for *her* enough that I want to tell her father that he should stop her from marrying me and giving up her choice for the sake of her country. At the same time, I'm selfish enough to be glad that it's *me* she's marrying.

And when she says softly, "This is what I want papa," warmth squeezes my chest.

I'm going to keep her safe. I'm going to ensure she gets what is most important for her—securing the future of her country.

I content myself with tucking her into my side and walking her to where Arthur is waiting for us. He looks between us, and a smile flickers across his features. I can swear there's a glimmer of moisture in his eyes. *Is the old coot getting sentimental?* His chin quivers, and he seems incapable of speech. *Huh.* I eye him warily.

He seems to have transitioned from the role of the hard-nosed businessman and conniving meddler in his grandson's lives to that of fond grandfather way too quickly for my comfort.

Imelda takes in the emotion on his face, and steps toward us. She curtsies to the princess. "Your Highness."

"Please, call me Aura," the princess murmurs.

"Aura." Imelda smiles widely. "Congratulations. I hope you'll forgive Ryot for not being able to speak what's really on his mind. Afraid we women must give the male of the species the benefit of the doubt at times, but especially when it comes to matters of the heart."

I gape at Imelda, then turn to find the princess staring at her, flummoxed. Then she chuckles. "A straight-talking woman. Do you realize how rare someone like you is?"

Imelda blushes, and that's something, because the woman's hard-nosed and takes life by its balls, and there's no demure bone in her body. "Aw, shucks." She dips her head. "You're being too kind."

"I don't think so. I hope Arthur realizes how lucky he is." She shoots him a glance.

Arthur's watching Imelda with a look of open adoration. *The old man's truly in love.* Another reason he wants to see the rest of us singletons paired off, no doubt.

Then Tiny woofs.

"Ooh, who're you?" Aura looks at the dog with interest. He

ambles to his feet, lumbers over to us, and butts the princess' waist with his big head. She stumbles, and I tighten my hold on her.

"What's your name, little puppy?" Aura coos as she extends a hand for him to sniff.

And now, I'm jealous of the mutt.

"Tiny," I murmur.

"No, it's not." She narrows her eyes.

"It definitely is." I snicker. "His name. Is Tiny."

She laughs before moving her hand under his chin so she can better see his face. "Hey, Tiny. You're such a good boy, aren't you?"

Tiny makes a purring sound at the back of his throat. He moves his big head so that her hand is next to his ear. She obliges by scratching around each of his ears. His eyes roll back in his head, and he groans. Then he slobbers all over her hand.

"Sorry about that, Princess. He can be expressive in his affections," Imelda explains. "C'mere, Tiny." She slaps her thigh, and he immediately walks toward her. Then he flops down on the floor next to Arthur with a sigh.

I pull out my handkerchief, take her hand, and wipe off Tiny's drool before folding it and pocketing it.

"Have you set a date?" Brody asks.

"A date?" We both look at him.

"For the wedding," Tyler clarifies. "It will be good to know so we can get the security arrangements in place for it."

I feel myself pale. This is getting all too real.

"Don't take too long. The more notice you give us, the better." Tyler's all business now. Somehow, in the last few hours he's become my right-hand man, in terms of protection detail.

The king walks over and sinks into the armchair next to Arthur. "The ceremony will have to be in Verenza."

"I don't suppose it could be restricted to close family and for the rest of the country to watch it when it's televised?" I widen my stance. "That would make things easier from a security standpoint."

Not to mention, I have no desire to be part of a circus that a royal wedding could become.

Her father shakes his head. "A royal wedding is a key reason for people from around the world to travel to Verenza. And tourism is what drives our economy."

"What about your daughter's safety?" Anger squeezes my guts. I don't care that he's the king and the man who's paying the massive security bill my agency has run up. Keeping my woman protected is far more important. You'd think he'd feel the same way too.

His expression takes on a haunted expression. "Her wellbeing is important, but a royal wedding will generate billions of dollars' worth of PR coverage and make Verenza a household name."

"I'd think Aura's welfare takes precedence over any money, and —" She squeezes my arm. I glance down to find her looking at me with shining eyes. There's tenderness, and something else. Something I don't want to examine closely or put a name to; that could complicate this situation a lot more.

"It's okay," she murmurs.

"It's not okay. I'm a little tired of seeing you constantly put yourself at risk for the sake of your country."

She angles her head. "Didn't you do the same?"

I open my mouth, then shut it. *Damn. She has me there.*

"What you described is the job description of being a princess," she reminds me. "Just like it was in your job description when you were a Royal Marine."

"Damn, you always know how to go toe-to-toe with me, don't you?" I mumble, then half smile.

She chuckles. "It's what makes the dynamics between us interesting."

We continue to smile at each other, until someone clears their throat.

She flushes and is the first to look away. "So yes, the wedding will be in Verenza, and I'd love for all of you to attend."

40

Aurelia

"Thank you so much for the invitation," Harper gushes.

"We really appreciate it," Grace adds.

"You're so very welcome!" I smile.

Ryot and I, along with Veronica and the security team, boarded a flight the day after we announced to the Davenports that we were getting married. The king and his courtiers were, of course, on board with the wedding. Not that they'd have an objection, given the money the Davenports will be pouring into the country.

Luckily, the public-facing announcements were limited to a joint press release that Ryot and I put out announcing our upcoming nuptials in a month. After which, I handed my phone to Veronica and had her deal with the flurry of questions coming my way.

I also briefed the palace's PR team on dealing with the publicity in the weeks leading up to the wedding.

"How are you doing?" Zoey hugs me, then takes a seat on the

chair to the left of the settee where I am. "Are you happy to be back home?"

We're in a conservatory within the Royal Palace in Verenza. The scent of flowers fills the air, but below it is the slightly salty air, reminding me that I'm never far away from the sea on this island. It's been a week since I returned here. I spent three weeks in London fulfilling various public engagements, and before that, I was on a European tour, stopping in five countries.

"I'm happy to be back in Verenza. But I already miss London."

"You do?" Grace asks, surprised.

I take a sip of my tea. "Verenza is where I will always be seen as a princess. London is where I went first, to boarding school and then, university. It's where I led as normal a life as I possibly could. Also, the media in England is more fixated on the British Royal Family, so with careful planning, I can fly under the radar, unless I am at a public engagement."

"I'd have never guessed that, but it makes sense." Harper nods.

"I do miss some things about my home country, of course." I place my teacup back in the saucer on the table. "The food, for one. The fish caught off the shore of Verenza tastes different from fish I've had anywhere else. I also miss the fact that everyone here speaks both Italian and English."

Given we're off the coast of Italy, everyone is fluent in both languages.

"And then, I like the slower pace of life. I'm also appreciative that, in many homes here, generations of families all live under one roof. Despite modernization we've kept the old ways alive."

Grace laughs. "And let's not forget the weather. It's gorgeous here!"

"I can't believe it's only three days to go to the wedding," Harper exclaims.

I laugh. "It's gone by quickly."

"A month is nothing in terms of wedding preparation time, let alone, enough to prepare for 'the wedding event of the century' as the media has been referring to it." Grace nods.

She's perched on the chair opposite me, with the coffee table between us. Zoey is on a chair which is twin to hers. Harper and I are on the couch facing the door.

"You should know, Ms. Morning Show host. I caught one of your shows when I was in London. You were excellent," I gush.

"Thanks." Grace seems pleased by the praise. "It's what I've always wanted to do. It's why I embarked on a journalism career. What they don't tell you is that you have to be up at three a.m. and at the studio by four a.m. to do your makeup and prep, so you're in the studio and on air by six a.m."

"Ouch." Harper winces.

"Not that working for a Michelin-starred chef means you're spared the early mornings." I turn to her. It's thanks to Zoey that I know about their professional accomplishments.

"My boss is a bastard." Harper scowls. "A beautiful bastard, but a bastard, nevertheless. He's so up his own arse, the only time he notices us is if one of us screws up, and then he'll chew us out. He doesn't even know our names and refers to us by numbers."

"He refers to his team by numbers?" Grace coughs on the sip of wine she's taken. "That's horrible."

"He says it's because no one on the team stays around long enough for him to need to learn our names. I'm determined to prove him wrong," she says with vehemence.

The fire in her eyes tells me she won't stop until she's brought him to heel. It also tells me, perhaps, there's more there than just hate for her boss, but I wisely don't share that. Instead, I ask, "He's a Michelin-starred chef. Is there a chance we know of him?"

"James Hamilton." She tosses her head. "He thinks the world begins and ends with him."

"James Hamilton?" I sit up straight. "He's the one in charge of the food at the wedding reception."

"Really? Well, thankfully, I'll be on holiday and attending the wedding as a guest. So hopefully, I won't run into him." She mutters under her breath, "He probably won't recognize me, anyway.

"He's invited to the reception," I warn.

"He is?" Harper seems taken aback. "I mean, of course, he is. He hobnobs with the rich and famous." She sniffs.

Grace clears her throat.

"What?" Harper scrunches up her forehead. Then her gaze widens as realization sinks in. "Ohmigosh!" She turns to me. "I didn't mean *you* by that. I mean, you are rich and famous, but I was referring to models and actresses and the kind of airheads he likes to date. Obviously, not you."

"Hmph." I raise one eyebrow. "I think you did."

Her jaw drops. "No, honestly, I didn't, I…"

She looks so mortified, I burst out laughing. "Relax, I was kidding with you."

She doesn't look convinced.

I reach over and squeeze her shoulder. "I know, you don't have a mean bone in your body, Harper." Which is why I was surprised to find out she was apprenticing to be a chef. It's not an easy path she's chosen. But then, none of the four of us are put off by challenges, are we?

"Ryot had arranged for James Hamilton to cook for us. That's when I was shot at."

"Gosh!" Harper looks stricken. "That's awful. Not that James cooked for you, but the fact that you were shot at."

I laugh. "No, the food was amazing prior to that."

"I'm glad you escaped unhurt," Grace exclaims.

The girls already know about the note that appeared in my room. They also know that someone tried to break into Arthur's place while I was there.

"Good thing Ryot was with you." Zoey scans my face. "Speaking of, how has he been coping with—" She waves a hand in the air.

"Honestly, I'm not sure." I reach over to nibble on a carrot stick. I eschewed a bachelorette party for the more mellow afternoon tea with my girlfriends.

"What does that mean?" Grace frowns.

I hesitate, wondering how much to reveal. She notices the expression on my face and holds up her hand. "You don't have to tell us. Especially not if it means breaking a royal confidence."

"Umm..." I choose my words carefully. I do trust them. And I want to share, since I want to have these women in my life.

"Ryot, he and I, uh... It's kind of a marriage of convenience."

Grace looks skeptical, but Harper nods. "Of course, it's common enough in some cultures. Especially among those with a lot of money to protect, and who want to manage who will inherit their wealth." She winces again. "Don't mean to sound insulting or anything."

I laugh. "You're not. Our alliance does have money at its heart."

"Oh?" Grace leans forward. "How's that?" Then her forehead furrows and she adds, "Again, you don't need to share anything that would put you in a spot. I'm curious because I'm a journalist. I love to get to the bottom of things. Not that I'd report anything you tell me," she adds quickly.

"It's what makes you a good reporter," I say with admiration. "And yes, it is confidential, but you're my friends, and I trust you."

Grace and Harper exchange glances, then Grace tips her chin in my direction. "We would never speak of this with anyone."

"Whatever you share with us will never leave this group," Harper says solemnly.

Tears burn the backs of my eyes, and I blink them away. "You guys are so good to me. I'm sorry I didn't make the effort to keep in touch with you."

"It's understandable. It's not easy being a princess, especially in today's world, where everyone wants a piece of those in the public eye," Grace murmurs.

Harper reaches over to take my hand. "We're here for you, honey, whatever you need."

I sniffle, then brush away the tear that escaped down my cheek. "I don't know why I'm getting this emotional. Ignore me."

"It's allowed. You've been under so much pressure; it helps to cry it out." Zoey rises from her chair and sits next to me, then puts her arm around my shoulders.

Grace's gaze is also understanding.

I take in their faces and feel relieved that I don't have to go through the next few days on my own. Of course, Ryot will be with me, but it's a different feeling from having girlfriends to lean on. A feeling, I realize, I've missed so much. I take a sip of my wine, allowing the tart Chardonnay to roll over my tongue, then place the glass back. "When Gavin decided to get aggressive with me, it's Ryot who came to my rescue."

"I'm so sorry you had to go through that." Zoey's lips tighten.

"Gavin took me by surprise." I rub at my forehead. "The man gave me the impression that he's a laid-back, spoiled heir to the family fortune. But for some reason, he seemed to find his balls when he wanted to get into my pants. No pun intended."

The girls laugh.

"Thankfully, Ryot intervened before things got too far."

"And now, you're marrying him." Harper sighs.

"Ryot says, this way, he has a reason to stay by my side all the time without raising suspicion. This way, he can protect me. It also gets his grandfather off his back about getting married. In return, he's going to invest enough money into Verenza to help us pay off our debts to the International Monetary Fund."

"Hmm"—Grace purses her lips—"and how do you feel about this?"

"Frankly?" I look around their faces. "The money he's investing is too important for me to turn down the offer. But if I put that aside, I honestly don't mind the idea."

"But does he love you?" Grace asks.

I glance down at my locked fingers then up at her. "He cares for me, a lot. As for love"—I pop a shoulder, trying to look unconcerned — "hopefully, that will come later."

"And what about you?" Harper tilts her head. "From the look on your face when you speak about him, I'm assuming you do love him?"

I wince. "I'm that transparent, huh?"

"Only because I'm a romantic." Harper smiles a little. "I want to believe that, while the two of you might have an unorthodox start, you're meant for each other. I truly hope that this marriage of convenience turns out to be the real thing."

"Hear, hear," adds Grace. "It's not for nothing we belong to a spicy book club. Aura is currently living the 'fake marriage' trope."

Everyone laughs.

I'd like to believe that too, but the fact is, I've only seen Ryot twice since we returned to Verenza. And that's only because I needed to update him on the wedding arrangements. He might have wanted to marry me so he could stay close to me, but the arrangements are taking up a lot of his time. He's trying his best to stay close to me, but he told me he doesn't trust anyone else with the arrangements and wants to oversee them as closely as possible.

He's roped Tyler in to stand in as my bodyguard whenever he's unable to be with me. He also drew up a cordon of handpicked guards around the palace, and given I haven't left the premises, I'm as safe as can be.

"So, are you ready for the wedding?" Zoey scrutinizes my features. "There's been very little time to plan for it."

She's right. The last three weeks since returning to Verenza have zipped by in a storm of preparations for the wedding.

Harper throws up her hands. "A month is very little time to organize any wedding, let alone, a royal one."

"There's a blueprint in place. One which has been followed for royal weddings for generations, and which I revisited with my father and brother not long ago. We updated it in anticipation of the next royal wedding, so all we had to do was activate the protocol. I've also brought in a wedding planner recommended to me by Zoey." I nod in her direction.

"Whew." Harper pretends to wipe her forehead. "That's good."

"It still feels like a very rushed timeline," Grace murmurs.

I pop my shoulder. "Arthur and my father agree that we don't want to wait too long. Especially since we need the investment to come in quickly."

"And Ryot was okay with that?" Grace asks with a shrewd expression on her face. Nothing gets past this woman.

"He was concerned that the time required to organize the security necessary for the event is very tight," I concede. "He argued for a more private wedding to better protect me but was overruled."

He's also managing operatives on the ground who are tracking the person who broke into Arthur's home, and who they believe is also behind the attempt on my life.

"And what about the man who's a threat to your life?" Grace scowls. "Is Ryot confident of managing that?"

"He'd have to get past me first," he interrupts from the doorway.

41

Ryot

"Empress." I hold her gaze as I prowl into the conservatory.

I have missed her so much. I've had to stop myself from throwing open the door that separates her suite from mine, stomping in, taking her in my arms, and kissing her.

I've been aching for her these past few weeks, but it's more important that I ensure nothing is left to chance around the security arrangements for our wedding.

I've spent every possible second working with Tyler and pulling in trusted security personnel to assist with the protection details around the wedding. I haven't been able to sleep at night, thinking of the woman next door, who is my life—I'll analyze that later—but I've stopped myself from going to her, knowing it was important to keep my attention solely on what matters. Her safety.

Her blue eyes light up before she reins in her pleasure, and it lights up something inside of me. I hold out my hand, and she places her much smaller one in mine. A frisson of sensations zips up my arm. I revel in the touch of her soft skin, draw in her sweet scent, gaze into those gorgeous eyes of hers, and feel like I can finally breathe.

She's my sustenance, the balm to my soul, the reason for my existence. I was spared in all those encounters when I was a Marine only so I could be here—with her, drawing the same air as her, being in the same space as her. She's a goddess, and I'm not worth the dirt beneath her feet.

I bring her delicate hand to my mouth and kiss her knuckles.

"Aww." The woman sitting in the chair on her right sighs.

The other two watch me with guarded expressions.

I want her friends and her family to like me. I want them to know that I have her best interests at heart.

I squeeze her fingers gently, and a shudder runs up her arm. She's affected by my touch just as much as I am by hers.

I need to keep my wits about me until we're married, and the ceremony has gone off without a hitch.

Aware of the eyes on us, and not wanting to make her self-conscious in front of her friends, I release her hand and take a few steps back. I survey the group. "Ladies"—I make eye contact and nod at each in turn—"it's a pleasure."

"Sorry, I should have introduced you." My Empress appears flustered. "This is my, uh…fiancé, Ryot Davenport."

"We know." The blonde woman who seemed taken in by my gesture earlier smiles warmly at me. "I'm Harper Richie, Aura's friend from university."

"A pleasure." I smile back, turning on the charm.

She flushes, and her smile broadens.

I turn to Zoey, who I met previously. "I'm so glad you made it for the wedding. I know the princess has been looking forward to having all of you here."

Zoey smiles graciously. The suspicion in her eyes is still there, though.

"Aura is a very dear friend, and it hasn't been easy for her to live her life according to the restrictions being part of the Royal Family has imposed on her. She deserves to be happy, and if you do anything to hurt her, you'll have us to contend with."

My Empress shoots her a look of surprise. She opens her mouth to speak, but I interject, "I care too much about her to hurt her. You have my word; I'll never do anything to break her heart." *And I mean it. I'd cleave out my own, before I'd allow anything to cause her pain.*

The princess whips her head in my direction. I sense the questions on her lips, the curiosity on her features. I want to say more, but I'm not sure how to form the words without giving away the depth of what I'm feeling. So, I walk over to stand behind her and place my hand on her shoulder. She hesitates, then rests her hand over mine. The softness of her touch melts something around my heart. Some of the tension goes out of my shoulders.

Zoey seems taken aback by my words. She looks from me to the princess, and a small smile plays around her lips. One which makes me shift my weight in discomfort.

The dark-haired woman sitting opposite us tips up her chin. "Grace McFee." She sniffs. Her voice is almost as imperious as that of the princess.

"I caught your exposé on the corruption at the local council level; very insightful and courageous reporting."

She nods slowly. Her gaze is still wary, but the skin around her eyes softens somewhat. A tough customer, this one. But I'm going to do my best to win her over.

"I've arranged for security for all of you ladies."

"Is that essential?" Grace frowns.

I incline my head. "I'm not taking any chances when it comes to the safety of my fiancée, or of any of her guests."

"But there haven't been any threats since Aura came to Verenza," Harper points out.

"The culprits are still out there." I run my fingers through my hair. I'd hoped to track them down before the wedding but that doesn't seem a possibility now.

Grace seems impressed, then presses her lips together. "Aura is very important to us."

"She's the most precious part of my life." I tighten my hold on her shoulder.

"If you were to cause her any unhappiness—"

"I'll die before I allow that to happen."

I'm going to do everything in my power to make sure she's safe. No matter that those behind the threats are smart and have proven they can get through stringent security measures.

The leads my team and I followed turned out to be dead ends. I'm convinced there's a leak within her inner circle. But the backgrounds of her employees and those on my security team, check out.

I've broadened the circle of people I'm investigating to include her friends and her wanker of an ex-fiancé.

It's one of the reasons I wanted to come by and meet them in person. I wanted to size them up. And yes, I also wanted to see my Empress.

Fatigue knocks at my temples, but I ignore it. I'm running on less than three hours of sleep each night. Nothing new to me. I've been on missions where conditions have been rougher. I can handle this.

I look down at Aura, then back at Grace, "I'll do everything in my power to make sure she's taken care of. I will not rest until I track down whoever has targeted her."

42

Aurelia

His words send a flush of pleasure up my spine. A throbbing pulse flares to life between my thighs. He sounds so sure, so confident, so protective. It's over the top, but it makes me feel safe in a way I've never felt before. I run my thumb over his thick wrist and sense the jolt that runs through him. I love that he's so affected by my presence. *So, why has he ignored me for so many days?*

Grace's eyes take in the gesture, and her eyebrows arch. Nothing gets by that woman. Zoey looks pleased, like she's been let in on a secret. As for Harper, she has a beaming smile on her face, and those damned hearts are back in her eyes. Jeez, I need to tell her not to get her hopes up. Not that her romantic outlook on life isn't infectious. But when you live a life most girls dream of and realize becoming a princess isn't the stuff of Disney movies, the scales are lifted from your eyes pretty quickly.

With a final squeeze on my shoulder, Ryot straightens. "I'll leave you to enjoy your tea."

He bends and whispers in my ear, "Later, Empress." He presses a kiss to my cheek. And it's very chaste, but the touch of his lips against my skin sparks off another trail of quivers in my stomach. He straightens and steps away, and I miss him so much already.

I'm not sure when I'll see him again. And I don't want the next time to be at the wedding. Before I can stop myself, I rise to my feet. "Uh, I need to talk to Ryot about something urgent."

Ignoring the smirk on Zoey's face, I walk around the couch, only making sure I hurry when I reach the doors of the conservatory. He's already walked through the living room and into the adjoining study.

"Ryot!" I hasten my steps. When I burst into the study, I can't see him. *Huh?* I glance around, when suddenly, I'm grabbed around the waist and pulled to the side and away from the doorway.

My heart somersaults into my throat, and I gasp. *OMG! Someone got in! What are they going to do to me?* Then, my back connects with a wide, hard chest, and his big arms wrap around me. One around my chest, the other around my waist, holding me immovable. *It's him.* The fear that twisted my belly fades away, leaving me shaking with relief. The heat from his body surrounds me, and his scent is so intense, when I draw it into my lungs, I feel like I'm going to combust.

"You called?" His dark voice plucks at my nerve-endings. Anticipation squeezes my lower belly.

Then he bites the tip of my ear, and I whimper, "Oh, God."

"Oh, Ryot."

"Hmm, what?" I'm too focused on how he's sucking on the fleshy part of my ear. My pussy clenches. My clit throbs. My panties are embarrassingly damp. Something rigid stabs into my lower back, and I gasp. He's so big, so thick, so everything. My breasts hurt, and my thighs tremble. I try to turn, but he doesn't let me.

"Have you been a good girl? Have you kept your orgasms for me, Empress?"

"Yes," I pant. "Yes. I haven't come, just as you ordered. I've been needy and come close to getting myself off, but I haven't."

"Good Girl."

His approval lights a fire in my belly. My thighs strain. My clit begins to hurt. I grind into him, not caring about how it might seem to him. He has me in the throes of such need, and the fact that he can hold me immobile with such little effort turns me on even more.

He drags his chin down the curve where my throat meets my shoulder, and I pant. I let my head fall back against his shoulder to give him better access.

"So impatient." He chuckles.

It's such a male sound, and he sounds so pleased with himself. It should make me scoff, but I'm too focused on how it feels to have the bristles of his five o'clock shadow graze my already sensitized skin.

I feel surrounded by him, consumed by him. The fact I can't see him means, when he bites down on the curve of my neck, I cry out. A trembling grips me. A climax threatens. That's when he releases me. *Eh?*

Before I can blink, he turns me to face him. He pats down my hair, tucks a few errant strands behind my ear, then sets me away from him. I stare into his face, taking in his gorgeous features, admiring those angular cheekbones, the defined jawline, the hooked nose, and those beautiful lips which have given me so much pleasure.

He cups my cheek. "You should head back," he whispers.

"You didn't let me come," I bite out. "Again."

"Trust me, it's only going to increase the pleasure when you finally do."

"I've been needy for weeks." I scowl.

"So am I." He smirks.

"You're leaving me like this?" I cry.

"You're leaving *me* like *this*." He takes my palm and places it on the tent at his crotch.

"Oh." Instantly, I squeeze and have the satisfaction of hearing him growl.

"Fucking hell, Empress." He places his hand over mine, stopping me from massaging him.

"But I wanna." I pout.

Tenderness flits across his face. With his free hand he cups my cheek, then bends and presses a hard kiss to my mouth. "And you will, I promise. But not until we're married."

"But—" My words are swallowed by his deepening kiss. Under my palm, his cock jumps. He swears against my lips, pries my hand off of him and twines my fingers with his, then moves my hand to my side. "Behave."

I huff. "I don't understand why we can't be together every night."

"Because I need every bit of my focus on tracking down these people. I can't let myself slip up, not when more than a billion eyes around the planet will be tuned into the wedding. If anything were to happen to you—" He sets his jaw. "I can't take that risk. I need to make sure we get through this ceremony safely."

The expression on his face brooks no argument.

I blow out a breath. "I... I'm not sure I can last like this until the wedding."

43

Ryot

She looks so frustrated and so damn cute, I almost give in. I want to let her come, but I also know if I hold back, the final pleasure will be above anything she's ever experienced. I place a finger on her mouth. "Trust me."

She scowls.

"You're adorable, baby."

She rolls her eyes. "You're turning on the charm and trying to distract me."

"Is it succeeding?"

She goes up on tiptoes and raises her chin, and because she has me wrapped around her little finger, I oblige and kiss her lips. She parts her lips, and I deepen the kiss. The feel of her mouth, the taste of her, the scent of her... All of it goes to my head. I feel all of my resolutions crumble and wrap my arms about her. Footsteps approach.

"Bro, are you ready to meet with the rest of the team? Oh—"

Tyler blinks, then turns his back on us. "Sorry, mate. Didn't mean to do that."

The princess squeaks and buries her head in my neck.

"I'll wait for you in the war room, and let them know…uh… That you'll be there soon." Tyler's steps recede.

I bang the back of my head against the wall. "Goddam Tyler," I say through gritted teeth.

The princess pulls away from me. I let her. "I should be getting back. They'll be wondering what I'm getting up to."

She takes a step back, but I stop her with a touch on her shoulder. "You okay?" I scan her features. Her cheeks are flushed, her lips swollen. It's clear what she's been up to, and while I don't want her to be embarrassed, I'm satisfied that I've left my mark on her.

She draws in a breath then composes herself. Once again, she's the haughty princess. "I will be." Her chin trembles, and I realize, no, she more resembles the girl I spotted at the bar and wanted to take home.

It elicits in me that same primitive instinct I had to possess her as soon as I saw her. The compulsion propelled me, for the first time, to see past my guilt at the events in my past. A compulsion which gave me hope and felt like redemption. It's what spurs me to confess, "You're the first woman I've wanted since Jane."

Her gaze widens. "So, when we kissed at the bar the other day—"

I nod. "I saw you, and I was selfish enough to want you."

A softness comes into her eyes. "You're not being selfish by falling in love. You deserve to be happy, Ryot."

"And you deserve to be with someone you choose to be with."

Say you chose me that very first night we met, too, I implore her silently. *Tell me you, too, have feelings for me. Give me a reason for this marriage to become something more than one of convenience.* Her expression grows wistful.

She looks at me with an imploring gaze but stays silent. The seconds stretch, then she looks away. "I'd better be off."

This time, when she leaves, I don't stop her.

I head off in the opposite direction, through the hallway, down the corridor, until I reach the room at the very end, which has been converted into our meeting space. I walk in to find the bank of computers set up on the tables pushed up against the wall on the right occupied by various crew members.

Upfront is a big screen, split into many windows, each of which shows the feed from different parts of the grounds. It includes all shared spaces from the palace, except for the suites of the Royal Family and the guests. The private suites of the princess, have additional cameras. Only I have access to via my phone.

There's a conference table on the left and Tyler, Quentin, and Brody are gathered around it. Connor's off on one of his research trips. I also recognize Karina Beauchamp, a friend who runs one of the leading security agencies in the world and whose expertise and team I've tapped into in the past.

Tyler watches me with concern on his face. Thankfully, he doesn't mention having found me with the princess. He's the most discreet of my brothers. Unlike Connor, who wouldn't have thought twice about telling everyone what I was up to.

"There you are," Tyler says with sarcasm. "Not even married to the princess, and already behaving like royalty."

I ignore him and turn to Karina. "Thanks for joining us."

She nods in my direction. "Arpad wasn't happy about my being away. But when I explained what it would mean to you, he agreed."

"Tell the big guy, thanks." I met Arpad and Karina at Sinclair's place and instantly hit it off with them. And when I found out Karina's background was in personal protection, and that Sinclair uses her agency to provide security for his own family, I knew I could rely on her.

"Including Karina's team, we have a total of five hundred operatives spread out around the palace grounds." Quentin nods in her direction. "We've also boosted the camera surveillance on the perimeter and have armed guards with guard dogs patrolling the area. On the wedding day itself, and the day following it, the number doubles to a thousand.

"Enough to provide security for all VIPs, as well as doubling the protective detail so no inch of the palace is left vulnerable."

"We're sewn tighter than a baseball's cover," Tyler grunts.

"Any more, and we'll be as tight as a duck's arsehole," Brody drawls.

"It's not enough." I fold my arms across my chest and scowl at them. I realize, I might be a tad unreasonable here, but when it comes to keeping my Empress safe, no security measure seems to be enough.

"You're joking," Tyler protests.

Brody stares at me like I've grown two heads. Only Quentin and Karina don't seem surprised.

"How many guests will be attending." Karina pulls up her tablet and swipes across the screen.

"Five hundred at the wedding in St. George's Cathedral. Two hundred of them will be at the evening reception." I rub at my temples.

"It's a security timebomb, is what it is," Tyler grumbles, his gaze fixed on his phone. His thick fingers fly across the screen.

"It's what the princess wants," I point out.

Aura wanted to leverage the PR generated from the wedding to bring in tourists, and it's working. Arrivals to the country have gone up. Restaurants and shops have reported an uptick in sales. The capital has hired hundreds of additional tour guides, leading to a rise in employment. And thanks to Arthur, the board of The Davenport group signed off on the investment proposal for Verenza. Her country's economic outlook has improved, and I know that makes her happy. Which makes me happy.

Tyler sends me a strange look. He's thinking I'm pussy-whipped. Hell, *I* think I'm pussy-whipped. But she is *my* Empress. *Mine.* And I'll do anything for her.

"Hmm." Quentin drags his thumb under his lip. "Most of the invitees are VVIPs—European and British royalty, and A-list celebrities. And then, there's the press."

"Two hundred of them will be in the press enclosure on the wedding day. Not to mention, the hundreds of onlookers in attendance around the cathedral."

"It'll be a miracle if we pull this off without a major incident." Brody rotates his neck.

I'm going to make sure nothing unexpected happens. Nothing that will spoil the wedding for my woman. It's bad enough she's going through this to ensure the future of her country is safe. I'm going to ensure she doesn't suffer the ignominy of a security glitch, as well. "A miracle is precisely what we're going to make happen." I look around their faces. "After all, we have the best security minds on this."

Quentin squares his shoulders. "You have my word. Given you won't be able to oversee the details that day, I'll do so personally. I'll do my best to ensure the event unfolds without a glitch."

"I've reached out to some more acquaintances I trust. They'll be here with their teams by tomorrow morning. That's another two hundred of the best security personnel on the continent." Karina continues to message on her phone as she speaks.

"And another two hundred former Marines, who've gone into private security since." Tyler looks up from his device. "Pulled in a few favors." He smirks.

"That takes the total number of security folk to nine hundred." Quentin's lips twitch.

That's more than one security person per new arrival, if you include the press.

Add in the mass of tourists coming into the island, the extra ferries being pressed into service, the additional sea and air traffic, not to mention the private planes and yachts expected during this, the scale is truly astonishing.

There hasn't been any further suspicious activity or threats since the assassination attempts on the princess. But instead of reassuring me, it's made me more nervous. It signals that whoever was behind the threats could be regrouping. But I'll be damned if they'll get through security at the wedding and do anything to disrupt the ceremony. My princess deserves a service fit for a queen. And with the number of security personnel deployed, we just might be able to mitigate the risk involved.

My shoulders relax slightly. "Now, we only have to rework the security arrangements and brief everyone."

"Good thing we have another seventy-two hours to the wedding."

Brody rolls his shoulders. "Hell of a bachelor's party you've got going here, bro."

I bare my teeth. "Never did believe in them."

Besides, I'm not getting drunk before the wedding. Not when I need to keep my wits around me. And no way, am I interested in going to a strip club or any of the conventional activities that bachelors seem to revel in. I'm not interested in any woman but her. So no, count me out of these boring rituals. I intend to channel all of my energy into making sure my woman is safe.

I walk around the table to the whiteboard and pick up a marker. "Here's how I propose we allocate our resources for that day."

44

Aurelia

"I can do this." I begin to rub my sweaty palms down my dress when Zoey cries out.

"Don't."

"Oh"—I glance down at my wedding dress and grimace —"thanks. I couldn't live with myself if I stained this beautiful gown."

We're in the room adjoining the main hallway of the Royal palace. The rest of the girls have gone ahead, and we're waiting for our pick-up to the cathedral.

"It looks vintage." She smiles at me, looking gorgeous in her peach bridesmaid's dress.

My dress is deceptively simple, with a V-shaped neckline and a lace bodice which nips in at my waist before continuing in a straight A-line skirt to my ankles.

"It is." I touch the intricate lace appliqué of the fitted bodice. "It really is beautiful." My arms are covered by the long sleeves, inspired by my mother's own wedding dress. It's modest, as befits a cathedral wedding.

I agreed to it because every generation of the Royal Family of Verenza, has gotten married here. While I'm not religious, I know my mother would have wanted this.

The lace design includes lily and sunflower motifs. The low-draped front neckline adds a touch of modernity. The classic, structured A-line silhouette, with a full skirt that elegantly flares from the waist, gives a regal, timeless shape, and is made of layers of soft tulle and underskirts.

The train is modest, by Royal standards, and I'm thankful for that because it already feels too heavy on my shoulders. In addition, a silk tulle veil is fastened to the tiara which belonged to my mother. It's a mix of ethereal and traditional, and I feel like my mother is here with me, in person, today.

"The dress belonged to my mother. Karma West Sovrano's seamstress tailored it to my measurements." I'm also wearing my mother's earrings. I've never felt closer to her.

The last three days went by in a rush of procession and ceremony rehearsals. Ryot was involved in security rehearsals. It means, I didn't see him outside of the wedding rehearsal. Even that was with the rest of the wedding planning and security teams in attendance, so there was barely any time to talk.

Except for the way his eyes flared when I walked down the aisle toward him, and the way he looked into my eyes when we rehearsed our vows—not to mention, how thoroughly he kissed me during the rehearsal—told me he missed me every bit as much as I did him. It's what has kept me going.

My PR manager conducted public and media rehearsals, coordinating logistics and coverage points with the press that arrived from around the world.

She's kept me posted on the arrangements, and if I fold in the online coverage to be generated and the number of satellite TV stations covering the event, it just might mean that my agreeing to marry Ryot is worth it. *You would've married him anyway, remember?* I push the thought aside. We both agreed we'd get what we want from this association. And then we'll move on. *But what you want is to NOT move on.*

My phone buzzes. I glance at where I placed it on the table next to me. Ideally, I shouldn't have sat down for fear of creasing my dress, but I need to save my energy for the day ahead. Besides, my feet in the stilettos were already killing me, and I needed to take my weight off them, so I decided to sit. I pull up my phone and read the message.

> Viktor: Landed this morning from my tour. So, sorry couldn't be at the rehearsal, Aura, but I'm at the church and waiting for you.
>
> Me: OMG, I'm so excited to see you.
>
> Viktor: I feel so guilty I was gone so long.
>
> Viktor: I should have asked you this earlier, but you weren't coerced into this wedding, were you?
>
> Me: No, this is what I want.
>
> Viktor: The news of your marriage came so suddenly. I wish I'd been here to help you navigate the intricacies that came with it.
>
> Me: You're here now. That's what matters.
>
> Viktor: You are going to be amazing, cara mia.

Our mother encouraged us to speak in Italian to her. Viktor and I kept up that tradition after she passed, and often use Italian words in our conversations. It's another thing we have in common. Unlike Brandon, who never picked up enough Italian to be conversant in the language. He also messaged me separately to wish me well and apologize for not being at the wedding.

I was disappointed, but not surprised. Given the bad blood between him and my father, as well as the fact that he and Viktor don't always see eye to eye, I knew it would create a strained atmosphere if he'd decided to come.

My phone dings again, and I check the message.

> Ryot: Are you okay? Soon, this will all be
> over, and you can relax. Just a few more
> hours, Empress.

For some reason, that brings tears to my eyes. Jeez, I'm more emotional than usual today. I suppose, it's allowed. I've always had to be strong, but when I'm with him, I feel I can lean on him. It's almost as if he knew I needed a pick-me-up and messaged me.

"He messaged you, didn't he?" Zoey asks softly.

I nod. "Is it that obvious?"

She smiles. "You get a certain look in your eyes whenever he's around or his name is mentioned."

"Do I?" I chuckle. "I didn't realize I was that transparent."

"It's okay to let your feelings show. Especially today."

I look at her gratefully, once again, feeling the emotions well up.

"Oh no, don't cry. You don't want to spoil your make up, do you?"

I shake my head and sniffle. "Thanks, Z, you're a really good friend."

"You bet." She grins widely.

There's a knock on the door and one of the waitstaff pops her head around. "The car is here, Your Highness."

———

"Ready?" Zoey studies me closely.

I nod, then take a deep breath. My heart is racing in my ribcage. My pulse is galloping at what feels like a million miles a second. *I can do this. I can.* I've prepared for this event my entire life. And at least, I'm going to marry the man I've fallen for, even if he doesn't completely reciprocate my feelings. And the chemistry between us is so strong, there's no need to pretend the attraction. Things could be way worse in a marriage of convenience.

I clutch at my wedding bouquet, which is a simple collection of Jasmine—a tribute to the flowers in my mother's bouquet—

Sunflowers, which are the national flower of Verenza — and roses. Because they begin with the same initial as Ryot's name.

The flowers are white, matching my ivory wedding dress.

The Rolls-Royce Phantom comes to a stop in front of the cathedral. The liveried driver opens Zoey's door. She walks around and waits for me.

One of the security guards holds my door open.

The pealing of the cathedral's bells washes over me, along with the cheering of the crowds. People lined the streets on the short drive from the palace, driving home the gravity of this event.

I struggle to slide out, and someone — I assume the guard — holds out a hand. I place my free hand in his gloved one and step out. He leads me a few steps forward, so my train fans out behind me.

Zoey smooths it out. When I pull at my hand, the man holding mine refuses to let go.

That's when I look up and gasp. "Viktor!" I want to throw my arms about him, but the cheering of the crowd reminds me we are very much in the public eye.

It wasn't mentioned in the protocol that he'd be the one helping me out of the car, but I'm not complaining. Having Viktor here is a huge support, even if it is breaking etiquette.

He grins down at me. "You look beautiful, sis."

"You look dashing yourself." I smile.

He's dressed in a fitted morning suit with a tailcoat and a blue tie. At six-feet-four-inches and with his wide shoulders, swept-back hair and brooding good looks, he looks amazing.

His gaze seems to shine with what looks suspiciously like tears. Then, he uses his thumb to wipe the underside of his eye, and I know, he's as moved by this moment as I am. "Oh, Vik, you're going to make me blubber."

"Don't you dare." He places his hand on mine, so the warmth of his hand engulfs mine, and squeezes. "You look so much like her."

I know, he means my mother. "I feel her presence so strongly today." Tears well up, and I, once more, manage to swallow them down. *This is a happy occasion, so why does my heart feel sad?*

"She'd be so proud of you." He smiles.

The cheers from the crowds around us rise.

"Your audience awaits."

"They might be here to see you as much as me," I tease. He releases my hand, and I wave. The noise from the crowd rises. Flash-bulbs pop from the press enclosure. Then, Viktor takes my hand and leads me up the steps of the cathedral to the entrance. Zoey follows, holding my train.

My father greets me at the top. He's wearing his formal dress uniform of a Royal Navy Admiral. He served in Verenza's navy before he took on the role of crown prince, and then king.

His face lights up; there's a soft smile playing around his mouth. And his eyes fill with tears. "My dear, Aura." He takes my hand in his and lowers his head to kiss my forehead.

He takes in my dress, and a flicker of recognition dawns in his eyes. He looks both stricken and happy. A bit like how I feel inside. "You look absolutely breathtaking." He looks into my eyes, and his own are filled with pain. "I miss your mother so much today, but I realize now, she lives on through you."

"Oh, Papa." My chest tightens. My throat hurts. I have a tough time controlling my tears.

"There, there—" He pats my hand. "Crying is not a good look for the press, dear." He winks at me through his own tears.

"I'll see you on the other side, sis." Viktor touches my hand, then walks away.

The wedding planner arranges the veil over my head, while Zoey places my train down carefully, so it stretches out behind me.

The prelate of the cathedral comes over to speak with me, and I become aware of the fact that the cathedral is full.

The nervousness that squeezed my insides in the car ratchets up. I'm aware of the prelate asking a question, and my father answering. The two of them laugh. Then, the prelate bows and melts away.

The orchestra begins to play "Wedding March" by Felix Mendelssohn from *A Midsummer Night's Dream*, and the choir joins in.

The same song was played when my mother walked down this very aisle twenty-eight years ago.

My father wipes away a tear. He's remembering the ceremony when he wed my mother as well.

Spine straight. You're a princess.

I take a step, knowing I'm following in hers. The hair on my arms rises, and I feel like she's blessed me with her presence today.

The murmuring of the guests increases in volume until every head has turned my way. Through my watery eyes, the faces blur into each other.

Ahead of me, two flower girls, daughters of distant cousins start down the aisle, scattering flower petals as they go.

The ring bearer, Fred's grandson, follows; behind him is Zoey, my maid of honor.

Then it's my turn. My father walks me down the aisle. My stomach twists in on itself, but I manage to keep a tight grip on my emotions. Swallowing down my nervousness, I smile and nod at the guests as I've been taught. Every single etiquette lesson I've taken since I came of age comes to my rescue, and I don't falter.

Halfway to the altar, a tingle runs up my spine. My heartbeat speeds up further. Of its own accord, my gaze rises and meets his silver-green one. He's standing with his back to the altar, watching me approach. The music fades, and the rest of the room seems to disappear, all of my attention captured by him.

He's wearing his ceremonial dress uniform, with a white jacket featuring his medals, ribbons and insignia. His pants are black. He has a white dress shirt, a black bow tie, and a white cap with a black peak and the Royal Marines' badge on the front. There's a sword at his side. He looks dashing and swashbuckling, like a knight ready to ride off into battle. Like he'll slay my dragons and ensure I'm always happy. Once more, my gaze is caught by his and held, and I feel like a moth drawn to a flame. A butterfly pulled toward a spider's web with no means of escape. A flower opening to the sun. I feel every nerve in my body tingle as every cell comes alive. My blood begins to pump faster. My feet seem to move of their own accord. Then, I reach him.

He keeps his gaze on me as he nods in my father's direction. I'm aware of my father asking something and of Ryot replying. But the words don't register. Then, my father places my hand in Ryot's much bigger, wider palm. His fingers grip mine, and his touch sends a spurt of electricity through my body. All of my senses snap to attention. My gaze grows super-sharp.

He brings my hand to his mouth and kisses my fingers. The touch of his lips sends an additional jolt of heat through my veins. My thighs quiver. And my panties dampen. *Damn.*

I'm standing in front of five hundred VIPS from around the world, and approximately a billion people who're tuning in live for this wedding, and I am so turned on. My nipples are hard; my toes curl in my designer stilettos.

I know I'm blushing, and I can't stop it. As if he reads my mind, one side of his mouth curls. There's a wicked edge to his smile. A promise inherent in the brilliance of his eyes that turns my belly into a tsunami of sensations.

We stare at each other, and the very air between us heats. With a last smoldering glance—that, surely, the news cameras must capture—he urges me to turn and face the archbishop.

45

Ryot

I take in my surroundings. The magnificence of the cathedral, the crowded pews, the fact that I'm in my dress uniform... All of it is so different from the rushed wedding at City Hall the last time. It brings home the contrast between my old life and the one I'm embarking upon now.

Jane didn't want to be tied down. She wanted to maintain her own identity, and I respected that. In retrospect, the warning signs that our union might not be everything we hoped for were there from the beginning. We were friends, decided to turn it into a friends-with-benefits situation, and then, she thought she was pregnant, so we decided to get married.

Not that it stopped her from going on the next mission. She messaged me a few weeks later to let me know it had been a false alarm. We should have annulled the marriage, but I foolishly thought we could work things out. Our married life—if you can call it that— was nothing like this connection I feel with my Empress.

Getting married to her, with half the world watching and my family in attendance? This is unexpected, and so very different from the last time. It makes me realize I've been given a chance to start over. I resolve to do everything differently this time. A lightness fills me. My thoughts no longer feel dark. I no longer feel like I'm being held back by my past. *Perhaps, I'm finally breaking free? Perhaps, I'm ready to move on?*

I sneak a glance at the light pouring in through the stained glass behind the altar. I'm not religious, but the beauty, and the hushed atmosphere of the space, make it easy to believe that Jane is resting in peace. *Perhaps, she doesn't begrudge me this chance at happiness, either. Perhaps, she's forgiven me... Perhaps, I'm ready to forgive myself?*

The archbishop gives a sermon about love being a choice and commitment needing dedication and effort, then something about the nature of marriage and the significance of our commitment in a public and private context.

I only half listen to his words, my attention on the gorgeous woman by my side.

As she glided down the aisle toward me in her beautiful white dress, I felt my world shift. She looked ethereal—an angel, a goddess from heaven sent down to rescue me. My Empress is every bit a queen. And it's my privilege to be here next to her, to be able to protect her. My senses stay tuned for anything amiss in the audience watching us. My internal radar, so finely geared to spot danger, remains silent.

The specially chosen security personnel including my brothers and uncle have been positioned within and outside the cathedral, at strategic points to observe the crowd. They're also embedded within the guests, the onlookers, and the press, and even within James Hamilton's catering team. They're ubiquitous and trained to blend in with the crowd, so their presence will not be noticed.

Trained snipers, hidden from view, have been positioned in elevated areas above the naves.

Tyler, himself, is by my side as my best man. This gives him a unique view to see direct threats to the princess.

After completing the homily, the archbishop turns to me. "Do you, Ryot Abraham Arthur Davenport, take this woman to be your lawfully wedded wife, to have and to hold, from this day forward, for better, for worse, for richer, for poorer, in sickness and in health, to love and to cherish, till death do you part, according to God's holy ordinance; and thereto do you pledge yourself to her?"

"I do." I nod.

He turns to her. "Do you, Aurelia Isabelle Verenza, take this man to be your lawfully wedded husband, to have and to hold, from this day forward, for better, for worse, for richer, for poorer, in sickness and in health, to love and to cherish, till death do you part, according to God's holy ordinance; and thereto do you pledge yourself to him."

"I do," she says softly.

Her blue eyes appear luminous, a tremulous smile playing around her lips.

I didn't think I believed in wedding vows. When I married Jane, we dispensed with vows. These are the same words we used during the rehearsal. But they take on a much deeper meaning, now that we're standing here in front of God, our family, our friends, and millions of people I don't even know.

Her hand trembles in mine.

Tyler hands the rings to the bishop, who blesses them. I take the simple wedding band I bought for her and slide it onto her ring finger.

She does the same.

The bishop then folds a scarf over our joined palms. "As these hands are bound together, so may your lives be bound together in love and harmony." The bishop removes the scarf and declares us husband and wife. "You may now kiss the bride."

It's not traditional for the Royal Family of Verenza to have the bride and groom kiss at the end of the ceremony, but I insisted on it. Arthur took my side during the debate that ensued during the wedding rehearsal, and the king gave in.

I lean in, and she tips up her chin. I gaze into her eyes for a few seconds, and when her lips part, I bend and fit my mouth over hers. I kiss her tenderly, softly, gently, yet deeply enough to taste her mouth.

The sweetness shivers through my veins, arrowing straight to my groin.

My cock twitches, and I realize I need to pull back or be seen sporting a chub on television screens around the world, and while I don't give a shit, I don't want my Empress to be embarrassed. I pull back. Her eyelids flutter open, the smile she gives me shy and dazed, and her gaze is tinged with lust. Good.

Applause breaks out from the audience. I take her hand in mine, and we turn to face the crowd who are on their feet. As we begin the walk back up the aisle, the orchestra plays Taylor Swift's Enchanted.

Surprise ripples through the audience. I arch an eyebrow at my Empress, and she laughs. This woman? She knows how to surprise me. Zoey picks up her train and Tyler joins her to follow my wife and me as we walk back down the aisle. The audience continues to applaud and smile. And as we reach the grand entrance of the cathedral, the bells ring out.

When we step out, Tyler walks past me. He takes his position next to the line of men who hold up their swords to form an arch for us to walk through.

"That wasn't in the rehearsal," my Empress muses.

I did it to differentiate this ceremony further from my last one. And because I wanted my Empress to be accorded that respect.

"You're not the only one who can surprise, Wife." I savor the word as it rolls off my tongue. It feels incredible to call her my wife. With Jane? She never wanted to be called that. She preferred we not refer to each other as husband and wife because it made her feel like a possession.

Tyler nods in my direction, and I acknowledge it. Then I lead my wife through the sword-arch. Familiar faces grin back at me: Brody, Nathan, Quentin, and other team-mates from my platoon who've flown here to attend the wedding. We emerge on the other side to more cheering from the crowds who've lined the square in front of the cathedral.

A gleaming carriage pulled by stately white stallions draws up.

I cringe at the thought of having to ride in it, but my Empress wanted to stick to tradition. She wanted to recreate the exact journey her mother and father made after they got married here, and her grandparents before that. She insisted that it makes for a better PR spectacle, and I realize, she's right.

Besides, I aim to please her. And while it's a security nightmare to ride through the streets of the city so exposed, I'll be there to protect her. I pull on my gloves, take my bride's bouquet, and help her in before following.

Another of my security team, doubling as a footman, shuts the door. I recognize the driver, too, as one of my men. Good. I also insisted on snipers being placed on the rooftops surrounding the square and along the route we're going to take. I hand the bouquet to my wife, take her hand in mine, and the carriage sets off.

"That might have been the most stressful hour of my life." Tyler sighs as he shrugs off his jacket and places it over the back of his chair.

"You and me both, brother." I pour water from the jug and hand him a glass before taking one for myself. The crowds lining the streets seemed to number in the millions. Every inch of the sidewalks was overrun with people waving the flag of the country, with many shouting out congratulations as we passed them by. Tyler drove in the lead security car ahead of us, and Quentin followed in the car behind. Despite that, even knowing I had my personnel stationed along the route, I was unable to rest. The fact that my internal radar didn't alert me told me that, likely, the person who targeted her saw the security and decided to pull back. Which made me more anxious. I refill my empty glass with water and toss it back before placing it on the counter with a thunk.

We are in the study in the cottage on the palace grounds which my wife and I will now share. Her father offered to lend it to us, but I insisted on buying it from him.

I wanted us to have a place that belongs to us, a space my wife could go to escape the influence of her father. Where she wouldn't have to feel beholden to the people of this country. Where she could be herself, with me.

Of course, with the amount of money the Davenports are investing in the country, I could point out that I already own part of the Royal Palace itself, but I chose not to highlight that.

"So, the Duke of Verenza, huh?" Tyler sinks his bulk into the chair.

Yep, that's the title I was granted, and the princess is now the Duchess of Verenza. The chair creaks as Tyler settles himself. "How does it feel?"

"That I am married again? Or that I'm royalty?" I shrug. "On the first, I'd say I'm surprised how good it feels. On the second, it's notional, as far I'm concerned. But if it makes my wife happy..." Hearing myself call her my wife sends my protective instincts into overdrive. I glance toward the door she disappeared behind, wondering how long she's going to be. We have another hour until the wedding reception we're expected to attend in the palace's staterooms.

Hosted by the king, and with the rest of her family and mine in attendance, it promises to be an absolute shit-show. I'm not looking forward to it.

"Hmm." He strokes his chin, as he watches me closely. "You're worried that since the person targeting her didn't show, he's regrouping to come back in a more dangerous fashion?" It's as if he read my mind. Which is why I trust Tyler's instincts almost as much as my own.

I shift my weight from foot to foot. I'm used to long days as a Marine, and functioning under enormous stress when on a mission, but none of it felt as personal as this need to keep her safe. It shows how entwined I am in this relationship with her. Something I'll worry about after I've caught the guy who's got her in his crosshairs. "I'll be glad when today is over," I confess.

Though likely, the day after could be worse, since whoever is targeting her might think security will be lax and try something. So, it's best to stay alert.

"Preach." Tyler rolls his shoulders. "How are you doing, really?" He peers into my eyes. "I was surprised when you agreed to Arthur's scheme."

Me too, bro, me too. "It was the only way to ensure she's safe."

"You going to change your entire lifestyle for her?" There's no judgement in his voice. Only curiosity.

"I'd turn my world upside down for her," I say with vehemence.

Before he can answer, his phone buzzes. His face lights up, and he answers the call, "Hello, poppet."

Serene's childish voice comes through, "Daddy. Look." She must show something to him, for he laughs.

"You're so clever, baby."

"Daddy, coming back soon?"

"Soon, baby. Uncle Ryot needs me here, but I'll be with you soon." He blows her a kiss. "You be a good girl for Aunty Summer now."

I hear other voices in the background, then Summer comes on the line. "We love having Serene; she's such a doll."

"Thanks for taking care of her; I appreciate it." Tyler murmurs.

"I owe you, Summer," I call out.

Tyler flips the phone.

I wave at her. "No really, thank you. It's been a godsend to have Tyler here."

Summer waves it off. "You keep the princess safe. And congratulations on the wedding. I'm sorry I couldn't be there, but I'll see the both of you in London soon." There are more voices in the background, then she signs off.

"Summer's been amazing, to step in and take care of Serene. But I need a permanent solution." He looks harried. "Why is it so difficult to find a nanny who Serene likes and who'll stick with us?"

The door to the room opens. A vision in white steps into the room. She's changed out of the wedding dress into an ivory satin gown with a square neckline and a fitted bodice that flares into a modest A-line skirt. The jeweled waistband accentuates her waist and shows off her curves.

She has her hair down with the tiara she wore earlier holding the strands back from her face. Other than her earrings, the only other piece of jewelry she has on is the wedding ring I placed on her finger.

I finger my own, remembering how it felt when she slipped it onto me. I felt connected to her in a fashion that rocked me to the bone. And when the bishop pronounced us husband and wife, a feeling of possessiveness—almost proprietary in nature—consumed me.

Seeing her standing there like an angel, I want to gather her in my arms, peer into her eyes and kiss her before I claim her all over again. I'm dimly aware of Tyler leaving us. The door snicks shut behind him, and I move toward her as if in a dream. When I reach her, I go down on one knee and take her hand in mine.

46

Aurelia

"My queen. My empress." He holds out his hand and when I place my palm in his, he kisses my wedding ring. "My wife." He enfolds my hand between his much larger ones. "You are beautiful."

He looks up at me with naked adoration in his eyes. There's something else there. Something possessive and primal. Something that sets off a flurry of heat pulsing through my veins and turns my pussy into a miasma of need.

"Ryot," I whisper.

His hold on my hand tightens. Then, he moves one hand to my hip in a gesture that signals ownership.

"You take my breath away." He scans my features, that look in his eyes turning into something fierce. "You make me want to scoop you up and hide you away from the world so no one else can see you."

I smile.

"You make me want to declare to the world that you're mine and that if any bastard dares to touch a hair on your head, I'll make them wish they'd never been born."

"Oh, Ryot." Those emotions, which seem to be so close to the surface whenever he is around, threaten to spill over.

"If I could wrap you up in cotton wool and protect you so no one could ever get to you, I would."

The pain in his voice sears through any remaining barriers I have left. I cup his cheek. "You make me feel confident and protected. If it weren't for you, I'm not sure I'd have gotten this far. You rescued me from Gavin—"

"—Don't say that arsehole's name."

"—and stood up for me against my own father. I didn't realize how much I was putting myself down until you came into my life."

He rises to his feet and takes me in his arms. "You make me want to be a better man, Empress."

I cup his cheek. "You make me…feel much more than I thought I could."

He frowns. "Is that a bad thing?"

"It's unexpected."

"Same." His lips quirk. "You make me want to kiss you, taste you, and draw in your scent until you're in my veins and in my very cells. You make me hope. You make me…believe." A shadow crosses his features. "If I could give you my heart…"

I touch his lips. "I understand. Jane was a part of your life. No matter what went down between the two of you, you were married to her, and that will not change."

The furrow between his eyebrows deepens. "I never felt like this about her. This…deeply. This…soul-shatteringly vulnerable. I never felt like if something were to happen to her, I would die. It's why, when her platoon was taken out, I felt so guilty. And finding out she was pregnant with someone else's child, when we'd married only because I thought she was carrying my child, felt like a cruel joke. Much as I want to get over it, I don't think I have. Much as the chemistry between the two of us is like nothing I've ever experienced before, and even though the connection I feel with you is searing—"

"—there's something stopping you from committing fully," I complete his statement.

I should feel deeply uncomfortable that my new husband is still not fully on board with us. That he's never once said that he loves me. That he's not over his past. That what happened to him with his previous marriage might have traumatized him so much that he's unable to lean into the attachment he claims to feel with me. I should feel uneasy that I'm going into this marriage not knowing if I'll have one in a few months. Or indeed, that within the year, we might no longer be married. But I know he's the one for me, enough to take this chance.

And a deeper part of me, the part which sees past his doubts and uncertainty, the part which is able to look beyond his words to the unsaid emotions I see in his eyes and writ into every angle of his body... That instinct feels confident that it's only a matter of time before he acknowledges his feelings for me.

It's there in his protectiveness, his possessiveness, and in the way he follows me with his gaze. He never lets me out of his sight when I'm with him. And when he isn't with me, it's because he's doing his best to keep me safe. No one has ever been this concerned about me. No one else can be this attentive to me. No, he's the one for me, and I'm confident he'll work it out for himself soon.

"I want you, Empress. I need you with every fiber of my being, but I fear I might be so badly burned from what happened that I'll never be able to love you the way you should be."

My heart thuds into my ribcage. It's the first time he's used the L-word, even if it's to say that he might not be able to love me. The very fact that he's thinking about it sends a rush of endorphins through my bloodstream.

"You need to work through everything you've been through. I understand," I say softly.

His clenches his lips together so tightly the edges turn white. "I want you to be able to live your life on your terms. Unencumbered by your duty to your country and your father." He drags his fingers through his hair, a look of consternation on his features. "I want you to fall in love and choose your own path. I just don't know if I'm capable of giving you the love you deserve. I don't want to hurt you, Empress."

A warmth squeezes my chest. He cares for me. He's half in love with me, and he's not even aware. It's only a matter of time before he comes to realize it too. It'd better be before our year together is up.

"You won't." I place my hand over our joined palms. "Just by being yourself and by being with me, you make everything seem possible."

He takes both of my hands in his, brings them to his mouth, and kisses my fingertips. "I don't deserve you. I'll do everything possible to protect you. I promise you, I'll track down whoever is after you and make sure they never bother you again."

"I believe you."

He moves my hands to one palm, and the other he wraps around my waist and brings me in. "You make me forget about everything else. You make me want to kiss you until you're breathless."

"Promises, promises," I say lightly.

His eyes flash, then he tugs me, so I squeak and fall into him. He brings his mouth to mine, and when I part my lips, he sweeps his tongue in. He kisses me, and I feel the sensation all the way to the tips of my toes. My stomach trembles, and my pussy clenches. My scalp feels like a thousand sparks are zinging across it. I hold onto him as he deepens the kiss, and it's so intense, so passionate, so fervent, I feel like I'm about to catch fire.

Someone clears their throat behind us, and I freeze. But my husband doesn't stop. He continues to kiss me, and when I push at his shoulder, he merely raises his head and stares into my eyes. My breath comes in short gasps as my chest rises and falls. Ryot's features, on the other hand, are granite hard. His jaw is set. His green eyes though, have turned to silver, and the nerve that pulses at his temple tells me he's far from unmoved by the kiss. This man... The more he tries to hide his emotions, the more I recognize them. "I see you," I say softly. "I see you, Ryot."

His gaze sharpens. His nostrils flare. He bends and nips at my lower lip, and I shudder.

"Sorry to cut in you guys, but there are three hundred VVIPs waiting for you, and no one is allowed to have a drink until you guys arrive, so if you wouldn't mind hurrying..." Tyler's amused voice reaches us.

A giggle bubbles up, and it feels so right. Ryot's features relax, a spark of amusement lighting up his eyes.

"I do mind," he throws over his shoulder, then leans back and surveys my features.

"Is my lipstick—" I raise my hand, but he grabs it. "You look perfect. A little flushed and like you've been kissed. Perfect." He links his fingers through mine. "Shall we?"

47

Ryot

"Congratulations." Arthur squeezes my shoulder. "You've made me proud, boy." Dressed in a suit, with his silver hair coiffed back from his face, he looks handsome. The tiredness I saw the last time has faded. He takes my wife's hand and bends to kiss it. "Congratulations, Duchess."

"Thank you." My wife smiles back.

"It was a beautiful ceremony." Imelda who's dressed in a suit which is a twin to Arthur's, right down to the bow tie, lowers her chin. "And mercifully short, if I might say so."

My wife laughs. "One of the things my father acquiesced to."

"There were others which he refused to budge on, I assume?" Imelda says shrewdly.

"He's a stubborn man, and a king." My wife's eyes shadow. "He has responsibilities."

"None more important than the one toward you." Imelda pats my wife's hand. "You're a dutiful daughter."

"And my wife." I put my arm around Aura's shoulders. I'm never going to miss a single opportunity to say that aloud.

She leans into me, and I can tell she's pleased. "A very happy wife today." She chuckles. "I hope the two of you will be staying on and taking in the sights of my beautiful country?"

"Alas, we have only one more day, which we plan to spend at the Fishermen's Islands."

She's referring to the mini archipelago of seven islands near Verenza, a favorite among tourists.

"Just a day?" my wife cries.

"You'd think this old man would enjoy his retired life and spend more time taking in the sights, but he insists he needs to be back for an important meeting." Imelda shrugs.

I turn to Arthur. "Is it because Nathan and Quentin are both staying here to oversee the security arrangements at Verenza and can't fill in for you?" I frown.

"Yes, it is —" Arthur begins to say but Imelda nudges him.

"What he means to say is that he'd have gone anyway. And it's right that they are here until we neutralize this risk to the Duchess' life." She turns to him. "Isn't that what you were going to say, dear?"

Arthur looks taken aback, then nods. "Yes, she's right. I'd much rather the men be here and support you."

"I am very grateful to all the Davenports for their help," my wife murmurs.

"You are one of us now," Arthur points out.

"I am," she agrees.

Arthur turns to me. "While you're here, you should take a look into the investment plan for the money being invested into Verenza."

I jerk my chin. "I've already touched base with the leader of the planning team."

My wife whips her head in my direction. "When were you planning to tell me?"

I scowl. "I wasn't aware I had to keep you posted about my movements?"

She firms her lips. "You were discussing how to invest the money being spent in my country over the next few years. Money which came into the country because I agreed to marry you. Money which will impact the future of my country."

Goddam, she has a point. I screwed up.

While I try to formulate a response, she squares her shoulders. "My father and Fred chose not to involve me in financial matters related to my country. I didn't expect my husband would follow in their footsteps." The skin stretches tightly over her cheekbones; disappointment turns her lips down.

"Excuse me." She pivots and walks away, back straight, anger shimmering off of her in waves. She's magnificent, this woman. My wife.

I definitely did mess up. "Fuck," I swear under my breath.

Imelda turns on Arthur. "Couldn't you keep your mouth shut?"

"What did I do?" Arthur looks genuinely puzzled.

Without another word, I head in the direction she's taken. And when she slips out onto the balcony, I follow her, then shut the door behind us.

She hears me but doesn't turn. Instead, she walks over to the far corner, which is in shadows, and sinks down on a bench. When I reach her, I sink down next to her. She turns her head away.

"I'm sorry, I didn't mean to come across as—"

"Arrogant and condescending?"

I wince. "You're right, and I was both. But old habits die hard."

She finally turns to me. The moonlight turns her blue eyes into a color as dark as the sapphire on the ring I had planned on giving her today. *So, why didn't I? What stopped me? What keeps me from being fully invested in this relationship, when I know I'm falling for her?*

"That's very candid of you."

"It's the effect you have on me." I hold her gaze, wanting to touch her but knowing it's not the time yet. "I'm not ashamed to say I have a big ego, and I have reason for that."

She scoffs. "If that's an apology—"

"That wasn't, but this is..." Once more, I go down on my knee in front of her. "I've never bowed to anyone, not man or woman, but I do to you." I bend my neck. "Only to you, my wife. And know that I'm sorry for what I said earlier."

Some of the tension goes out of her body. "You are?"

I nod. "We're husband and wife. A team. A partnership. And like any partnership, we need to keep the channels of communication open at all times. And that includes my telling you about my plans to be an advisor to the planning team for investing the Davenports' money in Verenza."

Her forehead smooths out. "I'm so sorry I got upset. I don't know what came over me. It's your money—"

"*Our* money."

"Our money." She nods. "You should definitely be involved in deciding how it needs to be channeled."

I rise up and sit next to her. "And *you* need to be on that planning team."

48

Aurelia

It didn't strike me until now how the balance of power between my father and me has changed. And it's all because of this man. My father has never treated me badly. But he's always favored my brothers before me when it comes to matters of state.

He preferred I focus on the marketing and PR for the country, while Viktor was involved in economic policy and developmental plans. He'd have involved Brandon too, except my middle brother kept his distance from the family.

I tried to fight it, and Viktor, too, tried to change my father's mind, but he was unshakeable.

I haven't been married even a day, and my husband has made a difference. He picked up on how much it bothers me to be cut out of the plans being made for the future of my beloved Verenza, and he wants to fix it. I lean in and kiss him soundly.

I must take him by surprise, for he goes still, then he plants his big palm on the back of my neck and, holding me in place, he deepens the kiss. Deep and drugging, it shoots heat through my veins.

My thighs wobble, and my toes tingle. Electricity courses through my veins, and I feel like I've stuck my fingers into a socket. We break apart, panting, and I gasp. "Wow."

"Indeed." He squeezes the back of my neck. "What was that for?"

"For—" I try to put the emotions I'm feeling into words. "For being in my corner. For knowing what I want better than I do. For respecting me and not taking me for granted. For recognizing what it means to me to be on that planning team, and being ready to fight for me, when not even my own family has done so. For"—I lift my gown and straddle his lap—"apologizing to me. For putting your ego aside and being willing to meet me halfway."

"What are you doing?" He frowns.

"What does it look like?" I place my hand on the tent at his crotch. "Whoa, someone's ready."

"A constant state around you." He smirks, then groans when I squeeze the rigid column I can feel through his pants. I begin to massage him, and he blows out a breath. "We're at our wedding reception, and there are three hundred VVIP guests out there. But I, know something, they don't."

I manage to string my thoughts together into a response. "Oh?"

"I know that their haughty Duchess is an exhibitionist. And that she derives great pleasure from praise kink, especially when it's spiked with the occasional degradation."

To hear myself described in such great detail makes me feel like I have his focus. That I am his center of attention. That he cares about me enough to know exactly how to elevate my desire.

His eyes gleam. "I know that if I touch you between your legs, you'll be wet, and that your pink swollen clit yearns for my ministrations."

I squeeze my thighs to stop moisture from seeping out. But I can't stop the gasp that escapes me.

"All I know is that you're my husband, and I want you." I toss my head. "Everyone else can go fuck themselves."

"What will your people say when they realize their sweet princess swears like a trooper?"

"That I'm human? Like them?"

He laughs. "I fucking love your spirit, you know that?"

"Can I say that I love your dick?" I flutter my eyelashes at him.

"You can do better." He jerks his chin. "Get up."

"Huh?" I take in the unyielding set of his jaw and realize he's serious. I rise to my feet.

He slides his legs apart, then he shrugs off his jacket, folds it, then drops it on the ground between his legs.

"On your knees."

Hearing him say those words in that hard, gravelly voice turns my pussy into a melting mess. My knees tremble, and I sink down onto the soft material of his jacket. "Thank you," I murmur.

"I'll never let anything hurt you, baby." He searches my eyes. "Except me. And that's only if you ask me to."

"Oh, god." I squeeze my thighs together. "Why do I find that so hot?"

I don't realize I've spoken that aloud, until he closes his fingers around the nape of my neck. His fingers are so long and so thick, they meet his thumb in the front. I feel shackled by him, shackled to him. I feel vulnerable and exposed, kneeling here in my very fancy, one-hundred-thousand-dollar reception dress. I feel... perfect.

And when he leans in, kisses my forehead, and whispers, "You like it because you're submissive, baby. Because you like to be told what to do when it comes to sex. Because *I* know what you like, better than *you* do, when it comes to sex."

My entire body lights up like I'm a human Christmas tree. A shiver squeezes up my spine, and I sense him smile. He leans back and eyes me lazily. "With your people, you may be the Duchess of Verenza, but when you're with me, you're my fucktoy. You feel me?"

The coarseness of his words is a delicious contrast to the bowing, the scraping, and the polite language I'm generally treated to. It's so different, so incongruous... It feels so natural, so right, that my need shoots up to fever pitch. I begin to slide my free hand under the skirt of my dress, but he shakes his head. "You don't come until I let you, remember?"

"B-but..." My pussy throbs. A heavy weight settles between my legs, and my clit feels like it's swollen to twice its size. "Can I rub myself, please? Just once?"

He shakes his head.

I scowl. I so want to defy him. But he's right; I can't go against his orders, not when he's my dominant. I raise my hand and place it on his thigh. "Fine, have it your way."

"Oh, I will," he says in a mean voice that pulses another wave of lust under my skin. "Unzip me."

The authority in his voice propels me to action. I reach forward and oblige him by sliding down the zipper. His boxers are tented, and the thick column of his cock is outlined against the fabric.

"Take it out." He raises his hips, and I pull down his briefs and his pants. His cock springs free. The swollen head is almost purple with arousal; it's thick and long and every bit as monstrous as I remember. My pussy trembles. My stomach squeezes in on itself. I curl my fingers around the base, and he groans. "F-u-c-k."

Liquid heat invades my blood stream. I lean in and, propelled by instinct, I lick up the underside of his shaft. Instantly, he digs his fingers into my hair and tugs. Pinpricks of sensation crowd my scalp. And when I close my mouth around the fat head, he shoots his hips up from the bench.

"Woman, you're killing me." His voice is gravelly, like he swallowed dirt, and when I look up at him from under my eyelids, his features are flushed. His lips are pressed together like he's barely holding onto his control, his green eyes burning with unbridled lust. He looks like a marauding devil, or a god who's on the verge of losing control. I lick my tongue over the velvety tip, and his nostrils flare. "You're going to pay for this, baby," he says through gritted teeth.

I merely swirl my tongue around the perimeter of the head, and he makes a growling sound at the back of his throat. It's so very male, so filled with desire, so hungry that it lights a fuse in my chest. Urgency grips me. I squeeze my fingers around the base and dig the fingers of my other hand into his thigh for purchase. Then I lower my head and take him down my throat.

"Fucking hell." He holds my hair back from my face, tightening his grip, and when I try to draw back, he holds me in place. The fact that I'm unable to move should alarm me, but my body seems to understand, for my muscles relax. My shoulders loosen, and once again, when I look up at him, he's watching me with naked possession. "Give in, baby. Let me guide you. Let me show you how good it can be for you." The husky promise in his voice makes me squeeze my thighs together. I order my body to slacken and give myself up to him.

"Good girl," he rumbles.

And I almost come with the approval. That's all I want. This man's validation. All along, I've been trying to please the world, when really, the only thing that matters is that I please this man. It's so simple. All my needs are centered right here where we are joined. All my wishes and hopes and dreams fall away. I'm reduced to my base self, which wants the pain and the pleasure he can bestow on me. He begins to maneuver me, pulling me back until his cock is balanced at the rim of my mouth, then forward until he slips down my throat. I swallow, and he blows out a breath. His dick thickens and presses against my throat. His thigh muscles tremble, and a current seems to run through his body. Then he pauses. "Change of plans." He pulls out.

"What are you—" I huff as I'm lifted onto the seat next to him. "Why—" I begin again, but he cuts me off by pressing his mouth to mine.

He must taste himself on me, for he makes that familiar growling sound in his chest. The next second, he slides down to kneel in front of me.

Then he pulls up the skirt of my dress until it's bunched around my hips. The material is going to crease which, in turn, is going to show when we walk inside, but at this stage, I'm beyond caring. He fits himself between my legs, forcing my thighs apart. Then, he hooks his finger into the waistband of my panties and tugs. It snaps.

I cry out, then gasp as he licks up my seam. Goosebumps pepper my thighs. My stomach jumps. Longing crowds my belly, my chest, my very soul. It overwhelms me, and I try to pull away.

But he grips my thighs and holds me in place. He hooks his elbows under my legs and pulls me to the edge of the bench. Then, he throws my legs over his shoulders and stuffs his tongue inside my cunt.

49

Ryot

She throws her head back and cries out, "Ryot!" And I'm sure everyone in the palace heard her. And fuck, if that doesn't make me feel a hundred feet tall.

This is *my* wife. My *life*. And she's on the verge of coming. Only I can draw this response from her. Only me. She's mine. A raw intensity surges through me. I lick up between her pussy lips and curl my tongue around her clit, and when she moans loudly and pants, and her entire body seizes up, I know she's close. I reach down, wrap my fingers around my dick, and begin to jerk off. Every time I thrust my tongue inside her sopping wet channel, she thrashes her head to the side. She grips my hair and tugs, almost pulling the strands from the roots. The sensations sizzle down my spine, and my cock grows impossibly hard. I curl my tongue around her clit, and when I bite down, her entire body jolts.

My balls draw up in response. That's when I rise to my feet and with jerky movements squeeze the length of my shaft over and over again. "Open your eyes," I snap.

Her eyelids are heavy with desire. She parts her lips, and I slip my cock in between them. "I'm going to come in your mouth, and you're going to take every drop, understand?"

My Empress nods. I slide my fingers into her hair to hold her head in place, then with a final twist and a tug, I pour my climax down her throat. I seem to come and come, and she closes her mouth around me and swallows. Her blue eyes are feverish with carnal need, and she sucks down almost every drop.

Some of the liquid escapes from the corner of her mouth. I pull out and, scooping up my cum, slide my digit in between her lips. She sucks on it, and my cock twitches. *And I just came.*

"You're so beautiful. I can't get enough of you. I'll never have enough of you." I sit down and pull her into my lap. She curls into me, her fingers pressed into my chest. Her breathing choppy. "I'm still horny." Her voice is uneven.

I chuckle. "Just a few more hours, baby."

"But you came," she whines.

"Only so I can keep going when I make love to you."

She considers what I'm saying, then scoffs. "You expect me to believe that?"

I notch my finger under her chin and tilt up her head. "I expect you to do what I say. I expect you to believe that I know how to wring every last drop of pleasure from your body."

"I do. And I'm afraid you know how to do that too well. I worry that when you finally let me come, it's going to be so good, I'm going to be addicted to you."

"I'm already addicted to you, baby." I kiss her brow.

She frowns and opens her mouth when Tyler's voice calls from the entrance to the balcony.

"Ryot? Duchess? There are people looking for you."

"Be right there!" I yell in his direction, then press my forehead to hers and groan. "Remind me why we're doing this again?"

"So, your investment and my country will benefit?" she says in a droll voice.

I lift her to her feet. Then, pressing a last kiss to her weeping pussy, I smooth her gown down. I pocket her panties then place my hands on her hips. "Each step you take, you'll feel the imprint of my mouth on you and remember who you belong to."

She gapes. "You're an—"

"Animal?" I nod. "Only when it comes to you."

"But I'm so wet, and so turned on," she gripes.

"You know how good it was when I made you come?"

She jerks her chin.

"Now, take that and multiply the effect by a hundred. That's how good it's going to be when I let you come again. I want it to feel incredible for you, baby."

"You're enjoying seeing me so needy," she accuses me.

"I like being in control. I like knowing I have so much power over your body, that you won't come until I let you."

"I want to be angry with you, but"—she shakes her head—"a part of me loves it when you order me around. And the fact that you haven't let me come yet is weirdly arousing." She knits her eyebrows, looking so very dissatisfied, and so very cute, I can't stop myself from chuckling.

"It's not funny." She slaps at my chest.

"It's not, but I promise, it's going to be worth it." I tuck myself into my pants and rise to my feet. Then, pulling out my phone and switching to the camera app, I hold it up so she can see her face in it.

"Thanks." She cleans up the sides of her lips and the corners of her eyes, then pats her hair down. "How do I look?"

"Like a gorgeous, sexy, confident Empress."

She laughs. "You have a way with words, husband."

A hot sensation squeezes my chest, and I take her hand in mine. "And it is my greatest privilege to be your partner. Never forget that." She looks like she's going to kiss me again, but I place a finger on her lips. "Come on, let's do this."

Our wedding reception includes a speech from the king, and another from Arthur. Halfway through the sit-down dinner, which seems to go on forever, and during which my wife seems to grow more and more tired, I make the decision to leave.

When I rise, pull my wife to her feet, and bid everyone at our table goodbye, no one bats an eyelid.

After changing into travel clothes, we leave within the protective cordon of the security team.

"I can barely keep my eyes open." She yawns.

I lead her toward the limousine waiting for us. I don't want to go anywhere else. I'd prefer to keep her in the suite where she'll be safe, but I don't want to deprive her of her honeymoon.

Besides, we'll be safe on the island an hour's boat ride from Verenza. It's private—owned by the Davenports—and we'll be alone. The island is also equipped with CCTV and thermal cameras around the perimeter, which are monitored by the off-island security team.

I've also deployed anti-drone technology that will jam signals, prevent footage from being captured, and disable any electronic foreign object that comes within miles of the perimeter of the island.

The measures are stringent enough to satisfy even me.

Our bags are packed and already in the car. Once we're inside, I pull her close, and by the time we reach the marina to board the yacht which will take us to the island, she's asleep. I carry her onto the boat and sit down in the cabin with her in my lap. I hold my precious burden close all the way to the island. When we arrive, I carry her out onto the jetty, then into the golf cart.

I hold her in my lap while Tyler drives us to the two-story house set back from the beach.

It's almost two a.m. by the time I carry her up the stairs and place her in our bed.

I remove her stilettos. Then, because I don't want to wake her up, I leave the dress she changed into before we left the palace. Finally, I cover her up with a duvet. She doesn't stir.

The dark circles under her eyes tell me she's wiped out.

I slip back out to talk to Tyler. He's already placed our bags inside the house and is waiting by the doorway.

I step out and shake his hand. "Thanks, bro."

"Anytime," he says in a gruff voice.

Then, because I'm overcome by brotherly love for this man, thanks to whom I am able to steal a few days away with my bride, I hug him. "I'm not sure how I can thank you."

"By getting some downtime and letting me and the rest of the team do the heavy lifting for a few days."

I squeeze the back of his neck. "I owe you. A lot."

"Oh, I'll collect on it." He smirks. Then his features grow serious. "We'll find this person who poses a risk to the Duchess. We're close; I can feel it."

"Are you sure you and Quentin want to be on guard duty personally?"

Both volunteered to lead teams who'd be on unmarked boats patrolling the waters around the island. He looks at me like I'm crazy. "Are you kidding? Of course, we want to be on guard personally. The wedding has been so high profile that you two are top of mind, even for those who might not have thought about you as a target. So yes, we'll be on the boats. We'll maintain distance, so we can give you guys your privacy while keeping an eye on any approaching vessels or unauthorized drones." He claps my shoulder. "Not even a fly can get in or out of the island without us being alerted."

Some of the tension bleeds out of my muscles. I hold out my hand. "Thanks, man."

"You bet." He squeezes my palm, then nods toward the house. "Best get some rest. You look beat." He steps back. "We'll be back in three days to pick you up. If you need anything —"

"I'll call." I jerk my chin.

He turns the golf cart around and drives off into the night. Tyler was the best of us in the Marines. But he left it all behind to look after his daughter. It's been an adjustment for him to become a single father, but there hasn't been a word of complaint from him. If anyone deserves to find happiness, it's him.

And me? Am I happy?

I look inside and realize I feel calmer than I have in years. Being with her feels right. It feels like I've spent my entire life searching for her, and now that I have her, I'll do everything to keep her safe.

I owe it to her to give her the most incredible honeymoon. The kind that will surpass all of her expectations. The kind that will satisfy her in every way and give her memories she'll never be able to beat with another man. I lower my hands to my sides and stare into the darkness. *Another man.* I'll never be able to see her with another man. Not when I'm the only one who can take care of her. No one else can protect her like I can. No one else can love her the way I do. *Love?* I stiffen.

When did that happen? Was it when I saw her walking down the aisle? Or when I slipped the ring on her finger? Or when I swore to love and protect her for the rest of my life? Or when I felt her come around my cock and realized nothing was as satisfying or as gratifying as pleasuring my wife. And it feels so completely different from what I had with Jane.

It feels so much more real with Aura. So much more earthy, and dirty, and fierce, and heartfelt. Every time I kiss her, my soul hitches. Every time I touch her, my body recognizes her. Every time I kiss her my heart insists she's mine. Only mine.

Footsteps sound and I turn to find my wife approaching. "I missed you," she says a voice husky with sleep.

A sensation unlike anything I've ever felt before—something so filling, so all-pervasive, so gratifying, something so caring it melts my heart, yet so tinged with lust, it turns my cock to stone—envelops me.

I bend and sweep her up in my arms. "You should be in bed."

50

Aurelia

"I missed you." I yawn hugely, then lock my arm about his neck.

I woke up horny and desperate for that orgasm. I'm so ready to consummate this marriage. The only thing more intense than the need to feel him inside of me is this ache in my chest.

It's this overpowering yearning to be with him, to feel his arms around me, to draw in his scent and be the focus of his attention, which drove me to leave my bed and find him.

His mouth curves. He bends and presses a kiss to my forehead, then carries me inside to the bedroom. He lowers me to my feet. Then, holding my gaze, he reaches around me to lower the zipper on the dress I'd changed into before we left the palace. My breath catches.

The neckline slips down over one shoulder, then the other. He bends and kisses the curve of one, then peels it down my arm. He repeats his actions on my other side. I let the fabric slide down to pool around my ankles. The air between us heats. A tremor shivers down my back. Then he reaches behind and unhooks my bra and pulls that off as well. He stares at my breasts. My nipples pebble.

"You're so beautiful." He kisses one breast, then the other, then trails his lips up my throat to my lips. He kisses me. That yearning sensation in my tummy catches fire, and I sway toward him.

He scoops me up in his arms again and places me on the mattress. I look up at him, befuddled, as he pulls the cover over me.

"You need to sleep." He begins to strip off his own clothes efficiently. The tie, followed by the jacket and shirt. When he reveals his wall-like chest with the dog tags around his neck, that fire in my veins is fanned into a full-blown inferno.

I lick my lips, taking in the thick biceps and the veins on his forearms which flex as he drops his clothes on a nearby chair. The jingle of his belt buckle, the r-r-r-ipping sound of the zipper as he lowers it, then the whisper of his pants as he shucks them off.

He straightens and lets me have my fill of powerful thighs, hair roughened legs, big feet, and neat toenails. My pussy instantly clenches, and my nipples pebble. He walks around to his side of the bed and slides in. Then he turns me over on my side, slides his arm under my neck and spoons me. With the heavy weight of his arm around my waist, and the heat of his body cocooning me, I'm surrounded by him, and it feels heavenly.

I'm sure I'm too turned on to sleep but I find my muscles unwinding. A heaviness steals over me, and I close my eyes. When my eyes open next, I find I'm in the same position. The pale light of dawn creeps in through the window whose curtains weren't drawn. I'm pinned under his arm, and I can feel his breath raising the hair on my head. I turn slowly and take in his features.

His thick eyelashes form a fringe over those cheekbones I'd die to have, that patrician nose, that full lower lip that drew me to him from the beginning, that strong chin that hints at his dominant nature, the beautiful cords of his throat that stand out in relief… I reach out and touch them. His skin is soft to the touch, but the strength underneath filters through my fingertips. I trace them up to his chin, then gently outline that gorgeous mouth of his. His lips part and he sucks on my fingertip. I shiver and raise my gaze to find he's watching me with that intent look I spotted in his gaze the very first day I met him.

His chest rises and falls but, otherwise, he's so still. That ability to keep completely motionless is unnerving. I lean in and, with my eyes open, kiss him.

Our lips meet, and our breaths mingle. He stares into my eyes, and it feels like I'm drowning in a storm-darkened sea. I slip my fingers around to tug on the hair at the nape of his neck. It must hurt, but he doesn't flinch. He also doesn't kiss me back. I straddle him, so the thick length tenting his boxers digs into my core. I begin to grind my aching center on that blunt instrument of torture.

He grows even harder, longer, if that's possible. I keep my gaze locked with his, then slide my hand down his front to brush up against his waistband. And when I slip my fingers inside to graze at the head of his cock, he moves.

He shoves me onto my back and plants his arms on either side of me, holding up most of his weight. His lower body, though, pins me down. "Remember what I said?"

Of course, I do. But I'm not giving him the satisfaction of admitting that. Besides, I want to incite him. I want to push him into losing control and taking me over the edge, because damn it, I'm tired of this crawling, empty sensation that's dug its claws into my insides and refuses to let go. So, I tilt up my chin and jut out my lower lip. "I'm sure you're about to tell me."

One side of his mouth curls, and something feral glints in his expression. I'm reminded, again, that this man is at his peak. An apex predator who likes to toy with his prey, who, in this case, is me. A shiver of anticipation jolts up my spine. My nerve-endings crackle. I try to pull away, but he has me pinned so that I can barely move. My breathing grows choppy. My heart rate shoots up. He lowers his head and licks up my cheek, and I whimper.

Oh god. His touch ignites little pinpricks of need all over my body. "Why are you torturing me like this?" I moan.

"Because it's so much fun to see you writhe under me, baby." He drags his whiskered chin down my cheek, and I whimper. And when he bites down on the curve of my shoulder, the explosion of pleasure in my blood stream almost shoots me over the edge.

"Ryot, please, please, please," I pant, knowing the more I ask, the more he's going to delay my gratification. It drives me out of my head with frustration, which turns my insides to a seething mass of need. He bends and runs his nose down my throat to between my breasts. He inhales deeply. I shudder.

"So, fucking sexy," he growls.

Another whimper works its way from my lips.

He drags his bearded chin toward a nipple, and the friction stabs little knives into my skin. Panting loudly, I throw my arms about his shoulders, but he twists one arm back and over my head, then the other. He holds my wrists in place and wraps my fingers around the bars in the headboard. "Hold on."

He rolls off of me and rises to his feet. I watch as he shoves his boxers down and kicks them off. Then he palms his massive cock and squeezes it from base to head. Little drops of precum glisten at the tip. I squeeze my thighs together to try to hold in the ache, not that it helps. And when he snatches the belt from where he dropped his pants last night, I widen my gaze. "Wh-what's that for?"

He merely smirks, then climbs back between my legs. He reaches over, loops his belt around my wrists, and ties my arms to the headboard. I tug to find they're secure, but loose enough that I can get free if I want to. But I don't want to. I want him. His touch. His kisses. His hands on me. His lips on mine. His dick inside me.

"I want you—" I swallow. "I want you to do anything with me that you want."

He quirks his head. "You sure about that?"

His tone is so serious, I pause to consider my words, then nod. "Yes." I nod again. "I want you to take me, fuck me, use me. I want you to treat me like your fucktoy."

He smiles. "You don't tell me what to do."

"I'm not telling you what to do; I'm telling you what I want you to do." I roll my eyes. "I want you to fuck me. Is that so difficult?" I cry out as he slaps my breast. "Oh my god," I groan.

I can feel the imprint of his fingers on my skin, feel the reverberations all the way to my toes. My clit throbs, and my pussy weeps. Once more, I try to squeeze my legs together but can't because he's there between them. He pinches a nipple, tweaking it so that a line of fire runs to my cunt. I whine loudly, and he laughs. *Asshole.* I scowl at him, but that seems to encourage him, for he delivers the same treatment to my other nipple. I cry out, then huff when he plucks on both nipples at the same time. My pussy seems to catch fire. A bead of sweat runs down my temple. I writhe and yell, and try to pull away, and when he bends and takes a nipple in his mouth, it feels like nothing in this world.

"I can't. I can't." I thrash around.

"You can." He releases his hold on my breasts, slides my panties — the pair I'd changed into before leaving—down my legs, and grasping my panties, reaches up. "Open."

"What?" I stare.

"I'm going to slide this between your teeth, so you have something to bite down on."

"Why should I need that?" I ask with suspicion.

His grin widens. "You'll find out soon."

"Not sure I like the sound of that."

He tilts his head. "You can say no."

I glower at him. "You know, I won't do that."

"Good girl." He cups my cheek. "I promise, you're going to love this."

I sniff. "I don't want to believe you—"

"But you do."

He knows me too well. I'm helpless under his ministrations. And I want that orgasm badly. Besides, he knows better than me what my body wants, I know that. I part my lips, and he stuffs my underwear inside my mouth. Then, he slides down between my legs. He hitches first one leg, then the other, over his shoulder —a repetition from last night—then licks me from seam to back hole. Just like that. Without any warning. Not a repetition from before, then.

The sensations are familiar yet foreign. No one's touched me there, and this man... He's eating me out in that very forbidden part of my body. He continues to lick into my forbidden hole, then slides one finger inside. The sensations are almost too overpowering. I can feel my cum slide out of my slit, and he scoops it up and smears it around my rosette. That's when I realize his intentions. He's going to fuck me there.

51

Ryot

I'm going to take her other virgin hole and make her completely mine.

She must guess my intentions for her body grows rigid. I look up to find her looking down at me with big eyes. Tension radiates from her, and I slide back up her body. "You okay?"

She nods slowly.

"We don't have to do this, if you're not comfortable with it."

She stays silent.

"Blink once for yes, twice for no. You okay to continue?"

She blinks. Once.

"You sure?"

She nods.

I peer into her eyes and take in the nervousness lurking there. But also, the lust.

"Good girl." I cup her cheek. "You won't regret it."

Then, I reach down and fit two fingers inside her back channel.

She shudders, and goosebumps pepper her skin. I work my fingers in and out of her, making sure her cum moistens her inner walls. I keep fucking her with my fingers until I'm able to slide in a third.

With all three of my fingers inside her up to my knuckles I stop. Little jolts travel up her body. Her eyes are so dilated, there's only a ring of blue around the irises. I curl my fingers inside her, touching a part deep inside of her, and a full body shudder grips her.

"You're so close, baby," I croon.

Pulling my fingers out, I fit my swollen head to her back entrance, then push inside.

She groans, the sound muffled by her gag. I stay there pulsing, waiting for her to adjust. I slide my hands up her arms and lock them over her palms.

Then I piston my hips forward and slide in through the tight circle of her sphincter.

"Breathe," I say through gritted teeth, fighting the need to fuck into her. "You're doing so well, baby. You're so tight. So hot. So everything."

The need to be inside her tightens my balls, but I won't move. Not yet. Not until she's ready for me. I squeeze my eyes shut and draw in a few sharp breaths, and when I feel more in control, I open my eyes. She stares at me with those big blue eyes, and I feel my heart melt.

I begin to move slowly, pulling out until I'm at her back entrance, then plunging inside her. I hit that part deep inside of her again, and she begins to shiver.

"Fucking hell, baby," I growl, willing my climax back.

I will not come, not until she's orgasmed. A few times. I begin to fuck her slowly, in-out-in. The blush from her cheeks extends to her chest and further. Her shoulders quiver. Her breasts are so swollen, her nipples little bullets of desire.

I hold her gaze and begin to push inside her again and again. The next time I thrust into her, she digs her fingernails into my palms. Her thighs undulate, and her hips shudder.

The climax swoops up her body, and when I pull her panties out of her mouth, she cries out. "Ryot. Ryot. Ryot."

Her eyes roll back in her head, and she comes on a loud keening cry. I continue to plunge into her. Her climax goes on and on. Tears squeeze out of the corners of her eyes trailing down her cheeks as her entire body quakes. Then she finally slumps. I stay inside her, throbbing, hurting, so fucking close to the edge that I see spots of black at the perimeter of my vision. Then, I pull out of her.

Reaching for the wet wipes on the nightstand, I wipe my fingers and my dick before grabbing a condom and sheathing myself.

When I fit my cock into the seam of her pussy, her eyelids flutter open. She takes in my condom, and the skin around her eyes creases. I can swear she's upset I'm wearing a condom, but before I can ask, she locks her ankles around my waist.

"I need you" — she swallows — "please."

I stay where I am, with my cock teasing her entrance.

"I want you so much" — I look into her eyes — "but I need to come to terms with my feelings for you. I need to work through what's holding me back. I don't want to hurt you, baby. But I need a little more time. Can you give me that?"

Understanding flits through her gaze, and her expression brightens.

"It's okay." She pushes her breasts into my chest. "It's okay." She tilts her hips, and the angle is such, I slip inside her.

"Jesus," I groan as the soft, melting channel of her pussy surrounds my shaft. "You're so tight. So soft. I don't deserve you."

I curl my fingers about her throat, and she shivers.

I begin to move in and out of her. Holding her gaze, I allow my feelings to come to the fore for the first time. Allowing her to glimpse how much this means to me. How much *she* means to me. I tighten my hold around her throat, then plunge inside her again.

I hold myself there, throbbing against her inner walls. She gasps, lips parted, hair in a golden halo around her features. I gently tighten my fingers around her neck, and her pussy flutters around where we're joined.

"This is going to be so good for you," I promise.

I pull out, and with a long, deep thrust, enter her again. And again. I feel the tension build inside of her, bleeding into her muscles, tightening her shoulders, her neck. Her eyes shine, her lips set in a firm slash.

"Give it up to me, baby. Lean into that feeling," I croon.

It feels incredible to be inside my wife. To feel her pussy clamp down on my dick. To feel her walls tighten around my throbbing cock. I look deeply into her eyes, and it feels like we're connected in a way I haven't been to anyone before. Body, to mind, to emotions. We're one person. It feels like we're melded together. Two beings. One soul. To give my wife pleasure, to make love to her, to gratify her, is the greatest feeling in the world.

As if she senses my emotions, a shudder ripples up her body. Her biceps tauten. The strain vibrates off her torso. She's reaching for that distant space where it's heaven. Where I'm going to lead her.

I squeeze down gently, around her throat. "Let go completely."

52

Aurelia

My body begins to vibrate. I sense my second orgasm approaching. He slides his other hand between us and pinches my clit. My entire body jolts. My back curves, and my eyes roll back in my head as the sensations swoop over me and I climax. My face is wet with tears, and my entire body is shaking. I gasp for air.

"That's it, baby. Let go completely. You're safe with me." His voice croons in my ears as I come down from the high. My scalp tingles, my toes curl. Even my teeth seem to hurt.

Another orgasm? That quickly? Jesus. I'm splintering to pieces, but perhaps, that's what he wants? To flay me open so I'm at his mercy. I should feel vulnerable and exposed, and I do, but it feels so good. It feels like I'm being reborn.

I open my eyelids to find him watching me with a tender look on his face. There's love and lust intertwined in a potent combination which warms my chest and ignites a pulse of pleasure in my bloodstream.

He reaches up to loosen the belt, and I lower my arms about his neck. Then, he begins to move slowly again, picking up speed, and when his pelvic bone brushes up against my clit, the telltale tightness in my lower belly signals the beginning of another climax.

"Not again. I don't think I have the energy," I moan.

"You don't have to do anything, baby. Let me do all the work." He picks up speed, holding himself up on his arms, biceps flexing, chest planes tensing. The sinews of his neck tighten, etched like cables under his skin. Sweat clings to his beautiful shoulders, a drop running down the cleavage between his impressive pecs. Once again, I'm struck by how chiseled he is. How sculpted. How God-like. And while I project a confident image to the world, I have often felt insecure about my tiny boobs and not-so-tiny butt. But he makes me feel good about myself.

He makes me feel worshipped. He makes me feel beautiful.

As if sensing my thoughts, he leans back on his knees, the angle causing him to sink even deeper inside of me. He hits that spot deep inside of me, and I cry out.

My body jolts with every lunge. My blood boils with such intensity, I'm sure it's going to evaporate. My chest hurts, my scalp prickles, and the sensation in my lower belly curls into itself, growing tighter and bigger until it seems to fill every part of me and encompass my entire body. Still, he doesn't stop. Long, smooth lunges when he sinks into me and hits my G-spot over and over again.

Damn, this man knows exactly how to drive me to distraction. And the fact that he didn't let me come for so long, then rewarded me with not one, not two, but with a third orgasm that threatens to overwhelm me, is too much to bear. Then, he looks deeply into my eyes, and with a final thrust, growls, "Come, right now."

The climax crashes over me with the force of a wrecking ball. The sensations sweep me up and away. It's so acute, so enormous, so powerful, I cry out. The orgasm blooms through me like a mushroom cloud which threatens to shatter me to pieces.

He holds my gaze, peering deeply into my eyes, and there's this connection, deep, and potent, and profound, and I know I've changed forever. And then his features turn fierce, and with a hoarse cry, he follows me over the edge.

I shiver as I come down from the high. My arms and legs are numb—my hands and feet feel like I have pins and needles stuck in them. My scalp tingles. All of my muscles feel lax. I feel like I've melted into a puddle and won't be able to move for a long time.

He collapses on top of me, the weight of his body pinning me in place, and I love that so much. He covers me with the musk of his scent and paints me with the heat that pours off of him. The drumming of his heart matches mine, and the throbbing of his cock inside me is a sweet pressure plucking at my nerve-endings and reverberating around the corners of my mind.

"I'm too heavy for you." He begins to back away, but I hold onto him. I dig my heels into his back and shake my head.

I don't trust myself to speak—not when what had happened between us felt so sacred, almost like an otherworldly experience. He presses his cheek to mine, and I sense him swallow as, inch by inch, he allows his body weight to sink into me.

My muscles relax, the tension squeezes out of my body, and my eyelids shutter down. I sense him kiss my forehead and pull out of me. I want to protest, but lack the strength to speak.

I'm aware of him rolling out of bed and his footsteps moving away. A few seconds later, the sound of water running reaches me, then sleep sweeps me under. When I wake up next, bright sunlight pours into the room.

I'm sprawled over him, the thundering of his heart a soothing background. I push my chin into his chest and raise my eyes to find he's watching me with a smirk about his features.

"You don't have to look so pleased," I grumble half-heartedly.

His arms close about me, and he pulls me up for a kiss, a soft kiss that deepens and grows drugging. His heartbeat accelerates, and his cock stirs against my waist. When we finally break apart, we're both panting.

"Wow," I breathe.

"Indeed." His touch is featherlight as he sweeps a wayward strand of hair away from my face.

I rub up against the column of wood that's grown steadily thicker and heavier between us. He groans, "I need sustenance before going another round."

"Do you?" I dig the heels of my hands into his shoulders for purchase, then swipe my pussy up and down that very impressive cock.

His grasp around me tightens. "Woman, have mercy."

"Nope." I continue to grind against him, then cry out when he slaps my butt. "What's that for?" I say breathlessly.

"Reminding you who's in charge, baby."

"Like I can forget." I bat my eyelashes at him, continuing to swipe my clit against that velvet-sheathed shaft of his.

I begin to pant in earnest, that familiar melting feeling radiating out from the point of contact. I squeeze my eyes shut, focusing on those incredible sensations slinking up my spine and down my front, circling my nipples, my belly button, and my clit, oscillating faster and faster until it pushes me over the edge in a gentle swell. I collapse against him, and he holds me closer, running his fingers through my hair.

"That was incredible," he rumbles.

"Mmm-hmm," I say sleepily.

His stomach rumbles, and I chuckle, then laugh when my stomach decides to join in.

He pushes up and, holding me in his arms, steps onto the floor. "I hope you're hungry enough to eat a full English breakfast?"

That was two days ago. He proceeded to cook breakfast for me, followed by lunch and dinner. We didn't leave the house that day or yesterday. He fucked me every way possible. On my front, on my back, sideways, and on almost every surface.

Two full days of bliss, and here we are on the third day, seated at the outside table on the patio. It overlooks the infinity pool, beyond which, the waves shimmer in the early evening sunlight. I see a boat in the distance, one of the two patrolling the waters to ensure we're safe.

Ryot told me Quentin and Tyler are on individual boats with their teams. They'll keep a distance and they'll be sure not to invade our privacy while patrolling the perimeter.

Every time I look out the window, I spot one of them. Between that and my husband's presence, I feel secure enough to relax.

Now, he sets the table for dinner for two, complete with a vase of flowers he picked from the garden. Daylight has started to fade, and the colors of a glorious sunset form a perfect background to the dinner.

He serves us starters, then pours champagne into two flutes, one of which he sets in front of me.

He raises his own. "To us."

I clink my glass with his. "To us." I take a sip, and the bubbles pop on my tongue. Zesty notes of green apple, laced with peach and raspberry, seduce my senses.

"That's so good." I take another sip and roll it round my tongue before swallowing it.

"It's from my personal collection," he tells me.

"You have a personal collection?"

A flush appears across his cheeks. "Not something I'd admit to, except to you."

"Why not?" I regard him with curiosity. "It's normal to collect bottles of wine and champagne that you like, no?"

He takes a sip of the champagne and contemplates his flute. "You already know how much I hate that I came from money?"

He laughs, the sound self-deprecating.

"When I joined the Marines, I didn't keep in touch with Arthur for nearly three years. I tried my best to disown my background. But when my team-mates were wounded in war and found it difficult to adapt back to civilian life, I realized I could use my money to help them.

"I began donating to veterans' funds to help them find a softer landing. That's when it hit home that if I embraced my inheritance, I could make a huge impact." He rubs the back of his neck. "It wasn't an easy thing to acknowledge."

"No, it isn't." I run my finger up the stem of my flute. "Not when you've spent your life running from who you are."

He looks at me with curiosity. "You seem settled in your role as Duchess of Verenza."

I blow out a breath. "It's different when you have a birthright thrust upon you." I take another sip of the Champagne. "When I was little, I would dream of running away and starting life as someone else. But every time, Viktor talked me out of it."

It's my turn to chuckle without humor.

"He knew how it felt, and the responsibility for him was, and is, much higher. It's a crushing weight, knowing everything you say and do can affect your family and your country. It was either let it get the better of me or come out fighting."

"And you fought." He reaches over and places his hand on mine. "What are the chances that the two of us would find so much in common?"

I turn my palm and twine my fingers with his, feeling that connection between us grow stronger.

"Can I ask you a question?" His voice is soft, but something in his tone makes me wary. "You don't have to answer it if you don't want to."

There's curiosity in his eyes, but I don't see anything that alarms me, so I dip my chin.

"You're not on birth control"—he clears his throat—"and you wanted me to come inside you."

I flush a little and look away. "I might have gotten carried away in the heat of the moment." I pop a shoulder. "I... I wanted to feel you inside of me without a condom."

"And if there were a child?" he asks softly.

I reach for the glass of water and take a sip before I tip up my chin. "I want kids, and if there were one, I'd keep the child. But truthfully, I wasn't thinking that far. All I wanted was to feel you without barriers." *Ugh, that sounds so irresponsible. But it's the truth.* "I know it must be difficult for you to talk about having children after what happened with your wife."

His gaze shutters, and his features set into hard lines. Then he sighs. "I'm sorry we didn't talk about this earlier, but being with you seems to blow my composure to smithereens."

"Me too," I say softly.

The silence stretches. I want to ask him what he thinks about having kids. I want to ask him if he'd stay married to me beyond the year he set as a timeline for us, if I did get pregnant. *To be a mother to his child, to see him as a father, to carry his child...* My head spins.

I'm unprepared for the surge of emotions that storm my chest. For the yearning that catches me unawares and forms a pit in my belly. I didn't realize how much I wanted to have kids with him. Until now. I was too consumed with the preparations for the wedding and, before that, with the emotional upheaval from the anonymous note and the assassination attempt. Maybe, a part of me thought we'd get around to talking about it; perhaps, even hoped we'd last beyond a year. Now, I realize how much I've left up to chance. Because the thought of being without him, of not having children with him, opens up a crater in my heart.

"Hey"—he squeezes my hand—"talk to me, baby. Tell me what you're thinking."

I'm not going to beg him to love me. I'm not going to plead with him to realize what we have here is so much more than temporary. He's going to have to figure it out. Hopefully, the more time we spend together, the more he's going to find we fit so well, he'd be crazy to give that up.

He dips his chin and peers into my eyes. I'm sure he can see the turmoil on my features and how my thoughts are racing ahead, and I want to look away but find I'm helpless.

He reads my features, and his own soften. "I do want kids," he says slowly in answer to my unspoken question. "And I've never wanted anyone as much as I want you. I just—" His Adam's apple bobs. "Just be patient with me. Give me a little more time to get over this...inability to trust in the future." A tortured expression takes over his features. Then, he seems to get a hold of himself. "If I could, I'd turn the world upside down to give you what you seek, but I can't make promises unless I'm sure I can keep them. You understand?"

I think I do. At least, I'm trying to. Even though a part of me wants to shake some sense into him and tell him that he needs to let bygones be bygones and move forward.

I'll never find anyone else I feel so much in sync with. Someone who makes me feel comfortable and turned on, all at once. Someone who I feel knows me almost as well as I know myself. And in some respects, *better*. Someone who knows exactly how to take charge and please me in bed.

He gets me. He sees through the façade I wear, the mask I present to the public. He makes me feel important, like I'm all that matters to him.

There will never be anyone else who can read my mind as if I were saying things aloud, and that is so special. So unique.

Our gazes meet and hold, and that chemistry between us spikes the air.

The sound of the waves on the beach, the lapping of the water in the swimming pool... All of it fades. The skin of my hand where I'm connected to him tingles. An electric current runs up my arm. I feel the pull toward him like it's a living force. I rise to my feet as if in a dream and walk around to straddle his lap. He places his hands on my hips, a curious look filtering into his eyes. He leans back in his seat, seemingly laid back, but his gaze is hawkish.

I bend and try to press my lips to his, but he holds me back. I try to lower my chin, but his hold stops me. I frown. "I want to kiss you."

"You don't set the pace," he warns.

I narrow my gaze, then reach forward and dig my fingers into his thick, silky hair and tug on it.

His lips twitch. Then, he raises his hands, curls his fingers around my wrists, and notches my arms behind my back. The position forces my chest forward, and my breasts jut out. I'm not wearing a bra, so I know my nipples can be seen through the almost transparent dress.

He rakes his gaze across my chest, and his pupils dilate. "You're so beautiful," he says in a gravelly voice, then leans in and closes his lips around one nipple. I groan and try to push more of my breast into his mouth, but he merely laughs.

What the— Before I can complete the thought, he bites down with enough force that I cry out, "That hurt."

"Good." He brings his mouth to the other breast and gives it the same treatment. Despite being prepared for the pinch of his teeth, it doesn't stop me from shuddering. Another cry escapes me. My thighs hurt; my pussy feels so empty.

I begin to hump the ridge in his crotch, trying to make myself come again, but he shakes his head. "Oh no, you don't."

"Aww, you're such an unfeeling man." I pout.

"That's not unfeeling"—he rises to his feet, and I wrap my legs about his waist—"but this is."

He walks over to the pool, and before I have a chance to figure out what he's up to, he steps in.

53

Ryot

That was a spur-of-the-moment decision. Mainly because I wanted to teach her a lesson. I wanted to surprise her, and I admit, I surprised myself too.

The water splashes over us, but we're in the shallow end, so it comes up to my shoulders and hers.

"Oh, my god, you didn't—" She glances at me in shock, droplets of water sticking to her eyelashes from where the water splashed over us. "How could you do—"

I close my mouth over hers and absorb the rest of the words. She tightens her hold and melts into me. The sweetness of her taste, the curves of her body trembling against mine, and the way her heart beats against mine, causes my body to turn to steel.

The scene around us begins to fade as we stare into each other's eyes, so when a column of fire explodes into the air, I'm sure I imagined it. The boom of sound sweeps over us, followed by the squawking of the birds from the trees. There's no mistaking that sound. Every muscle in my body snaps to attention.

"What was that?" She clings to me. "Ryot was that—"

"A bomb. On one of the boats," I say grimly.

Quentin! Tyler! Concern for them tightens my chest and turns my stomach into a churning mess. I have no doubt, whoever caused that is coming for her. I'll die before I let them hurt her.

I shove the panic away and reach inside to find that inner core of calm that will help me figure out what to do next. I move toward the edge of the pool and hoist, first her, then myself onto it, then head toward the house, pulling her behind me.

Another muffled boom reaches us, this time from the other side of the island.

Her grip on my hand tightens. "Is that—"

"The second boat." Adrenaline laces my blood. I pull her inside the house, shut the backdoor and lock it behind us. Releasing her hand, I take the stairs two at a time and reach our bedroom.

Ignoring the sex-scented sheets—now a reminder of just how much I allowed myself to be distracted—I head for the closet.

By the time she bursts into the room, I'm dressed in dry clothes and pulling on my shoes. I reach for the drawer on the nightstand next to my side of the bed, pull the drawer open, and grab my Glock. Checking it, I slip it into the back of my waistband then nod toward the closet. "Get dressed."

She races toward it, and once inside, begins to strip. I follow her, then draw in a breath. She's going to hate me for what I'm going to do, but it's the only way to protect her. As long as I can keep her safe, that's what matters. "I'm sorry."

She looks up at me, pausing midway to putting on a pair of jeans. "What do you—" Her gaze widens as I shut the door and latch it.

"What the hell, Ryot?" she yells. "You can't do this to me."

"I don't have a choice; I need to keep you safe, Empress."

"Damn you, Ryot." She bangs on the door with enough force that it rattles.

I wince. Then, not allowing myself to think further on it, I turn and grab my phone from where I left it charging next to the bed. Missed calls from Quentin and Tyler. *Goddam.*

I dial first one back, then the other, not surprised when I don't get a response. I call Brody, who picks up on the first ring. "Hadn't thought I'd hear from you —"

"Quentin and Tyler's boats were blown up. We've been compromised."

There's a beat, then he snaps, "I'm on it." The phone goes dead.

I slip it into my pocket and head down the stairs. Keeping to the wall I inch forward in the direction of the front door.

Through the open doorway I make out the burning wreck of one of the boats in the distance. There's no other movement around the house. But the prickling on the nape of my neck, the way the hair on my forearms bristles, the low hum in my ears... They tell me the worst is yet to come.

I pull out my gun and hold it in readiness as I take position by the front door. Sweat trickles down my spine, and my senses home in on scanning the scene in front of me.

Whatever happened on that boat, I have to hope Quentin and Tyler and their teams found a way to escape. They are too battle-seasoned not to have been alerted in time.

Clutching my gun, I bend, allowing my muscles to relax, getting into the zone, pretending I'm back on a mission. I peek out the door again, but nothing moves. The wind rustles the leaves on the trees, and the surf pounds in the background. Outside, the sun has set.

I flatten myself against the door, then slide out and against the wall of the house. I shuffle forward until I reach the next edge and peek around. The moon is beginning to rise. The patio and the pool stretch out in front of me, but I don't see anyone. I can bet they're around though.

I scan the surroundings, taking in any spaces where someone could hide, not that there are that many. It's one of the reasons I chose this island for our honeymoon. It should have made it difficult for anyone to get close without one of us spotting them. Still, they managed to get to the boats and are certainly on this island. But where?

My phone buzzes, I pull it out to see a message.

Brody: I'm on a helo with paramedics on board. We'll be out to you within ten minutes.

Thankfully, Brody stayed in Verenza, in case of just such an emergency like this. I just need to hold out until then.

A sound behind me has me spinning around. I spot a blur of white and shoot at the same time that a bullet whizzes past my ear. I race inside the house, managing to take cover behind the wall. I take aim at the place I saw the movement and fire off another shot.

It shoots through the dune grass, raising sand in its wake. Once again, I don't see anything out of the ordinary. *Goddam!*

Sweat trickles into my eyes, and I blink it away. My heart hammers in my chest. My pulse thuds at my temples. Every cell in my body is alive and vigilant. My shoulder muscles bunch. That low hum in my ears screeches out a warning, seconds before a hail of bullets is fired at me. *Fuck.*

One of them slams into the wall of the house; one whizzes past me and embeds in the furniture. A third buries itself in the door. Then there's silence. *All the bullets have come from one source. I'm fairly certain there's only one person out there.*

The moon hasn't fully risen yet. It's bright enough for me to see, but it still means there are patches of darkness wherever the ground dips. Staying low, I train my gun again in the direction of the firing and, letting my instincts take over, I squeeze out three shots in response. There's a yell, then silence. *Gotcha.*

I pull back and survey the landscape. The fire on the boat in the distance stands out like a beacon. I pull out my phone and glance at the time. Five minutes to go until the chopper arrives.

I scan the surroundings and make out what looks like a fallen body next to a grassy knoll marking the edge of the perimeter of the house which gives way to sand. The form on the ground is unmoving, which is not to say they aren't armed and dangerous. I stay still, watching them for any sign of movement, and there's none. I draw in a breath, then another. *I shouldn't go out. I need to stay here until help arrives.* And yet, the need to see the bastard's face, to find out who they are and make sure I've put them out of commission, builds in me. I glance at the burning boat, and anger grips me.

The people behind those attacks on the boats may have killed members of my family. It's because of their threats, my wife has had to seek protection. Their actions traumatized her and forced her to hide from the public gaze. Just for the torment they caused her, for the distress that, no doubt, will have left a mark on her psyche, I must make sure they can never cause her further agony.

Taking advantage of the growing darkness, I slip out of the house and approach the person without making a sound, gun at the ready to shoot. When I reach them, I take in their features and my jaw drops. It's a woman dressed in a scuba diving suit.

I've been trained to shoot to kill, but the fact that it's a young woman who has her life in front of her gives me pause. My fingers falter on the trigger, a costly error, for her eyes flip open.

She smiles, a grim, vengeance-filled thinning of her lip. Then, she raises her gun and shoots.

54

Aurelia

"No," I scream as he reels back.

I race across the grass toward him as he stands there with the gun aimed at the person on the ground.

When Ryot locked me in the closet, I was so pissed off. If he thought he was going to leave me there while he went in search of whoever had blown up Quentin & Tyler's boats, then he was dreaming. I heard him move away, then threw my bodyweight against the closet door over and over again. Luckily, the latch was defective and burst open.

I scrambled down the stairs, and when the sound of shots reached me, I almost had a heart attack.

This is probably the stupidest thing I can do. I have no weapon, no training, and no defensive armor. If I put myself in the line of fire, I'll likely put him in danger as well, because he'll be distracted.

There is no way I can stand by and watch him sacrifice himself for me either. He's in danger, and nothing can stop me from going to him.

I burst out of the house in time to see him reel back. My heart pounds like a drum against my chest. I run so fast my feet don't seem to touch the ground. In seconds I reach him, and grip his arm "Are you okay?"

He shakes his head as if to clear it, then cups my cheek with his free hand. "Are *you* okay?" he asks tenderly.

"Of course, I am. Though I'm pissed that you thought you could lock me in the closet and leave." I shake a finger in his face. "You and I are going to need to have a talk about your protective instincts."

He smirks. "We can talk about my instincts anytime."

I scoff and begin to turn, but he stops me with a hand on my shoulder. "You sure you want to see this?"

Something in his gaze tells me I'm not going to like it, but hey, I haven't come this far to lose my nerve at the last second. Not when the person who's turned my every day into a nervous reality, where I've had to second-guess my every step and jump at shadows, has been taken down. "I need to see who it is, so I can get some closure." I set my jaw.

He nods. "It's not pretty."

I square my shoulders, then turn and take in the figure on the ground. All dressed in black, with camouflage paint streaked across her features, her eyes are open and looking into the distance, already glazing over in death. There's a smoking hole between her eyes.

"Veronica?" I furrow my brows.

How? Why? I shake my head, not sure how to equate what I am seeing with the meek, excitable, and largely supportive woman who's been my personal assistant for more than a year. Suddenly, my mind starts flashing with memories of things she did that made me uncomfortable—the bowing and scraping, using my full honorific every time she addressed me, the fervency with which she viewed my position and her admission she wished she were a princess; going so far as to ask if I knew any single princes, followed by her concern about Gavin.

OMG! The signs were there, and like an idiot, I ignored them. My stomach roils. Bile boils up my throat, and I swallow it away. *I will not be sick. Will not.*

There's a sound behind me, then Ryot's arm circles me from behind. "I'm sorry, I know she was a friend of yours."

"Not that good a friend, apparently. And she was my employee, which means she was never really my friend." A distinction which is, once more, brought home to me. Another reality of my life which I need to be able to accept. There are very few people in my life I can trust, very few relationships money and my position haven't tainted. Ryot is one of them. His grip around my shoulders slackens. I turn to find him swaying. "Ryot!" I throw my arm about his waist. "Are you hurt?"

"It's just a scratch." He laughs, then coughs, a look of surprise on his face. He looks down at his chest. I pull up his shirt and gasp. It's a small circle of red, almost deceptive in its size. "You're hit," I cry.

He coughs again and stumbles.

I try to grab him, but his weight is too much. I manage to slow his fall, though not enough; the back of his head connects with the sand.

"Ryot!" I pull off my blouse and press it against the wound. There's a buzzing sound in the distance. That must be my heart racing and going into overdrive. The blood saturates the cloth I have pressed to his chest so quickly, I gasp.

I look up to find his features are pale, but his green eyes glitter. They look at me with almost feverish intensity. "If something happens to me—"

"No, nothing can happen to you." I taste salt on my lips and realize I'm crying. "I will not let anything happen to you."

He laughs. "My fierce, strong Empress." He coughs. More blood spurs out of the wound.

"Ryot, don't speak, please."

The buzzing sound grows louder.

"That's the chopper; you'll be safe now." Some of the rigidity melts from his shoulders. "If anything happens to me, remember... I love you." He closes his eyes.

"No, no, no, no." I continue to put pressure on his chest. "Ryot, open your eyes."

When he stays still, I slap his face. "Wake the fuck up. Don't you dare die on me, you asshole."

He coughs, then cracks open one eyelid. "Jesus, woman, taking advantage of me while I'm down, I see." He shuts his eyes again.

"Ryot." I cry. "Don't leave me, please."

There's no response. My heart feels like it's going to cleave through my ribcage. The pressure in my head feels unbearable. *No, no, no. This can't be happening.* "Wake up Ryot. I need more orgasms. Many, many, many more orgasms, which only you can give me."

His eyes open, and he laughs, then winces in pain. "Glad you have your priorities right, woman." His eyelids flutter down, and he slumps.

There's something about his stillness that sends my blood pressure shooting. I keep pressure on the wound and begin to cry in earnest. "Oh, Ryot...please baby...hang in there. I beg you."

I can't take my gaze off of his face. Not when the *whump-whump-whump* grows deafening, and the helicopter comes in for landing on the beach. Not when the wind from the rotors results in sand blowing over us. Not when the paramedics from the chopper race toward us and place an oxygen mask around his face.

Not when someone guides me to my feet, and I follow the medics as they rush the stretcher with him into the chopper.

I hold his hand all the way to Verenza and then through the doors of the hospital, letting go only when they rush him into surgery.

"How is he?" Zoey bursts into the waiting room of the Verenza Medical Center.

I open my arms, and she rushes over to sit next to me and hug me. "I'm so sorry this happened Aura." She rubs my back. Hearing her concern prompts a fresh burst of tears. I bury my face in her neck and sob.

"There, there, honey, he's going to be okay," she assures me.

I nod. *He's going to be fine.* I keep telling myself that. And I want to believe it so badly. "Sorry you had to cut your holiday short," I murmur.

While Harper and Grace returned to London, Zoey opted to explore some of the countryside of Verenza.

She huffs. "There's nowhere else I'd rather be than here with you."

Footsteps approach, then someone else sinks into the seat next to me. Someone else wraps an arm around my shoulder, and I look up. It's Imelda. She's been sitting with me almost since I arrived, only briefly leaving to take a break.

"Thank you for staying with me. I appreciate it." I manage a tremulous smile.

"Oh, hush, we're family," she squeezes my hand.

Then another thought strikes me. "I thought you flew back to London with Arthur?"

"When we heard the news, I asked Arthur to charter me a plane so I could get back here. You don't think we'd leave you unsupported in a time like this, do you? He'd have come too, but the old man's not as strong as he once was."

The warmth in her words brings forth another bout of tears.

"Oh honey, don't cry." She offers me the paper cup filled with a brown liquid, but my stomach cramps at the thought of drinking it.

"I'm good," I shake my head.

"How about some water?" Tyler prowls up. He twists off the cap, hands me a bottle, and I take a sip.

"Any word?" I ask.

He shakes his head, expression grim. "They're still in the operating room."

Tyler, Quentin, and the rest of their teams had discovered the bombs on their boats and managed to jump off before they'd detonated. A second chopper came along and fished them out of the sea. They survived with minimal injuries.

"Why is it taking so long?" I grip my fingers together.

"He's going to be okay." Tyler sinks down on his haunches and takes my hands in his. "He's a fighter."

His features seem tortured.

I know he feels responsible for not being able to stop Veronica from shooting his brother. "It's not your fault. It's no one's fault that she got to us. She had us all fooled. She's been in my trusted circle for a year, and I didn't suspect a thing." I shake my head.

"We checked her background, and nothing came up." His jaw hardens. "I should have been more vigilant. I should have been able to track her down before she got to the both of you."

"*We* should have been able to put her away much sooner than this." Quentin prowls over to stand next to Tyler. Despite my distress, I can't help but notice how these Davenport men are uniformly large and forbidding-looking and yet, also, hot.

"If anyone is at fault it's me." I lower my chin. "I'm the one who trusted her with the details of my location. If I hadn't texted her from the island, she'd never have found us. But—" Tyler opens his mouth to speak, but I hold up my hand. "But I know better than to blame myself. If it's anyone's fault, it's Veronica's. She betrayed me. Besides, I worked with her the closest, and I had no idea what she was up to."

A part of me does blame myself for it, but I push it aside. I can't afford to think like that. I need to stay strong for myself. For my husband.

"We looked into her background but, except for the fact that she went to a disproportionately large number of schools on account of her parents moving around, there was nothing that indicated she could be capable of what she did." Tyler drags his fingers through his hair. "She had a university education and did a stint in the army before she joined you."

"Knowing she was trained in arms and defensive protocol is what made me recruit her." I nod.

"Her training should have made her an obvious suspect, but one of our security team reported seeing only a man so we were focused on that," Quentin says grimly.

"We've since found out that team member was working with

Veronica." Tyler sets his jaw. "She was slim enough to dress in man's clothes and since the person on our team was colluding with her, he reported her as such. It's another reason we didn't suspect her." Tyler draws his mouth into a firm line.

"We also found a diary hidden in her room at the palace. Something we didn't find the first time." Quentin locks his mouth in a grim expression.

"It was the compromised member of your team who searched her room?" I make a guess.

Tyler nods, his eyes troubled. "In it, she talks about being jealous of the fact that you were a princess, and she wasn't. That she didn't think you deserved it. She wanted to find a way to scare you."

"Hence, the note on my pillow in the hotel room?" Which makes sense. She was one of the people who had access to my room."

"Turns out, she had something of a crush on Gavin, and when you broke up with him, she approached him."

"She did?" I ask surprised. Then, I remember her messaging him on our trip from the safehouse. Not to mention, I caught the way she looked at Gavin a couple of times, but I dismissed it as my imagination.

"We picked up Gavin for questioning." Tyler bares his teeth.

"That could not have gone down well with his family," I mutter.

Tyler scoffs. "The Davenports have more money and are more powerful than his family, and given he confessed to forming an alliance with Veronica to get revenge on you for dropping him, I don't think we have to worry about their feelings."

"We screened him earlier but couldn't find anything suspicious in his past," Quentin says grimly. "Nevertheless, we should have anticipated he'd act on the threats, he made against you. I take responsibility for the fact we weren't able to stop him before he teamed up with Veronica."

"You're not the only one who was taken in by them. They had us all fooled." My head feels like it's spinning. First, Veronica; now, Gavin. I shake my head. "Ohmigosh! That's how she got access to the money and the firepower to blow up the boats and the guns!" It almost cost my husband his life, and that of his brothers. The implications make me lightheaded. I take another sip of water and try to compose myself.

Tyler eyes my features. "You alright? We can always talk about this later."

"No." I shake my head. "Let's do it now. If not, I'm just going to fret about him. This way, it takes my mind off of him being in surgery."

Tyler nods; not that the concern on his face eases. "She has no history of erratic behavior. Nothing out of the ordinary to flag suspicion." He shuffles his feet. "Which is no excuse. We should have been more thorough in tracking her movements."

"Considering she was my assistant and had the highest clearance, you're not the only one who failed to spot something amiss with her."

"That's no excuse." Tyler frowns. "We should have stopped her, but we didn't. I'm sorry for what happened."

"Both of you took time out of your lives to help with the security arrangements at the wedding. I have no doubt, that's why the ceremony went off without a hitch. You put your lives at risk to guard the island. You were there in time to take him to the hospital. You didn't fail." I look between the men. Their expressions are serious. Both look exhausted, with dark circles under their eyes. "Thank you for taking the time to see this through. Thank you for being there for him… For us." My throat closes. A choking feeling squeezes my chest. I blink away the burning sensation threatening to overwhelm me.

"Hey"—Quentin eyes me with concern—"it's going to be okay. Ryot's a stubborn bastard. He's going to pull through."

The door to the waiting room opens, and a doctor in scrubs steps in. I rise to my feet, as does Tyler. The doctor's features are serious.

I swallow down the bile which coats my tongue and, ignoring my trembling limbs, I walk toward him.

The doc hands me his dog tags.

My stomach bottoms out. Oh no. *No, no. no.*

55

Aurelia

I walk into the hospital room. The scent of antiseptic sinks into my blood and whips my already churning guts into a heaving mass which boils up my gullet. I tamp down on the turbulent feeling, telling myself I need to stay strong. I approach the bed where he's hooked to various machines.

The intermittent beeping echoes the thundering of my heart. A pulse oximeter is attached to his finger, and a cannula delivering oxygen is strapped to his nose. His arms are at his sides, and he looks pale under his tan. I can make out the bandages on his chest which peek out from under the neck of his hospital gown. It's the sight of that which has tears squeeze out of the corners of my eyes. I swore I wouldn't cry when I saw him, but I can't stop myself. I stand next to the bed and take his palm between mine.

His eyelids flutter open, and he smiles. "Empress." His voice is raw, and his eyes show echoes of the pain he must have experienced when the bullet hit him.

Again, my eyes are drawn to the bandage on the left side of his chest, and I begin to tremble. So close. He could have been killed. A centimeter one way or the other, and he might not have made it.

"Your husband is very lucky," the doctor had said in a grave tone. *"The operation was successful. The bullet hit him an inch below his heart. It made a clean exit, and it missed any vital organs. He did lose a lot of blood, so he's weak. But he should make a full recovery."*

I sink down in the chair next to the bed, lower my head, and kiss his hand. "Ryot, baby—" I want to say so much, but the words get stuck in my throat.

The sense of relief that he's going to be fine is still sinking in. The vestiges of the anxiety, the helplessness, the sheer powerlessness I felt when I watched the medics trying to revive him on the way to the hospital, and then the wait as they operated on him, still clings to me. "I'm so glad you're okay." I clear my throat.

"Me too." He squeezes my fingers. "How are you doing?" He scans my features. "You look tired."

"I'm going to be just fine." I manage a small smile. "You gave me a scare."

"I remember being hit..." His forehead furrows. "And then... You talking about wanting orgasms?" His brow clears. A sly smile plays around his mouth. "I owe you a great many of them, considering you saved my life."

"It's the doctors who saved your life," I point out.

"You applied pressure to the bullet wound when you reached me. Your actions helped stem the blood loss, and improved my chances considerably."

"You took a bullet for me." A ball of emotion knots my throat. "If you hadn't been there—"

"There is nowhere else I could have been. I took a vow to look after you, and I take my promises very seriously. As long as I am alive, I swear nothing—and I mean *nothing* and no *one*—can touch a hair on your head."

The vehemence in his words triggers a tsunami of emotions within me. I've heard him say this before, but to hear him say this after seeing his lifeless body on the ground brings home just how much he means it. "When I saw you unmoving and the blood pouring out of your wound"—I shake my head—"I thought I'd lost you."

This time, he grins, a very confident, jaunty smirk. "And miss out on the orgasms I owe you? Nope, not letting you go that easily."

I half laugh. Then the emotions overwhelm me, and I begin to cry, great sobbing gusts that make me cringe, and yet I can't stop. I turn my head away, so he won't see me and, hold onto his hand like it's my only anchor in a storm.

"Hey, baby, hey. Look, I'm completely okay." He tries to sit up, and that shocks me enough that I pause mid-sob.

"Stop! You shouldn't be doing that; they just operated on you."

"It'll take more than a bullet to slow me down." He pulls me onto the bed, and I give in. The need to be near him, to be in his arms, to feel his skin against mine so I can assure myself that he really is okay is too overpowering. I climb onto the bed, taking care not to displace the various tubes attached to him.

Then, I lift his arm and place it around my shoulders and curl into his side.

Instantly, the beeping increases in frequency. "Proof of how you affect me, Empress." He chuckles.

I look up at him with worry. "Maybe, I should—"

I begin to pull away, but he holds me in place. "Don't you dare."

I bite the inside of my cheek, wondering if I should disobey him, but everything inside me insists I obey. Hurt as he is, his power over me hasn't diminished. The dominance that clings to him like a second skin has not been tempered by his wounded state.

He resembles an apex predator who's been temporarily laid low but is far from vanquished. With the bandages and his mussed-up hair, he's even more appealing. The vulnerability that I glimpsed when I held his hand as he was unconscious adds another dimension to him. It makes him even more attractive, sexier. But it's also a sign that he's human. That next time, he might not be this lucky. *If something were to happen to him*— I push the thought away, but it's lodged in my chest like an acid-tinged knife blade that's eating away at my flesh.

I press my nose into his throat and breathe deeply of his familiar dark scent. Not even the smell of the hospital pushing down on us is strong enough to diminish the comfort of it. I take in a few deep breaths, and he chuckles.

"Are you sniffing me?"

"Your scent turns me on. It's both reassuring and arousing," I admit.

He brings me in closer, and I melt into his side. I absorb the familiarity of his strength, the heat from his body surrounding me like a warm blanket. After what seems like hours of being stressed, this is the time for me to relax. But somehow, I can't. Somehow, I'm still on edge. A part of me wants more assurances that he's going to be okay. That we're going to be okay.

"You must be knackered." The rumbling of his voice across his chest is another sign that he's alive. *He's fine. Really.* I try to convince myself, but my stomach still hurts from the shock I experienced when I saw the blood spilling from the wound in his chest. That acidic bite in my chest widens to a full-fledged moat of concern.

"Ryot" — I look up at him — "are you really okay?"

He laughs. "This is nothing compared to some of the other wounds I've faced during tours."

I can't bring myself to smile.

He notices my seriousness and wipes the lightness he was striving for from his features. "I'm a former Marine. I promise you, I have survived worse," he says in a soothing voice.

"Don't dismiss my worries, please." I frown.

"I'm not, baby." He wraps his other arm around me, not caring that there's an IV needle sticking out from the back of his palm. "I'm trying to demonstrate that this is part of the life I've lived, and it doesn't faze me."

"Well, it fazes *me*." I look away from that shrewd gaze of his, not sure how much I want to reveal of what I'm feeling. *Strange huh? I wanted him to share everything with me and now that he is, I find myself pulling back.* "I... I didn't realize how much I was in love with you until I thought I'd lost you." As I say it, I realize how true my words are. "I love you, Ryot."

His features soften. His eyes shine. "I love you too, Empress." He brings me in for a kiss, and I meet his lips.

I revel in the softness of his lips, the syrupy sensation invading my bloodstream as he deepens the kiss, the strength of his arms, the ungiving breadth of his shoulders, and how, despite his injury, he still overpowers me with his size and makes me feel intensely feminine. My head spins with the overwhelming emotions that I've been grappling with since I saw him get shot. A shudder grips me. I can't stop my muscles from seizing up.

He instantly notices my body's response, for his hold on me tightens. "What's wrong?"

I shake my head. I'm not sure how to describe this turmoil I feel in my stomach, this tightness in my chest, this choking sensation in my throat that makes me feel like I'll never be able to breathe properly again. Perhaps, it's a delayed aftershock of seeing him wounded, and then praying for him in the waiting room, and now realizing that he's going to be okay.

"Hey, baby, it's going to be okay." The beeping sound of his heart grows more persistent.

"I'm so sorry I'm stressing you out," I say through my tears.

"Hush, Empress, you're what makes every moment of my life worthwhile. It's because I have you in my arms that I know I'm going to be okay. From the first moment I saw you, I knew my life had changed for the better. It's because I have you with me, that I can face down any challenge."

He notches his knuckles under my chin, so I have to look into his beloved emerald-green eyes.

"It's you, Aura. Only you. I've been waiting for you all my life, and I didn't even realize it. When I was shot and bleeding out, and I opened my eyes and saw you, I knew then, I found my reason for living. I knew I would survive because I wanted to live my life with you. I realized then, I had waited too long to commit completely to you. I swore, if I survived, I wouldn't waste a moment anymore. So, here I am, baby, all yours. I am all in."

I knew he loved me but that he was holding back. Here he is, having survived a bullet to his chest and feeling even more vital in many ways, telling me what I want to hear.

Hearing those words from his lips are a soothing balm to the tumult that the last few hours have wreaked inside of me. It feels like I've waited so long to hear him say that, and now when I hear his words, it feels perfect and real and momentous, all at the same time. Tremors grip me.

I hoped to find a man who'd be mine completely and utterly. Who'd look at me the way he is now. Who'd take in my features with that intensity in his eyes, that complete stillness about him which indicates he's giving me his complete focus. To be at the center of his attention, such that every nerve-ending in my body crackles with awareness. This is a feeling I never thought I'd have, and here it is.

My husband loves me. He adores me. He'll do anything for me. He'll die for me. And he's made it clear he's finally over the ghosts of his past... So why... Oh, why do I feel this anxious?

Why am I finding it so difficult to embrace what he's saying?

Is it because he almost died on me, and I felt...like my entire world was going to collapse? I didn't realize how much I'd begun to depend on him. To trust him. To want him by my side for the rest of my life.

As the ripples from what happened sink in, I realize, I'm irrevocably in love with him. If something were to happen to him, I'd never be able to withstand it. *Him... He's more important to me than... The country I've dedicated my life to.* And that's a shock.

It's a reversal of everything I believe in. My world seems to tilt on its axis.

I've changed. My priorities have changed. And I need to process this. I need to make some decisions.

The tremors intensify.

Spine straight. You're a princess.

And if I weren't anymore. What then? As this possible new reality for my future sinks in, I shake my head. The thoughts intensify and crowd in.

I need to sift through these conflicting emotions. I need to make sense of what I'm feeling. Of what I must do.

Ryot's looks me over, a shadow of unease crossing his features, "Everything okay?"

Of course, I can't hide anything from this man.

"Everything's perfect." I cup his cheek. "I realized that for the first time in my life, there's something I value more than my love for my country."

He inclines his head. "And what's that?"

"You," I kiss his forehead.

When I start to lean back, he clamps his palm around the nape of her neck and brings me in for a deep, drugging kiss.

"I love you so very much," he slows the kiss, nibbles on my lower lip, and my nipples tighten.

He licks into my mouth. "You're mine, Empress. My wife. My soulmate."

"Oh Ryot," A tiny moan escapes me. "You mean more than anything in my life. It's why..." I glance away then back at him. "It's why I need time and space to think things through."

56

Ryot

"Wait, what?" *Am I hearing things?* "What's wrong? Talk to me, baby."

Her gaze is troubled. She tries to move away, but I hold her in place.

I belong to my wife wholeheartedly... But my declaration has not had the desired effect.

The beeping of my heart monitor grows more insistent. With a grimace, I tear the sticky patches attached to my chest and throw them aside. Instantly, there's silence.

She looks at me in shock. "You shouldn't—"

"Fuck that. *You're* more important. Tell me what's on your mind."

"I..." She tries to speak, but no words emerge. "It's just..." She shakes her head. "I feel overwhelmed by everything."

"It was a shock when I collapsed in your arms bleeding. I understand that."

"It's more than that." Her gaze grows haunted. "I realized, if you didn't make it, if something were to happen to you, I'd never be the same again. The fact that I have become so dependent on you is something I'm going to have to get used to."

"I'm dependent on you too, baby. You're my heart. My life. You know that."

She purses her lips, and a shiver engulfs her. "It makes me feel so vulnerable."

"Tell me about it." I cup her cheek. "We can do this together. We'll be there for each other. Us against the world. I'll always be in your corner. When you fall down, I'll pick you up. When I lose hope, you'll be my shining light. When you lose confidence, I'll be your support. When I act like an asshole, you'll shut me down." I look into her eyes. "And then there are those orgasms."

She snorts through her tears, then laughs. "I'm sorry, I slapped you while you were out. It was the only thing that occurred to me to keep you awake."

"You can do anything you want with me, baby." I take her hand and flatten her palm into my face. "I'm yours. Body, mind, and soul. All of me is at your command."

Her gaze intensifies.

I wink. "Except when it comes to your pleasure. On that point, you obey what I tell you to do."

Her lips tremble, and a small smile curves her lips. "And I believe you. I do." She frames my face with her hands. "It's why I need to step back and revaluate."

Footsteps sound and a nurse comes running into the room. She stops when she sees me and the Duchess. "The heart monitor."

I wave a hand without taking my gaze off my wife. "I'm fine." Then, I force myself to swallow down the impatience welling up my chest. "Please, can you give us a few minutes, and then you can hook me back up?"

She hesitates. But something in my voice must convince her, for she leaves. The door snicks shut behind her.

"Time, you said?" I prompt my wife. I'm trying to make sense of her words. I have a sense of where this conversation is going, but I don't want to second guess her.

She lowers her hands, then nods.

"Just...a little while to process everything that's happened." Once more, her gaze turns haunted. "I'm not abandoning you, especially not when you're wounded. I promise, I'm here for you. But it would be wrong if I weren't open with you about this. For our future together, it's important that I think things through. I need a little time to come to grips with my feelings for you."

I want to say no. I want to say that now we've found each other, I will not spend one moment away from her. I was stupid not to recognize my feelings earlier. I should have committed to her right way, but I also recognize that she needs time—*just like I did*—to process what happened.

She needs time to work through seeing me shot and bleeding out in her arms. I can't begrudge her that. All I can do is make sure she understands what she means to me.

"I love you." I clamp my hand over the nape of her neck and bring her in for a deep, drugging kiss that has the blood draining to my groin.

I slow the kiss, nibble on her lower lip, and she shudders. I lick into her mouth, and a tiny moan escapes her.

I hold her gaze. "You're mine, Empress. My wife. My soulmate." I manage a smile, drawing on the diminishing patience inside of me, knowing I'm going to need that, and more, until she resolves the dilemma in her mind. "I'd slay your demons for you, if you give me a chance—"

She begins to speak, but I place a finger on her lips.

"—but I know this is something you have to work through on your own."

She looks at me with a grateful light in her eyes. "How can you be so perfect? How can you be so...so hot, and also so... So... Understanding? Even when you're an asshole, I like you." She rolls her eyes. "You're making it very hard for me to put this distance between us, you know?"

"Then don't."

"But I have to." Her expression turns beseeching. "I need to figure out a few things for myself, and the only way to do that is if I put a little distance between us. I need to process my feelings for you. How my entire life feels different. How my goals are no longer what I thought they were. I need...to figure out where I'm headed. I owe us that."

I'd go down on my knees and beg if I thought that'd make a difference, but the set of her features, and the glimmer in her eyes, tells me I need to allow her to be. If I respect her, I'll give her the space she's asking for.

I look deeply into her eyes. "I'll never hold you back. You'd better believe that I'll also give you space when you need it."

She stares, surprise evident on her face. "You—" She begins to speak but I shake my head.

"You don't have to say anything. Those are some big emotions you're dealing with. Trust me, I know."

She begins to tear up.

"Don't cry, sweetheart." My heart feels like it's going to burst with love for her.

"Thank you—" She clears her throat. "Thank you for understanding."

I search her features and understand how difficult this is for her. I'm not going to make it more challenging.

I'm going to stand by her. Whatever she needs I'll give it to her.

"You should know one thing though"—my voice turns determined—"I'm not going to *ever* be very far from you ever again. But I'm also not going to crowd you." I lean in and kiss her hard. "Go get some rest. And if you need to talk things out with me, I'll be here."

57

Aurelia

"Are you sure about this?" Viktor leans back in his chair.

I prop a hip against his massive desk. "Positive."

It's been a week since that discussion at Ryot's hospital bed. I've been in daily to see him since.

He's been getting stronger every minute, and it's taken a lot of cajoling to get him to stay until he's given the all-clear by the doctor.

I've used the time to think through next steps for myself, and having come to a conclusion, asked for this meeting with my brother.

We're in his study in the office wing of the Palace, which doubles as the administrative center for the Royal Family.

It's decorated in masculine colors to reflect Viktor's personality. With his dark brooding looks, and a gravitas he's only recently begun to wear like a Royal cloak, it's easy to see why the women love him and why the media adores him. If there's anyone born to be King, it's my older brother.

"You were born to be a princess. You were brought up to be the face of the Royal Family, and—"

"And I've done my duty. I helped save the economy of Verenza from possible collapse."

"You should have never had to use your marriage as a transaction to bring in money." Viktor sets his jaw.

I half smile, more than a little touched by my brother taking my side in this. "But I wanted to. The thought of marrying Ryot was never objectionable. I was secretly happy. I was attracted to Ryot as soon as I saw him at the bar."

Viktor freezes. "You and Ryot met at a bar?"

Oops, hadn't meant for that to slip out. But I suppose, there's no harm in revealing the details. "On my last trip to London. I needed a break from the boring official duties and hired a car."

Viktor blinks slowly. "You went to a bar? On your own?" His shoulders bunch. "And where was your security during this time?" His tone is ominous. Protectiveness vibrates off of him in waves. Gosh, he and my husband are so similar in their alpha-male instincts.

"They weren't a match for my machinations. That's why Ryot didn't want them to be part of my security team when he came on board."

Viktor's face grows granite hard. Veins pop at his temple. He looks about ready to explode.

"Either way, it doesn't matter, because Ryot was there. He saved me from unwanted attention. And now, we're married. And it's my turn to keep him safe."

Viktor's lips firm. He folds his arms across his chest. "I understand the sentiment. You care for your husband, and you don't want to have more crazies on your case or paint a bullseye on his forehead, either."

The one thing I love about my brother? He's sharp. You don't have to explain yourself to him twice. "I've never enjoyed being in the public eye. Never enjoyed dressing up and playing the role of a princess."

"You *are* a princess," he points out.

"Exactly. I've always felt like a fraud." I meet his gaze steadily.

"I'd rather wear jeans and a sweatshirt and be at my computer writing my next book."

His jaw drops. "You write books?"

I chuckle. Viktor has always been the older brother who I hero-worshipped. I quite enjoy being able to surprise him, for once. "It's my super-power. It's the one thing I know I'm good at, better than this princess gig."

He shakes his head. "Writing books? Who'd have thought?" Then his forehead creases. "So, is that your plan? Step back from Royal duties and become an author? Not that you'll have to work, given Ryot's personal fortune."

"I'm grateful that my husband can provide for me, but I intend to be financially independent. I have a deal with a well-known publisher. With the advance I received, I'm able to support the charities that are important to me."

His frown deepens. "I will never forgive myself for not keeping abreast of the true state of the financial affairs of Verenza." He rubs the back of his neck. "I should have been all over the economic woes of the country. I should have insisted father share the details of how he planned to invest money. I should have intervened while he was leveraging your potential marriage to fill in the funding gaps." He straightens. "I'm sorry for how he played with your future to fill the gaps. I failed you, Aura. The least I can do is help you live your life on your terms."

I smile. "You didn't fail me, Viktor. You were always there when I needed you. Besides, he didn't coerce me at all. Everything I agreed to was of my own accord. And what I want now is to no longer be responsible for Royal duties."

He meets my gaze and whatever he sees on my face seems to convince him, for he nods. "I accept your stepping back from the Royal Family duties, on one condition."

"What's that?" I ask cautiously.

"You'll continue to be on the board of the planning commission to decide how to invest the money brought in by the Davenports."

I nod slowly. "Ryot told me he spoke to you about that." I told Ryot I'd think that over.

"Your work with charities, and with the people, means you know what is most critical to the country. I hope you'll consider using it to continue to better their condition."

I'd hoped for a clean break from my Royal duties, but my past is too interwoven with that of the Royal Family. Besides, I'm only stepping down from my official duties, so I don't need to be the public face of the Princess anymore.

I still plan to support my father and brothers in any way needed. And if my country needs me—I incline my head. "You know how to play on my weaknesses, don't you?"

He doesn't seem repentant. "If it means I can continue to have you involved with the future of Verenza in some form—not to mention, it provides an excuse for me to see you—then I have no qualms."

I laugh. "You don't need an excuse. You simply have to pick up the phone and call me. Something you've been too busy for in the past."

He has the grace to look sheepish. "I'm sorry. I can be a selfish ass. But that changes now. You've taught me how important my role is for our country. It's time I fully embrace my duties as king-in-waiting."

"Hmm." I tap my fingers on his desk. "Does that mean you're going to fall in love, get married, and produce heirs soon?"

"Sure, I'll do what's needed to deliver on my duty and propagate the royal bloodline. As for love," he scoffs, "what's that?"

58

Ryot

It's been three weeks since I let her walk out of my hospital room. If I said it was easy to do so, I'd be lying. But I let her leave because my instinct told me it was the only way I could forge a future for us.

On the face of it, nothing has changed. She doesn't physically stay away from me. It's more of a mental and emotional distance she's put between us. It's there in the way she makes sure not to come too close to me. In how she doesn't take my hand anymore or makes sure not to meet my eyes directly. In the watchful look in her eyes with which she surveys me when she thinks I'm not watching her... *Which is never.* Being in the same space as her, there's no way I'm not aware of her.

I'd have left the hospital a lot earlier, but for the fact she convinced me to stay.

While the cottage I bought was being refurbished, I moved back into her suite, into my old room, the one next to her bedroom.

She gave me a grateful look when I told her about my decision.

Clearly, she doesn't want us to sleep together while she thinks through whatever is on her mind. That's fine. If space is what she wants, I'll give it to her. What pisses me off is that she's not sharing whatever is bothering her, and she thought she couldn't ask me to stay in a different bedroom while she figures things out.

At least, she's safe. I'm reassured she's safe in her bed every night, even if I spend most of each night in a state of raging arousal.

So what, if I miss her nearness, and her body, but mostly, just being with her. It feels like a very vital part of me is missing. There's a clawing need for her, a gaping Aura-shaped hole in my life which is only filled when I see her. If anything, this enforced distance between us confirms to me that I cannot go back to living life without her. I miss my wife, and I can't wait for her to realize how much we belong together.

"Thanks for helping identify who's going to be on the Duchess' permanent security team." I nod toward Tyler's face on my phone screen.

"Good, and how's Smith working out?" he asks.

The discovery of Veronica's and Gavin's involvement in the threats on the princess' life, resulted in a major overhaul of the Royal Security Team. It also resulted in a tacit peace agreement between the king's Head of Security, and me.

We set aside our differences so we could work together to keep the Royal Family safe. The fact that he was mature enough to push aside his resentment toward me for my muscling in on his role and realize it made more sense for us to combine our forces to do our jobs, made the guy go up in my esteem.

I resumed my role as the head of the Duchess' security team but acquiesced to Smith taking on more of the day-to-day duties.

Given Aura has asked for time off from her Royal duties while she takes her thinking time, I've stepped in on her behalf to help how to invest the Davenport money in Verenza. So, Smith's help in identifying additional training and tech upgrades for the security team has been welcome.

Tyler scratches at his whiskered chin. He has heavy bags under his eyes and, with his overgrown hair, is a far cry from the shaved and shorn Royal Marine I used to know. That was before his daughter came into his life.

"How's Serene?" I scan his features. "I take it she's not sleeping nights?"

"She keeps having nightmares and wakes up screaming. Then, she won't go to sleep until I've crawled into her princess bed with her, which is not exactly long enough for my length." He cracks his neck, then stretches his arms above his head. His joints creak.

"You're a good dad," I say softly.

He scoffs, "If I were, I'd know how to tie a French braid. Something I've been unable to master, despite watching online tutorials." He holds up his thick fingers. "I can load rifles and hit a target at three miles, but braiding my little girl's hair is beyond my powers."

"You changed your life around for her. You gave up your career in the Marines and work from home so you can keep an eye on her. It's me who should be apologizing for taking you away from her."

Tyler shakes his head. "She was well taken care of by Summer, and I'm glad I was there for you. Besides, I'd be lying if I didn't say, sometimes it's good to take a break from parenting." He grins.

"You almost died." I squeeze my fingers into a fist. I'm not over the boats being blown up. That moment of my stomach bottoming out when I realized my brother and uncle might be dead, then calling on all of my experience as a Marine to believe that they were veterans who knew how to take care of themselves and focus on saving my wife. "It's not an experience I want to repeat again."

"Amen." He lowers his chin to his chest. "We underestimated our enemy. But believe me, I'm in no hurry to go anywhere; not as long as I need to take care of my little girl."

He takes in my features. I must look as tired as I feel, for he asks, "Everything okay?" His shrewd gaze doesn't miss much.

I should have realized I couldn't hide my current state of mind from my brother. I want to tell him everything is fine, but I have a feeling that's not going to fly with him.

"Finding me shot and bleeding, and almost dying, was a shock to the Duchess. She needs a little time and space to process it; something I'm trying to give her," I admit.

"Hmm." He purses his lips. "And how do you feel about it?"

"I understand." I drag my fingers through my hair. "If anyone knows how it is to see your friends and platoon-mates get hurt and die, it's me. Doesn't mean it makes it easier to see her withdraw from me."

"It's because she loves you, and it's difficult to see your loved ones hurt. It makes you realize they're mortal, and that you're going to lose them one day. Nothing like seeing someone you care for almost die for your own mortality to hit home," he points out.

"When did you become so wise?"

"That's what becoming a father does to you. You realize how powerless you truly are, how little control you have over everyday life." He half smiles. "She'll come around; you just have to be patient."

Aurelia

"I am so sorry, I can't make it for your birthday celebrations," Zoey cries from the phone screen.

I'm in my suite, getting dressed for the grand ball that my father has insisted on throwing for me. Having completed my hair and make-up, I study my reflection. Not bad for someone who, until a year ago, had a full glam team at her disposal. Truth be told, it's so much more satisfying to dress myself. Now, I only have to get through welcoming the queue of celebrities and officials my father has invited.

"I wouldn't have expected you here, honestly. Anyway, it's an event my father's team has organized." For him, it's another opportunity to have Verenza in the news.

We have to use every occasion to drive publicity around the country. And weddings, birthdays, and funerals provide the ideal platform for this. But a part of me feels like I've had enough of living my life in the public eye. I want to scale back my appearances at such fluffy events and, instead, use my family's name to attract more attention to charitable causes. I'm not sure how my father would receive that though, so I haven't brought it up with him.

She frowns. "But it's your birthday."

"And I'm the Duchess of Verenza." I shrug.

"Not only. You're also Mrs. Ryot Davenport," she reminds me.

Like I could forget that. His touch, his scent, the feel of his body against mine, his cock inside me, the feel of his palm print on my ass as he spanks me... All of it is burned into my brain and into my very senses. Seeing him almost daily in the meetings when our teams meet to discuss the agenda of the day, and then having him hold my hand at various official functions we attend together, only reinforces that I am his.

There's not a moment when I haven't thought of my husband.

At night, alone in the bed in my room, images of how he worshipped me with his body crowd my brain. The way he dominates me and controls me during lovemaking and edges me to new heights, so when I orgasm it turns the act of sex into something almost sacred. It confirms to me that I'm doing the right thing in wanting to walk away from my royal duties to seek a life out of the limelight.

Unfortunately, it's also mixed with images of him lying bleeding; when my heart dropped into my stomach, and I was unable to breathe, and felt the world closing in on me.

When I dropped to my knees and whipped off my blouse, trying to stem the flow of blood. I was sure he was gone until I slapped him, and he opened his eyes. The relief that enveloped me threatened to pull me under. But I knew I had to stay strong, I had to maintain pressure on the bleeding gun wound. That it likely saved his life is of little solace, though. The gamut of emotions that cleaved my chest still haunts me.

I am still dealing with the trauma of having almost lost him. It's why I haven't been able to tell him about my decision to leave my royal duties.

"He was hurt protecting me—" I clear my throat.

She purses her lips. "Are you holding yourself responsible for what happened?"

I don't reply.

Her scowl deepens. "Honey, the only person at fault here is Veronica."

"But I trusted her. I was the one who brought her into my inner circle. It's because I messaged her that she could track down where we were."

She blows out a breath. "Surely, you can see how irrational you're being here. You checked her background before hiring her, and there was nothing in it that could have warned you about her or indicated she was the person out to get you."

I complete painting my lips and set down my lip gloss. "Logically, I agree with you. But the emotional part of me can't get past the image of him lying hurt after being shot by a bullet meant for me."

"He was also your head of security. It was his job to do that," she says slowly.

"That changed when I married him. I feel... like I've pulled him into my life and all the complexity that goes with it. And all because I wanted the money he and his family could invest in my country." I twist my fingers together. "If something had happened to him, I wouldn't have been able to survive it. Every time I close my eyes, I see him on the ground, bleeding out. And it's making me feel I need to do something about it. As long as he's with me, he's going to be exposed to the same level of threat I am."

"He's a Marine, and a scion of the Davenport family, who may be even more well-known than your family. He's used to being in the line of fire, as well as in the media eye."

"But I'm the Duchess, a member of the Royal Family of Verenza, with public-facing duties. I'm the one whose lifestyle people are envious about, enough that they want to take me down. The level of scrutiny he's come under is nowhere close to what I've faced. By marrying me, he's put himself squarely in danger, as well." I slip into my stilettos and grab the phone from where I've balanced it on the dressing table.

"Have you spoken to him about this?" she asks slowly.

I hesitate, then shake my head.

"Why not? It's clear, you're tying yourself up in knots. Nothing I say is going to help resolve the questions in your mind. You should discuss them with him. He's your husband, after all."

"You're right, of course. I need to be more open about my fears with him. But it's taken me a little time to even identify what was bothering me, you know?"

The lines around her eye softens. "Honey, that's normal. You had a shock. And it's normal to be so overcome that you pull back. Likely, you needed a little space to regroup. But he's your husband. And he was there when it happened. It must have been traumatic for him, too. He must have been just as upset to realize Veronica was the one who came prepared to hurt you."

"Not to mention that his brother's and uncle's boats were blown up, too. He probably feared they were already dead." Another thing that makes me feel guilty. "Thankfully, no one was hurt." Both men made it clear to me they were doing their job and, given a choice, would do it all over again. Which makes me feel lucky to have them as part of my new family. But that doesn't lessen the guilt of what I put them through.

"You really should talk to him—"

"Talk to who?" My husband's voice reaches me from the doorway of my suite. After what happened, he upped the security and installed locks outside my suite which now require a passcode. A passcode only he and I, and one member of my household staff responsible for the cleaning, have. No one else is allowed in here, or into the cottage he bought on the premises.

The security outside the palace was also increased, and all of the staff was subjected to more rigorous background checks and enhanced skill development. All of which makes me feel safer... But if I'm being honest, the only time I feel completely safe is when I'm with him.

"Hi, Ryot," Zoey calls out.

"Zoey." He nods at her "How's the job coming along?"

"As well as can be expected, considering so many of my authors have missed their deadlines." She rolls her eyes.

"I promise, I'll be done with the redrafts by the end of the month," I hasten to add.

She laughs. "Oh, I know you will. Despite all of the changes in your life, I know you're so professional, you'll stick to your deadline. Unlike some of the others I manage." Someone talks off screen, and she nods at us. "Okay, I'm late for my next meeting."

"Take care, Z."

She disconnects. I hang up and slide my phone into the tiny purse I'll be carrying. Then, because I need something inane to talk about, I step away and pose with one hand on my hip. "How do I look?"

He peruses me from the top of my head to the tips of my toes, and everywhere his eyes alight on me, it feels like he's touched me. Little sparks of heat dance off my skin. Tiny stings of pleasure nip at my nerve-endings. His gaze is so hungry, so admiring, so lust-filled and tender, all at once, my heart swells in my chest. A heavy sensation squeezes my pussy. When our gazes connect, I feel like I'm being pulled in his direction.

As if in a dream, I take a step in his direction, and another, until the tips of my stilettos bump into his dress shoes. It's my turn to scan him, from the razor-sharp crease of his black pants, to the crisp white of his shirt, and the emerald green tie which brings out the silver highlights in his eyes. The breadth of his shoulders stretches his jacket. The dark, spicy scent of his aftershave crowds my senses and turns my nipples into pinpoints of need. The lack of his five o'clock beard indicates he recently shaved, and his hair is combed back, with an errant strand falling over his forehead. My fingers tingle and, unable to stop myself, I go up on tiptoe and brush it aside.

His gaze widens, and as I pull back, he plants one big palm on my hip. The heat of his fingers burns through the fabric into my skin. "You look beautiful."

"You look beautiful," I murmur.

He slides a hand into his pocket and pulls out a ring. He releases me, only to take my left hand in his and slide a ring next to my wedding band.

"Oh!" I take in the large, oval sapphire in the center of the ring.

It's deep blue, with a sparkle. *So, like my eyes.* My heart stutters. A warmth squeezes my chest. Surrounding the sapphire are brilliant cut diamonds that enhance the beauty of the sapphire. It's simple, yet elegant, and very regal.

"Fit for my Empress." He kisses the ring, then holds my hand between both of his.

"It's gorgeous." My throat aches with unspoken feelings.

"It belonged to my grandmother. She left a piece of jewelry from her collection for each of us brothers to give to the woman we love. She'd have wanted you to have this."

"It's beautiful." A pressure drums at the backs of my eyeballs. I can't take my gaze off the beautiful stone. "It feels… Perfect."

"You're perfect," he says with such feeling, I raise my gaze to his.

On his face, I see the wonder, the love, and the tenderness. That look which marks him out as mine. *Mine. Mine. Mine.* His green irises spark. That underlying current of lust that underpins our interactions flares.

I take a step toward him and tip up my chin. He lowers his chin, and a buzzing sound interrupts us.

59

Aurelia

"Ignore it." He brushes his lips over mine.

Soft and sweet. Then, he deepens the kiss, and it's urgent and hot, and the flick of his tongue into my mouth sends shivers all the way to my toes. I moan deep in my throat, and his muscles bunch. He sweeps me up to my toes and into him. My breasts flatten against his chest. The muscled strength of his thighs, the throbbing length at his crotch... I feel everything. I dig my fingers into his biceps and hold on as he ravages my mouth and turns my insides to jelly. The buzzing grows more insistent.

He groans, and when he lifts his head, his green eyes have turned into a sea of emerald fire. My lips throb, and my breath comes in pants.

My phone vibrates in my purse again, but I ignore it.

Zoey was right. I should talk to him. I should tell him what I've decided. I should explain to him why I needed the time to process everything that happened. And why I decided to leave my official duties as a duchess.

He's my husband. He loves me. He'll understand it.

"Ryot"—I whisper—"I missed you."

"I missed you so fucking much, it feels like a part of me was torn out. I feel so fucking incomplete without you, baby."

"Me too."

My phone buzzes again. Then his phone vibrates.

"Goddamn." He releases me, then snatches up his device. "We're on our way." He disconnects the call and looks at me. "They're waiting for us. Can't start the festivities without the birthday girl."

"I love you so much." I reach up and press my lips to his.

He deepens the kiss, and when he sweeps his tongue inside my mouth, my core quivers. I melt into him.

He pulls me close enough that I can feel his heart slam against his ribcage. The kiss goes on and on, and when he finally pulls away to press his forehead into mine, both of us are panting.

"Now I wish I could keep you to myself." He pockets his phone, and reaching down, swipes his thumb around the edges of my lips, removing any smeared lipstick.

"I need to refresh my makeup." I turn, but he grips my arm.

"What if I want them to look at you and realize you've been kissed soundly by your husband."

His words are so possessive, my blood turns to lava. When the buzzer to the suite sounds again, he twists his fingers with mine. "Let's get out of here."

"Thanks, baby." I take a flute of champagne from him and sip from it. Cold bubbles burst on my tongue. "Mmm, I needed that." I take another sip. "If I had to pretend to laugh at another joke by that senator, I'd have to kill myself," I say only half-jokingly, then proceed to toss the rest of the champagne back.

"Take it easy, Empress," my husband cautions.

"I need to be a little drunk to get through the evening." This, I say seriously.

He gives me a funny look, then takes my flute and sets it aside.

"Hey, I thought you were going to fill me up," I pout.

He takes my hand and leads me off to the side. Of course, we're stopped by the Queen of Spain, who kisses me on both cheeks and wishes me a happy birthday. She goes to kiss my husband, but when he scowls at her, she blinks and steps aside hurriedly. He hustles me to the end of the room where a chaise is pushed up into the shadows. There are potted plants around it, which give us some degree of privacy. He sits down then pulls me into his lap.

I squeak, "What are people going to say?"

"That we're newlyweds?" He raises his shoulder in that nonchalant way I've come to love. "Frankly, I couldn't give a damn."

I giggle.

"God, I love that sound. If I could spend every moment of my life making you happy, it wouldn't be enough."

I fasten my arms around his neck. "I never would have thought someone as alpha and as stern as you was such a romantic."

"And I thought you'd know by now not to try to stereotype me."

"I'd never." I look into his beloved features. "Now, why is it that you pulled me aside?"

He looks taken aback, then laughs. "Am I that transparent?"

"Only to me."

He nods, a thoughtful look coming into his eyes. "If you hate this, why do you do it?"

"What do you mean?"

"Clearly, being here at an official reception for your birthday, meeting and greeting dignitaries, is not something which appeals to you."

"Am *I* that transparent?" I ask surprised.

"Only to me, baby." He places his palms on my hips, and the heavy weight feels both secure and erotic at the same time.

"There was a time when I enjoyed it, but I very quickly tired of having to put on a face and pretend I'm having a good time." I shuffle my feet. "Instead, I'd preferred to be at my desk writing, or in my PJs watching a series on television."

"And now?"

"Now, I'd rather spend time alone with you."

His expression turns thoughtful. "So, why aren't you?"

"What do you mean?" I try to understand what he's trying to say.

"If you're finding it such a chore, don't do it anymore."

"Okay."

He stares at me. "Okay?"

I look away, then back at him. I've been wanting to tell him about my decision to move away from my official duties within the Royal Family and now seems like the right time.

"As you know, I was brought up to be a princess, and now, a Duchess, to play my role within the Royal household and help my father fulfill his duties to his subjects. As were my brothers." I nod toward where Viktor is holding court, surrounded by a bunch of women of all ages. "Obviously, it didn't really take in Brandon's case." She laughs.

I recognize the Princess of Spain, the daughter of the American ambassador to Verenza, the first cousin to the Prince of Wales, as well as a well-known actress, an Olympic gold-winning athlete, and a model who has millions of followers across social media platforms. In the middle of them is my brother, with a smirk on his face. And that cold look in his eyes signifying he finds them all too easy and is planning to take, at least, one of them to bed tonight.

"Clearly, he laps up the attention." My husband snorts.

"As he should, as the future King. As for me, my role first as Princess and now, Duchess of Verenza pales in comparison to my most important identity, your wife."

He jerks his chin in my direction. "You are the most important person in the world to me."

At his words, my heart does that little flip in my chest. I'll never get used to hearing that from him. For once, it's not Verenza that comes first, as it does with my father and oldest brother. For once, it's me who's the most important to someone.

"As you are to me. Which is why I have decided to—"

Someone coughs behind us. I sigh.

He looks past me and arches an eyebrow at the new arrival. "I believe that's your new assistant."

Yep, I hired someone recommended by Zoey, whose background my husband vetted before giving me the green light to hire her. I'm happy to say that, so far, Yaz has been amazing, if a little shy.

"Uh, sorry to bother you, Duchess, but there are a few more people who want to meet you."

I glance at her over my shoulder, and she blushes, but she doesn't look away. "I held them off, but it's probably best if you come and meet them before they come looking for you."

I nod, then turn to my husband and kiss his cheek.

"What were you saying? It sounded important." He searches my features.

I allow myself a small smile. Internally, I'm sure now, I've made the right decision. "I promise, I'll tell you later."

He stares at me for a few seconds more, then nods. "I'll hold you to it." He kisses me hard, and by the time he lets me go, I'm flushed. I slip off my husband's lap.

Viktor approaches us. He walks past Yaz, who blushes deeper, but my brother doesn't seem to notice.

"The troops are getting antsy for the birthday girl. I've entertained them for as long as I could, but best you get over there and talk to them." He smirks.

I roll my eyes. "Like it was such a chore for you to flirt with the women."

He holds up his hands, an innocent look in his eyes—as if I'm going to be taken in by that. "I was simply doing my job as host and being polite."

"My ass," I snort.

"Why, Aura"—he shakes his head—"how frightfully impolite of you."

"Ha!" I toss my head and am about to leave, then look between them and hesitate.

My husband interprets the expression on my face correctly. He leans over, takes my hand in his and kisses my fingertips. "Go on. Viktor and I are due a catch up."

60

Ryot

"I'd say you were pussy-whipped, except it's my sister you're married to, and it's evident to everyone who comes within a mile of her, how happy she is." The Crown Prince of Verenza remains standing. At six feet three inches, he's as tall as me. And as broad.

We both come from money and have had privileged childhoods. The only difference is, I chose to forge my own path when I joined the Marines. And chose not to join the Davenport Group as CEO. The only reason I embraced my wealth was because it was going to help her country, and that was important to her. The crown prince, though, has no such compunctions. He's in line to succeed the throne. He has no qualms about owning his birthright as the successor to the King of Verenza.

"I'm the one who's deliriously happy that she accepted me as her husband." I sprawl back in my seat. "I consider it my duty to help her fulfill her dreams, her goals, and her aspirations. To bolster her when she's down. To lift her spirits when she needs a reminder that she's got this."

I mean every word I said. I want her brother to realize I don't take Aura's happiness for granted. That I'll do everything in my power to take care of her.

He blinks slowly, a look of such comical surprise on his face that I chuckle. "You haven't got a woman in your life, I take it?"

He scoffs. "Not going there, mate. I have enough on my plate, focusing on the country. Verenza is a demanding mistress."

"Wait until you meet and fall in love; that will change your mind-set, and your life," I say with a knowing smirk.

"Which is why I plan on getting married only to perform my duty. None of that falling in love bullshit for me."

I could point out he's tempting fate, but that would have no effect. Sometimes, you need to go through the ups and downs that come with finding your soulmate to realize they are the most impor-tant thing in your life. Not money. Not power. But love.

The kind of love that has you sacrificing everything, so your other half is happy. The kind that makes you do anything, so they can fulfill their dreams. The kind that makes you put them in the center of your life and do everything in your power to protect them, to keep them safe and to provide for them. The kind where, every time you're in the same space with them, you can't stop yourself from touching them to feel their skin with your fingertips and reassure yourself they're fine. The kind where, when you're not with them, you miss them. The kind where you respect them enough to give them agency to make up their own mind and believe in the power of your love that they'll find their own way back to you.

"Only time will tell." I tilt my head.

He must read some of my thoughts, for a flush steals across his features. Then, he sinks down next to me. "Nothing personal, of course."

"Of course." I smirk.

"What you and my sister have is different."

"Hmm..." I drag my thumb under my lip and stay silent.

He moves around, trying to make himself comfortable. "I mean, it's clear the two of you love each other. And there is a deep bond between the two of you. And thanks to you, Verenza's future looks far more promising than it did a month ago."

"I did it for her." I hold his gaze. "If she wanted me to burn the world down—"

"Let me guess, you'd give her the match and not stand in her way?"

I bare my teeth. "And after it's reduced it to cinders, build her a brand new one in which she never has to do anything against her will. I'd take my own life, if it meant she could live hers in a way that makes her happy."

His jaw drops, then he rubs at his neck. "Damn, you have it bad, mate."

"You mean I have it good, don't you?"

"If that's what you want to call it." He chuckles, then grows serious. "I do want you to know I appreciate what you and your family did for Verenza. The money your company invested will make a huge difference to the futures of our children and boost jobs for families. You have my word that it will be invested where it's most needed."

"I have no doubt." I nod. "This is a good time to let you know that I will be withdrawing from my role as the head of the task force responsible for investing the money."

He does a double take. "It's money the Davenport group pumped into the economy."

"I'm aware."

"It's the most reliable way to ensure it's invested the way you think is right."

"A job my wife is more than capable of managing," I point out.

His eyebrows draw down, then he nods. "I agree with you. In fact"—he squares his shoulders—"I've insisted that my father make Aurelia the lead on that planning commission. She's more than capable of chairing that group. If she wants that responsibility, that is."

"Good man." I clap his shoulder.

"And what are you going to do now?" He eyes me curiously.

"Without your responsibilities on the task force, you could—" His next few words are drowned out by a series of gunshots.

My heart slams into my ribcage. My body reacts on instinct, and I find myself crouched on the floor, putting the settee between me and the window. Viktor must follow my lead, for he's next to me.

"Did someone fire?" He pulls out his phone and begins to dial someone. His head of security, no doubt.

Without bothering to reply, I'm on my feet and moving in the direction she headed. *She's safe; she has to be. Nothing has happened to her.* I scan the people milling about, most wearing confused looks on their faces. *I can't see her. Where is she? Why did I let her leave? I should have gone with her. I—* Suddenly, she elbows her way through the groups of people milling around and races toward me. *Thank fuck. She's safe.* Something inside of me relaxes. I hold out my arms, and she jumps into them.

"You're okay." She throws her arms around my neck and presses her nose into it. "I was so scared." She trembles, and I pull her in even closer. She lifts her chin, and I press my lips to hers.

Outside the window, there's a high-pitched whistling. We look to the side to find fireworks zipping through the sky then exploding in a burst of colorful stars.

"It's only fireworks," she breathes.

I remember, now; they were arranged to go off at the end of the evening. It's a testament to how wrapped up I am in her that I forgot about it.

The tension drains from my body. My head spins with relief, and I bury my nose in her hair, drawing in her scent, enshrining it in my lungs. I squeeze my arms about her, reveling in every curve, every dip, every flare of her gorgeous body. "Jesus, baby, that was a hell of a scare. I thought something had happened to you."

"Me too." She hiccups, then looks up at me through relief-filled eyes which are beginning to tear up. "Will you please get me out of here before I break down and make a complete fool of myself?"

61

Aurelia

He rushes me out of there, sidestepping those who try to stop us, shouldering past others. The curiosity on their faces is too much for me to bear. Not right now, when my heartbeat hasn't returned to normal, and my pulse drums at my temples and at my wrists. Every beat of it trying to convince me that he's *safe*. That *I'm* safe.

I'm unable to stop trembling and realize what I mistook to be shots fired catapulted me right back to when he was shot, to when the bullets narrowly missed me. A pressure grips my chest. My throat seems to close. I try to breathe, but my lungs burn. I realize I'm hyperventilating and, rather than allow people to realize what's happening to me, I turn my face into his neck and draw deep breaths of his scent. So familiar. So safe.

My heartbeat finally slows. While my pussy begins a different kind of trembling. I hear voices. Viktor's, asking the guests to let me pass. Then my father's, asking if I'm okay and saying I can't leave without bidding people goodbye. To which my husband firmly says that I'm not feeling well and I'm in no shape to stay. Then, we're stepping out into the corridor, and I hear his footsteps and those of someone else up ahead. We reach the entrance to the palace and step out. Cool air flows over my skin. I shiver; he pulls me closer. Then, there's only the rustling of the breeze, and I realize we're walking toward our place.

I look up to find Viktor walking ahead of us. Cole brings up the rear.

We reach my husband's house—*our* house—and Viktor opens the door for us. As we pass, he presses my shoulder. "Rest up." He exchanges nods with my husband, then steps back. The door closes behind us.

My husband carries me up the stairs, down the hallway, to the open double doors at the end. He steps through, walks over to the bed, and places me on it. When he begins to straighten, I shake my head and grab his hand. "Don't let go."

"I'm not." He kisses the back of my palm, then sinks to his knees and slips off my stilettos. I sigh and wriggle my toes.

"Better?" he rumbles.

I reach for his tie, but he squeezes both of my hands. "Let me take care of you first, baby."

His gruff voice brings tears to my eyes. And I let them slide down my cheeks.

He reaches up and wipes them away. "Does this mean you don't need space anymore?" His throat bobs as he swallows.

I cry harder and he holds me and rocks me until my tears slow. I sniffle, and burrow further into his chest.

He reaches behind me and unzips my dress. The fabric slithers down my shoulders. I rise to my feet, and it slinks down to catch around my waist. I shimmy out of it until it pools around my ankles. The tendons of his throat flex. He drags his gaze up my thick thighs, over the roll of my stomach, to the valley between my breasts, then the hollow of my throat, and to my face. Little flickers of heat arise in his wake.

"You're so beautiful," he whispers.

"You make me feel beautiful," I confess.

He scoops me up in his arms and walks toward the ensuite bathroom. Putting me down, he runs a bath, dropping in a couple of my favorite bath bombs. The scent of honeysuckle, vanilla and strawberries fills the air. He walks around lighting the candles set up at strategic locations around the bath, and when he switches off the light, a soft golden glow fills the space.

"It's so gorgeous," I murmur.

"Not as much as you." He turns to find I've removed my bra and panties and tossed them aside. Even in the shadowy light, his green eyes glow. Color smears his cheeks. He reaches me and bends to kiss, first one nipple, then the other. I shudder, then gasp when he presses little kisses down my stomach to my belly button and further down until he reaches the space between my legs. He licks at my clit, and the burst of pleasure in my veins threatens to undo me completely. My knees knock together, and I dig my fingers into his hair for support.

Already on his knees, he sinks to his haunches and urges me to part my legs. Then he swipes his tongue up my weeping slit, and I cry out. He licks and sucks and holds my pussy lips apart. Then curls his tongue around the swollen nub between them. Shivers of ecstasy course up my body. And when he squeezes my butt cheeks and bites down on my cunt, I cry out.

The orgasm hits me so quickly, my lungs burn. My nipples tingle. My scalp feels like it's splintering into tiny pieces, each of which carries his name on it. As I slump, he rises to his feet. He holds me up until he's sure I'm able to support myself, and then he strips.

I take in his magnificent chest planes, the dog tags, the scar from the bullet he took for me—I swallow. The sight of that will never cease to affect me. It's proof of how much he loves me. But the scar isn't as obvious as I thought it would be. It's partially covered by a tattoo— *A tattoo?* I blink. Then reach over and trace the name he's carved into his chest over his heart:

Empress of my Heart

Wow. I swallow. "Is that…"

"It's so I always have you with me, wherever I go."

I rise up on my toes, and he picks me up like I weigh nothing. He always makes me feel so small, so delicate, so protected. He gets into the bath and lies back, places me between his legs, then reaches forward and shuts off the water.

In the silence that follows, I sink back against his broad chest. And when his arms come around me, the weight is so reassuring, so right, I know I'm home. "I love you." I place my hands on his and squeeze. "I love you so much."

He tucks my head under his chin. "I can't live without you. You're my heart. My soul. My everything. Without you, I'm nothing."

I turn my chin into his chest, relishing the vibrations of his voice across his ribcage. "When I heard those shots—well, what I thought were shots—the panic that gripped me—" I shake my head. "I thought something had happened to you. Not that the shots had been fired from inside, but in that moment, I remembered how it'd been to see you on the ground and bleeding. To hold you in my arms as you struggled to breathe. To feel like I was going to lose you, and knowing I could not go on without you. It was at that moment I realized my life as I knew it could be over."

I sense him stiffen and look up to find a quizzical expression in his eyes. I sit up, and when my breasts jiggle, his gaze drops to them. His breath quickens, and a sense of elations fills me. To know that this powerful man is so affected by me, that he feels so much for me, that he loves me, and respects me, and thinks the world of me, fills me with immense joy. I feel so light, I could be floating.

"I'm stepping back from my duties to the Royal Family."

His gaze widens, and he seems momentarily stunned. "But—"

I put my finger on his lips. "I want to do this. I *need* to do this. I've needed to do this for so long… and what you said earlier struck a chord with me. You gave me the courage to accept that I don't enjoy what I do. I don't want to wake up every day, dreading the next official engagement. I don't want to be in the public eye. I want to live for myself, and for you. I want to be safe, and I want *you* to be safe." I draw in a shuddering breath. "That's not possible as long as *I* am in the public eye. As the Duke of Verenza, you will be at my side at these public functions which puts *you* in danger—and that"—I shake my head—"that I cannot bear."

"I can take care of myself. And I can take care of *you*," he growls.

I trace the outline of his mouth, and the pulse at the base of his throat speeds up. "I know you can. But so long as I'm in the public eye, it's inevitable that there will be danger associated with my movements. Which puts you in the line of fire, as well. If something happens to you, I won't survive. I can't live with the specter of god-knows-what hanging over us. I can't, Ryot. I choose you. I choose *us*. I choose my freedom." When his cock throbs against my core, I know I've said the right thing.

He cups my cheek. "Are you sure?"

"I am." I nod. "I've done my bit, getting you and the Davenport group to invest into Verenza. It's up to Viktor to steer the country to the next stage."

"You shouldn't do this for me—"he begins, but I shake my head.

"I want to do this for *us*. So we can have a future together. So we can have a life where we can build a family"—I swallow—"if that's what you want..."

The creases around his eyes relax. "I want you. I want a family with you, baby." He lifts me up until I straddle him and lowers me onto his erect cock. The swollen head breaches my entrance, and I groan. I grab hold of his forearms and dig my knees into the sides of his waist. He throbs against my seam, and when I try to lower myself down further, he shakes his head. "Not until I allow you."

I pout—"But I wanna"—then gasp when he squeezes my butt. Sensations course up my spine and back down to my throbbing clit.

"Who do you belong to, baby?" he growls.

"You—" I swallow. "Only you."

"That's right." His grip on my hips grows almost punishing, and I can feel the brand of every single fingerprint on my skin. I feel the swollen head of his cock at my slit. I want so badly to tilt my hips and take him in, but if I try to do that two things will happen. Number one, he'll stop me and he's too strong for me to override him. And two, he'll make me wait longer for my orgasm, and damn, I won't be able to.

I dig my fingernails into his forearms and wait. I wait until he jerks his chin as if coming to a decision.

"You do as I say, you feel me?"

I nod.

"Good girl."

His praise shoots liquid heat through my veins. My thighs tremble, my entire body turning into a storm of need, of desire. Of needing him inside of me. And just when I think I can't stand it anymore, he punches his hips up and impales me.

"Ryot," I cry out as he begins to fuck up and into me.

His forearms bunch, the planes of his chest turn to stone, and he grunts as he, once again, kicks his hips forward and slides in to the hilt. "Jesus, baby, you feel so bloody good." He holds me in place, so I can feel every throb of his cock, every ridge, every hard inch pushing against my walls. He feels so thick, so big, enough for little pain-filled pockets to radiate out from where we're connected.

"Okay?" he asks through gritted teeth.

I nod, focused on how he's filling me completely. He stays there for a few more seconds, giving me a chance to adjust, then he begins to move again.

He fucks me in earnest, pushing in until his monster cock hits the spot deep inside of me. The explosion builds up my legs, up my spine, and I'm so close.

Oh, god. "Ryot," I whimper.

"With me, baby; stay with me."

He thrust into me over and over again, and the orgasm grows bigger, larger than life, filling me, stretching me, becoming something so much more immense, so much more everything. The shudders speed up my body, increasing in ferocity, pushing me higher and higher, and when it peaks, I cry out. The climax crashes over me, my orgasm spinning me through a funnel and spitting me out the other side. I feel his guttural cry as he pours hot streams of cum inside of me and follows me over the edge.

I come down from the high and slump against his chest,

becoming aware of the warm water lapping around us, of his arms banded around me, of his shaft pulsing inside me. He rises to his feet and, still joined, steps out of the tub. I struggle to open my eyes and when I look up at him, my eyes at half-mast, the ferocity of coming together still clinging to my senses, he smirks. "I am going to fuck you again."

EPILOGUE

Statement by The Duchess and Duke of Verenza

It is after much consideration that we have decided to step back from our duties as working members of the Royal Family. We will continue to fully support His Majesty, The King.

We now plan to balance our time between Verenza and the United Kingdom, continuing to honor our duty to King and Country, and to our patronages.

This geographic balance will provide us with the space to focus on the next chapter, including the launch of our new charitable entity.

We look forward to sharing the full details of this exciting next step in due course, as we continue to collaborate with His Majesty, The King, The Crown Prince of Verenza, and all relevant parties.

Until then, please accept our deepest thanks for your continued support.

EPILOGUE 2

Three months later

Ryot

"I'd say welcome to the neighborhood, but it's as if you've always lived here." Sinclair narrows his gaze on his cards.

It's Friday night, and the first time I'm hosting poker night at my place. A tradition Arthur started at his place. One of the few my brothers and I decided to keep because we enjoy it so much. We moved it out of Arthur's place when he was diagnosed with the big C, at Imelda's request. She'd hoped it would mean he'd stop smoking his cigars. In deference to her wishes, we've forgone our cigars at the poker table. Replacing it with whiskey, and nachos, and guacamole, which my wife rustled up for us.

Aura has discovered a love for cooking. Something she was unable to do earlier when she had a chef on her staff. We agreed that, while we'll have a housekeeper come in regularly to help keep the house clean, we'll be hands-on in the kitchen.

She mentioned to me that Viktor was supportive of her stepping back from her Royal duties. Her father, less so. The king told her she was making a mistake, but if that's what she wanted, he wouldn't stand in her way.

Her brother Brandon, too, backed her decision. He's the one member of her family I don't know well at all, considering he didn't make it to our wedding. She was upset about that, but I'm willing to forgive him because, it turns out, the guy has his heart in the right place.

Both Viktor and Brandon, separately, wished my wife the best for her move away from the monarchy.

It took another week to draw up a plan to help her separate her future from that of the Royal Family. She agreed to honor the public appearances she'd already committed to, and indicated she wouldn't take on more. If the Royal Family needed her to do so under extenuating circumstances in the future, she'd consider them on a case-by-case basis.

Which means, she has a year's worth of engagements to get through in countries around the world. All of which I'll accompany her to, along with a top-notch security team.

I'm not taking any risks with her protection, no matter that the person who threatened her life is dead. My wife is too precious, and I won't leave anything up to chance.

Then came the public announcement by the Royal Palace. By then, we'd moved back to London, and that helped cushion her from the worst of the media scrutiny to follow.

I bought a place in Primrose Hill and ensured the house is under round-the-clock surveillance. This is where Sinclair lives, as do Tyler, Nathan and Quentin.

"This is a great neighborhood. Aura loves getting to know her sisters-in-law and Summer, and she's thrilled to spend time with Serene." I nod in Tyler's direction.

"Serene's over-joyed to have her dropping by so often." He rubs the back of his neck. "Pass," he murmurs, eyeing his cards with a frown.

"I'm sorry I took you away from her," I apologize again.

He scoffs, "I wanted to be there for you. Besides, Serene was delighted to spend time with Summer and Matty." He tilts his chin in Sinclair's direction.

"Summer loved having her over." Sinclair looks at Brody. "And how is it that we have the pleasure of your company today?"

Brody smirks. "Figured the only way I was going to meet you over-the-hill men was by crashing your poker session."

"Over-the-hill?" Tyler frowns. "Who're you talking about?"

"Given these two are married"—he nods between me and Sinclair —"and since you've got to make it home by a decent time to put Serene to bed—" He shrugs. "The three of you are no fun."

"Walking up to my bedroom where I can sleep with my wife, in my bed, in my house? I'm not complaining." I laugh.

"Same." Sinclair raises his beer bottle, and I tap mine to his.

Tyler and Brody exchange looks, both wearing matching smirks.

"You guys have no idea what you're missing," I murmur.

"Nope, not going there. I'm out of the marriage game, was never in it to begin with. And with responsibility for Serene, I'm never getting married."

I eye him with curiosity. "Why is that?"

"First off, the relationship piece. I have enough in my life with taking care of Serene. The last thing I need is some high-maintenance woman marching in and demanding I give her attention. I only have space for Serene. And any time I have left is spent on taking care of the business."

"What if you find someone who fits into your life and who Serene likes?" Sinclair asks. His voice is casual, but I read the seriousness under his words.

"That's not going to happen." Tyler scowls at his cards.

"Why not?" I exchange another glance with Sinclair.

"Because—" Tyler rolls his shoulders. "Because I'm not the easiest man to be with. And Serene will always come first. It's not fair to expect any woman to accept that."

"There might be someone out there who'll love Serene as much as you and who you find makes your life better," Sinclair murmurs.

Tyler makes a rude noise. "And Arthur turns into a loving, cuddly man overnight."

Brody laughs. "Now, that'd be a sight."

"He has changed since meeting Imelda. Not that it stopped him from trying to interfere in my love life," I throw down my cards.

"You're folding?" Sinclair lowers his chin.

"Best to quit while I'm ahead."

"Agree." He follows my lead.

"Hmm." Brody considers his cards, then lays them face up on the table.

A slow smile curves Tyler's face, then he turns his cards face up.

We take in the cards. It's an eight of hearts, a seven of hearts, a six of hearts, a five of hearts, and a four of hearts. "A fucking straight flush?" Brody glowers at him.

Tyler moves the poker chips closer. "Better luck next time." He rises to his feet, then yawns.

"You're leaving?" Brody looks disappointed. "I was hoping you'd have another beer before you head home."

"That's my quota for the day."

"You're not driving, so why not have another?" Brody seems genuinely taken aback.

"Because I need to be up early? Serene's up at five a.m. most days, and I want to be able to get her dressed and feed her breakfast before I drop her off at school."

"You're a wonderful dad." My wife glides into the room. She's dressed in jeans and a plaid shirt, but her stance is regal. She halts next to me and puts a hand on my shoulder. Warmth seeps into my bloodstream. My heart kicks up into high gear, as it always does when she's around.

I look up at her. "Missed you, baby."

She bends down, and we kiss. Soft and sweet, and so fucking erotic. Her scent fills my senses, and my pulse rate spikes. I wrap my arm about her waist and pull her closer.

"Jeez, you guys, get a room," Brody says in disgust.

My wife trembles, and fuck, if I don't want to pull her in my lap. She straightens and looks at me with shining eyes. Her features are flushed, her lips swollen, and damn, if that doesn't fill me with pride.

She smiles, then looks at Tyler. "I may have found a nanny for you."

"A nanny?" He looks at her with skepticism.

"You're still looking for one, I assume?"

Tyler nods slowly. "Though, at this point, I've given up hope of finding anyone Serene likes."

"She's an old friend; I can vouch for her. I gave her your address, so she'll be at your place for an interview tomorrow at five p.m. Hope that's okay?"

"Oh, that's good." Tyler yawns again. "Although, I'm not holding my breath."

"You might be surprised," my wife says with a small smile.

Tyler merely laughs, then looks around at the rest of us. "Right then, I'm off." He pockets his phone, meets the others at the door, and walks out.

"That's an evil smile." I scan my wife's features. "What are you up to Empress?"

To find out what happens next read Tyler & Priscilla's story in *The Rejected Wife. Scan this QR code to get the book*

How to scan a QR code?

1. Open the camera app on your phone or tablet.
2. Point the camera at the QR code.
3. Tap the banner that appears on your phone or tablet.
4. Follow the instructions on the screen to finish signing in.

READ A BONUS SPICY EPILOGUE FEATURING RYOT & AURELIA.

Bonus scene

This takes place a few days after Aura and Ryot move to Primrose Hill

Aurelia

"Oh honey, I need to finish writing this book," I whine.

"You've been working all day; you need a break," my husband reminds.

I raise my arms above my head and stretch. The soreness in my forearms and my shoulders reminds me I've been hunched over my keyboard most of the day. Sure, I'm a little tired but I couldn't be happier. I am so enjoying the freedom that comes with working for myself.

To be able to get up every morning and write is a real treat. To not have to put on a dress and heels and trudge off to another public engagement in my former role as the Duchess of Verenza is something I wouldn't have thought possible in my wildest dreams. Yet here I am, wearing my yoga pants and an oversized sweatshirt, writing spicy novels under a pen name.

No longer am I Aurelia Isabella Verenza, former working member of the royal family of Verenza, who had to represent her country in boring state dinners and diplomatic missions. I retreated from my public-facing role and my official duties nearly three months ago, and I couldn't be happier.

I wake up without an alarm clock, naturally. And isn't that a treat? To open my eyes with my husband's big, warm, muscular body wrapped around me, in our bed, in Primrose Hill, where I am Mrs. Ryot Davenport—is nothing short of heaven.

Then, I make us both breakfast and head to my study where I work until noon. Most days, my husband works from home too. In which case, we order in and eat lunch together. That's when we catch up on news, and oftentimes, it leads to a little quickie—a fringe benefit of both of us working from home. Then, it's back to the writing desk for me.

Today, I lost track of time as I raced to write the latest quarter of the novel I'm working on. I reached the climax of the scene but then, couldn't write the climax between the characters—in other words, when the two finally made love, because yeah, this one turned out to be a slow burn novel. Some readers aren't fond of it, but it's what the characters demanded.

So here I am, staring at the screen, trying to figure out their positions, when my husband stalks in and demands that I stop writing so he can take me out to dinner.

I turn to him. "I'm sorry. I know I've been so focused on getting this novel completed. It's always like that when I'm inching toward the end. I just want this book done with, you know?" I peer up at him from under my eyelashes.

He gives me a half tender-half proud look. "You're amazing, Empress."

"And you, Mr. Davenport, are the sexiest man in the entire freakin' world." I take in his button down with the loosened tie, the rolled-up sleeves which show off his muscular forearms, and the tailored pants that encase those powerful thighs and never cease to turn my core into a mass of melting need.

My breathing grows choppy. My pulse rate speeds up. *Damn, I only have to look at the big guy and I want to jump his bones.* He's totally aware of the effect he has on me for he all but preens. He slides one hand into his pant pocket, stretching the crotch tight. Of course, my gaze drops there. And I swear, I can discern the outline of that long, thick column I've come to know so intimately.

"Like what you see, darlin'?" he drawls.

I can hear the smirk in his voice. With good reason. I don't begrudge him his ego... At least, not when it comes to his prowess in bed. And not otherwise either... Because as much of an alpha that he is, Ryot is also the kindest, gentlest, most caring husband I could have asked for.

"You know, I do. The problem is I like it too much. So much so that I'm finding it difficult to work up enthusiasm for this sex scene I'm writing."

"Eh?" He blinks slowly. "Come again?"

"All you have to do is put your penis in my vag, and I'll come as many times as you want," I say sweetly.

His jaw drops. Yep. I managed to surprise Ryot, a freakin' Davenport, and I count that as a win. Not that I'm counting. But it feels good to know I can.

"I keep imagining your cock instead of the hero's pecker, and I get distracted," I explain.

"So, you're writing this smutty scene, and thinking of me is leading you astray?" His smirk broadens.

"Umm, yes. And you don't have to look so happy about it."

He lowers his hand from his pocket, walks around to lean a hip next to me at the table. "Perhaps, what you need is something to spark those creative ideas on how they can have sex?"

Hearing him say 'sex' in that hard, dark, raspy voice sends a flurry of sensations coursing through my veins. "I'm not sure I follow," I say in an innocent voice, when I know perfectly exactly what it is he's hinting at. "Maybe I need you to explain it to me?" I flutter my eyelashes at him.

"Do you, hmm?" He drags his thumb under his lower lip, and my god, my entire body grows hot. All the cells in my body turn into little flames of need. My clit throbs. My nipples tighten until they hurt. I've turned into a miasma of lust. And want. I want to jump up and climb him but decide to play it cool.

So, I tip up my chin. "What're you gonna do about it, *darlin'*?"

He shakes his head. "Oh no; you don't get to direct what's going to happen next, baby."

I pout and open my mouth to protest, when he reaches over, grabs my shoulders, and lifts me bodily from my chair, placing me on my feet. He does this without blinking or his breath growing choppy. The only sign that he's lifting a full-grown, one-hundred-thirty-two-pound woman is that his biceps bulge and the cords on his neck stand out in that way I love.

Then he straightens, takes a step forward until his shoes brush my sneakers. "You're so fucking beautiful. Every time I see you, you take my breath away."

That melting sensation spreads from my core to my chest. This man is going to turn me into a sobbing mess. I reach up on my tiptoes and throw my arms about his neck. "I love you so much."

He grips the backs of my thighs and boosts me up. I lock my ankles around his waist. He pushes the papers off my desk and lowers me until my back touches my desk.

He plants his palms on either side of my neck and stares into my eyes. I'm aware of that fat column at his crotch digging into my core. He begins to fuck me slowly through our clothes. A long, flowing, almost poetic swipe up that has him hitting my throbbing clit. Sparks sizzle out from the contact. A soft sound of longing breaks free from my lips.

His green eyes spark with those sliver-gold sparks that are a tell of how aroused he is. He locks his fingers around one of my wrists, then the other, and lifts them over my head before shacking them with one of his hands. With the other he pinches one of my nipples.

The unexpectedness of it lights a fire under my skin. The yearning in my body shoots adrenaline through my veins. I try to reach up and kiss him, but he pulls back just enough that he's out of reach. He places tiny kisses on my forehead, over my eyelids, on my nose, my cheeks, my chin. Everywhere except my mouth. *The tease!*

"Ryot," I whine.

"I'm here, baby." He continues to press his lips down my throat, and over my sweatshirt to my cleavage. Goosebumps pepper my skin. I tremble.

"Ryot," I moan.

"I'm here, baby." He closes his mouth around one swollen nipple, and I cry out. He continues to knead the other one with his fingers and doesn't stop rubbing that long pillar in his crotch against my core. My pussy lips tremble with desire. My core clenches. Moisture pools between my legs, and when he hits my throbbing clit, vibrations of need sweep through my body. I begin to pant and tremble. My breathing is embarrassingly loud. My heartbeat ramps up until I'm sure it's going to jump out of my ribcage. And still, he doesn't stop.

He continues to tweak and play with my nipple, as he dry-fucks me through our clothes. My desire swells my belly, spreads to my chest, and to my extremities. I'm one big mass of melting yearning. My entire body begins to vibrate. That's when he releases his hold on one nipple, reaches between us to squeeze my clit, and growls, "Come."

I shatter.

The combination of his harsh, demanding voice and the way he's playing my body is too much. I scream as I tumble over the edge. Sparks shoot behind my eyes—green and silver and gold. They soar through the air and me with them. As I slowly float to earth, my entire body relaxes. Any tension I had from my long day dissipates. My eyelids feel heavy, as do my arms and legs. But the rest of me thrums with the remnants of that over-the-top orgasm. I flutter open my eyelids to find him watching him.

He releases his hold on my wrists and straightens.

There's enough space between us that he's able to yank down my yoga pants and my panties. He lowers the zipper on his trousers and the sound of the metallic teeth scrapes over my nerve-endings. My pulse rate leaps, and my stomach clenches. And when he fits the blunt head of his cock against the seam of my pussy, a wave of anticipation overcomes me.

He holds my gaze and looks deeply into my eyes, his lips but a hair's breadth from mine. Then in one thrust, he buries himself to the hilt.

Ryot

Her softness. Her warmth. The way her blue eyes turn into clear pools of desire in which I can see myself, and our future together. The way her lips part. Her sweet breath mists over my lips, and her pussy clamps around my cock in the most intimate of embraces. My balls tighten, and my thigh muscles turn to stone. Sweat beads my forehead as I stay there, allowing her to adjust to my size. "You feel so fucking good," I growl.

In reply, she digs her heels into my lower back and twines her arms around my neck so tightly, I know she'll never let me go. And I won't her, either. She is my wife. My soulmate. My love. My everything.

"I love you," I say through gritted teeth.

"I. Love. You," she says in a voice hoarse from screaming — because I made her. With my love. My touch. My cock. I worship this woman.

I'd do anything for her. I'd set the world on fire to protect her. "I'm so lucky to have found you." I lower my chin and brush my mouth over hers. I swipe against the seam of her lips, and when she parts them, I sweep my tongue over hers. Her taste — honey, powdered sugar and candy — it goes straight to my head in a rush.

"I can't get enough of you," I whisper. "I want to fuck you and stay buried inside you until we become one."

Her eyes spark. "Then do it. Take me. Own me. Do to me as you want. I'm yours. Only yours, Ryot."

Before the words are out of her mouth, I pull back, then plunge into her with enough force that the table shudders. Something crashes to the ground, and a giggle bubbles up her throat.

"These little noises you make... They make me feel like the king of the word."

"You are my king. My lord. My master. My *everything*." She smiles.

The fire of desire in my loins turns into an inferno roaring through my blood. I tilt my hips and change the angle so this time, when I fuck into her, I hit that spot deep inside that makes her eyes roll back in her head.

She cries out. Her spine arches. And when I do it again, she wails. "Ryot, please."

"That's it, baby. Give into the pleasure. Give into me."

I thrust into her with enough force that my balls slap against her inner thighs. This time, her entire body jolts. Her chin trembles. Her eyes are blind with lust. And I know she's so very close. That's when I slip my fingers between us to toy with that knot of flesh between her butt cheeks.

"Ryot." Her gaze widens.

Yep, it's not like this is the first time I'm going there, but my princess—while loving anal—likes to pretend she's scandalized when I venture there.

"You know you love it." I smirk.

She pouts. "You don't have to rub it in," she mutters.

"How about I—" I tease the opening of her back entrance—" I rub it there?"

She gasps, then flushes. The red stains her cheeks and spreads to her throat. Her pupils dilate. And when I slip my finger inside her back channel, her pussy clenches down further on my cock. My balls harden.

"Goddam." I clench my teeth. "You're making me forget everything else in this world but where we're connected."

I glance down at where we're joined, and the sight of my thick cock seated inside her cunt is enough to push me over the edge. But not before I make her come one last time.

I pull out and drive back into her again and again, holding her hips so she's pinned down. She moans and whimpers and writhes under me. But I don't let go. I watch her carefully as she shudders, and when I impale her again, she cries out. Her shoulders jerk. She squeezes her eyes shut as she orgasms, her lips parted, chin tipped up as the climax crashes over her. I wait, rooted in her, one with her, with my cock pulsing against her inner walls. Her body convulses with aftershocks. Seconds pass, and she relaxes further, then opens her eyes. I look deeply into them and affirm what I know. She's my home. Mine. My wife.

I tenderly push into her welcoming wet pussy, never taking my gaze off her. And when I'm unable to hold back any longer, I groan as I empty myself into her.

I rest my cheek against hers, taking most of my weight on my arms, my body covering hers. Not wanting to move from my position as peace steals over me.

She drags her fingers up and down my spine and into my hair. "I love you," she whispers into my ear, then bites gently on my earlobe.

A shudder squeezes my balls, and my cock jumps.

She stills. "Again?" she whispers.

"I might need a little more time to recover," I admit.

"What, really? Mr. Macho Alphahole can't go another round so quickly?"

I chuckle. "Now that you mention it, I'm sure I can dig into my reserves of strength and—"

Her phone vibrates from somewhere on her desk, and she groans. "That must be the girls calling. I'm already running late."

Aurelia

"Have all of you met Priscilla?" I glance around our little group. Skylar, Summer, Harper, and Zoey take in the fifth girl who's joined us.

"Priscilla Whittington." She holds out her hand.

The girls introduce themselves.

Zoey looks at her with a quizzical expression. "Whittington. Are you one of *the* Whittingtons?"

She winces but jerks her chin down.

"And haven't the Whittingtons and the Davenports been embroiled in some kind of family feud?"

I glance at her. "Look at you, all up to date with the gossip columns."

Zoey scoffs. "It's not gossip when the business media is always happy to speculate about the state of affairs between these two families."

"Your sources are correct," Priscilla says in a light voice. "Generations ago, a Whittington and a Davenport fought over a woman who belonged to another business family, the Madisons.

The Davenports settled it by selling five percent of a group company to the Whittingtons.

The Madison's tried to buy a portion of the same company in retaliation, until my brother Toren stepped in and helped the Davenports stave off that threat. Since then, there's been a tacit truce between the two families." Her gaze clouds.

She seems to be recalling something that makes her uncomfortable.

"You okay?" I touch her arm.

She shakes her head, and the look dissipates. "Of course." She nods. "Thank you for asking me to go bowling with you."

"You bet." I smile.

Ryot had mentioned to me that there was some history between Priscilla and Tyler, but that was before Tyler's daughter was born. No one knows who Tyler's daughter's mother was. Arthur and Toren decided that Priscilla would marry Knox in an attempt to build ties between the two families. But then, Knox fell for June, so that didn't work out. Priscilla and Knox remain on friendly terms though.

Since then, the Davenports have, adopted Priscilla as one of their own. That is, except Tyler who has made sure he's not around whenever Priscilla is invited to Arthur's place to join the weekly family lunches.

I met Priscilla first at boarding school. She was a few years ahead of me, so I never got to know her well. Then I met her again at one of the Davenport family lunches, and we renewed our acquaintance. There's something about the soft-spoken woman with the lingering anguish in her eyes that reached out to me. She sat quietly at a corner of the table, her gaze flickering around the assembled faces as if she were searching for someone. *Tyler, maybe?*

The family tried to involve her in conversation, including Knox's wife June, who seems to harbor no ill feelings toward her, either. In fact, the two sat next to each other. I was on Priscilla's other side. During a lull in conversation, I asked her to join me and my friends on our bowling sojourn, and she agreed. June was going to be busy, so she couldn't make it.

I'm glad to introduce her to my tribe. The woman looks like she could do with some friends in her corner.

Skylar flashes a warm smile at Priscilla. "I'm so happy you could be here. This way, we even out our numbers. I'd love for us to team up."

Priscilla's lips curves. Her shoulders seem to lose some of their tension. "I'd love to be on your team."

※ ※

"200 points!" Skylar jumps up and down, then throws her arms around Priscilla. "Two-fucking-hundred points; we win!"

Priscilla's features are wreathed in a smile. It's bigger than the previous smile, but it still doesn't reach her eyes. There's something bothering this woman. Something that's eating away at her and not allowing her to enjoy life. She seems haunted... By something that happened in the past? Is it what happened with Tyler?

I should probably butt out of her business. But the fragility that clings to her makes me want to protect her. It makes me want to do something to do something for her.

Maybe it's because I've found my own HEA, and I want to help her get her own? Either way, I don't question my instinct to want to get to know her better. To do what I can to ease her misery. *Isn't that what friends are for?*

I grab the pints of beer from the bar and walk over to where Skylar is dancing around a pissed-off looking Zoey.

"We won. We won." Skylar smirks.

Zoey rolls her eyes. "Okay, all right. Not need too sound so happy."

"Ooh, someone's a sore loser." Skye chuckles.

"I'm not, doofus." Zoey smacks Skye lightly on her shoulder.

"You are too." Skye sticks her tongue out at Zoey. Summer giggles helplessly, while Priscilla watches them with an amused look on her features.

"Here you go," I hand one of the pints of Guinness to Priscilla. "Nice to find another woman who enjoys Guinness. Cheers." I touch my glass to hers and take a sip. "Mmm." I lick the foam that sticks to my lips. "This is so good."

She takes a sip. "That hits the spot."

"Guinness always tests better in London than in Verenza. I have no idea why." I laugh.

She takes a few steps to the side and sits down on the seats at the lane start and a little away from the girls. "Tastes even better at the Guinness factory in Dublin."

"You've been there?" I ask, curious to find out more about her.

"Yes. Once. With my family. When my brothers and I were younger."

"How many brothers do you have?"

She takes another sip. "Five."

I widen my eyes. "You have five brothers?"

"I'm the youngest." She laughs.

"Wow, they must have been protective of you."

She pops a shoulder. "They were. But mainly, it came down to me having to fight to get my voice heard around the kitchen table."

I give her a considering look. "Funny, I pegged you as shy."

"Guess I've been withdrawn lately." She smiles, a thread of sadness running through it. "It's—" She hesitates.

When I stay silent, giving her space to speak, she blows out a breath. "You may have heard that Tyler and I have a history?"

I sit down next to her so we're both facing the girls. I'm so pleased she's confiding in me. But I don't want to say anything that'll cause her to go off track. So, I give her my full attention but refrain from commenting.

"It's not something I want to dwell on but... You've been so nice to me. And I can see the questions in your eyes every time we speak."

I bite down on my lower lip. "Am I that transparent?"

"Oh, I don't mean to upset you or make you feel uncomfortable. I think you're lovely, a great addition to the Davenport family. And it's natural that you'd want to know what happened between me and Tyler, but—"

"But you still have feelings for him?"

The widening of her eyes tells me I'm right. I hadn't meant to ask her that outright. But given she's broached the issue, and it's clear she's not going to tell me more about what had happened between them—not that it mattered, really it was their business— I do want to help her. Somehow.

I don't question that instinct either. I'm a princess. I've met enough people in my lifetime to be able to judge them quickly, and I'm confident that Priscilla is an amazing person. Whatever happened between her and Tyler is, likely, a misunderstanding. I'd like to do my bit to get them together—but how?

She glances away, then back at me. "Am *I* that transparent?"

A shout from the girls has us turning in their direction. Zoey is glaring at Harper, who's doubled over with laughter. Summer is looking between them with a big grin on her face.

"These girls. I swear, they fight like they're children when we get together," I say in an amused voice.

"It's nice," Priscilla replies in a soft voice. "I had a few friends from boarding school and, later, university. But, I've lost touch with them." She gives a self-deprecating laugh. "I haven't been in the frame of mind to go out much," she confesses.

I want to ask why that is, but it could have come across as impolite. So instead, I ask, "And do you work in the Davenport family business?"

She takes another sip of her Guinness before setting it down on the small table in front of us. "I opted to leave home at eighteen and take out a loan to put myself through university. Only, I dropped out."

"You did?" I knit my eyebrows.

When she laughs, it's a sound of resignation. "I was too busy playing the rebel. I kept skipping classes, hanging out with friends, drinking and smoking, and doing all the things you'd expect someone who's misguided in life to do. I guess, I was too taken in with the idea of being anti-establishment. I thought of myself as being somewhat of a free spirit. Someone who looked down on the moneyed past I came from."

She shakes her head, a self-reproachful expression on her features.

"You'd think, considering I was putting myself through university, I'd have been more respectful of the rules. But no. I broke enough of them to be expelled. Only good thing is it brought me to my senses."

"Oh?" I'm spellbound by her story. And the regret on her face for her actions? It tugs at my heart. I want to reach over, take her hand and comfort her, but I have a feeling it's not time to do so.

"What did you do next?" I prompt her.

"I grew up. I enrolled in an online course for a degree in education and graduated while working in a non-profit organization that focused on supporting children with special needs. I credit them with finding myself. After graduating, I couldn't find a job as a teacher. So instead, I work as a nanny.

Only, I'm between jobs at the moment." She takes another sip of her beer, drains it, then makes a face. "Didn't mean to bother you with my story of woe. In fact, I can't remember ever telling this to anyone else. You're the first." Her expression turns to one of amazement. "You're easy to talk to, you know that?"

"I hope it helped." I raise my glass and take another sip.

"I do feel lighter. So, thank you. But hope I didn't bore you?"

"You didn't." I tap my fingers against my glass and survey her. "In fact, I think I might be able to help you. You're a nanny, you said?"

She nods.

"And you're looking for a job?"

"Right again." She tilts her head. "Why? Do you have any leads for me?"

"I might..." The thought forms in my head, and I consider it.

If I told her, it was Tyler looking for a nanny, would she be open to accepting it? Or would she be pissed off at me for suggesting it?

But if I don't try, I'll never know.

And perhaps, there's a reason I invited her to go bowling with us today. Perhaps, this was meant to be, and I'm playing my little part in getting these two together, eh? I have to, at least, try, right?

"So—" I choose my words slowly. "There *is* a job available, but it depends on how much you need it."

To find out what happens next read Tyler & Priscilla's story in *The Rejected Wife*
Read an excerpt from *The Rejected Wife*

Priscilla

He curls his tongue inside me, and little balls of fire erupt under my skin. My blood feels like it's boiling. Sweat beads my temples. I grab at the bedclothes on either side of my body, push my head into the mattress, and try to stop myself from coming again so embarrassingly soon. But when he grazes his whiskered chin up my pussy, I wail. The sound is so vulnerable, so heavy with lust, it turns me on even more. I'm aware of my inner walls pulsing. Of moisture sliding out from between my legs.

He licks up my cum, then proceeds to suck on my pussy, using just enough of his teeth to cause a combination of pain and pleasure to squeeze my lower body. "Tyler, please. Ty," I whine.

In response, he drags his tongue down my slit to the crease between my thighs, almost to my forbidden back hole, then back up again to my cunt. Then, he pries my pussy lips apart and focuses solely on my slit. He sips and slurps and draws on the swollen bud until I'm out of my head with wanting. My toes curl, my hips quake. Full body shudders oscillate up and down my length. "Tyler, please, please, please."

"What do you want, baby?" he whispers into my cunt.

"You." Half out of my head with need, unable to bear the emptiness clawing deep inside of me, I yank on his hair, desperate to have him, kiss him. To have him replace his tongue with the part of him that I haven't yet seen. "I need you, please."

The longing in my voice must finally get through to him, for he pushes off of me. In a fluid move which has his biceps bulging and the planes of his back stretching his shirt, he rolls off the bed and straightens. With more than a little swagger, he unfastens the sleeves of his shirt, and a couple of his buttons, then reaches behind his back and, in a very quintessentially male gesture, he pulls off his shirt and throws it aside. I greedily drink in the expanse of his chest planes, the dog tags which nestle between his pecs, the eight pack which corrugates his chest and turn it into a work of art, and then that Adonis' belt. *Oh my god.*

My mouth waters. A jangle of metal as he undoes his belt, lowers his zipper, and then shucks off his pants and his briefs in one sweep. When he straightens, I take in the powerful thighs corded with muscle and the heavy organ jutting up from the nest of hair at his crotch. *Jesus.* He's bigger than I imagined. I felt the length of him pressed up against my core, but seeing his cock in its full naked glory ignites those balls of fire in my blood stream and turns them into flaming cannon balls.

"Holy shit." I take in his thickness, the proud jut of his penis, the throbbing vein which runs up the length, the swollen bulbous head, and shake my head. "You're too big."

He smirks. "I'm aware."

I scowl. "You're huge."

"Thank you." He dips his head.

My annoyance increases. Whatever I say, it seems to only add to his already inflated ego which, given what I'm seeing there, he has reason for, but still. My scowl deepens. "That's a monster dick you have there."

"You're welcome." His grin widens.

"Oh no, no, no." I close my thighs. "You're not putting that thing inside of me."

"Now, honey—"

I throw up my hand. "Don't try to sweet talk me. You're going to impale me with that, and I'm likely to feel you all the way in my throat, and it's going to bloody hurt."

"What's pleasure without pain, huh?" He arches an eyebrow.

He begins to move toward me. With every step, the muscles of his thighs ripple, and I swear, his giant penis seems to grow even bigger in size. I jump up on the bed and take a step back.

"I... I'm not sure I want to do this."

"You do," he says with confidence. "Trust me, baby, you're going to love it. You just have to let me...squeeze this"—he grips himself and swipes from root to head—"inside of you."

I stare at that anaconda-like organ and end up slapping both of my hands over my center. "No, thank you."

He chuckles. "You know you want it, baby. Aren't you the one who insisted that we spend the night not-only-talking?"

I swallow. He's right, of course. "That was before I realized you were hiding that—that purple helmet warrior in your pants."

He pauses. A strangling sound reaches me. It invokes enough curiosity for me to tear my gaze off his cock and look up into his face. His feature are twisted, and he seems to be choking.

"Are you okay?"

He holds up a hand. His shoulders shake. Why, that bastard, he's laughing.

And it's so infectious I can't stop a small smile from tugging on my lips. "I suppose that did sound funny," I admit.

He wipes the tears from his cheeks and seems to compose himself. "If only you'd seen your face." He chuckles.

His features are softer, his eyes shining with mirth. Laughing Tyler, with his gorgeous face alight with amusement and his big body almost relaxed, *and* with that thick, baseball bat-shaped thang jutting up from his center is... a fucking vagina destroyer. My pussy clenches, already resigned to feeling sore for weeks after this... interlude.

He stops laughing and holds out his hand. "Come here, baby. I promise, I'll make sure you're wet enough and relaxed enough so you'll be able to accommodate me."

I frown. "You sound like... you've had a lot of experience with this."

He hesitates, then slowly nods. "I have."

My heart sinks. An ugly feeling squeezes my chest. "How many women have you slept with?"

He frowns. "What does that have to do with anything?"

It shouldn't. Really. Not when I only just met him. But I'm so attracted to him. The more I get to know him, the more I like him. And my instinct says I have a future with him, so... Yes. I want to know. And yes, I'm very, very jealous. That feeling in my chest tightens.

"You wanted to talk, didn't you?" I tip up my head. "Well, this is your chance, talk."

He drags his fingers through his hair, then sighs. "I'm not a monk, and as you can tell"—he points at his still erect penis—"I have an appetite."

"No kidding," I say dryly.

"I'm not going to apologize for my past. I have been with women," he says softly.

Of course, he has. I know it. I knew it before he said it. I knew it as soon as I saw him. You don't get to look like ad for GQ, and Country Living, and Sports Illustrated without having women fawning over you. But I'm a possessive bitch. I've always hated the idea of sharing the man I'm going to end up with, with anyone else. I also know that's an irrational hope. Doesn't stop that jealousy in my chest from growing harder. I glance around, then snatch up my blouse and pull it on.

"What are you doing?" He frowns.

"Getting dressed." I pull on my skirt. My panties are on the ground, so I leave them for now. I slide off the bed to stand with the length of the mattress between us.

"How many women, Tyler?"

A frustrated look comes into his eyes. "That was in my past, Cilla, you… You are my present. And my future."

"Future?" I blink.

"You don't think, given this"—he gestures to the space between us—"this incredible connection between us, I'm going to let you go, do you?"

Pleasure pinches my nerve-endings, but it's immediately tempered by this wariness knocking at the edges of my subconscious mind. "How many, Ty?" I ask again.

He stares at me steadily, then walks over to his clothes and pulls on his boxers, hiding that glorious, XXL-sized, baseball bat-shaped column he calls his penis…

And a part of me mourns it. My pussy is both regretful and slightly relieved. Okay, only one percent relieved, because secretly, I trusted what he said. He'd have made sure I came a few more times and that I was soaking wet. And while I'd have had to stretch to take him inside me, considering women have pushed out babies, I'd have probably accommodated him, ultimately. No doubt I'd have had the biggest orgasm of them all when we fucked.

So... Yeah, I'm more than a little disappointed. But I also know this conversation is very important. Especially if, as we both sense, there's a future here for us. Not something I've felt with anyone else before.

He pulls on his pants, and damn, I wish I'd had the chance to feel him skin-to-skin, naked first—only, that would've meant there'd have been no way I could've stopped us from fucking. He shrugs on his shirt, but thankfully, he doesn't button it, so flashes of that very impressive, drool-worthy, pecs of his remain visible.

He walks around and holds out his hand. I glance at it, then up at his face. There's resignation and understanding, and lust and...more than a tinge of tenderness. *Tenderness*. It's what I associate most with this man, along with that dominant, bossy, take-charge attitude I've found so hot from the very first time he opened his mouth and ordered me around. There's no question of refusing him. I slide my hand into his.

He relaxes. I realize then, he was worried I'd refuse him. As if I could? I still want him. But he was right; this thing between us is serious enough that I also want to get to know him better.

"Come on, let's get something to drink."

Priscilla

"You've got to stop feeding me like this." I chew another forkful of the pasta, savoring the creamy, complex textures of the dish. Turns out, he was hungry. So, he wanted, not only to have a drink, but also to eat dinner.

I didn't demur when he began to whip up what turned out be an Aglio Olio e Pepperoncino—Pasta with olive oil, parmesan cheese, cream and pepper, in very little time.

After pulling on my blouse and skirt, I was content to sit at the counter and watch his graceful movements around the kitchen. I was right. The man can cook. And given how clean the space is, he must have a very efficient housekeeper, too. For someone who's so keen to jump into bed with him, I have so many questions.

He pours us both a glass of white wine; it's clean and dry on the palate. I may have left home at eighteen, but my tastes were already refined by then. Enough to appreciate the kind of quality ingredients which only money can buy.

"I love taking care of you." He takes a sip of his wine and places the glass down.

He's already inhaled his pasta in a few efficient mouthfuls. Maybe a hang-over from his military days, when he had to eat on the go and, likely, in shared dining rooms? And now, I have myriad questions about this very handsome, very rich, rescuer of my bag who's made me come more times in one day then I ever have, even with my vibrator. Speaking of… No doubt, he's come many, many more times, and with different women.

I finish the last bite on my plate and place my fork down. When I look at him, he nods. There's touch of —*worry in his eyes?*—which he banks. His expression turns almost bored, but he doesn't fool me. He is concerned about my reaction.

"That many?" I ask softly.

He groans, "Fuck, woman, why are you putting yourself through this? They didn't mean anything to me."

I nod miserably. "I know it's different for a man. And of course, it's stupid for me to expect whoever I choose to be with hasn't been with anyone else. Especially not someone as attractive as you. And who's been in the Marines. You probably had a different woman every night."

When he stays quiet, I stare. "You *did* have a different woman every night?"

His expression turns uncomfortable, then he composes his features into a mask, so I can't decipher what he's feeling. "They didn't mean anything. I promise, there was no emotional connection with any of them. You, on the other hand—" His Adam's apple bobs. "You've begun to mean so much to me in the little time I've already known you, baby."

The muscles in his jaw flex.

"There was a time, when I first joined the Marines and was back from my first mission... When I saw upfront friends being killed and innocents among the enemy being slaughtered... When the clarity of what I'd signed up for... When the futility of what I was embarking on became clear to me... I... I might have lost it a little."

There's anguish in his voice and a pain that shines through and thaws the ice which had begun to settle around my heart. Whatever he's feeling, whatever he went through, tested him. It changed him. It made him grow up and become the man he is today... The result of which I'm attracted to, hugely.

I sigh. "How... How old were you?"

"Eighteen when I joined; twenty when I went to the Middle East on my first call of duty."

The mask is in place, but something in his eyes is in shadows. Echoes of the past which were difficult. Which he had to survive to get here.

"I'm sorry." I'm not sure what prompts me to say that, but it's the right thing, for a little tension bleeds from his shoulders.

He nods. "You don't need to be. It was my choice. And I don't regret it. I'm proud of my service. Proud I could come to the defense of my country and my fellow citizens. But there was a price to pay for it."

"The sleeping around?"

He nods. "It provided a temporary relief... Very fleeting, but it's the only thing that kept me going. Some kind of reaffirming of life, in a twisted way. When I was between missions, I slept with a different woman almost every night."

I wince. Well, I did ask him to tell me. And he was clear he'd never lie to me. So, here's the truth. Except, it doesn't relieve that burning sensation in my chest any.

"Especially in the early days, when I also used alcohol as a crutch. I'd often be blind-drunk enough to wake up in a different bed every night, with a different woman, who I didn't recognize. A name-less, faceless person I'd used to try and get the frustration out of my system. Not that it helped much." He shrugs. "By the time I realized that, a few years had passed. It was Brody, my younger brother, who gave me a talking to and told me to pull myself together." He half smiles. "We got into a fight, which I was too drunk to win. But his thrashing me was the best thing he could have done. I—"

The doorbell rings.

We look at each other.

"Were you expecting company?"

He shakes his head. "No one was announced, so it must be someone security recognizes." He looks around and swears. "I left my phone by the bed, so I don't know if any of them called me, either."

The doorbell rings again, then again. The sound is harsh, jarring, almost insistent. A shiver runs up my spine. A frisson of discomfort stabs into my breastbone. Not sure why I feel like it's an alarm bell, a warning.

I shake my head and attempt a smile. "Guess whoever that is, is impatient."

"Sorry about that." He rises to his feet and walks out of the kitchen. Unable to sit still, I jump up and follow him through the living room to the front door. He throws it open and looks around. "There's nobody here," he says in a puzzled tone. Then he looks down, and his entire body freezes.

Something about how motionless he is—the bunched muscles of his torso, the way his shoulder blades stand out with surgical precision against his shirt—fires another ripple of alarm through my blood stream. I hurry and close the distance to him. "Who is it?"

I draw abreast, stand next to him, and look down at a basket with an oversized bag left next to it. *Huh?* Does the basket have clothes in it? No, not clothes. Wait, that's a diaper bag! Now, I can make out the curve of a tiny head with downy hair peeking out. My heart leaps into my throat. My mind recognizes what I'm seeing, but the connection between my brain and my mouth seems to have been lost.

It's Tyler who recovers first. "It's a baby." His voice is surprised. He looks around the short hallway, a stunned expression on his features. The noise of the elevator's engine running reaches us.

He springs into action, walks around the baby carrier and toward the elevator. The numbers count down as the elevator descends. He spins around, rushes into the apartment, then reaches for what I assume is the intercom hooked into the wall next to the door.

"Someone came to visit me just now. You need to stop them from leaving."

He listens to whatever the voice on the other end says, then barks, "Yes, they are on their way down in the elevator. Intercept them and keep them there. I need to talk to them."

I glance down to find there's an envelope tucked between the clothes. A stone forms in the pit of my stomach. I can't let myself give shape to the possibilities which are crowding my mind. *Take a breath. Don't let your imagination run away.* I calm myself enough to bend and pick up the envelope.

I'm half-aware of Tyler saying something else to whoever is on the intercom. Then he hangs up and walks back to me. I silently hand over the envelope with his name written on it.

He glares at it, then takes it and rips open the flap. He pulls out a single piece of paper. Whatever he reads in it makes the blood drain from his face. As if in a dream, I reach over and take it from him and read it.

Tyler,

She's yours. Her name is Serene.
She's better off with you. Take care of her.

It's unsigned. My heart stumbles in my chest. It's not what it seems. It can't be. There must be a simple explanation for it... Except... There's a baby in a carrier on his doorstep, and that note tells me everything I need to know. I look up to find him staring at me.

"Did you know about her?"

To find out what happens next read Tyler & Priscilla's story in The Rejected Wife here

Scan this QR code to get the book

How to scan a QR code?

1. Open the camera app on your phone or tablet.

2. Point the camera at the QR code.

3. Tap the banner that appears on your phone or tablet.

4. Follow the instructions on the screen to finish signing in.

Read an excerpt from The Unwanted wife - Skylar & Nathan's story

Skylar

"I can't do this." I lock my fingers together and narrow my gaze at my reflection. I'm in the tiny bathroom adjoining my office at the back of my bakery—my baby, my enterprise into which I've poured my life savings. And now, it's going to shut down. Unless I find the money for the rent next month... And for the utilities to keep the lights on so the sign on the shopfront continues to be lit up in pink and yellow neon... And for the supplies I need to continue baking. *The Fearless Kitten* is more than my dream; it's my whole life. What I've worked toward since I was sixteen and knew I was going to become the most phenomenal baker in the world. And now, I'm going to lose it.

"Sure, you can do it." My brother encourages me from the doorway. "You can do anything you set your mind to."

"That's what I used to think. It's why I started this pastry shop." I was twelve when I discovered I was good at baking. That, combined with my love for desserts, meant I knew what I wanted to do with my life.

Two years ago, I moved to London to work at a well-known patisserie. I began scouting for a location for my place while I saved every single penny I could.

A year ago, I found the perfect place, and my little artisan bakery with coffee shop seating was born. Of course, I work eighteen-hour workdays, which means I have almost no social life. I barely manage a few hours of sleep in my little apartment over the shop. But nothing can dampen my spirits. I'm spending my days churning out cakes and pastries. It's what I've dreamed of for so long. Only issue?

I don't have the money to advertise, and despite having a social media post go viral—which is when a lot of people look at your social media feed—and result in a surge of customers, I'm not making enough to salvage my business.

"Don't give up. You have to believe this can take off." Ben's voice is confident. If only I shared his optimism.

"Oh, trust me, I want to believe. But blind faith in yourself only takes you so far." I wish I could do better at spreading the word about the place and bringing in new customers. I seem to suck at everything outside of baking. It's why my business is on the decline.

"Success is what's beyond the dark night of the soul," my brother, ever the wise one, remarks.

"Is that a saying among you Royal Marines?" I scoff.

"It's—"

The bell over the door at the front of the shop tinkles.

"—your destiny." His lips curve in a smile.

"What?" I blink.

"The bell—it's your future calling."

I roll my eyes. "If you say so."

"Go on, your customer is waiting." My brother walks over and kisses my forehead. "Good luck. Remember, when one door closes, another one opens. Or the one I prefer, she who leaves a trail of glitter is never forgotten."

"Eh?" I stare. "What does that have to do with my situation?"

"Nothing, but it did cheer you up."

I roll my eyes, then can't stop myself from chuckling.

"That's my girl." He pats my shoulder.

Yep, that's my brother. The ever-cheerful, never-surrender person. "You'll see; it will work out." He turns me around and points me in the direction of the doorway leading to the shop. "Go on now."

"Whatever you say, big bro."

I was ten when my father passed, and Ben became the de facto father figure in my life. I'm fifteen years younger than him, an "oops baby," born when my mother was in her early forties. I hero-worshipped Ben, who, in turn, took care of me and never let me feel the loss of my father. And when my mother passed away, he took a leave of absence and came home and stayed with me, until he was assured I was ready to pick myself up and move on. He's the most important person in the world, in my life, in so many ways. And the fact that he fights wars so I can be safe is a source of the utmost pride for me. It's one of the reasons I feel terrible about being on the verge of bankruptcy. I want Ben to be proud of me.

"This is my last chance to get things right. If I can't find a way to pay off my debts, I'll have no choice but to shut down." I hear my words and realize I'm being negative. The exact opposite of my brother. I expect him to tell me off, but there's no answer. I turn to find he's left the shop. Not that I blame him. He has a two-week break before he has to ship out again. I suspect he's gone to meet his current squeeze. Ben never lacks female companionship.

As for me? I need to face whatever's in my destiny. If only my every decision didn't impact Hugo. If only I weren't running out of money to keep him in the care home that provides round-the-clock attention for him. If I can't pay next month's fees—no, I'm not going there. I will not contemplate the repercussions of what would happen if I didn't come up with the money, and fast.

With a last tug at the neckline of my blouse, which dips a little too low in the front, and which I wore to try and cheer myself up — big fail, there — I march out of the kitchen and go behind the counter. And all the air whooshes out of my lungs.

The man standing in the middle of the bakery is so big, he seems to occupy all of the space in my little bakery. He's so tall, I have to tilt my head back to meet his gaze. And his shoulders — those shoulders I once held onto — are wider than I remember. They're broad enough to block out the view of the rest of the space.

His biceps stretch the sleeves of his suit, which must cost my entire annual rent to buy, given its tailor-made finish. He's wearing a black silk tie, and his jacket is black. Wait, a suit? I've never seen him in a suit before, but OMG, does he do it justice. I take in that lean waist, and those massive thighs, which seem ready to burst the seams of his pants, and between them, the tent that was the object of my obsession for so long. He prowls over to the counter and whoa, that predatory walk of his, the way he seems to glide across the floor with the gait of a barely tamed animal turns my bones to jelly.

"There was no one at the counter when I walked in. No wonder, you need a cash infusion," a familiar voice growls.

What the — ? How dare he say that! I wrench my gaze up to his face. And any remaining thoughts in my head drain away. I was prepared to give him a piece of my mind, but all of the pieces have scattered.

Those eyes — one piercing blue, the other an amber brown. Those heterochromatic eyes, which have always had the effect of reducing me to a mindless blob of need, stare into mine.

My entire body hurts. My shoulder muscles turn into cement blocks. My stomach twists. It feels like I've run into a wall. Frissons of shock reverberate down my spine, and when he rakes his gaze down to my chest, his entire body seems to tense. He brings his gaze back to my face, and it feels like I've been punched in the gut. Again.

"What are you doing here?" I manage to croak around the ball of emotion in my throat.

"What do you think I'm doing here?" His jaw tics, a muscle spasms in his jaw, and he curls his fingers into his sides. There's so much tension radiating from him, I feel faint. Apparently, he doesn't like what he sees.

That makes two of us. Nathan-bloody-Davenport. My brother's best friend. The man I've had a crush on for more than half my life. The man who turned me down when I threw myself at him the day of my eighteenth birthday party. Not before he kissed me, though.

He hauled me to him, thrust his tongue between my lips, and ravaged my mouth. He squeezed my ample butt and drew me against him, and I felt every inch of what he was packing. The kiss seemed to go on and on. My head spun. My knees gave way underneath me. I stumbled, and he straightened me. Only to tear his mouth from mine and stare into my face, his chest heaving, his breath coming in gusts that seemed to swell his shoulders. He raked his gaze across my features, like he was seeing me for the first time. Like he wanted to throw me down and mount me right there.

"Nate..." *I breathed his name.*

"Starling," *he whispered against my lips. The sound of his voice seemed to cut through his reverie, for the next second, he released me and jumped back.*

A look of confusion, then regret, then anger swept over his features. I felt his rejection even before he blanked all expression from his face. "I'm sorry, I shouldn't have done that, Skye." *He turned on his heel and walked out of my birthday celebration, and our house. And my life.*

That was it; he cut off all communication with me. I never saw him again. Over the last five years, I've heard about his progress in the Marines from my brother, but I never set eyes on him. Until today.

"You're the last person I want to speak to." I cross my arms over my chest, thereby pushing my breasts up higher. His eyes move down before he forces them back to my face. *It's not that I want to flaunt my double-D tits. Okay, okay, maybe I do. Maybe, I want to make him realize what he's been missing.* I'm proud of my assets. I might be a size sixteen, but I've never tried to conceal my full figure. So what if I want to run and hide right now?

"The feeling's mutual," he growls.

And the sound is so freakin' hot, so caveman like, my ovaries seem to quiver. Just because my body can't control itself doesn't mean I find him attractive. Nope, it doesn't mean anything that I haven't stopped thinking of him all these years.

I draw myself up to my full height. Not that it helps, considering I'm five-feet four-inches tall, and he's a good foot taller than me. Still, this is my space. "This is my shop, and you need to leave."

"Trust me, I wouldn't be here if I had any other option," he sneers.

"What's that supposed to mean?"

"You're looking for a bailout."

"Excuse me?" I gape at him.

"Your business is in trouble. You need money to pay off your debts."

My flush intensifies. Heat crawls up my cheeks, all the way to the roots of hair, followed closely by anger. *How dare he walk in and throw my failure in my face? How dare he not talk to me all these years, only to reappear at the worst possible moment? And right after my brother told me it was my destiny come-a-calling when the bell to the shop rang.*

"Wait, did Ben put you up this?"

"Eh?" He stares at my lips. His gaze is so intent that the frisson of awareness, which has crackled up my spine since he arrived, flares into a full-blown shiver. I shake my head, ignoring the buzz of electricity that has always hummed between us. "Are you here because Ben asked you to help me out?"

A weird look comes into his eyes. He shifts his weight from foot to foot. "I'm here because my grandfather is the chairman of the Davenport Group of companies, and he thinks your bakery would make for a good investment."

"He does?"

"I'm yet to be convinced." He crosses his arms across his chest.

So that's how it's gonna be, eh?

He glances toward the counter, taking in the various desserts on display, and his frown deepens. I follow his gaze and take in the tray of cupcakes displayed: Splcy Scene, Red Room, Velvet Ties, Purple Patches, Cave Wonder, The Vanilla Vajayjay, The Earth Moved… You have to admit, they're innovative names for the treats.

I named the first one in jest, but it proved to be a hot topic of discussion among fellow spicy book readers like me. Before I knew it, I'd ended up naming many of my desserts in a similar vein.

In fact, the dessert shaped like the backside of a woman and called Spanked is one that customers seem to love. Then there's my other hit, a chocolate cake shaped like a vibrator and called Clitasaurus. Yep, they love that one. Also, another raspberry-infused one in the shape of a peach called Moist Goodness, not to forget the honey-glazed fruit cake in the form of a beehive called the Honey Pot, and the strawberry and cream-topped, fig-shaped shortbread I named Sweet Bits. Finally, the doughnut-shaped dark chocolate glazed treat called —you guessed it —AlphahOle, which readers love when I cater at book events.

You'd think business is booming, and I certainly have my share of loyal customers, but it's not enough to keep me in the black. I need to bring in new customers, and a lot more of them.

He stabs his forefinger at the display. "Is this a joke?"

Skylar

A-n-d that was the absolutely wrong thing to say. No one insults my baby —my bakery, my dream —and gets away unscathed.

"I can assure you; they are popular amongst my customers."

He turns those searing eyes on me, and it feels like I'm looking into the depths of a frozen lake. The surface seems able to bear my weight, but one wrong step, and I'm going to fall right through and find myself trapped. I try to breathe, but all of the oxygen in the room has been sucked out by his presence. My pulse crashes in my ears, and my nerve endings are so tightly stretched, I fear they'll snap any second. And when he shoves a hand in his pocket, pulling the fabric of his pants taut over that bulge between his legs, a slow thud flares to life between mine.

I *cannot* find him attractive. Cannot risk acknowledging this chemistry that thickens the air between us. Not when I need his help to save my business. Not when I know who he is, and he's definitely out-of-bounds. Forbidden. Sirens go off in my mind. *Back away. It's not worth taking on the humungous backlog of complications that are going to come with having anything to do with him.*

Then a look of boredom crosses his face. He yawns, and my pulse rate shoots up.

Strike out everything I felt earlier. It's definitely worth taking on every challenge that comes with getting him to cough up money, because by God, he needs to realize the world doesn't revolve around him. How can anyone be this full of himself? This insensitive?

Anger squeezes my chest. Adrenaline laces my blood. *And how dare he turn the most important meeting of my life into... into... something that doesn't merit even a few seconds of his attention?*

"I've seen everything I need to see. Goodbye." He turns to leave.

What the—? He's leaving? Does that mean he's decided against investing in the bakery? Think! You need to say something to stop him. You cannot afford to piss off the one guy who might be able to help save your bakery.

"Wait, don't you want to taste my wares?" I burst out.

He freezes mid-step. His shoulders seem to swell. The planes of his back rise and fall, and the jacket pulls even tighter. *Is he going to burst out of his skin and go all Hulk on me?* I swallow. And when he turns slowly and makes a growling sound at the back of his throat, I have to stop the yelp that almost spills from my mouth. Every single cell in my body has woken up and is doing the hula. *Stop that. You can't feel this drawn to this... To this arrogant beast who rejected you.*

But I also need his help. I have to save my business from going bust. And if that means swallowing my pride, then so be it. I tip up my chin and straighten my back. "I... I mean, maybe you want to taste my Honey Pot?" *Ugh. Didn't mean it to come out like that.*

His left eyelid, the one covering his blue eye, twitches, and he seems one step closer to either having a breakdown or walking away. Neither of which is desirable.

"Oh, *Fraggle Rock*. What I meant to say is, you'll definitely like the Purple Patches." I point to the range of cupcakes showcased under the counter.

"Did you use *Fraggle Rock* as a swear word?" He stares.

"I did. It's because my mother hated me swearing—being a girl, and all that." I roll my eyes. That condition had *not* applied to my brother. "So instead, I began to use names of TV series as swear words. Also, you could try the C!itasaurus?" I look at him hopefully.

"The whatasaurus?" He tilts his head. His gaze is, once again, fixed on my mouth. My thighs clench, and moisture laces the flesh between my legs. I push away the burst of awareness which seems to have stuck its claws into my skin. No way am I going to succumb to his magnetism, which has multiplied in the years since I last saw him. Especially not when his jerkhole factor hasn't reduced, either.

It's always been a mystery to me why I found his arrogance such a turn on. Now, I'm also reminded of how he always managed to get on my nerves. Not that it stopped me from throwing myself at him. A mistake I'm not going to make again. When I named that cupcake, it seemed like a stroke of genius. Having to pronounce it aloud in front of the Hulk, however, negates any laughs I've had about it so far.

"Uh, you know what I mean?" The color of my cheeks deepens and spreads to my chest. My entire body seems like it's on fire.

"No, I don't," he says in a low, hard voice.

I shiver. "You know that…that…pink pastry between the blue cakes that looks like…" I glance around, then slide open the glass door to the under-counter area. I pull on a pair of disposable gloves, reach in and, instead of the C!itasaurus, slide one of the fig-shaped desserts onto a plate. I place it on the counter. "Actually, I think you should eat my Moist Goodness, and everything will be clear to you, and—"

I hear a gnashing sound, and when I dare to peek at Mr. Grouchy Face, I see the muscles of his jaw ripple. *Oh no, at this rate, he's going to crack a molar. Or two.*

I blink rapidly. "Maybe we should start afresh?"

"Start afresh?" he asks in a tone that implies he'd rather have never met me.

Yeah, me, too. Unfortunately, I don't have that luxury. "You know, pretend we don't know each other. Pretend the last few minutes never happened?" *Pretend that kiss is not seared into my brain, and into other parts of my body I'm not going to think about.*

I pull off my gloves and hold out my hand. "Skylar Potter." Then, because I hate my life and because, apparently, the connection between my brain and my mouth has been lost under the force of his glower, I smile. "No relation to Harry, as you're aware."

"Harry?" He looks at my slim, pink-tipped fingers, then back at my face, and makes no move to shake my hand.

I set my jaw. *Oh, my god, he's so rude, I should slap one of the pies baking in my oven into his face. Only, they're too good to waste. Also, I can't risk messing up a pie when I need every sale I can get.* Every part of me wants to turn and run out of here. But I can't. I owe it to myself, to my dream, to give this one last shot. *I will not give up easily. I will not. I will stay polite, even if it kills me.* I manage to bare my teeth in the resemblance of a smile. "You know, Harry Potter? Boy wizard? *Evanesco.*" I pretend to flick my wand in his direction.

His jaw hardens further.

Ooh, he looks pissed. The tips of his ears have turned white. Also, the end of his nose. Also, the vanishing spell on him didn't work. His Royal Dickness is still here, larger than life and glowering at me.

"I'm sooo immersed in the Potterverse. Oh, and Taylor Swift. I love Taylor Swift." I beam at him.

His frown deepens.

"I'm guessing you're not a Swiftie?" I nod.

"What's that?" he asks in a contemptuous tone.

"Those of us who love Taylor Swift call ourselves Swifties."

"Sounds contagious," he sneers.

I ignore his cantankerous attitude because I need to charm him. And because I desperately need him to fork over the money I need. "I love her songs, don't you?" I chirrup.

His fingers curl into fists at his sides. Which is not a good sign. Then, because I love to go from the sublime to the surreal, I smile even wider. "Guess which Hogwarts' house Taylor Swift belongs to?" I toss my hair over my shoulder.

"Hogwhat?" He seems like he's about to have a cardiac event. Or like he went to sleep and woke up in an alternate reality. This is bad. So bad.

And I have to go and put my foot in it by prompting him, "Hogwarts."

"Hogwhat?" he snaps again.

This time, the light goes on in my brain. "Oh, you haven't heard of Hogwarts?" I titter. "That's okay. I wasn't alive when *Titanic* hit the cinemas, either…" *Don't say it, don't say it.* "Unlike you."

He blinks slowly.

"I meant the movie, not the actual event when the Titanic hit an iceberg and sank."

His jaw tics.

"Not that you were alive when the Titanic sank." I cough. "Even *I* know you're not *that* ancient."

A nerve pops at his temple. That's not a good sign, is it? *Zip your lips. Just shut up already.*

"Not that I'm implying you're old or anything." I try to contain my laughter and end up snorting—ugh, bad habit. "The grey in your hair adds to your distinguished appearance. Besides, you're only fifteen years older than me." *Oh no, I don't think that makes it better.*

The veins on his throat stand out in relief. I try to swallow, but my throat is so dry, it feels like sharp knives line my gullet. I flick out a tongue to wet my lips, and his eyes gleam. He watches my mouth with a rapacious gaze. Every part of his body seems to have turned to stone. Watching me with such intensity, he seems to have turned into a predator who's planning every possible way to jump me. If he had a tail, I think it'd be swishing from side to side.

The silence deepens. It doesn't stop me from shaking a finger at him. "You, mister, need a crash course in pop culture. Although, I suppose, I shouldn't expect someone who has grey at his temples to have a sense of the zeitgeist."

"The fuck you prattling on about?" he bites out through gritted teeth.

"Whoa, hold on, no need to show me your horns." *Although, I'd love to see the one between your legs.* "In fact, you look so angry, I'm expecting you to breathe fire at any moment." *You can turn into a dragon and carry me away anytime.* "And seriously, you should taste this." I push the plate with the moist, pink-and-white, fig-shaped shortbread in his direction. It has a button between the lips made of edible silver leaf and there's glitter around it.

"My desserts are awesome; one bite, and you'll be a convert."
I nod.

He stares.

"Unless you're worried you'll get addicted to my Sweet Bits." I
tip up my chin.

Did I say *my* sweet bits? I did say *my* sweet bits. "I meant the
dessert that I've named Sweet Bits, not *my* sweet bits." I hear my
words, and argh, didn't mean for them to sound so... provocative.
But I'm not going to apologize for that. Hell no.

"Well? You going to taste it or what?" I scowl.

He must see the challenge in my eyes and, alpha male that he is,
of course, he doesn't back down. Without taking his gaze off of my
face, he licks the cream from the hollow in the center. A thousand
little fires flare to life under my skin. I swallow; my breath grows
shallow. He bites down on one of the plump lips, and a shiver grips
me. I clutch at the edge of the counter. The pulse at the base of my
throat speeds up. And when he pops the other lip into his mouth, I
gulp. He brings his thumb and forefinger to his mouth and sucks on
them, and a breathy moan leaves my lips.

"Not bad." He shrugs.

I stare. "What do you mean, *not bad?!* *That* is my best-seller."

"It was okay." He looks down his nose from his superior height.
"I admit, the names you give your baked goods are creative, but I'm
not sure that's enough for me to approve the takeover."

"Takeover?" I stiffen. "Who's talking about a takeover?"

"It's the only way I'd consider investing in your business."

"I only need help," I say through gritted teeth.

"That's putting it mildly. I reached out to the bank you took the
loan from—"

"You reached out to my bank?" I burst out.

"You don't think I'd be here without due diligence—"

I cut in, "The terms of my deal with them are confidential." I lock
my fingers together.

"Not when you're about to go bankrupt. When they realized the
Davenport Group was considering an acquisition—"

"An investment; a loan; that's *all* I'm looking for. Something to tide me over and buy me some time until I get back on my feet."

"Keep fooling yourself. You might be a good baker—"

"So you did like my dessert," I declare in a triumphant voice.

"—but you're not a businessperson, by any stretch of the imagination."

Oh, my god! What I wouldn't give to wipe that smug look off his face.

"There are ups and downs in any business." I lock my fingers together. "Things will bounce back."

"There are ups and downs, and then, there are downs and more downs," he drawls.

Anger thuds at my temples. *I will not lose my temper. I will not.*

He slides his hand into his pocket. "Not that I don't understand your reluctance to sell out."

"You do?"

"Of course. You've invested your sweat and blood, and likely, your entire savings into the venture. Too bad you didn't have a financial person advising you."

Of course, he'd say that. Nate's always been a numbers whiz. I heard that from Ben. It's why, even when they were in the Marines together, Nate oversaw strategy. He was the person coming up with the game plan for their team. It was Nate's sharp brain which helped them both stay ahead of the enemy; or so my brother informed me over the years. Too bad his best friend's temperament leaves much to be desired.

"I would be willing to consider a merger instead of an acquisition of your little business." His gaze flicks about the place and back at me.

"*Little* business?" I curl my fingers into fists. *Breathe, count back from ten. Do not give into the impulsive need to throw a pie in his face.*

He wipes his thumb under his lip, a considering look in his eyes. "Of course, I don't have to do anything. But given you're Ben's little sister, and he wouldn't want me to leave you in the lurch, I might have a proposition that could help both of us."

"Of course you do."

My sarcasm is lost on him, for he looks me up and down. "Marry me."

To find out what happens next read Skylar & Nathan's story in *The Unwanted Wife*

Read Liam and Isla's marriage of convenience romance where the bridegroom marries the wedding planner in, *The Proposal*

Read an excerpt:

Liam

"Where is she?"

The receptionist gazes at me cow-eyed. Her lips move, but no words emerge. She clears her throat, glances sideways at the door to the side and behind her, then back at me.

"So, I take it she's in there?" I brush past her, and she jumps to her feet. "Sir, y-y-you can't go in there."

"Watch me." I glare at her.

She stammers, then gulps. Sweat beads her forehead. She shuffles back, and I stalk past her.

Really, is there no one who can stand up to me? All of this scraping of chairs and fawning over me? It's enough to drive a man to boredom. I need a challenge. So, when my ex-wife-to-be texted me to say she was calling off our wedding, I was pissed. But when she let it slip that her wedding planner was right—that she needs to marry for love, and not for some family obligation, rage gripped me. I squeezed my phone so hard the screen cracked. I almost hurled the device across the room. When I got a hold of myself, for the first time in a long time, a shiver of something like excitement passed through me. *Finally, fuck.*

That familiar pulse of adrenaline pulses through my veins. It's a sensation I was familiar with in the early days of building my business.

After my father died and I took charge of the group of companies he'd run, I was filled with a sense of purpose; a one-directional focus to prove myself and nurture his legacy. To make my group of companies the leader, in its own right. To make so much money and amass so much power, I'd be a force to be reckoned with.

I tackled each business meeting with a zeal that none of my opponents were able to withstand. But with each passing year—as I crossed the benchmarks I'd set myself, as my bottom line grew healthier, my cash reserves engorged, and the people working for me began treating me with the kind of respect normally reserved for larger-than-life icons—some of that enthusiasm waned. Oh, I still wake up ready to give my best to my job every day, but the zest that once fired me up faded, leaving a sense of purposelessness behind.

The one thing that has kept me going is to lock down my legacy. To ensure the business I've built will finally be transferred to my name. For which my father informed me I would need to marry. Which is why, after much research, I tracked down Lila Kumar, wooed her, and proposed to her. And then, her meddling wedding planner came along and turned all of my plans upside down.

Now, that same sense of purpose grips me. That laser focus I've been lacking envelops me and fills my being. All of my senses sharpen as I shove the door of her office open and stalk in.

The scent envelops me first. The lush notes of violets and peaches. Evocative and fruity. Complex, yet with a core of mystery that begs to be unraveled. Huh? I'm not the kind to be affected by the scent of a woman, but this... Her scent... It's always chafed at my nerve endings. The hair on my forearms straightens.

My guts tie themselves up in knots, and my heart pounds in my chest. It's not comfortable. The kind of feeling I got the first time I went white-water rafting. A combination of nervousness and excitement as I faced my first rapids. A sensation that had since ebbed. One I'd been chasing ever since, pushing myself to take on extreme sports. One I hadn't thought I'd find in the office of a wedding planner.

My feet thud on the wooden floor, and I get a good look at the space which is one-fourth the size of my own office. In the far corner is a bookcase packed with books. On the opposite side is a comfortable settee packed with cushions women seem to like so much. There's a colorful patchwork quilt thrown over it, and behind that, a window that looks onto the back of the adjacent office building. On the coffee table in front of the settee is a bowl with crystal-like objects that reflect the light from the floor lamps. There are paintings on the wall that depict scenes from beaches. No doubt, the kind she'd point to and sell the idea of a honeymoon to gullible brides. I suppose the entire space would appeal to women. With its mood lighting and homey feel, the space invites you to kick back, relax and pour out your problems. A ruse I'm not going to fall for.

"You!" I stab my finger in the direction of the woman seated behind the antique desk straight ahead. "Call Lila, right now, and tell her she needs to go through with the wedding. Tell her she can't back out. Tell her I'm the right choice for her."

She peers up at me from behind large, black horn-rimmed glasses perched on her nose. "No."

I blink. "Excuse me?"

She leans back in her chair. "I'm not going to do that."

"Why the hell not?"

"Are you the right choice for her?

"Of course, I am." I glare at her.

Some of the color fades from her cheeks. She taps her pen on the table, then juts out her chin. "What makes you think you're the right choice of husband for her?"

"What makes you think I'm not."

"Do you love her?"

"That's no one's problem except mine and hers."

"You don't love her."

"What does that have to do with anything?"

"Excuse me?" She pushes the glasses further up her nose. "Are you seriously asking what loving the woman you're going to marry has to do with actually marrying her?" Her voice pulses with fury.

"Yes, exactly. Why don't you explain it to me?" The sarcasm in my tone is impossible to miss.

She stares at me from behind those large glasses that should make her look owlish and studious, but only add an edge of what I can only describe as quirky-sexiness. The few times I've met her before, she's gotten on my nerves so much, I couldn't wait to get the hell away from her. Now, giving her the full benefit of my attention, I realize, she's actually quite striking. And the addition of those spectacles? Fuck me—I never thought I had a weakness for women wearing glasses. Maybe I was wrong. Or maybe it's specifically this woman wearing glasses... Preferably only glasses and nothing else.

Hmm. Interesting. This reaction to her. It's unwarranted and not something I planned for. I widen my stance, mainly to accommodate the thickness between my legs. An inconvenience... which perhaps I can use to my benefit? I drag my thumb under my lower lip.

Her gaze drops to my mouth, and if I'm not mistaken, her breath hitches. *Very interesting.* Has she always reacted to me like that in the past? Nope, I would've noticed. We've always tried to have as little as possible to do with each other. Like I said, interesting. And unusual.

"First," —she drums her fingers on the table— "are you going to answer my question?"

I tilt my head, the makings of an idea buzzing through my synapses. I need a little time to flesh things out though. It's the only reason I deign to answer her question which, let's face it, I have no obligation to respond to. But for the moment, it's in my interest to humor her and buy myself a little time.

"Lila and I are well-matched in every way. We come from good families—"

"You mean rich families?"

"That, too. Our families move in the same circles."

"Don't you mean boring country clubs?" she says in a voice that drips with distaste.

I frown. "Among other places. We have the pedigree, the bloodline, our backgrounds are congruent, and we'd be able to fold into an arrangement of coexistence with the least amount of disruption on either side."

"Sounds like you're arranging a merger."

"A takeover, but what-fucking-ever." I raise a shoulder.

Her scowl deepens. "This is how you approached the upcoming wedding... And you wonder why Lila left you?"

"I gave her the biggest ring money could buy—"

"You didn't make an appearance at the engagement party."

"I signed off on all the costs related to the upcoming nuptials—"

"Your own engagement party. You didn't come to it. You left her alone to face her family and friends." Her tone rises. Her cheeks are flushed. You'd think she was talking about her own wedding, not that of her friend. In fact, it's more entertaining to talk to her than discuss business matters with my employees. *How interesting.*

"You also didn't show up for most of the rehearsals." She glowers.

"I did show up for the last one."

"Not that it made any difference. You were either checking your watch and indicating that it was time for you to leave, or you were glowering at the plans being discussed."

"I still agreed to that god-awful wedding cake, didn't I?

"On the other hand, it's probably good you didn't come for the previous rehearsals. If you had, Lila and I might have had this conversation earlier—"

"Aha!" I straighten. "So, you confess that it's because of you Lila walked away from this wedding."

She tips her head back. "Hardly. It's because of you."

"So you say, but your guilt is written large on your face."

"Guilt?" Her features flush. The color brings out the dewy hue of her skin, and the blue of her eyes deepens until they remind me of forget-me-nots. No, more like the royal blue of the ink that spilled onto my paper the first time I attempted to write with a fountain pen.

"The only person here who should feel guilty is you, for attempting to coerce an innocent, young woman into an arrangement that would have trapped her for life."

Anger thuds at my temples. My pulse begins to race. "I never have to coerce women. And what you call being trapped is what most women call security. But clearly, you wouldn't know that, considering" —I wave my hand in the air— "you prefer to run your kitchen-table business which, no doubt, barely makes ends meet."

She loosens her grip on her pencil, and it falls to the table with a clatter. Sparks flash deep in her eyes.

You know what I said earlier about the royal blue? Strike that. There are flickers of silver hidden in the depths of her gaze. Flickers that blaze when she's upset. How would it be to push her over the edge? To be at the receiving end of all that passion, that fervor, that ardor... that absolute avidness of existence when she's one with the moment? How would it feel to rein in her spirit, absorb it, drink from it, revel in it, and use it to spark color into my life?

"Kitchen-table business?" She makes a growling sound under her breath. "You dare come into my office and insult my enterprise? The company I have grown all by myself—"

"And outside of your assistant" —I nod toward the door I came through— "you're the sole employee, I take it?"

Her color deepens. "I work with a group of vendors—"

I scoff, "None of whom you could hold accountable when they don't deliver."

"—who have been carefully vetted to ensure that they always deliver," she says at the same time. "Anyway, why do you care, since you don't have a wedding to go to?"

"That's where you're wrong." I peel back my lips. "I'm not going to be labeled as the joke of the century. Not after all the media has labelled it 'the wedding of the century'." I make air quotes with my fingers.

It was Isla's idea to build up the wedding with the media. She also wanted to invite influencers from all walks of life to attend, but I have no interest in turning my nuptials into a circus. So, I vetoed the idea of journalists attending in person. I have, however, agreed to the event being recorded by professionals and exclusive clips being shared with the media and the influencers. This way, we'll get the necessary PR coverage, without the media being physically present.

In all fairness, the publicity generated by the upcoming nuptials has already been beneficial. It's not like I'll ever tell her, but Isla was right to feed the public's interest in the upcoming event. Apparently, not even the most hard-nosed investors can resist the warm, fuzzy feelings that a marriage invokes. And this can only help with the IPO I have planned for the most important company in my portfolio. "I have a lot riding on this wedding."

"Too bad you don't have a bride."

"Ah," —I smirk— "but I do."

She scowls. "No, you don't. Lila—"

"I'm not talking about her."

"Then who are you talking about?"

"You."

To find out what happens next read Liam and Isla's marriage of convenience romance where the bridegroom marries the wedding planner in, The Proposal

💜 *Want to be the first to find out about my newest release? Join my newsletter. Use this QR code*

How to scan a QR code?

1. Open the camera app on your phone or tablet.

2. Point the camera at the QR code.

3. Tap the banner that appears on your phone or tablet.

4. Follow the instructions on the screen to finish signing in.

MARRIAGE OF CONVENIENCE BILLIONAIRE ROMANCE FROM L. STEELE

The Billionaire's Fake Wife - Sinclair and Summer's story that started this universe... with a plot twist you won't see coming!

The Billionaire's Secret - Victoria and Saint's story. Saint is maybe the most alphahole of them all!

Marrying the Billionaire Single Dad - Damian and Julia's story, watch out for the plot twist!

The Proposal - Liam and Isla's story. What's a wedding planner to do when you tell the bride not to go through with the wedding and the groom demands you take her place and give him a heir? And yes plot twist!

CHRISTMAS ROMANCE BOOKS BY L. STEELE FOR YOU

Want to find out how Dr. Weston Kincaid and Amelie met? Read The Billionaire's Christmas Bride

Want even more Christmas Romance books? *Read A very Mafia Christmas, Christian and Aurora's story*

Read a marriage of convenience billionaire Christmas romance, Hunter and Zara's story - *The Christmas One Night Stand*

FORBIDDEN BILLIONAIRE ROMANCE BY L. STEELE FOR YOU

Read Daddy JJ's, age-gap romance in Mafia Lust HERE

Read Edward, Baron and Ava's story starting with Billionaire's Sins HERE

READING ORDER

Download your exclusive L. Steele reading order bingo card. *SCAN THIS QR CODE TO GET IT*

How to scan a QR code?

1. Open the camera app on your phone or tablet.
2. Point the camera at the QR code.
3. Tap the banner that appears on your phone or tablet.
4. Follow the instructions on the screen to finish signing in.

ABOUT THE AUTHOR

Hello, I'm L. Steele.

I write romance stories with strong powerful men who meet their match in sassy, curvy, spitfire women.

I love to push myself with each book on both the spice and the angst so I can deliver well rounded, multidimensional characters.

I enjoy trading trivia with my husband, watching lots and lots of movies, and walking nature trails. I live in London.

Follow me:
On Amazon
on BookBub
on Goodreads
on Audible
On TikTok
Join my secret Facebook Reader Group
on Pinterest
My YouTube channel
Read ALL my books
Spotify

Made in United States
North Haven, CT
13 September 2025

72859035R00245